The Tamil Dream

The Tamil Dream

Koom Kankesan

QUATTRO BOOKS

The publication of THE TAMIL DREAM has been generously supported by the Canada Council for the Arts and the Ontario Arts Council.

Author's photograph: Jacob Hoffman
Cover design: Natasha Shaikh
Cover Photograph: Drummond Wilson
Editor: Luciano Iacobelli
Typography: Jared Shapiro

Library and Archives Canada Cataloguing in Publication

Kankesan, Koom, author
The Tamil Dream / Koom Kankesan

ISBN 978-1-988254-30-2 (Paperback)

I. Title.

PS8621.A55T36 2016C813'.6
C2016-906371-2

Published by Quattro Books Inc.
Toronto, Ontario
www.quattrobooks.ca

Printed in Canada

To all the teachers who took an interest
or saw something in me

and

a classmate and generous friend,
Nilesh Chohan,
and his wonderful family

SEMESTER ONE

DANIEL

My father was a very difficult man, and I suppose this has made me one also.

Lynn, my girlfriend, avoided him and my mother like the plague. Those Sunday dinners took up half the day at my parents' new home, a low squat bungalow paid for with little money down, nestled between the hills and ravines of central Scarborough, subdivisions and concrete dreams carved into the slow fertile Rouge Valley. Their new house was not far from the school where Lynn and I taught, but Sunday evening is always a sacrosanct time for teachers. It's when we plan most of the coming week. I, however, have always been loyal to these family dinners. I value loyalty to myself and others above all else – without it, where would we be?

I visited my parents the Sunday before the 2008–09 school year started, the Sunday before Labour Day. On Labour Day, Lynn and I would parade down University Avenue as part of the teachers' union, near the new condo we had bought. The waterfront condo was her idea. An inveterate artist at heart, I had been hesitant about our investment. Later on in the year, University Avenue would play a major role in our lives – to me, what happened there would be a feverish dream, a source of wonder. To Lynn, it would be nothing more than an irritation.

It took me an hour and a half to get to my parents' place by transit because Lynn kept the car. I took the subway, then the dreaded Scarborough RT before taking another bus and walking through the ravine to get to my parents' small bungalow. Acres of wild grass, spruce and pine, pointillist beads of buttercup and dandelion flashed by as I stood impatiently on the RT train, waiting for it to reach Lawrence station. The chemical sheds stood to my right, and I tried not to look at them. Here my father put on his tired security guard uniform every day and made his rounds, wrote his reports, trying hard not to ingest the toluene, the tannic acid, the god-knows-what-else drifting in the air.

The Lawrence bus rolled east past crumbling apartment blocks and dried-out strip malls, past low squat bungalows that showed little variation or distinction. Everything was brown and grey and tan, except for the patches of green where the Rouge valley, its network of parks and fields, showed through. The electrical towers ran through the Gatineau Hydro Corridor, and my parents lived beside them.

I thought about Lynn gazing out the window of our sixteenth floor corner unit. I imagined her staring out the wall to ceiling glass, her thick braided dreadlocks falling over her high shoulders. Her view would be of the lake, waters calm as sailboats and the island ferry skimmed across in the summer evening light. She might see the Gardiner Expressway wending, an overcongested and bulging artery cutting through the sinews and thews of downtown. It loops and curlicues into the Don Valley Parkway, bisecting the city in half. A grid of straight roads and avenues that extend east and west, north and south, capturing the city's vegetation in a net. What did she think of when she was alone? Did she plan our future lives? Did she miss me in the same way I missed her? Or was she glad to have these free times, patches of solitude that had become rarer and rarer since we had moved in together?

I got off the bus and cut through the electrical fields, the wires and conductors crackling above me, stepping through the ravine. A small trickle of water flowed through, connecting to the stream that flowed behind our school, Leonard Cohen Collegiate. I crossed on the footbridge and approached my parents' house from behind like some kind of interloper. In the driveway stood my sister's Yutani Neutron hybrid, a beast of a station wagon whose pristine black shine and soft leather interiors boasted affluence. Malathi and her husband Mahesh had acquired it, though they did not yet have children. Since my parents and I didn't own cars ourselves, the Neutron was the only thing taking up space in the driveway.

As usual, my father was bent over, knees of his old trousers encrusted with dirt, potting trowel in hand, flowers laid out upon the lawn. He wore a straw bonnet with a red ribbon that had once belonged to my sister. He dug up soil and transferred the peonies and mums he had bought from the garden centre to the small, loamy patch in front of the house.

"Their cherry tree looks good this year," he said, jutting his chin towards the Chinese neighbour's fragrant tree behind the adjoining house. Its thick branches were dark, and the blossoms had long blown away, but its musky smell of acetone and sap drifted upon the air, making us dizzy.

"You can plant one too," I said. "I'll buy you one."

"You don't need to buy us anything!" He laughed, straightening up quickly as if he shouldn't be bent before me. He dusted the mud off his knees. It was meant to be a smooth casual gesture, but I could see his hands and knees shake. The arthritis sent a quiver from his elbows right up to his chin. "Flowers need time and care," he said. "You don't just buy your garden at once – not like your condo life."

We left the trowel and remaining potted plants in the scant shade and went towards the house where my mother, my sister, and Mahesh waited. But there were other voices too.

"Who's inside?" I asked. Sometimes there was a latent dread about Scarborough that I couldn't place. Even in the summer, it felt as if it were already fall. A tension that seeped from the ground and seemed to hum in the electrical wires above the house.

"Thambi and his mother are here," replied my father. "They've been waiting for you."

When Malathi and I were young, my father had been a moody man. We had left Sri Lanka during the mid-eighties to escape the civil war, fleeing as refugees. Our father began his security job as a temporary stopgap; in time, it became permanent. Like acid, it wore on him, it ate away at him slowly, but he stayed faithful to that job. He wore his battered serge uniform, stained and corroded with fumes suppurating its threads, like a badge of honour to hide his shame.

On a day off and when home from work, his brooding heavy presence filled the air. Out of the security guard's uniform we so hated with its stink of corrosive acid and toluene, he stood out. Freed from his job at the chemical sheds, he wore a freshly laundered banian and saram, the pleats folded stiffly, falling across his knees as he sat in our used armchair and read the newspaper. He made us do math problems way beyond our grade level – equations in algebra, problems in geometry, exercises in calculus – as an attempt to get ahead in school. I would have to suffer his smell of talcum powder and sweat as I approached him with the solutions to the questions and he looked over them.

I used to be interested in scientific things then, before film and the arts found my heart. I used to think about God, the forces of the universe, holding us together yet pulling us apart as I stared at the slow second hand on his heavy Seiko watch while he checked my solutions, its interminably slow progress around the dial cutting away slices of time, demarcating the loss of joy in our household. I wondered how the Gods could abandon us to such cruel fates. I'd have to focus on the light glinting off the clasps of his watch because I could not bear to look at his stern unhappy face.

"We've been waiting for you, the food's getting cold," said my mother in the doorway of the kitchen. Her eyes examined my face and eyes, trying to guess what we'd been talking about. *Nothing* was my silent reply. She always looked to me to explain something about her husband, to pass on to her some secret that I was privy to. The secret was that I knew no secrets. Amma and Appa were as different as chalk and cheese and why they had been thought to provide a suitable match now seemed long forgotten.

Like Appa, Amma carried the weariness of the last twenty-five years within the soft tallow of her face. She was younger and fairer than him, and you could see in the old photos that she had possessed a radiating beauty. Now her figure drooped, and an ashen pallor clung to her face. The beauty no longer radiated from her chubby cheeks, her upturned nose, her dry scarred skin, but spryness remained in her eyes. Amma's head had been filled with a thousand and one schemes over the years – Amway products, a real estate license that never materialized, lottery trees for Tamils – and they had all come to nothing. The detritus of these projects filled the boxes crowding the basement of my parents' new bungalow, competing with the garlanded and gilded pictures of Sai Baba and the Gods.

Malathi, my sister, had inherited Amma's beauty. They were both short with curly black hair, and both possessed the delicate upturned nose, as if they were forever trying to sniff at something which eluded them. Two years ago, Malathi had married Mahesh Jayapalan. She and Mahesh had met in undergrad when they both tried to get into med school. Mahesh had gotten in; Malathi hadn't.

I watched them now, sitting on my parents' love seat and looking through old photo albums, leaning against each other as if still engaged, a power couple embarking upon their life of adventure and wealth. The couch and love seat, like the bungalow, were new acquisitions, and my parents had left the set wrapped in plastic. This was normal for Tamil households – they warded off the deterioration and despoilment of furniture. For similar reasons, the TV and DVD remotes were encased in layers of wadding. The couch, upholstered cream and embroidered with a pattern of large red and green tulips, could only be felt through the plastic. Our lives were in mothballs, and the feeling that the decor was temporary filled the living room – it was like a showroom or warehouse that they lived in, not permanent at all. The fear existed in the back of our minds, as immigrants, that we might have to flee at any moment

Sliding around on the plastic covered-couch were Thambi and his mother, Mrs Navaratnam. They were neighbours, our close friends from long ago when we all lived in the same apartment building, the Gilder Block. The Navaratnams were still there. Thambi, his elder brother Roshan, and their mother had lived on the floor below ours. We would walk down the stairwell, or they would come up, and we'd dine together, my mother and Mrs Navaratnam sharing cooking duties. It was the closest to extended family that we got. Thambi and Roshan's father was still stuck in Sri Lanka; they'd had to leave without him years ago. Some of our family had died during the war, but my father's brothers were still in Sri Lanka; they were the closest family we had.

Thambi was the one in the Navaratnam household I found easiest to talk to. He was frank and earnest, and did not guard his thoughts like some other Tamils you meet – for better or worse – but he was closer to my sister's age. He was still in his twenties and possessed that twenty-something assurance and impetuousness, an assurance which told you he knew everything. His brother Roshan was closer to me in age, but I'd always found him cold and distant, a hardworking and unfriendly professional.

They all looked up at me as if with one glance.

"We haven't seen you in some time," said Mrs Navaratnam. "You must come round and visit us."

"Where's your father?" asked Thambi.

I pushed my hand through my long hair and indicated he'd gone downstairs to clean up and pray.

"About time you showed up," muttered Malathi. Her eyes narrowed. She was always like that, always trying to get the upper hand at the beginning of a conversation. She possessed a quick angry gleam in her eye, and her voice rose towards a point. I used to call her 'Napoleon' and she hated it. She was short like my mother, shorter even. When she stood on chairs, Malathi still could not reach the tops of high cabinets. When she'd gotten her driver's license at sixteen, an ample cushion was necessary for her to see over the steering wheel. When she shopped for clothes and make-up on the third tier of the Eaton Centre, she always bought the highest heels she could find. When I called her 'Napoleon', she fumed, all of her fury pressed into the tight corkscrew of her soul. She was forever angry.

"You didn't bring Lynn?" asked Mahesh as I nodded and looked around. Nobody got up.

"Well," I pushed my hand through my hair again – it had gotten too long over the summer and desperately needed to be cut – "she's preparing for the week."

"Uh-huh," said Napoleon.

"How are you liking your place?" enquired Mahesh, talking over her. Mahesh was always cordial to everyone in our family. My parents adored him – he had tilted at and obtained the ultimate brass ring: he was a paediatrician with his very own practice.

"It's nice, if a bit overwhelming," I replied. "I'm used to simple apartment buildings, you know."

"You should spend and enjoy a little," stated Mahesh, smiling with his polished teeth that sat high in a long curved crescent on his face, muscles pushed forward to project confidence. He was the physical opposite of my sister. Everything from his feet to his fingers to his spectacles was drawn out, tall as if the impression of him had been formed in a convex mirror, some old Tamilian's dream. Always pleasant and cordial, he was one of those camouflaged stick insects that could turn their profiles away from you and disappear, wearing his longness with a minimum of fuss.

"Come on, time to eat," said my mother, wiping her hands on the hem of her house dress, which had faded and was stained from many hand-wipings. Her hair was wispy and dry, pinned back over the shoulders of the stained blue dress. In the old photos, her hair was long and lustrous, but now she looked like one of her pictures going out of focus, the chemicals upon the paper burning and fading, not agreeing with exposure to the Canadian climate.

The sound of Appa intoning his thervarums came up from the basement. The creaky yet steady voice rasped through the air ducts and rattled round the vents:

"Please God, protect my wife and children.

Let them do well and continue to be healthy.

Let no illness or harm befall them or cause them pain.

Please help us to help our loved ones in Sri Lanka, however we can.

Please provide for us so that we may serve you.

Show us how to become better so that we may worship you and observe your will."

"We should go say our prayers," stated Mrs Navaratnam, rising and pulling Thambi with her. They all trooped downstairs, their footsteps carefully falling on the narrow stairway that led to the basement. Garlanded pictures of

Shiva and his family, the afroed orange-clad Sai Baba, and various statuettes awaited them.

I listened from upstairs, all their voices in chorus coming up through the vents, the ducts emitting prayer combined with the recirculated air.

Waiting, I examined the photo albums that my sister and Mahesh had set down. My father's parents, now dead, their land and house in the background, long ago sold off during the war that had raged for decades, the war that pressed on still. The famed red Jaffna earth and mango trees behind them. Whom did I resemble more – my mother's or my father's parents? There was Appa and his brothers as young men. His brothers were laughing, but he, the eldest, held a firm and serious expression. So severe and lacklustre was that expression, so serious and devoid of joy. So characteristic of him as a whole.

A more recent photo of my father showed his face haggard and drawn. He used to be a train conductor back in Sri Lanka, puffed up with pride, sure of himself. But in his security guard's uniform, he was nothing more than just another former refugee, working some dead-end job in Canada. He was dark skinned with a long pointed nose, almost a beak, and a lower lip that swallowed the upper in a permanent underbite. He possessed pockmarked, weather-beaten skin and a fringe of balding hair around his ears. Against his dark skin, his hair was startlingly white, as if the very bone was pushing in tendrils out of his pores.

He came into the kitchen ahead of the others, changed into his freshly laundered saram and smelling his smell of aftershave and sweat and talcum powder, and for a second I was twelve again. I was handing over a sheet of completed sums. I stared at the glints off the clasps of his Seiko watch.

"Why didn't you pray?" he asked.

"Martin Scorsese is my Shiva and Francis Ford Coppola is my Vishnu," I replied. "Kurosawa is my Jesus. You know that."

He sighed. "I'll never understand you."

I didn't want to look too hard at his pockmarked weather-beaten pores, even if they had been scrubbed clean. I felt that I could fall so easily into that sea of sadness and despair that lurked below the surface. All that hard work and bitter struggle and pain clogged up in his arteries.

The others came up, having said their prayers, and milled around the kitchen counter, serving themselves the rice, curries of dahl, eggplant, spinach, and onion, okra, sliced vegetables, fried chilies, and yogurt that my mom had prepared. They heaped it all together in one clustered pile upon their plates. Bowls of pappadams and vaddais sat on the table. My mother poured us all glasses of water.

"So, what are you teaching this semester?" asked Thambi, the least self-conscious, the least tense person in the room. He spoke as he continued to chew, not closing his mouth. It was a very Tamil thing to do, as Lynn often reminded me. She sometimes found our habits disgusting. My sister, when we were children, would purposely and unguardedly sneeze on me when she had a cold.

"The grade tens like last year," I replied. "Grade Ten Civics. An English class. Media's grade eleven though. You're still working at the same place?"

"Yep, still stuck there. I want to look for a new contract, but with this economy…" He wedged some string beans into his mouth. "My brother's the ambitious one."

"Teaching is a very important role," said Mahesh. He could afford to be smug because he would never stoop to being a teacher. "You're moulding the future citizens of our country."

"Besides, you get the summers off ," added Mrs Navaratnam.

I've heard this line again and again. Almost all the people I meet seem to think that teachers ride in the lap of luxury. We're always on strike and never grateful for what we get. So I just sighed and agreed. "It's true. Teaching's a secure middle class job with benefits and pension. One of the few that's left. But it's hard work. No one ever understands how much hard work it is, how stressful it can be. The marking and the prep time. They just think you get to play with kids all day and take vacations."

"Ugh – you couldn't pay me enough to do that," said Malathi, shaking her head and grimacing. "Not with teenagers the way they are these days."

"Speaking of teenagers," interjected my mother, trying to be subtle, "have you heard anything from Niranjan?"

"I've been moving for the last couple of weeks," I replied bluntly. "You know that. If I hear anything, don't you think I would tell you?"

I put my hand down for a moment beside my plate and wiped the rice crumbs from my fingers with a paper napkin. We could see the dark branches of the neighbouring cherry tree through the open kitchen window, and its heady smell of sap seemed to permeate the house, obliterating that of my mother's cooking. Intoxicating. Birds picked away at the smashed fruit that lay on the grass beneath and cried out.

Niranjan was a cousin to Thambi and Roshan. He was the younger son of Mrs Navaratnam's younger sister. The sister's family in Sri Lanka had sold their gold to get Niranjan out and over to the Navaratnam household. At fifteen, he had endured an arduous journey through North Africa and the less scenic parts of Germany and Norway. Since Thambi and Roshan's father was also stuck in Sri Lanka, my father had stepped in, joined their mother, and helped her to get Niranjan over here. My father's honour and pride were at stake too. I knew that very well, because my parents reminded me every time I visited. Niranjan had been a promising student back home, but something had happened to him after coming to Canada. The lack of supervision and parental control does something to a young man. Now seventeen, he had left their apartment.

For a while last year, he had been at Leonard Cohen Collegiate, where I taught. I had leaned on Lynn, and she had pulled some strings and gotten him admitted so that I could keep an eye on him. That was the plan anyway. We had tried our best – we even took him away to camp with us the previous year at the end of summer with the leadership students that Lynn coached – but there was only so much I could do. I couldn't watch him every second of every day. Boys will be boys. He had his own ideas.

Dealing with a teenager is like pushing on a string. A bunch of strings. A bunch of tangled strings. What could I do?

Everybody was looking at me now, and I realized that I'd been sitting for a while, just staring out the window. I moved my hand and resumed eating.

"I'm really sorry, Aunty," I apologized. "He's seventeen. Under the law, he's not a minor anymore. We can't make him do anything he doesn't want to."

"That's the problem with this country," hissed Mrs Navaratnam. "All these so-called freedoms, and people go nowhere. They forget who they are. They forget who their families are."

"We do so much for them, and do they remember?" asked my mother sympathetically. "One can only do their best and serve their responsibilities in this life. You are right – people in this country are nowhere when it matters. They will let their parents die on the streets."

I looked at Thambi and Mahesh, hoping for an ally to stem the tide of maternal ruefulness, but they were silent and looked away. Cowards. Surprisingly, it was my sister who spoke. An emotional tremor made Napoleon's eyelid flutte , her voice quiver, as she broke out, "That's completely unfair. How dare you! Mahesh and I do everything for you. Just last week, we paid for the man to come fix your drain. Isn't that right?" She worked for the government now, making more than I did, but her emotions were always close to the surface.

Amma just steamrolled over her. "Yes, yes, we weren't talking about you. You take everything so personally! Why do you immediately assume we're talking about you?"

Malathi directed one of her withering Napoleonic glares at our father. "Come on, what's the matter? Don't you want to get in on this too?"

But Appa said nothing, just stared at his food, mouth slightly open as if he wanted to say something and could not find the words. I glanced at the pores in his dark skin, the bone-like hair coming out in tendrils, and quickly looked away. "What am I going to say? You talk enough for all of us."

"That is so insulting!"

My gut had been clenched for the better part of an hour now, sphincters tightening. I remembered why I dreaded Scarborough so much.

"Still, you must do something," rolled on Mrs Navaratnam, not missing a beat and staring me in the eye, pointing a finger in my face. A poor grain of rice stuck to the end of that finge , unable to fall away. "You're their teacher. If you can't do something, who can?"

"At least try to talk to him, Dan," reasoned Thambi. "We don't even know where he is."

"What do you want me to do? Hunt him down?"

"That wouldn't be a bad idea. You have resources at your disposal." Thambi and his mother looked at each other, then looked back to me. "Maybe he'll come back to school this year," said Mrs Navaratnam. "If he does, you must… catch him!"

I put my hand up to cover my face. "Say he comes back, what do I do?"

"Make him return home! His proper place is with his family!"

I excused myself and went to the bathroom. I did not really have to go, of course, and just stood there for a minute with my hand against the locked door. I hadn't even had a chance to bring up the thing with Lynn yet. Lynn wanted us to have a baby. A baby! And we weren't even married. Or engaged. How was that going to go over? I could smell the smashed cherries stronger than ever. There was no door thick enough to lock these people out of my life – these people, my family, my parents. They were my life, my destiny.

Leaving the door, I opened the cabinet under the sink and saw the tray with vials, boxes, tinfoil strips, all of my parents' over-the-counter and prescription medications in it. Some of the aspirin pills had expired, and the combined smell of ointments and powders was sickening.

Closing the cabinet, I stood up, flushed the toilet, and returned to join the melodrama.

NIRANJAN

I carry my garbage bag of clothes slung over my shoulder. It's everything I own. Tied it myself. Slung it over my shoulder and got going earlier today. Bag'll probably break before I get to Rageev and Soothy's apartment. My flip flops are at the bottom, and they dig into my back. A belt and a mug too. Strains against my shoulder, and I hump it past Leonard Cohen Collegiate.

Behind our school are the Tuxedo Court apartments. Rageev and Soothy live there. Now I will too. I cross the football field and walk along the track, still dry and dusty red from the summer. Kick pebbles along the way. Dust flies up. At the end of the field is the old chain-link fence, rusting. That little hill. In one direction the Tuxedo Court, the poorest of the poor. Me and my friends. In the other direction, the tennis courts and the children's playground. The subdivisions where richer kids live. In between, the ravine with the trees. The trickling water you can just hear.

Going to have to go left eventually. The Court. But first, I lug my garbage bag containing my garbage life down to the playground and put it down. Panting. I sit on one of the swings and swivel around. The chains twist, and I push it as far as I can go till I feel their tightness. I feel it through the chains, corkscrewing into my gut. All around me that gummy smell of pine needles and dried grass – it's the end of summer and here I am moving from my aunt's apartment into the Tuxedo Court. Ass-backwards. Dopers, fiends, and criminals. And immigrants. The poorest of the poor. Rageev and Soothy of course – my brothers. If I didn't have them, I'd have nothing.I finally let the swing go, and it whips me around, spinning the other way, making me dizzy, throwing the thoughts from my stomach to my head.

How did things get this way? So complicated?

The Tigers had recruited my older brother, Karuna. My parents didn't want to see the same thing happen to me. My brother hated people comparing him to the 'traitor Karuna', the soldier who used to lead in the Eastern province before he broke off from Prabhakaran. Anna wanted to prove himself. He was pretty fierce that wa .

After a while, we never heard from him. My mother used to go to the Tigers' local camp when I was twelve and plead with the commander to let her eldest go. That was when she knew where he was. My brother told me he was joining so they wouldn't recruit me, but he wanted to be there, I could tell. I used to go with Amma and wait in the yard outside the Tiger camp. Every week she'd go in and plead. Girl soldiers in uniform played with a volleyball but no net. I sat with stray dogs on the side, watching them. There were always lots of stray dogs in Sri Lanka. I'm like that now – a wild stray dog belonging to no one.

I pick up my garbage bag, heave it against my shoulder, and walk down towards the Court. The apartment is on the fourteenth floor of the 40 Tuxedo Court building. The apartments are crumbling, grey, and weepy. It's still summer. There's pigeon netting over the rusting balconies. Everything has that rusted gritty feeling.

You can see a clear view of the whole Court from Rageev and Soothy's balcony, all right. Who's coming. Who's going. The football field in the distance, the school behind it. A little too close, but who cares?

"You must be strong to carry that bag all the way over here by yourself," says Yalini akka once I take the elevator up and get inside. Yalini is Rageev's girlfriend. She holds their baby against her hip and rocks her. Baby Geetha. Yalini and Geetha.

"I took the bus for part of it," I reply. "I'm just glad my bag didn't break."

I wish one of them would have drove down and picked me up, but they're already doing me a favour, letting me crash. Soothy doesn't drive well anyway. I wouldn't dare ask Rageev to leave his girlfriend and daughter to pick me up.

The apartment looks the same. Yellow walls with brown stains. A string curtain with red beads dividing off the hallway where the bedrooms are. In the living room, Rageev sits on a faded grey corduroy sofa. The sofa's old and soft, the corduroy faded long before I ever visited here, maybe even before Soothy moved in. Rageev's couch isn't covered in plastic. The plasma flatscreen TV that Rageev's watching – the one that Soothy and I have played Xbox on – that's new. WWE wrestlers on the TV right now in high def. Rageev's in a banian and jeans, bare feet propped up on the little glass table, scars running across his soles. Rageev's like a wrestler himself. He's been working out, and there's always sweat dripping from his hair and sliding down his face. He's got a couple of empty beer cans on the table beside the soles of his feet. I can see the blistering skin on those feet, all pink and hard where the scars are.

He looks up at me without moving his face; his eyes stare up from the scar tissue, worse than his feet. It's on one of his hands too. He's in his thirties, but I've never asked him exactly how old he is. I wouldn't dare. All that Soothy's told me is that he's from the old days, the gang days when the AK Kannans ran this area, that he was part of Kannan's gang. Kannan's gone now, like most of the others. Dead, deported, locked up.

Rageev doesn't care about keeping his sofa wrapped under plastic because he's got other things to worry about. If you see his face, you'll understand. His face is like plastic. It's been scarred and hardened so much it looks like a rubber mask you could pull off. Once again, not something I'd say out loud. There's a massive scar running all the way down the left side. Where they tried to stitch him up and make the skin look nice. They failed. Failed even harder than the way I failed school last semester.

Some of the skin is light where he burned. Like a map of his past. Other parts are dark just like the rest of him. And us. But when you see it – you don't want to make any Michael Jackson jokes – it doesn't make you laugh. It terrifies you. Like he's part of a new species. Part of the flesh tried to bubble out from under the skin but froze instead. I never get used to it. The muscles are dead, stiff, hard like leather and bone. They don't move. His expression doesn't change. But his left eye works just fine. When it turns around to look at you but the rest of the face stays still, ice slides down your back.

"Alright, machan?" he says gently, nodding at me.

"Alright," I say. Nod back. Soothy helps me with the garbage bag, and I sit down to face Rageev. "Get him something to drink!" Rageev shouts to Yalini who's still rocking the baby against her hip. Then to me, "You want a beer?"

I shake my head. "He doesn't drink," says Soothy.

"You don't drink? You sure?"

I shake my head again.

"How come I didn't notice? That's good. Stay that way. Use your head." Rageev points a finger to his head where the dried leather and bone bubble out. I've never asked him how it happened, but I know it was a car crash on the highway. The Gardiner. VVT crashed into him and overturned his car. It made the news. Rageev was the only one who survived. Even Soothy doesn't know the whole story.

Yalini akka brings me some tea – milky, sugary, a spoon in it. I stir the tea and am grateful for it. "Thank you, Akka."

As I sip – it's still hot – the WWE announcer's booming voice interviews some guy, all muscled and oily – fireworks are going off in the ring – and I think about how fake wrestling is. Not like real life. Photos of Rageev and his girlfriend and baby are on the wall. Some old photos of Rageev, in Jaffna I think. One nice studio portrait of Geetha in a gilded frame, just after she was born, crawling on a pink blanket on an ancient Greek style column.

Yalini seems tired now. Always hurried and overworked, you can see worry lines on her face. When I first met her, she was all businesslike but still formal, polite. She's more friendly now. Wiry like Rageev, she's almost taller than him, very tall for a Tamil woman. She wears jeans and a check shirt like a woman back home, long hair tied back in a strong thick braid. I like her okay, but really, the only one I know well is Soothy.

"So, what are you going to do, now that you're here?" asks Yalini akka.

I scratch my head. I didn't think that far. "Probably get a job."

Rageev laughs and looks away from the wrestling. "You're a refugee, machan, who's going to hire you?"

"I'll get a job under the table," I mumble.

"What's that?"

"I'll get a job under the table!"

Soothy and Rageev look at each other and smile. Soothy's standing up and slaps his knee, his little ponytail jumping up and down.

"Why not?" I ask. "Soothy's not going to school anymore. He's working, isn't he?"

"He's working for me," smiles Rageev after his laughs die down, "but he's hardly working." It's a weird feeling seeing half his face shake with little laughs while the left side is dead still. The left eyeball shakes though – eyelid blinking fast – it moves around just fine. Soothy begins smirking all over again, and Rageev has to tell him to stop. I've never been in the apartment long enough to see Rageev laugh before. Ice goes down my back again.

"You'd better go back to school," says Rageev, half smiling, his face split in two. "I don't want you sitting around, doing nothing, wasting your life like this one." He points his finger at Soothy, and Soothy looks away, embarrassed. "Soothy, take him to the room and show him where to put his things."

It's a two bedroom apartment. All the walls are painted yellow. The brown streaks are from cooking I suppose. One of the rooms belongs to Rageev. His girlfriend and daughter stay there when they visit, but they have another place. I don't know where, know better than to ask. The other bedroom belongs to Soothy. And me now. There's a bed in it that's Soothy's. They've laid out a single mattress beside it for me. Hardly room enough to walk in between. It's a small room holding a closet and bookshelf. On the bookshelf, there are no books. The highest shelf has both an Xbox and a Wii, with controllers for both. They belong to Soothy. There are some rolled-up socks, Maxim magazines, and Rizla papers, also Soothy's. A couple of old textbooks from school – one English text that says Sightlines 10, and a Physics 11. Soothy didn't even bother going to his review meeting when they kicked him out of school.

When was that? At least half a year. Soothy and I had met in the school's office, but I'd seen him around before that. I knew who he was. He had a reputation for being a fool. I'd gotten in trouble because I used to pretend I'd lost something, then ask the secretaries if I could go into the lost and found, looking for stuff I wanted. Nice clothes, nice shoes. A lot of Canadian kids got whatever they asked for; some had so much that when they lost their stuff – nice stuff – they didn't even miss it. Not just clothes. I'd search through all the pockets for change. If I was really lucky, I found bills. I never got spending money at my aunt's – she controlled everything.

Mr Raptis found me searching through pockets one time. He reported me, got me in trouble. From then on, I was on their bad list. Soothy was in even worse trouble than I was. He used to pick fights, take on the black guys who were bigger than him, Macedonians and

Greeks too. He'd flunked most of his courses by then, didn't give a shit.

For me it was harder. Used to do well in school back home. Wasn't used to finding it so hard. Soothy didn't care whether people thought he was a fool. Whether he failed or not. He was full of rage and ego. He just didn't care.

Soothy showed me how to crib other people's locker combinations. You pretend to be doing something or looking for stuff in your bag, but out the corner of your eye, you watch your target's fingers move the dial. Later, you fiddle around with it until you hear tumblers lock. It's easy. We got too greedy. My aunt wouldn't even give me two dollars to buy a McDonald's cheeseburger.

After Soothy's third suspension, they kicked him out. I was kept on. A sort of probation. My guidance counsellor, Ms Varley, wasn't too happy. She always gave me stink-eye when I went to her office

"What are you thinking about?" asks Soothy as I sit on the thin mattress with the garbage bag.

"Nothing. A few days ago, I'm at my aunt's, boxed in, hating my life. Then you ask if I want to stay with you guys, and here I am."

"Look!" Soothy's face goes serious. "I really had to beg Rageev to accept you. You'd better appreciate what I've done. Don't fuck it up."

"I'm not going to fuck it up. But I don't want to go back to school."

"It's his place. His rules. You'd better listen. What are you going to do? Argue with him?"

"Of course not, but…"

"But nothing." Soothy gets up and pushes a bunch of his clothes to one side of the closet. The empty hangers at the other end shake nervously. "Hang your clothes and shut up. On Tuesday you're going to school. That's it." I'm about to say something, but he puts his finger out. "Shut up. Do as you're told. Then wash up. Yalini akka's made dinner."

After Soothy leaves, I take everything out of the bag. Everything that belongs to me. You can put it all in two piles. In one pile are the three pairs of jeans and five shirts that I own. A few superhero T-shirts that my aunt let me get at Walmart. My socks and underwear. The only pair of shoes I own, a pair of no-name runners, is sitting on the mat at the entrance where I took them off. I have a pair of flip flops, or slippers as we Tamils call them, that I took from the Navaratnams. A belt.

In the other pile is the ID I own – everything that shows who I am – a health card, my Sri Lankan passport, a copy of my refugee claim. One white mug that says 'Toronto' on it. There's a notebook I wrote some stuff in when I went to school last semester. Three DVDs: The Terminator; The Good, The Bad, and The Ugly; and Raiders of the Lost Ark. They're movies I've seen with my dad, my appa. They make me think of him, working in the fields under the hot sun. I bought them with some of the money I boosted from lockers last year. In the pile are also, tied up neatly, a few photos of my parents and me. They're old, colours starting to bleed. One of my parents with Karuna and our younger sister, Vasuki. That was a happy time – years ago, before Karuna joined the Tigers. Vasuki's so small that my dad's carrying her. She's in a little blue dress, got her arm around his neck. Vasuki was always the happiest in our family. The youngest and a girl, our father loved her. She was in school until the school got shelled last year.

That three room building with its pink walls, courtyard, and palm trees – hard to believe it's all gone. Vasuki misses it more, I think. Now she stays home and helps my parents. My parents teach her on their own, I suppose. I used to teach her too. She's a fast learner, a better student than me. There was a time when their biggest worry would have been how to find a husband for her. But that's another life.

Here's a photo of my father and his brothers, their entire family in the old house before it was destroyed. My parents live in a much smaller house now, outside of Jaffna, thatch roof instead of stone. They do what they can to get by. The last thing in the pile is the stack of my mother's letters. She was always the one to write, never my dad, after I came to Canada. But I can hear his voice in them, standing over my mother, looking over her shoulder, sending me love and hope. Vasuki would sometimes write a little bit at the end, but she's still only thirteen, not that old. The same age I was when Amma dragged me to the Tiger camp to beg Karuna to come back.

Why then did I disappoint Amma, run away from her sister's apartment? The pain and shame she must feel. Perhaps I am a horrible son.

My mother wrote blue aerogramme letters every month, letting me know what was happening. Her sister, my aunt, would tell me what to write back. She would dictate, "I am well and hope the same with you. Aunty is treating me well, and I hope you are well also. We think of you and send you all our wishes and love." I wish she had let me write my own letter, just once. Just once. That's one of the things I hated about her. So controlling. She'd never let me get my own haircut, never give me the money for it. She would cut my hair with a pair of rusty scissors that hurt every time she snipped. The haircut was never even. It would have to grow out before I could stop being embarrassed about the way it looked. Will Amma continue writing letters to me, even though I am gone? I'm sure her sister must have told her by now.

That's it. That's all there is to my life. Two piles. Everything that defines me is here. No cellphone. No money. Nothing. Just a few pieces of ID and blue aerogramme letters.

I listen to the voices outside in the hall. Soothy's excited giggle. Yalini akka's deep heavy words, low to the ground. Rageev's speech, selective and short.

This is my life now.

The choice I have made.

DANIEL

Leonard Cohen Collegiate sat between low rolling hills on the edge of the ravine system. From my classroom on the second floor, I could view the pleasant meadows and grass, the hillock at the end of the football field. On early summer days, the smell of the cut grass drifted through my window. You could just see the edge of the subdivision with all of its bucolic sounding streets: Par Avenue, Cumberland Drive, Linnett Crescent. At the edge of the fields, in the ravine, was a dwindling stream. A copse of maple and birch trees on either side. Musical burbling as thinning brook slapped against rock, moss, and sand. The result was friction between liquid and solid; matter became liquid and liquid evaporated into gathering air.

I looked at the Tuxedo Court towers as we walked into the school. They rose up, invasive. I lived there once, but Lynn didn't know that. We had just moved to Canada. It was before we moved to the Gilder Block, where the Navaratnams were neighbours.

Many Tamils lived in the Tuxedo Court. Many of our students lived there. If you are too poor to place a down payment on a house, this is where you live. If you are new to the country and don't know anyone except for a Tamil who is a cousin's aunt's friend, this is where you live. My parents now lived near the ravine again, the proverbial piece of Heaven that floated into Scarborough and made it tolerable. It backed onto their property. The lush green scar stretches between Thomson Memorial Park and Morningside Park. The Gatineau Hydro Corridor runs along it, passing close by Leonard Cohen Collegiate, large hydro towers buzzing and crackling with stray ions, surges of electricity. Maybe that's what made our students so boisterous, so crazy. As I have said before, it always felt like fall in Scarborough, even though it was technically still summer.

As you enter the school, a scrap of verse attributed to Leonard Cohen is mounted, framed beside the auditorium. They are blue words scrawled on a napkin, unused in any poem:

As a branch shakes
when a bird alights, departs
So I continue trembling
long after you are gone

A strange invocation. The words, beside the framed photo of Leonard Cohen looking haggard and wolfish, leave you with a melancholy feeling as you pass into the great hall. Lynn and I kissed, and then she broke left to go to the Guidance office and I proceeded right towards the Communications office. I tried to stop my stomach from squeezing into a tight rictus of despair, a feeling I always get at the beginning of school, this dread that puckers into your gut before the actual classes begin. The beginning of a roller coaster ride, the sense of imminent and unnecessary doom.

The Communications office was already teeming with activity by the time I got there. Pete Cram, who was younger than me, had his desk adjacent to mine. We had team taught courses the previous year and knew each other fairly well. John Raptis, who wasn't in our department, stood by Pete's desk, and they were involved in an easy conversation, smiling and laughing with each other. The other teachers milled about, shuffling stacks of photocopies, checking over their course outlines, waiting for the very slow computers to load. Janarius Brent, our curriculum leader, stood over his desk, watching us all.

"Hey, there he is!" laughed John Raptis as I entered the Communications office. "Daniel Boone! How was the camping trip?"

I responded with a lame fist pump, and it was good to see Raptis, although he sometimes scared me. Raptis was an old man, beyond his eligible retirement, who continued to work because he had nothing else. There was a photo of him in his office – younger, holding the reins of a horse – he did not drive a car. One of the old guard, he had never been married. He cursed technology and clung to the rote methods of teaching. Students told me that he still used acetate sheets on an overhead projector.

But he was spry and full of life. Ideas and knowledge buzzed around his head like mayflies. Cram and I shared lunch with him in the staffroom, and he was always entertaining. The administration hated him, but that was part of his charm. Cram was a very popular teacher, especially with the girls. Blonde and lean, he coached football and pored over his lesson plans. He was often there late in the day prepping, when Lynn and I went home. He wore neatly pressed shirts and tan pants, and Lynn said he looked like a Hudson's Bay model.

"So, what's the rumpus?" I asked.

"The new lab'll be ready this year," said Cram.

"The Yutani lab?"

"Oh yeah," replied Cram, "finally, we get some decent technology in our school."

"Boring!" Raptis imitated stifling a yawn with his hand. "I need caffeine. You guys are putting me to sleep."

"I think they have some coffee downstairs in the staffroom."

We walked down to the staffroom, picked up a coffee for Raptis, then made our way past the scrap of verse penned on a napkin and Leonard Cohen's wolfish photo to the auditorium, where the first staff meeting of the year was underway.

We sat near the back of the auditorium, in the shadows. On stage sat Badlamenti, Bud Ackerman, the vice-principal who helped Badlamenti implement his school-wide plans, Joanne Stevenson, the other vice-principal in charge of discipline, and Joyce Heidelberg, the head of guidance. Lynn sat to their right in her cream blouse and herringbone skirt.

Our auditorium was large – our school population had been larger in the old days – but now numbers had dwindled. Families had taken their kids and moved out to surrounding school districts because the prices of houses had risen steeply in the GTA. Things had gotten to the point where houses were going for almost a million dollars in Toronto, and in Scarborough, it wasn't much better. Though banks were giving mortgages, two income starter families were having a hard time paying and keeping up. Smaller school populations meant fewer teachers. They were scattered throughout the auditorium. It was possible to scan their identities and scrutinize each face.

Raptis poked me in the ribs, "Hey, exactly how Italian is Badlamenti?" he asked.

"I don't know," I dutifully replied. This was an old schtick of Raptis's; he would change the answer every time.

"Badlamenti's so Italian that when he needs a little olive oil for his bread, he opens a vein."

As if he knew we were talking about him, Principal Badlamenti cleared his throat and began speaking. "Thanks to all of you who came on time to the school's first staff meeting. It's important to start the school year off on a good foot! It would have been a little nicer if more of you had come out to the barbecue at my and Mrs Badlamenti's house during the summer. The leftover food means that there's another five pounds I'm going to have to try and burn off before the holidays." He chuckled, but nobody else did because Badlamenti really did have a weight problem; it was awkward when he made jokes about it.

"Looking around the room," he continued, "I can see that more than a few of you went away this summer – it's good to see you rested and refreshed. As you're all aware, we're still dealing with some of our problems from a year ago. We're also transitioning to the MarkBook system board-wide to enter marks, so the old systems will no longer be a choice. Some computers have been repaired. Others have been replaced. The new lab will be up and running." Many of the older teachers groaned at this point.

"Now, now, technology is the way of the future, isn't it?" Badlamenti chided. "We must all embrace the ways of change, and the Toronto Board of Education is no exception. A twenty-first century teacher is a connected teacher. He – or she – must find a way to reach students on their level.

"Try to actually say something," muttered Raptis.

"This school is a community nested within a larger community. We sit square in the middle of the greatest country in the world, ladies and gentlemen," intoned Badlamenti. "Our greatest resources are the people in our community – the students but not just our students – our families, our teachers! You are the ones who make this school, this school board, our very society, work. You are the last line, the thin red line between responsible society, citizenship, and chaos. We have to teach them how to become global citizens, responsible members of society. We are in the business of character education. Never forget that."

It was a good speech, and I wondered if he had rehearsed it.

Waxing at length without going into specifics, Badlamenti plopped back down and settled into his chair. He pulled out his PDA and let the others carry the rest of the meeting. I thought about the time he had interviewed me for my job, in his office. He had been much the same – genial but noncommittal. A mounted poster of the Scorsese classic Goodfellas hung on his wall, and I gathered he was proudly Italian. Boxes of camcorders, tripods, and cables were piled behind his desk. On top of an antique case were two Italian duelling pistols. He told me they had belonged to an ancestor and had been passed down through the generations. He waxed large then as he did now. There was something of an exaggerated Italianness to him, and I tried to focus on the grim faces of De Niro and Pesci in the Goodfellas poster in order not to burst out laughing. In the end, I think they only hired me to work at Leonard Cohen Collegiate because of its large Tamil population, so who was I to criticize someone for broadcasting his ethnicity?

Joanne Stevenson stood up in the auditorium. A short and stubby middle-aged woman, she wore a burgundy blazer and grey charcoal skirt. By contrast, given it was the end of summer, most of the teachers were dressed in cheerful colours. Even Badlamenti was sporting his blue suspenders with the drifting clouds that he wore often. Stevenson had curled permy hair and carried a walkie-talkie that she continued to hold as she stood up to receive the microphone from Badlamenti. She held the walkie-talkie like a weapon, and it crackled and beeped, sending electronic signals that were caught by the microphone and warped, continuously warbling, while she spoke. She talked about the gang problem, which still persisted even though the worst days were behind us. A kid called Seelan had died last year, and it had shocked the school. It was in the papers – you might have read about it. The fights and the statistics at our school were displayed on a PowerPoint graph, showing that expulsions, suspensions, and infractions were down. The red and blue graph lines jagged down over the last few years.

"Just like my RSPs!" retorted Raptis loudly and slurped his coffee. A few teachers near us laughed.

We all knew that the only reason the expulsions and suspensions were down was because the administration refused to administer them. Whenever possible, they softened the punishments. The more students they could show successfully registered in the school, the more money they were entitled to get from the province. Last year, two boys had broken out in a violent fight in my Grade 11 Media Studies class: a collarbone was broken, and blood was spilled across a desk. They sent the bleeding kid to the hospital and gave the other a week of in-office detention. He was kept there, then allowed back into my class the following week.

Bud Ackerman stood up. He was affable and kind – I liked him. He was old. I had no idea how long he'd been vice-principal, but he was the most approachable of the three. He was useful to them because he presented a warmer face on the administration. Many of the teachers hoped that Badlamenti would be promoted to the office of school superintendent and that Ackerman might be promoted to principal. Ever since the Harris years, the structure of school society had changed. Teachers and administration no longer belonged to the same union. The admin patrolled the halls less and less, stopped communicating with teachers over policy, and a growing distance made the two parties inimical to each other. John Raptis, part of the old guard who had taught for many many years in the old system, was one of the most vocal resisters to these changes; he was a constant thorn in their sides.

Raptis put his coffee cup down, interlaced his fingers over his belly, and asked: "Hey, how Italian is Badlamenti?"

"I don't know. How Italian is Badlamenti?" replied Cram.

"Badlamenti's so Italian that tomatoes ripen and fall off the vine as he passes by."

"Joyce and Lynn have done a lot of good work with the troubled kids last year, especially the Tamils," said Ackerman.

Lynn stood up and cleared her throat. I was so proud of her – the utmost professional in a herringbone skirt and cream blouse. Her stockings led to polished black shoes, almost as pointy as Badlamenti's. She talked about taking kids to camp and the positive influence it had – the fruits of leadership and success – the well-being for our whole school. Photos from the summer's camping trip projected onto a white screen that lowered from the stage's ceiling.

In one photo, Lynn and I stood, near but not touching, our backs to the camera, watching a group of kids play soccer. When teachers around us clapped, I felt embarrassed as well as proud. The blood in my cheeks became warmer till I was sure it would bleed out my pores. "Stop looking at me like that," I said to Raptis and Cram. Lynn talked about some of the challenges in our school – the fights, the violence, the groups of students who hung around the hallways. Many of them were Tamil and did not go to class. Of course, there was a strong contingent of Tamils who were the opposite too – they were studious, mark fixated, ambitious. Lynn openly favoured them. Many filled the ranks of her Student Council and Prefect associations.

"What about the clothing issue?" asked Mr Stewart, the head of history, a man whose voice grated like a creaky old rocking chair that had sat out in the Muskoka sun for summers on end. "I've been saying for a long time that many of our problems would be solved by a school uniform. It's still warm, and I want to know how we can stop these kids from revealing nine-tenths of their bodies."

"Not just the girls," said Myra Solikowski, our union rep. "The boys too. Their pants hang so low you can see enough to bring your lunch back up." Myra's always been direct and outspoken that way.

"Plumber's butt," concurred the head of history, all the sawdust around his rockers floating off as he sat back down.

"Well," drawled Badlamenti, "first I'd like to know how to stop my own son from doing the same." He threw his hands up in the air.

We got up to leave. The kids would be coming in to pick up their timetables and find their classes

NIRANJAN

I sit through all the first classes, short periods in the afternoon. I collect their class outlines and file them in my binder. I sit at the back and try not to make a sound. They all get my name wrong – Niranjan Sittambalam – when they try to pronounce it, but I put my hand up anyway.

It's beautiful outside when I leave school. I can't wait to get out. I wish all days could be like this – warm, but not too hot, long and beautiful. The good months in Sri Lanka, after the monsoon season, are like this, except there's a cool breeze. When there isn't fighting nearby, you can go to the beach, and it's like the war doesn't even exist. Like it never existed. But there are reminders on the way – you can see bullet holes in the buildings. People don't have things: food, books, petrol to run their cars. When I was young, my whole family used to go to Point Pedro for the day, but we hadn't done that in many years, not since Karuna joined up to fight

When I get back to Tuxedo Court, Yalini akka is cooking in the kitchen and Geetha is in her stroller, buckled in, beside the kitchen table. Normally Geetha doesn't like being buckled unless she's being pushed but now she's strangely quiet. Rageev is sitting talking to someone I don't know, an older guy with a beard. He's bald and wears a red polo shirt and older style trousers, creased and wide at the bottom. They both stop talking as soon as I come in.

"That's the boy you're talking about?" asks the older man.

Rageev nods to me, "Vannakam, thambi!"

I stand there with my backpack almost half off my shoulder, removing my shoes. He doesn't introduce me. I'm not sure what to say.

Yalini akka calls me over to the kitchen. "Come here! Help me with this." The other two watch as I walk to the kitchen. There's something strange about the way the bald guy shakes his right leg. They start talking again once I'm gone, but they talk low. I can't make out what they're saying.

"Where's Soothy?" I ask Yalini akka. She's checking on the rice in the rice cooker and turning off the stove. Fried chilies and potato slices and mushrooms are emptied from the pan onto a paper napkin, which will soak up the oil.

"He's gone to fetch some things. I have to go get some milk and groceries now. Do you want to come with me? You can push the stroller."

They stop talking again as we walk through to the hallway to put on our shoes. "The food's ready," says Yalini akka. "I'll be back in an hour and we can eat. If you get hungry, just serve yourselves. Don't let the paruppu get cold."

Rageev nods. Bald guy shakes his right leg, and just the way it sits on the floor, withered, I know there's something wrong with it. It leans away at an angle from the rest of his body.

Geetha looks forward to being outside. She makes noises of excitement – Rageev kisses her as I wheel the stroller over to the door. I like buckling up her shoes around her little feet. They're like little doll's feet, but they kick excitedly.

I push the stroller across the sidewalks and road, being careful not to bump Geetha. She's Rageev's only child – he'd kill me if anything happened to her. We go to the Tamil grocery store across the street, which looks like it's permanently under construction. The packaged food's in open shipping boxes with their tops cut off like they've just been dumped. Even the plantains and coconuts and other vegetables just sit in boxes. They've got some shelves and a cooler where Yalini akka picks up the four-litre bag of milk. She gets some vegetables and some jaggery and cashews, and then I carry the groceries while she pushes Geetha out of the store.

"You didn't pay for those groceries," I say as we cross the road.

"They know us there. We've got credit."

I don't say anything – thoughts run through my head about whether I can go in there and pick out stuff on credit too.

"Let's go up to the park with Geetha," Yalini akka says. "You know, the baby's only four months old and she cries if we aren't moving." She pulls my hand towards the park, and we trudge up the driveway towards the rusted chain-link fence and then turn left over the grass. She has to go slowly with the stroller there because it's all hills. We walk past the tennis courts and go to the children's playground. The warm sun beats down on us, and there are a lot of kids at the playground already, screaming and shouting on the swings. Some parents as well.

Yalini akka stops before we get to the playground, parks the stroller, and tells me to sit down. She takes Geetha out of the stroller and bounces the baby on her lap to keep her moving. Yalini akka is sharp and serious; Geetha is happy and stares around. She's still a baby so everything's new, I guess.

"What do you think we do here?" asks Yalini akka.

I don't know what she means so I shake my head.

"What do you think Rageev does all day when he's not at the apartment?"

"I thought you and him had another apartment, so I guessed that's where you were."

"Where do you think Soothy is?"

"You said that he's out picking up some things," I reply.

She laughs. "Soothy is out collecting money from donors. That's what he's doing. Here, take Geetha. She likes you."

I take the baby and bounce her as steadily as I can in my lap. She bounces up and down in her red dress and buckled shoes and kicks her legs and sticks out her fists and drools, but she's laughing. I wait for Yalini akka to continue.

"Soothy didn't tell you what we do?"

"I thought maybe you stole stuff – he showed me a couple of things." I don't want to insult her. "What do you mean donors?" I ask.

"In the old days, before I met up with him, Rageev was into that gang business. He used to run around with those guys – drinking, stealing, fighting, they were doing some drugs. But now all his friends are gone. He's started working with the Tigers here. You'd better not say anything to them about it, but that's what they're doing. The guy you saw – Muruges – he used to fight with the Tigers. That's why he limps. A mine blew up near him – he has shrapnel in his right leg."

"Really? He fought with the Tigers?"

"Yes, of course! I fought with them too, did you know that?"

I did not. I do not. I can hardly see it. Is she serious?

"Yes, I was one of the Freedom Birds!" she laughs. "Can you believe that? A lifetime ago."

I still can't talk. Clutching Geetha to make sure she doesn't fall takes all my effort. "Yes, it's true!" laughs Yalini akka again, and maybe this is the first time I've seen her laugh. "Can you see me in camouflage uniform, ammunition pouches on me, a kuppie around my neck, an AK in my hand? Yes, that was me. My hair was short then. Many, many lifetimes ago. Long before I met Rageev, of course, and had Geetha. All I wanted then was to become a Black Tiger. Now everything's different – all that matters is Geetha."

I can only think of Yalini akka over the stove, stirring chilies and garlic into the curries. Geetha calling out for her attention. I can't think of her as a soldier, the black kuppie with poison – the suicide pill every soldier wears – around her neck. I can't think of her firing a rifle at people and wanting to be a Black Tiger, the elite of the elite, carrying out a suicide mission with a bomb strapped beneath her clothes.

"You can't think of me that way, can you?" she asks. "Well, that's what I was. A very different life. Here – let

44

me take the child. She's getting hot." I know better than to ask her why she's no longer a soldier, why she came over here. She seems to think it's funny rather than tragic. She betrays no regret, no sadness, does not seem to miss Sri Lanka. Like I do. I pass the baby over to her, and she straps Geetha into the stroller. "I'd heard of your brother too."

"You knew my brother?" We begin to slowly push the stroller over the hilly grass. The sun starts to go down.

Sweat runs down my neck. Flies bite at me. It's all too much to take in.

"I didn't know your brother, but I heard about him. His real name's Karuna, right?" I nod. "He has a good reputation – we've all heard of him. Why do you think you're here? We wouldn't just let anybody sleep here in the apartment. It's only because of your brother that we accepted Soothy's suggestion and took you in."

"Do you know where he is?"

"That I don't know, thambi. I left four years ago now – that part of my life is over. But we're doing some good work here. It's not fighting for the motherland like the soldiers, but it helps the struggle. You have to be brave."

I think about my brother. The last time I saw him was when Amma went to the recruiting station and tried to get him back. How long ago was that? The girls playing volleyball without a net, the dogs lying around on the dusty ground. If only I could see him again, get word to him. If only life could go back to being the way it used to be, before he joined the Tigers, before Amma and Appa became miserable all the time, before they sent me here.

"I'd like to help," I say. The words are out before I even realize that I'm saying them. "Anything if it means I can find my brother again.

Yalini akka looks sideways at me. Geetha is extremely quiet in her blue stroller as if she knows that what we're talking about is serious. "It's a big responsibility, Niranjan,"

Yalini akka finally says. "Be sure it's what you want. You may need to carry a gun. In that way, we are the same as our soldiers back home."

"Give me a gun," I say.

DANIEL

My mother phoned me up and begged while I was helping Lynn unpack the last of our things. "Come to Richmond Hill temple with us, mahan – it's been so long since you went. People will say we didn't raise you right."

I closed my hand over the phone and mouthed to Lynn, "They want us to go to the temple with them."

"Tell them no!" Lynn mouthed back, vigorously shaking her head.

On the weekend, Napoleon drove my parents and myself out to Richmond Hill in her Yutani hybrid. It was a smooth ride – I'll give her that – all the flashing consoles and digital aids made the front look more like a cockpit than a car.

In the same way I called her 'Napoleon' inside my head, she called me 'Dan' to my face. She knew all too well that this was a sign of disrespect in our culture. She wished to emphasize that we were equals, that as far as she was concerned, age didn't matter. It was also to mark the fact that she had triumphed in life whereas I had failed – she could address me any way she wanted and not worry about our father saying a thing. If I said the least thing disparaging about her on the other hand, he would fall on me – a ton of bricks. But it was Napoleon's car – I was just along for the ride.

Though our father had studied some engineering at school in Sri Lanka, he had ended up as a conductor on the railway lines. Government quotas during the seventies restricted his ability to push further. Still, he had had a government job with a pension, not something to be sneezed at. Everybody had thought him mad to give it up and move us out to Canada, but that's how strong willed he'd been. Decisive. Before disappointment and despair set in. Eventually, the Tigers tore up the steel and wood in the train tracks and used them to reinforce their bunkers.

"You both don't know how lucky you are to be living here," stated our mother from the rear seat. "Just think – if you were back home, what options would you have? We came here and sweated our blood for you! We went without so that you and your sister could have opportunities – remember that!" Her well-honed script. When they were on this tack, they tended to talk in exclamation points. Well, to be honest, my mother spoke like that. Our father's health and despair had slowed him down. In comparison, my mother's sly pastmastery of guilt, how cunningly she laced even the simplest conversation with that sly thread, was unrelenting.

Luckily, the temple soon rose before us, two monumental white stone-carved blocks above the landscape. The temple had grown over the last two generations so that it was now resplendent with decoration and work. Stones shipped from India, it was the inverse of a Gothic cathedral, so gleaming and alabaster white that the sun reflected off its walls and illuminated the ground.

"You know, our people had already built cities while *they* were still living in jungles," my father muttered.

The parking lot was hot with the reflected sun from over a hundred cars, few of them as nice as my sister's Neutron. My mother shooed away the money collectors with their red tin cans. The painted and colourful image of Ganesh astride his rat greeted us as we entered.

People lined up for prayers in front of the various statues while priests intoned their pujas. My mother greeted the priest at the window beside the entrance. With his beard and holy thread, he looked like a Brahmin straight out of the Mahabarata. My mother paid for them to perform three pujas: one for our family, the second for Napoleon and her in-laws, the third for me to come to my senses, leave Lynn, and move back in with them.

My parents and Napoleon walked around the smaller statues to pay obeisance while I sat down with Amma's purse. They ambulated in clockwise fashion around the alabaster statues painted in vivid colours. The smell of camphor and incense had seeped into the temple's very pillars. Smoke wafted in front of deities with skin as black as basalt, blue as primary school paint.

Napoleon followed our parents closely, shuffling her feet in imitation pilgrimage. She had adopted the way of custom while I had moved out. As Lynn said, Malathi knew which side her bread was buttered on. Napoleon resented me for moving out, for leaving her at home to contend with our parents and their expectations. She was modern, but had inherited something of the superstition, the narrowness, of our parents. She did not like the number two. She wouldn't begin new endeavours on days that were not Mondays or Wednesdays. Tuesdays were particularly bad. And – she would not travel in a car with three people.

The basalt statues, so heavy, so featureless, always represented Shiva and Parvati and were like the Tamils themselves, craggy and immobile. They were scarred with the past, with history. Fractured families. Lives of pain and sadness. The calamity of an age. The lingam stones were heavy pillars invoking Shiva's fertility. They were set in the ground in every village and town from Trincomalee to Mullaitivu, from Kappudu to the Hill Country.

People moved forward to have the priest circle the flame in front of their faces and bless them. They formed only the most recent line of countless worshippers who stretched back through time, two hundred thousand years, to the ascension of our species over the australopithicenes and neanderthals. The supplicants moved forward, backs doubled over, bent, shuffling through history, to receive their vermillion and ash. Amma and Appa urged me to move forward and take the ash, but I would not budge. I stayed rooted while they all lined up to smear the baked cow dung on their foreheads.

"You know you're embarrassing them," said Napoleon, nudging me in the ribs. "Go forward!"

I let her guilt me into joining the line but immediately resented her for it. The priest daubed my forehead with sandalwood paste. Amma and Napoleon were the more vocal ones, but Appa said nothing. He just shuffled forward and grunted his thanks after taking the ash and paste. The flame passed over his head, and for an instant I saw him evanescent, glowing, light in his eyes, the halo of white hair around his bald pate. The misery in the pores of his face burned away like camphor. He even seemed to lift his shoulders and straighten his back. This must have been what he looked like when he was young, I thought, a conductor on the trains, neem and mangosteen trees flying past; a man erect, secure, confident. I thought of the photos of him with his brothers. Then the moment passed, and the flame had gone – the spirit vanished, and he was made corporeal again.

"The least you can do is not embarrass him in public," said Napoleon curtly as we put on our shoes.

"I thought that was your job," I replied. "You're the one he always loved."

She shook her head. "No, he thought you were smarter. You were the one he counted on to win all the scholarships. You broke his heart when you left, and you don't even realize it. If he's sad and depressed, it's because of you."

"He succeeded with you!" I countered. "I can't think of a couple more successful at achieving the Canadian dream."

"Oh, grow up!"

That's rich, coming from one so small, I wanted to say, *who's always trying to overpower others and get the better of them.* Why did we always talk like that, more quarrelling than discussing, more arguing than agreeing? None of us had ever hugged or told one another that we cared. But we did, didn't we? It would have been out of character, I suppose; the implied assumption of our arrangement was that care was present. Surely this was what it was all about – familial love? Thambi Navaratnam had once said to me that the only things which existed were guilt and obligation? Shiva's law. Was he right?

Religion was only a punishing rod, like racism and sexism, homophobia and authoritarianism, a feature of the twentieth century to be packed and shipped away with the rest of its relics. Wasn't it? The best value one could hope to find in these relics was to consider them museum pieces: intellectual objects of curiousity and wonder, like my parents' abhorrence of Tuesdays and the number two, their belief in the evil eye.

"Do you remember the time…" I asked.

"Yes?"

"Do you remember the time Canadian Tire had a sale on bamboo curtain rods? You were very young. He took us all there and pointed them out, in the aisle, dyed in red and blue 80's colours. He said he was going to use them to beat us if we misbehaved, but he allowed us to pick the colour of the canes he would buy."

"You're making that up!" she whispered. "I don't remember that at all."

"You chose the red and I chose the blue," I continued, my shoes laced up. I could still smell the camphor and smoke, taking care not to let my face twitch. We never talked of those years, that period when we were young and imprisoned, when unhappiness was at its most concentrated.

"You're wrong," Malathi cried. "That never happened." And crossing her arms, she walked away to find her ca .

"Okay, pretend it didn't happen, Napoleon!" I shouted after her retreating body.

NIRANJAN

Soothy and I are playing his Xbox one evening, when Rageev drops in with someone else.

Rageev's upset. I don't know what it is. There's something different about him tonight. Maybe he misses his friends. I know how that feels. As if all the dogs are howling when you walk down the street.

He's comfortable with the guy standing beside him though. They're not friends exactly. The guy has very dark skin, almost black, as dark as a Tamil can get. He's wiry and wears a red shirt with flowers on it. Tan pants. Wisps of hair stick up like he was in too much of a hurry to comb. Dark sunglasses, a thin moustache. The moustache is a slit, almost like a frown. Rageev doesn't introduce him, but in my mind I start calling him 'Dark Moustache'.

We all take the elevator down. A couple of residents from the tenth floo , a small boy and his grandmother, also Tamil, get in. They stand in the elevator, keeping as much distance as they can. They know who Rageev is. His photo's been in the paper.

Walking into the ravine, we kick the dead, dry leaves as we go down. The chill air settles in. Rageev stays at the entrance to the path and keeps watch. The dark skinny man leads us down to the water. We make our way between fallen trees and pine cones and needles and rocks. Shopping bags and bottles and junkie needles and other disgusting things are in the shallow water.

Dark Moustache walks ahead of me. I follow. Soothy brings up the rear. Dark Moustache carries a large plastic case. What's in it?

He doesn't say anything, just tells me to stand near the water. I'm all jumpy, and my foot keeps kicking at the stream.

Dark Moustache frowns, tells us to be quiet.

I think about following orders. Whether it's better to follow orders most of the time, or not follow them most of the time. I look at Soothy, all calm. For someone I live with, how well do I know him? How can he be so calm? He isn't my brother, he isn't my cousin, what is he? We're just Tamils who've had it rough and ended up in the same place.

Dark Moustache tells us to stand up straight, extend our hand, make it into a grip. He adjusts our postures. He tells us to brace ourselves, adopt a defensive stance. Looks at our hands once more. As he opens the case, I'm the most worried I've been since I came to Canada. But finally I understand what's going on. A lot of guns – black, gunmetal, silver – in that case. Cartridges of rounds. Some ammo clips. Even two pairs of headphones. All packed tight inside that foam padding. He tests different guns in our hands until he finds ones that are right for our grips

For me, I get a really small pistol, silver plated. I didn't realize my hands were so small. The gun looks funny, like a prop from some old movie. Other handguns in the case are really big.

"Don't worry," he says from behind his dark glasses. "You can do a lot of damage with a small gun."

He takes away the pistol and settles on a gun that's even lighter. It's plastic, and he puts it together from two parts. The main part of it is hardened plastic. It's really really light, and it only becomes heavier when he feeds a clip into the handle. He takes out the clip, and it goes light again. Dark Moustache shows me the rounds inside the clip, little jacketed bullets, which are forced up against a heavy spring.

"This is a Glock 9 mm," he says. "It can evade some metal detectors, chariyo?"

He pulls back the sliding mechanism. We have to practice our stance. Then I'm shown how to hold and aim the gun.

"Relax, machan, relax into the stance. You're not flying a kite. Squeeze the trigger calmly. Don't think of it as firing a gun. Think of it as making a punch. Your enemy's coming at you so you have to make the first punch. If you think of it as firing a gun and killing someone, you won't be able to do it. Think of it as striking a blow. Defending yourself. Don't be fancy and try to shoot for the head or the hand or the leg. Shoot right dead in the centre."

I wonder why he's mainly talking to me. Why doesn't he look at Soothy's stance and talk to him? Is my nervousness that obvious?

He hands us each a pair of headphones to protect our ears.

I'm still standing there when Soothy fires off the first round. I'm still pointing and practicing my stance like an idiot. The noise of Soothy's shot is deafening, even with my headphones. His arms jump with the gun.

Dark Moustache laughs. Soothy says nothing. He's far gone – really into it. Just a few minutes ago, we were playing on the Xbox.

Dark Moustache tells us to put our guns down. He places their safeties on. Down by the water, where the moon shines through, there's still some light. It bounces off his glasses, shows up ripples in the water. How does he see? Dark Moustache picks up beer bottles from the ground, abandoned from dead campfires. He washes the brown bottles in the water, then sets them up on rocks in the middle of the stream. Maybe four or five perch in a wobbly line on flat rocks. He asks that we step back, take the safeties off, shoot them.

There's hardly any light. I have to search for the moonlight glinting off the bottles to sight them.

I look to Soothy, but he's somewhere else. I finally fire. Try my best. Round after round roars in the darkness. My arms kick. Like a donkey's leg. In the movies, on TV, they look like Robin Hood. You think you can be Robin Hood too. Only, Robin Hood's bow doesn't jump half a metre every time he shoots an arrow. I try to keep my arms stiff, but the recoil makes them jump. Like my arms are pulled by strings; I'm not in control of my body. And the sound! We unload against these bottles and some hit, but it's not because we pull master shots. No way. We hit maybe a couple of those bottles because our guns are semi-auto and keep feeding bullets every time we cock the trigger. All we're doing is aiming artillery in a general direction. Two more bottles fall simply from sheer wobbliness. The vibration of the other bullets striking the water. There's one bottle left. I try and try. Cannot take it down.

Soothy just pauses, lifts up his gun, exhales, brings it back down again. Breathes in. Breathes out.

Crack!

His arms jump.

The bottle's no longer there.

Just pieces ruined, jagged, lying with the others between rocks on the floor of the stream

Our clips are empty. The smell of barium and lead is in the air. It's hard to see smoke in this darkened light, but I sure can taste it.

Dark Moustache laughs and laughs. "You've learned the first thing," he says. "Like I said, you don't shoot at the opponent's heart or his hand or his head. You shoot in the middle and keep firing. You take him down."

He gets us to hand back our guns, then help him pick up all the shells we can find. Soothy seems reluctant to give up his gun, like it's a new favourite toy.

"Where'd you learn to shoot like that?" I ask.

I don't see it, but I feel him smile in the darkness.

I can smell Dark Moustache. He doesn't smell of cumin or sweat like Yalini akka, he doesn't have that smell of tension like Rageev. He smells of machinery and oil. I find it hard to look him in the eye. When he collects my gun, he just grunts a laugh. Even his laugh is wet and electric. I shiver. I must have said something because Soothy laughs at me too.

"Are you cold?"

I shake my head.

I fall in line between the other two as before. We march to the top of the ravine silently. Work our way around the fallen pine cones and needles in the silt. Can't smell the gummy pine any more. Barium and lead fill my nostrils. Rageev waits for us at the top.

"Nobody?" asks Dark Moustache.

"Nobody," says Rageev.

"Chariyo," says Dark Moustache.

DANIEL

The kids were noisy in the hallways, boisterous. The administration had stopped walking the halls long ago, though Stevenson still made a show of agitatedly striding through with her walkie-talkie. The hall monitors employed by the schools were rubber-toothed bulldogs, at best.

Raptis and Cram were in the science lab. Lunch for me was sometimes spent with Lynn, or as she became increasingly busy, with Raptis and Cram.

"If they'd only walk through the halls, kids wouldn't have an excuse to skip class," muttered Raptis, his large meal spread out on the science bench in front of him. He had a formidable appetite and had loosened his belt and splayed his legs so that as he leaned over the bench, he looked like a jeweller with a loupe, examining a tray of diamonds. The pickled eggs he was eating sat in a plastic container of their own. They smelled something awful; they even overpowered the whiff of sulphur that clung to the lab.

Cram ate a large sandwich, exquisitely packed, made with proscuitto, ham, brie, avocado, and alfalfa sprouts. He ate slowly and carefully. The food had been assembled in such a way, with its accompanying carrot sticks and side serving of granola, that you might be forgiven for assuming it'd been purchased at a fancy deli. I looked at my two friends; they couldn't have been more different. Raptis, his lab coat open like a bath robe, sprawled over his food and masticated loudly. Food stains adorned his clothes. Cram was careful, considerate, and leaned back in his cleanly pressed powder blue shirt and tie. Even the manner in which he ate suggested that he had factored the activity into that day's lesson plans.

"I've never seen them patrol the hallways," stated Cram. "Not since I started teaching."

My own lunch was made of leftovers that Lynn had packed.

"The previous guy was better – you'd see him out in the halls – but he was a prick too," said Raptis. "They've all been pricks since Harris changed things in the nineties. Used to be part of the same union. Principals and vice-principals listened to us. I had a passion to teach a particular subject – they'd let me. Now everybody's just number crunching; they're middle management. I don't know what it'll be like when you guys get older. Luckily, I'll be dead by then."

Though elder to Cram, I hadn't experienced the sea change that constituted the Harris reforms. The educational system we had gone to school under was not the same one we worked in.

"Everything's deflated," continued Raptis, "the quality of education, the standard of behaviour, expectations, and examples, everything winds down with time. It was a good thing in the sixties, seventies, even the eighties were okay, but what do you get now? An 'A' isn't worth an 'A'. They just stamp 'em out. Teaching used to mean something. Now it's a factory of mediocrity."

"Well, I don't know," Cram countered, "it depends on the way you look at it. It's not all bad. Technology for one thing. Kids are way more adept, faster, with technology than we were at their age. They pick it up. Second nature."

"You're talking about that fancy new computer lab Badlamenti's pushing, aren't you? He takes being a prick to new heights. Hey, how Italian is Badlamenti?"

"How Italian is he?" I asked dutifully.

"Don't encourage him," said Cram, putting down his sandwich. "Yeah, why not the computer lab? Why is that bad?" Cram straightened his tie. "Why shouldn't kids have access to modern technology? In private schools, they have interactive whiteboards and a mounted projector in every classroom. Have you looked in the Communications book room? We've still got the same novels, the same copies of books, as when I was in high school: The Stone Angel, Lord of the Flies, Streetcar Named Desire. They're great books, but progress isn't always a bad thing."

"I argued against that lab!" shot back Raptis. "Think of all the things we could have done with that money. Repaired classrooms, gotten supplies, gotten a decent breakfast program going for the kids. What do we need a flashy computer lab for? Just optics, isn't it? We're supposed to be teaching kids to think for themselves. All the software in that lab – it's the antithesis of thinking. Kids can't learn anymore. They're on their cellphones. Stripping away the last brain cells they have. You sit those kids in front of a computer and you're only rewarding them for bad behaviour. School should be about learning – books, enlightened discussion – not video games."

"You still don't have a cellphone?" I enquired.

"Look who decided to join the discussion. Yeah, I don't have a cellphone – so what? What's wrong with that? Am I missing out? Is there a national emergency?"

I could smell the hydrochloric acid in the lab. It wasn't as strong as the sulphurous eggs, but perhaps it was more ingrained. Years and years of student experiments, spilt acid from pipettes and flasks etched into the heavy benches. It was the same smell that clung to my father from the chemical sheds. Where did Raptis order his materials from?

Raptis was a bit older than my father, but had no children of his own. He wasn't close to his family either – he had a sister somewhere, some nephews or nieces, but never talked about them. The smell in the lab reminded me of the smell that sometimes hung over my father; it was a co-mingling of bitterness and regret, like bile regurgitated from the stomach.

"How are your students?" I asked Cram.

"Good," he replied thoughtfully. "I have that one general learning strategies class that's a nightmare, but the others are good." If Raptis was bitter, Cram was upbeat.

"Same as last year," sighed Raptis. "Hey, that kid you were interested in is in my science class."

"Niranjan?" I asked. "Since when?"

"Dunno. My class is at capacity, but they put him and a couple of other numbskulls in. I don't have benches for them. So I borrow some chairs from next door. I've got 'em sitting at the side of the class. How do you like that? How am I supposed to do lab experiments with this?"

"They're expecting some of them to drop so they overenrol the classes," sighed Cram. "All of mine are thirty or more, except the locally developed of course."

"Of course!" snorted Raptis, sarcastically. The locally developed class was filled with kids with behavioural issues or learning disabilities – the types of kids that Raptis hated. He also hated the Tamils who caused trouble, and others. These discussions were fraught with tension. I was cautious and tried to tread carefully.

"Anyway, Niranjan," I said. "What's he like? I guess Lynn forgot to tell me about it."

"Wait a minute," interjected Cram, "did you say Niranjan? Tall, thin, never smiles? Yeah, I've got him too. Both in my English and my GLS class."

It seemed that I was the only one who hadn't seen the elusive maladjusted object of our discussion. "What's he like?" I inquired of them both.

"What's he like?" echoed Raptis. "He just sits off on the side, is all. Sometimes takes notes. Doesn't say anything.

He's at the back, where all the troublemakers are. I'm not giving him a textbook – not until he returns the one from last year. Well, two, if you count him and his friend – what's his name?"

"Soothy."

"Yeah, him – look to your right, next bench over."

I looked to my right as Raptis directed. The lab bench was identical, black with scratchings and scars over the years. There was a tap and a sink, the customary Bunsen burner ports with their gas valves. Cram peered over my shoulder.

"See that burn mark – can you make it out?" asked Raptis. I could not. "That's where your boy's friend, Soothy, wrote his name in cyclohexane and set it on fire.

"Why?" I asked.

"To see his name in flames – what else? That's the type of knuckleheads I deal with now. Not students – thugs. Didn't you take Niranjan up to camp with you last year, Daniel Boone?"

"Yeah, that's right. You did, didn't you?" Cram straightened his tie as he leaned back in his seat.

"Yeah. I thought it was a good idea. Good for the kid. Lynn fought against it – she was right."

"What happened?"

"We went out on a hike through the fields. At night. I took the boys, and Lynn took the girls. Niranjan was with my group of course. There were some woods and fields – that's pretty much it out there – no people, houses, or cars. It was dark, and we had to use flashlights. There are wild animals out there – you can hear 'em at night. Niranjan had a panic attack. I don't know why. He'd lived near animals and grown up near the jungle, but it was different out there – kid was freaked out. He thought we were going to leave him there – he'd never been outside of Scarborough, I guess. He curled up into a ball in the middle of the field. I didn't even realize he wasn't with the group until I did a head count about ten minutes later. We had to go back, combing with flashlights until we found him. For the rest of the trip, he just lay curled up on the sofa, same as in the field.

"Yeah, Lynn really doesn't have patience for that kid, does she? She likes those alpha types. Isn't that right, Daniel Boone?" Raptis ribbed. Cram laughed. He nodded and talked about Niranjan in his classes, but didn't have anything new to relate. When Niranjan showed up, he sat at the back and was silent, much like in Raptis's class. Unlike Soothy, Niranjan was not a talker, and that was one of the reasons Lynn distrusted him.

When I started working at LCC, I had never in a million years thought I would end up dating Lynn Varley. You might as well have told me that I'd end up dating Badlamenti. The idea of dating *anybody* at work wasn't particularly appealing. The school was a fishbowl, and teachers tend to be a mouthy, judgemental set. Lynn was attractive of course – anyone could see that – and had a strong personality. When I joined, she was moving from teaching to guidance. It was my first year teaching the media studies course, and there was a kid called Seelan who hardly ever came to class – he and I used to fight when he did occasionally show up. I was more strict then.

Anyway, Lynn was his guidance counsellor in second semester, and she got him to try and make up some of the assignments he'd missed. The semester came to a close, and he still didn't have enough to pass. Lynn came to see me. She importuned me to pass him, give him a technical fifty, so he could obtain the credit. It was meaningless, she said, to keep failing him. Anyway, no one would think his technical fifty was a good mark. I argued with her and held my ground. Relatively new to teaching, I used to go along with what people such as Raptis said about marks needing to be earned.

More than a year later, Seelan died while waiting at a TTC bus stop. Somebody gunned him down. Badlamenti had referred to it at our inaugural staff meeting this year. But back then, I had to log onto MarkBook to see what grade I had given him. Students had come and gone, and I couldn't remember what mark I'd given Seelan. It was a 46 percent. Forty-six! So close to fifty! That was when I realized that grades are meaningless. Are they not? How can a number truly take the measure of a person's abilities, their worth? Did my failing him really accomplish anything, given the short span of his life?

Even before that, some air of contrition would waft me up, urge me to volunteer my services to Lynn. She seemed to know where things were at. She couldn't get any males to help her take kids away to camp and asked me to join in.

It was that second night, the first time we had really been away together, when things changed.

There was an all-pervasive stillness, a silence, to Albion Hills. It had been there in the gathering wind as we arrived, in the land around us. It took us the better part of a day to settle into it. A warm tonal atmosphere, this silence was full and thick, like waves of milk. It sat comfortably upon the air, rustling the stalks of grass, brushing the needles of the conifers. The staff from Albion Hills had gone home, and it was just us, far from the city. You could hear the cicadas if you listened carefully. There were some wild turkeys around too, the kids had spotted them. But all in all, it was peaceful and complete. This was my first time up there, a whole year before Niranjan joined us.

After our hike, I'd done the rounds on the boys' side of the dorms, made sure everyone had turned off their lights. I found Jayanath and Allan, two of the grade tens, still up. They were giggling, and I could see a little bit of light coming from underneath their door. I thought they might be watching a porno or something on a laptop, but that wasn't the case.

The camp was in a valley, and it was hard to get a signal anyway. We really did feel isolated from the world, in a pocket of space and time separate from real life. The boys were passing a small bottle of Malibu rum back and forth, taking sips, and whispering.

When I opened the door suddenly, surprised them, and took their bottle away, they were crestfallen and embarrassed. As if I had caught them with a porno. "Aw, please don't tell Ms Varley," pleaded Jayanath. "If she phones my parents, I'll be dead! I didn't even drink any!"

"C'mon, Mr N, you're cool, right?" said Allan.

Their roommates were asleep and hadn't been in on it. "Go to sleep," I said, and took the bottle.

I walked the contraband over to the girls' dorm and knocked on Lynn's door. She took a while answering. When she did, she put her hand across the doorway, blocking the entrance as if I shouldn't enter. I got the feeling that I'd woken her and she might be upset.

"You had anything like this?" I asked.

She shook her head and said, "No, they just wouldn't go to sleep – that's all. Trying to email and get a signal out here, keeping each other up talking – you know how girls are. Well, do you want to call their parents, or should I?"

I didn't say anything and looked down at her pyjamas. They had little cartoon pictures of cats, also wearing pyjamas. The drawings were either funny or horrendous, depending on your point of view. They made her look softly childish and vulnerable, although her hair, a neat wave of colour in it, was combed straight. I guess she had to comb it before answering the door.

"There's always one, Dan. We have to call their parents by law."

"They're kids," I said, "and we've had such an eventful day already. They hardly drank any of it. If this is the worst that happens, I'll be relieved. One of them seems really worried – Jayanath. It'd be a shame to make their parents drive up here in the middle of the night over this. We don't want to ruin the trip completely."

She frowned, and I could see that she didn't like my logic, but she ushered me in. "You could lose your job behind thinking like that," she said. "You should really be careful what you say. We've got to get rid of that bottle – the other kids shouldn't see it."

"Who's to know?" I smiled. I think being away from the regular world had made me bold. "Between you, me, and your cat pyjamas, let's just tell the boys we threw it out and give them a break."

Her cheekbones lifted as if she were about to say something, then fell back down, the thought actually passing over her face before her lips settled into a thin smile. She had lovely cheekbones, sharp and angular, large eyes. In general, she was in good shape, although you'd be hard pressed to tell with those flannel cat pyjamas covering her. Mostly, during the day, she wore pantsuits and blouses, but once in a while, as at the camp, she would wear jeans, and I'd notice her when she walked away, or when her back was turned to me. I discovered later that she went to yoga at least three times a week.

There was something criminal about how assuredly, how stealthily, we crept into the kitchen and got a couple of cans of Coke from the fridge and styrofoam cups. It had been a long time coming, but we had finally become relaxed around one another. We were our real selves.

We took these things back to her room, and she sat on her bed above me while I sat on the floo , and we drank our rum and Cokes. It was a strange misdemeanour, and the thrill of doing it, defying the students and our roles that way, was a huge part of what made the transgression enjoyable. We had to keep the lights off and drink in the dark so as not to wake the kids. Her room had no window, and therefore it was an absolute dark that enveloped us – her voice, in lilting whispers where usually it was businesslike and sharp, and her smell, which also seemed to arrive in whispers, was a mixture of the oil in her hair, a kind of heady linseed smell, and the sweat from her body. Our talk was sparing and punctuated by quiet sipping from the styrofoam cups. I wasn't a big drinker of alcohol anyway, and I'd never been fond of rum and Coke – it ruins the taste of both the rum and the Coke. It always seems to me that people drink the Coke against their will, a way of justifying the rum. Sour and sweet, the two drinks could not be more different – the weird concoction giving edge to our conversation, lending it a medicinal flush

"You know what I'm saying," she whispered, and when I didn't reply, "I know you see Raptis doing it all the time, but he's got a lot of history in the school, he can retire whenever he wants."

"Well, Raptis isn't really…"

"You spend too much time hanging out with him and Cram. It's about time you found a sense of adulthood – you can't keep talking to the kids like you're one of them." She poured me more of the rum, but I couldn't keep pace with her. "Do you know what I'm saying?" she asked in stage whispers. I'd only started drinking in my twenties; it wasn't an activity I was very good at.

"You know that the only reason they hired me is because I'm Tamil?" I asked.

"I know – you wanted to be a filmmake ." She leaned forward and whispered so that I could smell the rum on her breath, those thin lips modulating the air so that it tripped over her teeth and bounced on her tongue, warm outbursts of sonic rum-soaked meaning in the dark.

"Well, the joke's on them because I don't even speak the language!"

"You're more than the colour of your skin or where you come from."

"Coming from you?" I said. She hated it when I reminded her she was black, but I secretly enjoyed it, pretending not to notice the faux pas.

I was sick of talking about school anyway, but the conversation drifted to our families, which was worse. She told me that I was an adult and must take charge of my life, that I could not play the 'blame game', whatever that means, that I could not adopt a 'victim's mentality'. I tried to tell her what it was like being Tamil, that you grew up expecting to be seen, expecting to perform, but never be heard. That you were always at the behest of those more powerful than you: those who were older and in positions of authority. All the expectations that it entailed.

"Well," she said – again the rum and Coke–soaked whispers came my way – "from what you've told me, your sister didn't feel like that, and women have it lots worse. No, don't deny it, that's one universal constant – women always have it worse."

The discussion had become too intense, too serious. I was being too much of a sop, it was true. I did not like feeling vulnerable and exposed like that about my family, so the next time her foot brushed past my knee, I grabbed it. With ferocity, in the darkness, I began massaging it and worked every toe, every muscle at the ball of her foot, the tendons, the ankle, and pushing those ridiculous flannel pyjama legs up, massaged her shapely calves.

She would not have brushed her foot past my knee repeatedly if she did not mean to, I reasoned to myself as I removed the rest of her clothes; no one makes that many misjudgements, even if it's dark. Besides, she could have resisted me at any time, told me to stop.

But she did not.

Without the dark, I don't think we could have done it; the darkness provided a cover and even lubrication that the entire bottle of rum could not have supplied on its own. She pulled her pillow over her face to stop herself from crying out in the darkness, and I kissed the other side of the pillow, biting its fabric with my teeth. I imagined the pillow to be her strong cheeks, her thin lips. After all the talk about our parents, how could I not imagine my mother sitting at the end of the bed in the dark, shaking her head and saying, "Son, what are you doing?"

It almost made me not come, and I had to shake my head against the pillow to dispel the illusion of my mother. "We're just trying to have fun and not get pregnant," I whispered in response.

"What?" whispered Lynn into the pillow.

I pressed on.

All sex is strange and powerful to me, and I'm always grateful when it comes my way. We lay there afterwards, naked, salty beads of perspiration strung between our torsos, the sweat winnowing and breaking apart as she separated herself from me. I could almost smell my sweet joy spreading itself into her chest and lungs, cooling in the valley between her throat and shoulders, evaporating like liquid on a hot stone.

"What did you say just then?" she asked.

I shook my head, "Nothing." As I lay back to give her room and pulled off the condom, she sprang alive with fury. I could feel her jump like a bird above me, the mattress sinking underneath the weight of her feet and folding into a V. "Listen," she hissed, placing one foot on my throat, holding it there to let me know she could crush me if she wished. "You won't tell anyone about this, will you?"

It was the foot I had massaged so tenderly.

I would have shaken my head, but I couldn't. Her pressure was too great.

"You took advantage of me," she shout-whispered. "You got me carried away with the alcohol. It's all just fun and games with you, isn't it? Isn't it?"

She eased off a bit, let me breathe, and I repeated her words after they had tripped across her hot tongue and pointed teeth, assuaging her guilt.

The next day, when we took the kids back, we sat at opposite ends of the bus, hardly acknowledging each other.

It took a while to smooth things out between us, to convince her I was really attracted to her, to begin dating normally. But now, two years had passed, we were as solid as could be. Jayanath and Allan were the president and vice-president of the Student Administrative Council. All the kids from that trip were older, scrunching their way through the last year of high school, hungry for scholarships and admissions to competitive universities. Lynn and I lived together.

And Seelan, poor old Seelan, was dead.

I only thought these things of course, didn't say anything to Raptis or Cram. I don't know that they'd have understood. Like I said before, I value loyalty and discretion in myself and others.

I picked myself up and gathered my lunch container and fork. "I'd better go and have a word with Lynn about Niranjan. I think you teach him during my prep period. Is it okay if I drop in and have a word?"

"Why don't you just call him down to the office?" asked Cram.

"He'll never come down."

"Be my guest," said Raptis, with a flourish of the hand

I said my goodbyes and left and thought about the strange profession I was in. When my dreams of becoming a filmmaker dried up, I fell into teaching

It was like choosing between the rods at Canadian Tire. My sister had chosen the red and I had taken the blue. By teaching, I simply chose the blue bamboo cane instead of the red.

NIRANJAN

Rain smashes against the windshield. Soothy and I have been given guns. Before giving us guns, Rageev made us pray in front of the God cupboard. Now he's driving us downtown to a meeting. Wish they'd at least play some music in the car. Everybody's tense as if we're going to a fight. Worries start racing through my head. What if the Glock I've been given isn't enough? Nobody will know how I died.

Finally, Rageev turns off the highway. Our eyes meet when he turns around to check his blind spot. "Hide that gun," he says quietly. "I don't want police to see and pull me over."

We stop in an area that seems mostly Korean. Somewhere I've never been before. There are English language signs too: Korean Bookstore, Korean Grocery Market, Bi Bim Bap. Rageev parks in front of an old rundown apartment building. Not like ours – there's only nine floors. We climb stairs instead of using the elevator. Rageev tucks his gun into his jacket. Soothy puts his inside the waistband of his jeans, so I do the same. Feels strange with it pressed against my belly and thigh.

I hang behind as we walk down the hall, try not to let my fear show. They keep looking all around, on high alert. I can smell Chinese cooking, or is it Korean? It stinks up the hallway, making me gag. Rageev looks back, his scarred and burned face warning me: hold it together.

They pause at the door. Rageev tries to look in through the peephole before he knocks. What's waiting for us in there?

An Asian guy opens the door. We all go inside. Should we take off our shoes? But this guy's dressed in a suit, wearing shiny dress shoes. Rageev says nothing. He recognizes a guy at the back: the old guy in a wheelchair, doing a jigsaw puzzle on the kitchen table. The old guy's bald, but he wears a grey suit, a nice green shiny handkerchief in the breast pocket. The other guys in the apartment are all young. Everybody's Asian. A couple of them wear suits, but the other three are dressed like Soothy and me – casual. They shut up soon as they spot Rageev. Hard for them not to stare at his face. Two of them smoke, and the smoke is thick. I start to cough. I wish they'd open the curtains or the windows. Dark as hell, and the smoke swirls blue against black curtains.

"You're late," says the old man in the wheelchair, looking up.

"Traffic," replies Rageev gruffly.

The old guy puts down his puzzle piece. The picture on the box is a lake and mountain. "I hope you're not going to ask for more time," says Professor X finall , narrowing his eyes. "You people – never reliable…"

"Let's discuss it – in private."

Rageev turns away from Professor X, looks at us and says, "Wait here till I come back." He goes behind the bald guy's chair, turns him around. They disappear into a bedroom. Rageev pushes while Professor X smooths out his blanket and sighs.

What's going on? Soothy sits down on the sofa. I follow. We look at the young Asian guys. They never stop looking back. The ones wearing the suits are almost identical. I think they're related, brothers perhaps. The other ones seem more menacing. They're older than me and Soothy, definitely in their twenties. They speak to each other in Korean, grinning once in a while. I think it's Korean. They whisper-shout their words and chuckle. Sometimes, one of them looks back at us. He nods, points his cigarette as if indicating me. I don't know if it's friendly or a challenge. Hard to read his grin. He wears a basketball jersey. His buddy wears a vest. The third wears a tracksuit top and jeans. They could be university students on a break between classes. I try not to cough, despite the smoke.

Soothy and I don't say anything, we just look ahead. There's a clock on the wall. Below it is the jigsaw puzzle – undone. The lake and mountain seem far away. What does the writing on the box say? Is it in Korean or Japanese? The longest fifteen minutes of my life. I can feel my balls itch. What will I do if I need the toilet? If I really have to go? Clench my thighs and hold it in.

"So you drive a Yutani? Nice Japanese car," says one of the suits in thick English.

I look at Soothy. He nods but doesn't say anything – crosses his arms.

"We know the guy who makes your Japanese car," says the guy in the tracksuit top. "We get you a good deal." They all laugh.

Then we go back to saying nothing. Smoke continues to thicken the room. One of the guys offers Soothy a cigarette. For a second, he looks like he might take it. Then he whispers "No," and coughs, mutters a thank you. But his eyes stay on the packet, the hand that holds it. He looks into the guy's eyes, coughs again.

They blow smoke. I feel it irritating my lungs. In an odd way, they're like us, aren't they?

Finally, Rageev comes out by himself. He nods to the Asian guys sitting opposite us. They can't seem to take their eyes off his burned skin. It shuts them up. "Come on, guys, let's go," says Rageev. "Let's get some food." We get up and follow him.

My guts are heaving inside my stomach.

I tell them I need to run to the toilet bad.

"What's wrong with you?" asks Soothy.

"I can't breathe – this Canadian air – think I may have athsma." The words are out before I've thought them through. They might even be true. Never felt so exhausted before.

"Give me your gun," demands Rageev.

"What?"

"Give me your gun."

I give it to him. He looks around carefully while I'm handing it over. "You're useless," he mutters. I run for a nearby McDonald's to get to the washroom. They follow as quickly as they can, not running themselves. I really do have to piss, but it's also smoke in my chest, nervousness in my belly. My bowels feel coated with lead. That smell from the ravine. Barium and lead. Metal and gun oil. I want to throw up. All that comes up is dry heaves. I splash water over my face to feel halfway normal.

The smells of the bathroom finally filter through. Register, bringing me back to reality. Here and now. I've been around Tigers before. What is the problem?

The Koreans (or whatever) are probably sitting in their apartment, laughing.

At me.

Rageev and Soothy waiting for me at a table with food. Are they laughing?

A quarter pounder cheeseburger for me, with fries and Coke.

I could turn around, walk away. Use a different exit. Never come back. My stomach heaves again at the thought. I can't go back to my aunt's. No. Never. Not her. Not ever. The lack of freedom, lack of control – she is a nightmare.

Go over, join them. They're already talking about something else.

"Who were those guys?" I ask. "Were they Korean or Japanese, or what?"

"Look at him," grins Rageev, chomping a mouthful of fries.

"First he thinks he's got athsma, now he wants to know who they are," laughs Soothy.

"They're people who'll tear your eye out and eat it for dessert," laughs Rageev.

"What do you care who they are?" asks Soothy. "They're all Orientals anyway – they all go back to the same triads."

"They do stick together," nods Rageev, now looking out the window. He had gone in with nothing, come out with nothing. What did they talk about? "You ever heard of Asian Assassinz? The FOB killers? No? Then don't worry. Eat your food."

I look at the quarter pounder. My stomach shrivels to the size of a peanut. Smoke's still churning in my bowels. Lungs feel like plastic bags that someone's burnt holes into.

Why do we pray to God if He moves all the pieces, gives us such few choices?

Are we just football players praying before a game? Did we just see the opposition in that living room?

I feel as if some unseen hand is moving the pieces in my life and I have so very little choice.

DANIEL

The school system had crumbled. Literacy had plummeted and numeracy was down. Raptis was correct. Numbers and funding were more important, as were optics and public relations. And the kids knew it. We settled for massaging the grades of the glut in the middle, passing them with technical fifties. The keeners were fine – they left school with eighties and nineties, mercenaries made mercenary by a mercantile world – but the others were essentially useless for the academic and economic realities that lay before them. They were armed with little more than pieces of paper that verified they'd passed, and courses like Civics here.

What did I care? I didn't really bother too much over grades, not since the thing with Seelan. Like Lynn said, why make things worse than they already were? In our early thirties, we had already begun to count down towards our eighty-five factors, when we could take full pension. When I was their age, fourteen, fifteen, I couldn't wait to be an adult, grown up with a grownup's rights and responsibilities, to be out of the home. Now here I was, already thinking of retirement.

During my prep, I went to find Niranjan in Raptis's room. I had feared they would be immersed in some intricate lab, but they were only discussing gravity. On the board was a diagram of the CN tower and a figure dropping a penny off the top. I remembered the urban legend: If there was no wind resistance, the penny would achieve the momentum of a bullet due to gravity. It could bore a hole through the head of an onlooker standing below.

On Raptis's wall was the poster of Einstein smiling above his quote, "Gravitation cannot be held responsible for people falling in love." It was a cute quote. I could see Niranjan sitting off to the side, dutifully taking notes, attempting to be as inconspicuous as possible. He stood out with his massive dry wispy hair, his scraggly beard, older than everybody else. His face so gaunt that the skin strained over his jaw. He gripped his pen with such tension that veins bulged out on his knuckles.

There was a lull in the discussion and I went in, the smell and aftertaste of sulphur and hydrochloric acid hitting my nostrils, my tongue. Niranjan looked cornered and glanced out the window more than once, wanting to escape.

He took his sweet time coming out of the classroom. "I didn't know you were back at the school," I said. He just stood there, maintaining silence, arms folded.

"Everybody's worried about you, your aunt especially," I continued. "We are too. Your aunt's very upset. She calls every week to ask if I've seen you or not."

"That's the only reason you're here, right? Because you don't really care what happens to me. It's just because they're getting on your case, right?"

My hand unconsciously went out to him, but he backed away immediately. I quickly gave him space. "We want the best for you."

"The best for me?! I didn't notice you saying anything when my aunt put me down in front of everybody. She treated me like shit. Man, what am I telling you for? You all knew it – and you didn't care. She's not my aunt. She's just a crazy person that my mother is related to."

He really had a winning personality. "You're not getting it worse than anybody else, you know? That's the way Tamils are. Tons of people back home would love to be in your situation."

"Well, now you don't have to worry about me no more."

It was becoming a loud conversation. I tried to hush him, but he only grew more irate. "Look," I said, "you've got to come home. Where you gonna go? You belong with your family. Where you living now?"

"I'm not going to tell you that! I know the law. I'm seventeen. Nobody gets custody of me!"

"You know the law. That's great."

"And anyway," he said, unfolding his arms, pointing those bony fingers at me, "didn't you move out and leave home when you were young? Aren't you being a hypocrite?"

"That was a different circumstance."

"Different how? My aunt doesn't care. She treats me like crap. The only reason she's interested is because of the money my mother sends. Amma's not doing that anymore, is she?"

I didn't really know. Out of breath, he began to wheeze. Had the conversation exerted him that much? Niranjan pulled an orange plastic inhaler out of his pocket, shook it, took a couple of drags. "How are you going to pay for things?" I asked.

"None of your business."

"There's no point talking to you. I can see that you don't want help! Get back into class!" I pushed him into the classroom. Niranjan had gotten under my skin and ruffled my composure.

Some of the students heard my words. Raptis looked up, concerned. I didn't know what to say. I closed the door after Niranjan and stormed out of there.

At lunch, I apologized to Raptis. It was just him and me, as Cram was away for a football game. "Oh, they're all the same," he said. "That kid you're interested in – he hangs around with another kid in there that's a real piece of work."

"Soothy?" I asked, digging up a name from somewhere.

"Nope." Raptis paused to wipe flakes of bread from his beard. He cleaned his hand on his acid-stained lab coat. "Soothy was from before. Remember when I showed you where he'd lit up his name in cyclohexane?"

I nodded.

"This is another kid. Black. Janelle Rochester. Her and her mom – useless, real pieces of shit. Niranjan doesn't sit by her, but he sort of encourages her. She's nice to him, flirts with him, could be fucking him for all I kno ."

I pulled a face. I didn't like when Raptis talked like this. It was taking things too far. "I don't think Niranjan's involved in anything like that."

"Anyway, what can I say? You get enough bad seeds in the class, it ruins the atmosphere for everybody. Nobody can learn. It's chemistry. Just like what I used to teach in my grade ten classes. You mix the wrong elements and the whole solution's blown."

"My dad would say that one drop of ink can ruin a vat of milk," I said.

"There you go. Anyway, she wasn't there when you dropped in today, thank God, but some days... She's got a mouth on her. She shouldn't be in that class. Problems up to here. She storms in late, fights with people, argues with me, says stupid things. I try to put her in her place, but it doesn't work. What can I say? I'm fucked if I do, fucked if I don't. This is what teaching's come to."

"And Niranjan's involved with her?"

"Who's to say what these kids get up to?"

NIRANJAN

Soothy and Rageev don't give me back the gun. Instead, they get me to clean up the apartment. Go for food. Run their errands. They don't kick me out of the apartment either, so I should be grateful. Wish they'd give me another chance. If they want to test me, it'd be nice to tell me what I'm being tested on.

I keep my mouth shut and do what they say. Rageev says I have to stay in school. I listen to him. He says, for now, he's just going to get me to drive. I'll wait in the car. The Yutani's a nice car after all, equipped with satellite technology. I've got a G1. I'm good with mechanical things. Driving isn't a problem.

A week later, Rageev tells me to drive him and Soothy to Lawrence Avenue. The clouds are out. No moon. We sit in the car outside a Tamil takeout shop. We wait for the couple who run it to close up. They're new – I've never seen this shop before. Customers shuffle in to buy their stringhoppers and sambol. Not many. One of them just stands there. You can tell he has no car because he got off the Lawrence bus earlier. All he buys is a couple of samosas. He stands there talking to the husband and wife, gossiping for almost an hour. They want him out more than we do. Underneath his old winter jacket from Walmart, his big peaked hat with ear flaps, I imagine his skinny aiya body, reminds me of people back home. They all look like they've lived five lifetimes. Bodies worn out and tired. Old before their time. This guy came over recently. Like me. He could be my grandfather, my uncle.

Everybody leaves their family back home when they come over. It's the price you pay. Soothy and Rageev are my family now. They sit in the front of the car. I look at the streetlight shining on the patches of Rageev's skin where no hair grows. Almost like an almond, peeled raw. Almost soft white, bubbling out from the inside.

What was that night on the freeway like for him? Rageev would have been in the car roughly where I'm sitting, half his face burnt, windows shattered in pieces around him. The car careens and flips against the railing. Rageev has to unloosen his seat belt, reach for his iron, then come out blasting while holding up part of his face, which is trying to burn and peel off. Telling himself it doesn't hurt. The glass falling away from his face like a jigsaw puzzle. Maybe, when it burns that hot, that intense, you don't feel anything. Maybe it's beyond fear and pain. His face cut open. Everything inside and outside coming together. A folk story. Wisdom, like a flame, glowing within.

"Pay attention!" Rageev's whisper catches me off guard. Sitting beside them in that Yutani Quantum with its V6 one-hundred-and-seventy-horsepower engine, it's hard not to let my thoughts drift away.

We wait and watch. Watch and wait. October, 2008, and I don't know what I'm doing. Sodium glare from the streetlights shines down even though the moon does not. I take out my inhaler, take a hit as quietly as possible. The other two make fun of me.

The last customer goes home. By that time we know everything there is to know about the shop. What their cooking routines are, what kind of people come in, how many in a stretch, the traffic patterns on the street, what hours this hardworking couple keep. Doesn't look like they've hired anybody else – doing everything themselves. No credit card terminal. Many of our people don't use a credit card anyway. In fact, far as I can see, the couple aren't doing proper receipts. They're running two different registers – one for most of the customers, the other one with a receipt roll for tax stuff. Everybody's running some game.

Still, I feel a little sorry. They're young. He has a giant moustache, each half like a sword. He's tall and awkward with his apron on. She's a short little thing. Back home, I might have called them uncle and aunty. They have no idea we've been clocking them.

Her hair's tied with a floral scarf. I don't know if they're in love or not – who can tell these things? They seem happier than most. I wonder if Rageev and Yalini akka are happy. At night, sometimes the baby cries in their room. Rageev shouts at Yalini akka to quiet Geetha down, and then she starts yelling at him. We hear everything through the walls.

Now I understand why the Tamil store across the street from our building gives them credit. It's going to be the same deal with the place we're watching now.

When I get married, I'm going to marry someone pretty. She can be as dark as the car we're riding in, it doesn't matter, but she has to be pretty. I don't want one of those Tamil girls with the buck teeth. Call me superficial if you want.

The couple work around the clock. Cleaning, baking, washing, stirring the pot, talking to customers.

About one in the morning, they have everything scrubbed down and are counting receipts. They bundle them with rubber bands, place them in a shoe box. They would get home at what, two? Then be back here in the morning to start all over again. What kind of life is that?

Rageev tells me to go ask them for three packages of kottu roti. I nod my head, happy to get out of the car.

I look down the road towards Bellamy in the east. On the other side, it dips towards McCowan. Except for one time my aunt took me to Niagara Falls and that time at camp, everything I've ever known in Canada is within a few minutes drive of this place. Occasionally, cars zoom by on Lawrence. All the other restaurants, the Jamaican jerk place, the KFC, are closed. You can feel the people sleeping in the bungalows and apartment buildings, like they're graveyards. The weight of all those bodies in the cold October night.

I go inside to get the food.

"Hello uncle, aunty," I say politely, respectfully. "Kottu roti, please."

The man looks up from his receipts, sleepy eyed. "I'm sorry, thambi. Most of our food is finished. But here, we have same vaddais left if you're just looking for short eats." He packs them up in a paper bag, greasy with oil, hands them to me with a wad of napkins. When I offer up the loose change I have, he waves it away. "No, it's okay. Come back earlier next time."

When I was living with my aunt, I wouldn't have had loose change in my pocket.

I take the vaddais, eating one as I leave the shop. The red chilies and sharp onions and coconut hit my rumbling stomach as I walk away. I think about what Mr Narayan said about doing something with my life. How condescending can you get? It's too late anyway. I'm here now. Rageev and Soothy are all the family I've got. I've seen what there is to see in the shop. They have no cameras or security system. Rageev sent me in, not Soothy, because it wasn't a job for guns. I'm good with electronics, and I notice things. They're running a small operation here. This couple's taking in hundreds of dollars a day, maybe thousands, off the books.

They have a small shelf beside the door with a picture of Lakshmi and Saraswathi, the goddesses of wealth and the arts. Half a banana with incense sticking out of it. Just like Rageev's God cupboard back home. The incense is still burning. I could smell it. Why did they have to have those goddess pictures beside the door? I could feel their eyes following me. I know what I'm doing is wrong, but I can't help it.

Rageev will pay them a visit tomorrow. They'll come to an agreement. They get peace and quiet, we got a steady donation starting next week. If you want success, you have to pay for it. Tamils understand that – you've got to have strict hierarchy. Chain of command. Conduct. Obedience. Nobody lives without it. Everybody pays. Everybody's happy. Even Lakshmi and Saraswathi.

Still, I feel sorry for that pathetic couple.

DANIEL

Raptis came into the Communications office, all agitated, smelling like Windex. Cram and I extricated ourselves from the stack of photocopies we were sorting out for various classes. It was a full office during the lunch hour. A few teachers, already around the lunch table in the middle of the room, had opened their tupperware, heated up leftovers, brewed tea; they were deep into gossip. Only Cram and I and another teacher were mad enough to work through lunch hours. Pete Cram was non-stop busy because of the football season. Hours of practice with the ailing team left him scrambling to keep up with school. Me, I was just disorganized. Janarius Brent, our awkward CL, squatted in the corner but rarely joined in group discussion. A middle aged Guyanese man, he had once been ambitious but now settled for CLship. He spoke in a lilting Caribbean accent with a good natured inflection, but an odd tension existed beneath his words. He swept in, heavy handed, Hawaiian shirt flapping, cologne overpowering, trumped up pronouncements dropping from his loud mouth. Something artificial and anxious about his reprimands: the computer monitors hadn't been turned off, stray books had not been returned to the book room, the room wasn't kept tidy. He never asked about people's families or what they thought. Brent was a jobsworth, and people avoided him if they could. It was difficult to talk about anything too personal in the Communications office

"You won't fucking believe it," cried Raptis.

"What happened?" Cram and I were startled out of what we were doing, curious even, while we were aware that talking in the Communications office was not a good idea. We gathered around him, but the others kept talking, their chatter taking on an uneven, stilted murmur. There were many pauses, and it was obvious that they were listening too.

"That kid. That kid – you won't believe it."

"Who are you talking about?" I asked, "Niranjan?" I had asked some of my students to find out where Niranjan was living, but they didn't know.

"Janelle Rochester. Pain-in-the-ass Janelle Ro-ches-ter. You know what she did today?"

Cram and I waited for an answer.

"She threw a flask at my head.

Now there was absolute silence. No one spoke.

"What, like a flask of tea?

"A lab flask with ammonia in it.

"Did it hit you?" asked Cram in his pressed shirt and tie, hands in his pockets. The Windex smell made sense now. Cram fidgeted with his tie, trying not to laugh

"It's not funny," said Raptis.

"Yeah, I know," replied Cram, straightening up. "But did you say something to set her off? What made her throw it?"

"It wasn't anything that we don't do every day," emphasized Raptis, his mouth working around the words. His lab coat drooped and the smell almost obscured his movements; his hand gestures, normally wild, seemed unusually modified. "Every day she gives me a hard time, and every day I put her in her place. Today, she throws lab equipment at my head."

"Did the flask hit you?" asked Alice, one of the teachers at the table. In her fifties, with grey hair, she had taught at LCC for almost twenty years.

Raptis shook his head. "Some of it splashed my coat, but that's not the point. It could have hit me if I'd been a foot to the right."

"Pity. You could get her suspended if it'd hit you."

"They don't want to give suspensions these days," snorted another teacher. "When was the last time you saw a suspension?"

"Yeah, they need you bleeding, lying on the floo , when it's too late, before they're willing to do anything."

"I called down to the office," answered Raptis. "It takes Stevenson ten minutes to get to the lab, swinging her big walkie-talkie. They can't even send a couple of hall monitors."

"Hall monitors don't do anything, you know that," said Alice.

"Stevenson takes Janelle out of my class, but brings her right back before the period's over. Before the period's over. Can you believe it? Not even the next day."

We couldn't believe it. This was something new. They'd been holding kids in the office instead of sending them home with detentions, everybody had experienced that, but this was new. "Did they run out of space in the office?" I asked.

"I don't know. I don't know – I just don't think they wanted to deal with her," said Raptis, still fazed. Normally, he would never speak to these women, and they wouldn't talk to him, but this was a novel circumstance.

"How do they expect us to do our jobs with objects flying at us?

"They don't do anything and then wonder why kids shoot and stab each other."

"So, what are you going to do?" asked Janarius Brent, standing up. His Hawaiian shirt flapped over his belly as he waddled over. Brent cocked his head and stared at Raptis. I'd never seen the two talk before; Raptis wasn't part of our department – he resented Brent.

"I don't know. What should I do?" asked Raptis. "I don't want her in my class."

Raptis's smell of ammonia mixed with Janarius's strong cologne. The combination was nauseating.

"Go talk to Myra," said Alice thoughtfully. "She'll know what to do."

Raptis looked around at the others and nodded, searching for understanding. It surprised me that he could be so vulnerable. He was probably still in shock. Raptis had always seemed indomitable to me.

The next day, Raptis asked Cram and me to meet him in the staffroom for lunch. I guess the Communications office was no good, and he told us later that they were watching his comings and goings. Meeting in his lab might seem suspicious.

He was agitated yet more subdued than before. His foot kicked against the small lunch table. We sat wedged in a corner. The light was poor in the staffroom, and its large potted plants were continuously wilting and dying. A couple of large ferns partially obscured us from the rest of the chatter; their browning leaves gave us cover. Normally, Raptis would have made a joke – like the declining standards in education were causing the vegetation to give up and die. But now he was subdued, not jovial.

We talked about our classes that morning. I knew he must have had his science class with Niranjan and Janelle already. Cram was tired from football practice. Though his clothes were as neatly pressed as ever, there were pouches under his eyes, and his skin looked rough. It was left to me to bring up what we were both wondering. "John, what happened with Myra? Did you talk to her about the Rochester girl?"

Raptis sighed, running his fingers down his lab coat. He patted the sides of his mouth for crumbs, then stared at us. "Yeah, I talked to Myra, but not because I went to her. She came to me."

"What do you mean?" I looked sideways at Cram. He wasn't eating. My own zucchini had started to dry out and tasted overly bitter.

"Somehow those fuckers knew what I talked to you about. Yesterday at lunch. Beat me to the punch. Before I even go talk to Myra, before I go to the admin, the admin comes at me with a charge saying that I talk to kids inappropriately, that I swear at them."

"Well, do you?"

"Yeah, but it's nothing new. They swear at me, I swear at them. Been doing it for years. All of a sudden, it's a problem? You've got to talk to those animals in a language they understand. They're throwing rat guts around the lab instead of dissecting them – what do you want me to do?"

"The Rochester girl," asked Cram, "she complained against you?"

"It doesn't make sense," Raptis shook his head. "They already had her down there yesterday morning. I'm sure she complained about me then. But I talked to Myra this morning. And they didn't set a time for the meeting until today. To discipline me. I've been teaching for more than forty years. They can't discipline the kids, but they're going to discipline me?"

"What did Myra say?"

"Oh, the usual. It's a slap on the wrist, something to go into my file. To be honest with you, it's happened before. They can't do anything to seriously threaten me. I've got too many years. There's nothing they can really take, is there? Myra was a little worried. She said a lot more kids have been claiming false allegations lately. That Rochester girl is a born liar. Myra also said that if I had gone to her earlier, she'd have gotten me to file a form claiming that the conditions I teach in aren't safe. Then the Board would have to bring in somebody to investigate the situation. Stevenson and Badlamenti'd be up shit creek. They couldn't do anything to me then – do you get what's going on?"

I agreed with what he was saying but wasn't sure.

"Somehow they knew I would have filed that form. I don't have anything to lose, and Badlamenti knows I hate him. But they brought me up on a charge before I coulda done something. This isn't the first time Badlamenti's had to deal with this. Remember last year when all those kids were in the hallways and weren't going to classes? What did they do? The hall monitors didn't do anything. Teachers were shouted down when they asked kids to go to class. And before that a few years ago, with the black West Indian kids? Did the admin go out and handle the situation? Badlamenti just hides in his office behind his video cameras and computers."

"They're afraid to look racist," said Cram, putting his finger on it. He unwrapped his sandwich. No one spoke. The sandwich looked a little sloppier than usual, and it was packed in tinfoil instead of immaculately arranged in tupperware with alfalfa sprouts and chopped veggies.

"Yes!" whispered Raptis. "So they're breaking my balls over it? I'm going to fight them!

"You've got Myra going with you to the meeting? When is it?" I asked. "In a week?"

"Yeah, of course. They didn't even tell me she should come. I had to ask," replied Raptis. "They're scared of Myra. She doesn't mess around."

Raptis possessed the martyr's zeal. He relished these fights with Badlamenti. It didn't matter; with Myra on board, Raptis was on solid ground. She was a generation younger than Raptis and almost a generation older than me. There was something about her swagger, the way she palled around with the older teachers, that made her one of them: a 'good ol' boy'. Something hardy and masculine about her, something fearless. Often, there was a whiff of whiskey about her breath. Cram thought it could have been the alcohol in her mouthwash. Though she didn't seem drunk, it was distinctly whiskey I smelt. I imagined her pouring a slug of booze into her tea every morning and again at lunch. She and Raptis would be formidable. Stevenson and Badlamenti had their work cut out.

"But how did they know to slap you with that before you could fill out the workplace safety form?" I wondered aloud.

"Somebody in the Communications office who heard me talk about it yesterday," said Raptis. "Myra figures it was Janarius."

"Really?"

"Janarius is a toady for them. Been doing that for years. You know, he wears those Hawaiian shirts and lounges around, but he's just eyeballing everything, figuring out what he can use. Well, someone in that room had to tell them something."

"You should be careful what you say around him," I cautioned.

"What? Around Janarius? Janarius is a pimp! He's a walking cunt. It's the people he reports to that I worry about." There was the Raptis I knew. A little talk, and all the solicitude was gone.

I mentioned our conversation casually to Lynn that night while she practiced some of her yoga asanas on a mat. Her black leotards were damp, and her shoulders glistened with sweat.

"Stay... away... from Raptis," she replied, breathing hard.

"Why?" I asked. "Have you heard something?"

"Stay... away from him. He's a black hole... and he's going to take you and Cram right down with him."

Lynn hadn't answered my question, but the fact that I was distracting her during her workout made it unfair for me to press her.

"And another thing," she mentioned casually as sweaty palms were brought together over her head, left foot up to her inner thigh to do the 'tree', "watch out for Cram too. He seems all quiet and docile, but he's an ambitious one. He coaches, does a lot of stuff with the kids, even asked to shoehorn in on my Student Council once, but I said I could manage. He wants something."

"He deserves it," I said. He was genuinely a great guy.

"Everybody wants something."

NIRANJAN

Something bad has happened at the apartment. I leave school after Raptis's physics class to go home. I've been eating lunch with Janelle Rochester and her crew. Sometimes guys hang out with her, but mostly it's Janelle and her girls. I don't tell them I won't be there – Soothy's texts are very urgent.

"What's up?" I ask as I enter the apartment. Drop my bag on the floo . Rageev's here, wringing his hands, sitting on the sofa. Muruges, the guy with the limp, sits beside him. Soothy stands in the corner, staring at the laces on his high tops. Yalini akka paces back and forth. There's anger on her face.

What's different?

It takes me a while to realize what's missing: Geetha.

I don't see the baby anywhere. No stroller, no carrier, no gurgling. No smell of cooking either, that's unusual. Yalini akka's usually in the kitchen, grinding, stirring, chopping, tasting. I associate the smell of fried chilies and boiled rice with Yalini and Geetha. It floats around them. Now, it's like watching a movie with no soundtrack. The balcony door is open. A cold breeze blows in.

"Thambi, sit down," says Muruges uncle.

I sit.

"Tell him," says Rageev, his head in his hands.

"This is all your fault!" Yalini accuses from her corner. My hair stands up. I've never heard her yell at him in front of us.

"You're the one who let her out of your sight!" snaps Rageev. He raises his head, sits up, but cannot look at her.

"Where were you? It's my responsibility, is it? Always me? Call yourself a man?!"

Muruges watches everything. His right leg twitches, but that's the only movement he makes. There's something appealing about him. Something gentle. I'm trying to be the same as Soothy: invisible. When nobody says anything, I quietly ask Soothy, "What's going on?"

"It's baby Geetha. Someone's stolen her." He looks up at me, something in his face I've never seen before. Fear.

Grabs my shoulders. "Why would anybody want to take Geetha?"

I don't understand what he means.

"Do you know something? Do you know where she is?" asks Rageev.

It takes me a second. "Why would I know?" I reply. "Soothy didn't even talk to me on the phone! The first I'm hearing about it is right now."

Yalini akka's face twists with anguish. She cuts Rageev off before he can fire another question at me. "It's your fault!" she cries. "You and your fucked-up face. Now you've fucked up our lives too! And that baby, the poor, innocent baby! I knew I should never have gotten involved with you."

"Sit down!" shouts Rageev. "Don't you see – having a fight now s no good. Not now! Think about the baby."

She sits down and he tries to hold her, but she won't let him.

"Tell me what happened," I say calmly. "Maybe we can figure out what happened." I still can't believe anybody would snatch a baby.

"I took her to Scarborough Town Centre," says Rageev, head in his hands again. "I go to get them a snack – New York Fries, you know how it's always busy there – no place to sit down. She's got the stroller and is looking at stuff in one of the stores. Which one, Yalini?"

"Indigo Outlet."

"Indigo Outlet. I come back with the fries, and she's running around screaming."

"I had her right there!" Yalini akka points at the floor with her hands. "Right there! I turn around. She's vanished! Stroller and everything."

"Stroller too, huh" I just repeat their words. It doesn't seem possible. How? For what reason? "What did you do then? Did you look where you were before? Did you call security?"

"Of course we looked everywhere," she shouts at me. "Are you stupid? She's not a shopping bag. We didn't forget her!"

"Of course I can't call security," Rageev snaps. "They know who I am. You think they're going to help me?"

"So what did you do?"

"They called me," Muruges says quietly. He leans forward and puts his hands together. In all the times he's come by, he's never spoken to me. He's just a 'friend of Rageev's'. I mean, of course he's LTTE – Yalini akka's confirmed that much. His leg damaged in a mine explosion. Like Rageev, who climbed out of a melting car, these men are defined by the wars they've fought. The mine jumps and blows up next to him. Metal springs four feet in the air, spraying shrapnel. According to Yalini akka, a piece of shrapnel is still stuck inside that leg. They weren't able to operate. He carries the war around inside his body.

"Muruges says we should wait," states Rageev.

"Do you have experience with stolen babies?" I ask, hoping he won't be offended.

"No!" laughs Muruges. "In all my life, I've never seen something like this."

The call comes two hours later. A blocked number so Rageev and Muruges can't trace the call. They try their best to record it. "Uh-huh," says Rageev. "Yes, yes. I... thank you for calling... The baby's safe?... I understand but... Wait... Hello?"

He has to wait again until they call back a half hour later. Muruges thinks they're moving locations and changing phones. Whoever it is doesn't know whom they're dealing with. After all, this is the one person who survived a burning car. Shot his way out. I've never seen him get mad. I mean, really mad. What would that be like?

When they call back, they're very short with Rageev. Muruges has coached him not to say anything. He's too scared of losing Geetha forever to not obey. They tell him how much money they want: thirty thousand dollars.

Rageev shakes his head when the call ends two minutes later. "I don't get it. Why go to all the trouble of kidnapping Geetha if they only want thirty thousand dollars. I mean, thirty thousand dollars isn't nothing but still – what'll that get you?"

"A down payment on a house – but only in Scarborough!" laughs Muruges. "What else did they say?"

"They said they didn't trust me to bring the money. They want one of the boys."

"Did the caller sound Tamil?" asks Muruges.

"I don't think so, but maybe familiar. Maybe he disguised his voice."

"Hmm," Muruges puts his hands together and thinks. "We can't track them. They want the money delivered by one of the boys, he said?"

"Let me go," Soothy stands up. "I'll crack their heads open with a baseball bat. Let me be the one."

"That's what I don't want," says Rageev. "There might be ten of them there! Think!"

"I'll take them all on, I don't care," Soothy states with false bravado.

"A baby's involved," says Rageev quietly. "Our child."

"I don't want him going," Yalini akka shakes her head.

"But why?" asks Soothy, disappointed.

"I don't want him going – that's that!"

Muruges speaks to me. "Thambi, can you do it?" All eyes turn on me. What can I say? Of course I don't want to do it. Of course I think Soothy should go. He's older. He's got something to prove. Why me?

But I don't say that. I remember who lets me live here. Who buys food and pays the bills. So nod my head. I look to the floor as if there's an answer somewhere beneath the fake wood linoleum.

"I'd go if I could," croaks Yalini akka, her voice scratchy from shouting, "but they want a boy. You need to do this for us, Niranjan." Gone is any softness in her voice. The Yalini akka who was the nicest one in the apartment is now replaced with a different Yalini. This Yalini is willing to tear trees out by their roots because of her rage.

"They know a lot about you," says Muruges carefully, "at least whom you have living here. It's not wise to do anything rash. They know more about you than you do about them."

"I hope they've been able to feed her," says Yalini, staring at the men on the couch. "Geetha's very particular about formula. What if she's dead? You should have asked them to hold the phone by her mouth. You idiot! Could you hear her crying in the background?"

"Relax," Rageev tries to calm her and again takes her shoulders. This time, she lets him. "We'll get our daughter back. All they want is money. That's obvious."

"Do you have thirty thousand?" asks Muruges. When the others don't reply, he shakes his head, scratches his leg, then his beard. "I see, I see." He scratches the bald spot on his head, then goes back to the leg, and again to the beard. It's like a cycle he can't stop.

"Won't you help us?" pleads Yalini, nicely as she can. "You can see it's an emergency. We wouldn't ask if… you understand."

Muruges stares at Rageev. Now, his leg stops shaking. He becomes still as a coiled snake. His eyes are bullets. "I'm only doing this because Yalini is like a daughter to me." I can see relief start to enter Yalini's eyes. Muruges keeps staring at Rageev, talking to the burnt part of his skin. "We've given you some help, money, in the past, that's true, because you work for us. Because of that, but mostly because of Yalini, we will overlook some of the other things you've done. This is not our business, and we would be nowhere if we gave out lakhs just because fools got themselves in trouble. We do this favour, make you a loan without interest, only for a short while. We lend it to you only so that you can get your baby back. Understand? We expect it to be repaid."

Rageev nods. He is relieved. It's strange to see Yalini so upset, but Rageev is taking it as it comes. His daughter has just been kidnapped. He seems to be a person who doesn't expect much in life.

"Now what did they say?" asks Muruges, his leg twitching again.

"They said to get the money together, that they'd call in an hour. They said they'd give him directions where to take it on the subway. What if we get Niranjan to call us on a cellphone from the subway as he goes along? We could follow, then get the baby back and still keep the money."

Muruges shakes his head. "Niranjan won't be able to get a signal in the subway. That's why they're asking him to take it. No, no. Do you want to lose your baby? You'd better not make them think you're up to any tricks. Grab a bag – get prepared – I'll call somebody about the money."

"I'll make some formula for Geetha," says Yalini, pulling herself away from Rageev's shoulder. She pieces herself back together with hope, sounds like the Yalini akka I know.

Dark Moustache fetches the money. Instead of a case full of guns, he brings a satchel. He shows us: inside are rubber-banded bundles of twenties. Why twenties? They're not clean bills either. Where does he get them from? Each bundle has fifty twenties. There are thirty bundles. That's fifteen hundred twenty dollar bills that Rageev takes from Muruges to put into my backpack. He shakes my backpack clean. Notes and loose papers fall out. Pens and pencils. A couple of Spiderman comics. He cleans the food crumbs out, then puts the bills in a plastic bag, ties up the plastic bag before putting it inside my backpack.

What's to stop me from running away with the money myself? All I'd have to do is take the subway to a GO station, and take the first train to god-knows-where. Rageev and Muruges can read my thoughts on my face. Rageev gives me a look that says he would kill me without thinking twice. Hunt me down and kill me before he even hunted down the guys who took his baby. Yalini akka wraps a bottle of heated baby formula for Geetha in a cloth, puts that in my bag too. Should I take a gun? No, I know better. Their baby's life is at stake.

We wait for the call.

While we wait, Rageev urges us all to go to the God cupboard to pray for the baby. "What's that going to do?" asks Muruges. "Stop acting like a hysterical grandmother. It's actions that matter now!" Rageev ushers me and Soothy and Yalini akka towards the God cupboard anyway. We try to sing thervarums. Our voices are shaky. I can't remember the words. Yalini akka breaks down crying halfway.

There is nothing we can say or do. Dark Moustache leaves. Muruges begins scratching his leg and head again.

The call finally comes

They tell me to take the money to Kennedy station. I must go down to the subway level alone. There's a phone there at the east end of the subway platform. It'll ring in half an hour.

"Good luck," says Yalini akka, kissing me on the cheek. "Bring my baby back home."

Rageev and Muruges drive me to Kennedy in the Yutani. Soothy volunteers to come, but they tell him to stay home. I really shouldn't, but I feel that pride again.

"You know, you're probably thinking that thirty thousand is a lot of money," says Muruges softly as Rageev drives. "But I don't need to tell you why cheating us would be a bad idea." I nod my head. Nobody talks as Rageev pulls into busy traffic on Markham Road. He turns onto Ellesmere, which is way less congested. "Why are you doing this?" asks Muruges, looking at me through the rearview mirror.

"To get Geetha back." The bag is tight in my fingers

Rageev clutches the steering wheel as tightly as he can. Tension flows through us both. "No," says Muruges, shaking his head, scratching his bald spot. "Why are you helping Rageev? Why have you moved in with them? What do you hope to gain?"

I consider telling him about my aunt, who would tear me down, make me miserable, but he already knows. I cough nervously. "Yalini akka says that you knew my brother. I haven't heard his voice in years. My family hasn't heard from him. She says you can put us in touch."

"Yes, I knew your brother. A good fighter. We defended Elephant Pass in 2000, before this happened." Slaps his right leg. "I can see a bit of him in you. He was brave, a very intellectual young man. Yes, yes, I can put you in touch. I will try my best to help you out."

Rageev has turned onto Kennedy now. We're almost there. The sky is turning dark. Wind feels cold. Can even feel it through my jacket. There's no music, no radio on. I hold the backpack even tighter. We're silent the rest of the way to Kennedy station. Rageev lets me out at the passenger drop-off.

Muruges gives me lots of change for the subway. "Do exactly as they say," he tells me.

I nod, hold up the bag as a sign that I understand. Close the door behind me and look past Muruges to Rageev. "Don't worry about the money," he whispers. "Just get back our Geetha."

"Hurry up – they're going to call any minute now."

Downstairs on the subway platform are three phones. I wait, guarding them. People come and go, getting into trains or leaving them. They move in waves, leaving me like a rock after the tide goes out to sea. I clutch the backpack, feel the tension in my knuckles and knees. Thankfully, more people have cellphones. No one uses the phones.

Fifteen minutes later, the phone in the middle rings. Snatch it up with my left hand. "Hello?"

"Who is this?"

I give my name.

They hang up.

A minute goes by. The phone rings again. I snatch it up again, listen without saying anything. There's breathing on the other side. Finally, a voice says, "Take the subway to St George station. There's a phone near the middle of the platform on the northbound line. We'll call you there in thirty-five minutes. Hurr ."

Line goes dead.

There's one train in the station and the bells are chiming. Letting the phone drop, I clutch the backpack and sprint for the train. Don't want to lose time waiting for another train. The doors close on my chest as I'm halfway in. Wedge them open, get inside, take a seat at the back.

Train finally leaves. It's not very full. No one's sitting beside me. I look outside the windows as we pull out of the tunnel. The sky is dark now, a very dark metallic blue. I am cold and alone. Other kids from school go downtown all the time. I never do. The subway flashes by Scarborough, goes back into tunnels again after Victoria Park. I know a lot of Tamils live in the apartment buildings around here.

We don't come out in the light again until after Broadview station. The subway travels underneath the bridge that goes over the Don Valley. I imagine the train suddenly going off the rails, dropping.

Finally, I get out at St George, find the phone in the middle of the northbound platform. Once again, I'm lucky – no one's using it. I wait, clutching my pack. All those twenties, rubber banded, inside. Hard not to want to open the bag, peek inside, touch those notes. This station's a lot busier than Kennedy. Platform's smaller too. Lots more people rushing around. Makes me nervous.

The phone rings. I quickly pick it up.

A couple of people notice me doing it. They watch me. No privacy at all. "Hello?"

"Who's that?" asks the same voice. Gruff. Bit of an accent. Familiar maybe? Don't know. Hard to tell. All these people rushing, trains coming, going.

"Niranjan," I say.

"Niranjan. Good. Are you alone?"

"Of course!"

"Not pulling any tricks?"

"I promise you on the life of that baby, I'm not."

"Okay, I'm glad you said that," says the voice. He chuckles. "Means I don't have to say it for you. Now, take the train to…"

"What?" I scream, "I can't hear you! The trains are loud."

He stops. I worry he'll hang up. Smell of grit and oil and fumes. Tunnels so dirty. I focus on the mild green colour of the subway walls. This calms me. Green is like twenty dollar bills. "Okay, can you hear now?"

"Yes."

He's yelling, but I remain calm. "Good! Go – take the northbound train – now. One stop to Spadina station. It'll be quiet there. We'll call you at the phone when you get off." Line goes dead.

I place the phone back in its receiver properly. Gulp some sooty air. Clutch the backpack. Get on the northbound train.

It's a long travel time to the next stop. The phone on the platform is already ringing when I get there. Have to run down to get it. Somebody's already picking it up. Some older guy with a raincoat and woollen hat. I shove him out of the way as I wrestle for the phone. "Hey!" he falls over. His hat gets knocked off. He has to go grab it before it blows onto the tracks. Curses me as he goes, leaves me with the phone in my hand. A few people get off the next train and watch us. Pretty soon, they're bored. They begin walking to the escalator.

"Who was that?" asks the voice on the phone.

"Just some guy. You phoned before the train stopped," I say, out of breath, nervous again.

"You're sure?" says the voice. He's almost become friendly with me now, casual. "You sure you don't have somebody helping you?"

Heart beats in my throat. That baby's life is in my hands. "Why would he pick up the phone if I did?" I argue.

Silence on the other end. This station smells cleaner. No one around. Walls have little circular orange tiles. I feel like I'm a million miles away.

"Okay," the voice on the other end says. "I'm going to trust you. You better not be fooling us. You don't want that. Okay?"

"Okay."

"Leave the platform and walk up. Don't leave the station. There's a tunnel that will take you away from the northbound line, where you are now. You walk through the tunnel till you get to the Spadina station on the green subway line. See? That's where you exit."

The voice gives me the address of a house, softly, as if he's sorry. Then additional directions from the subway. He hangs up. I worry I might miss something, say or do something wrong. What am I going to say when I meet them? What will they be like? Will I have to fight somebody? How will I get the baby home?

I open the backpack just to make sure everything is there. That I haven't lost the money through a hole while rushing around. All thirty bundles are present. For a moment, I think of getting back on the train, taking it to the end, then taking a bus even further. Getting as far away as I can. But some kind of loyalty kicks in. Where would I go? The formula that Yalini akka heated up for Geetha has gone cold.

I go to the escalator, ride it up. Walk down the tunnel to the other Spadina station. A long walk.

I am glad. I am glad this is the last phone call. No more rushing up and down stairs. No more. Feels like I'm in an airport. Frankfurt airport, where I had to change planes after I left Africa.

Eventually, I come out, into sunlight. As I walk west along Bloor like the voice said, I'm surprised by how different this place is from Scarborough. How close together everything is. The shops, the restaurants, the gift shops, the bookstores, the art places, the narrowness of the main street, the fact that all this closeness just seems to stretch forever. What's even more amazing is the number of people outside. A lot of university students. Other people too. Hanging out on the street, talking, sitting outside a restaurant. All packed together. A few black people, some Asians, mostly white. No Tamils. There's nothing in Scarborough like this.

A car pulls up. A very familiar car. "Adai!"

Rageev and Muruges in the black Quantum. "Hurry up, climb in the back!" yells Rageev as the car pulls to the curb.

All the excitement and anticipation goes out of me. I do as I'm told.

"Give me the bag," says Muruges. Takes it from me before I can hand it over. Counts the money, closes up the backpack.

"Everything okay so far?" asks Rageev, watching me in the rear view mirror. His half burnt face looks horrible. Still anguish in his skin.

I nod my head. "How did you find me?"

Muruges laughs. "I had one of my guys follow you. We weren't going to let them take you and the baby. Not with thirty thousand dollars."

"You had somebody follow me on the subway?"

Muruges grins. "You didn't recognize him, did you? He called us from payphones while you were talking at the other end of the platform!"

"Don't play the fool!" says Rageev urgently. "We've still got to get Geetha safe and alive. They give you the address?"

"Yeah." I tell them the place.

"I should have known," says Rageev. He begins to drive, fast. As the shops and people go by, I finally realize where we are. I should have known, too. I've been close to here before. With Rageev and Soothy. Yep, there's the Honest Ed's. McDonald's down the street.

Rageev pulls into a side street. "We know them but that doesn't mean it'll be easy."

"I can't go in there with you," says Muruges. "We can't be seen together. You know that."

Rageev grunts, then looks at me. "Just you and me. Come on."

Can't move myself just yet from the car. "You're going to come in with me? But they said really strictly – they asked me about it on the phone – they said no one else. They're going to think I was lying."

"She's my daughter," says Rageev. "Whatever happens, I'll take responsibility for her, not you. I'm not going to sit here while they're holding my daughter." He takes the backpack from Muruges, gets out of the car.

Force myself to get out, follow Rageev. So little control over things. I pull out my inhaler, take a drag in preparation.

Not the same building we visited before. The same neighbourhood, though. A house. Rageev and I walk right up to the front door, press the bell. Old baldy's sitting inside in his wheelchair, doing a jigsaw puzzle just like before. A different one. A cottage with a waterwheel turning in the river beside it. Professor X looks up, crinkles his eyes, puts his hands on top of his blanket. "I told you to come alone."

"It's my child," says Rageev, holding the bag. Tosses the bag onto the table. Lands on the jigsaw, breaking up the picture Professor X has been building. The suddenness of the movement makes the old guy lean back, his chair turning away. Grabs his blanket so it won't slip off, leaving him exposed. A couple of jigsaw pieces fall off the table. The cottage looks like a bomb hit it.

The house is empty of furniture. Just the table, a couple of chairs. The walls are stripped, only partly painted. A tray with yellow paint sits at the side. Its roller, still wet, lies in the tray. I recognize the young guy behind Professor X. Basketball Jersey, the one who kept smoking and pointing at me in the apartment building. He's not smoking now. Standing very serious behind the old man. To the right of the old man is Geetha. As quiet as a mouse. Her eyes are open, she knows something's going on. A woman, also Asian with short black hair, sits on a chair holding Geetha. Feeding her actually, with a bottle. The woman holds her firmly, almost lovingly. Geetha just keeps sucking, quiet as a mouse. The woman wears a cream coloured suit. She watches us carefully. In her breast pocket is a green handkerchief. Professor X has one in his pocket too. The woman doesn't even look away when she sees Rageev's burns. She seems to find them interesting.

"My daughter," says Professor X. "I know what it's like to look after children, what losing a daughter might mean. My daughter is taking care of your daughter."

"You could have just asked me for the money like a normal person, with respect," states Rageev, through clenched teeth.

"We did ask you. Again and again. You needed a little reminder. We're not here to lose money."

"I would have given it to you. Just a little bit of time. You didn't have to do this."

"It's not for you to decide the terms to pay us!" The old man slams his palm on the table. Geetha cries. The woman soothes her, puts the rubber teat back into the baby's mouth. "You had obligations, yet you did not meet them. What kind of father are you? What kind of man does not take care of his family, does not take care of his obligations? You needed to be reminded. You see, life is a very fragile thing. Anything can happen. A strong man, a man who works for us, uses everything in his power to take control of his life. It's a very precious thing.

"The man who used to own this house also had many debts. He lost control of things to the point where he couldn't get them back. He used to live here with his family. Now, no more. Do you know what these houses are worth? Invest in houses, my friend. They are the only things that are safe."

Rageev strides towards Professor X. Basketball Jersey pulls out a revolver and holds it above baldy's shoulder, levelled at Rageev.

"Shota, show our friend the position he's in," says the old guy. Shota points the gun at Geetha, two feet away, sucking the bottle. Shota grins at me like he did before on the couch. I realize that I cannot read the grin any more now than before. Shota cocks the revolver. The hammer pulls back.

In one swift movement, Rageev has his hand on the revolver. He tries to pull it away, but Shota's grip is very strong. They wrestle over the gun. Struggle crosses their faces. Rageev inserts his index finger in the space between hammer and revolver. Shota cannot fire. As Shota pulls the trigger, the hammer lands on Rageev's finge . He screams in pain. We all hear the crack. That finge 's broken. Rageev manages to hold on. Doesn't cry out again. "If you're going to kill anyone, kill me. But leave my daughter alone. Please."

Professor X watches them, then finally nods towards Shota, telling him to stand down. Rageev's finger is a bloody mess. He holds his hand up to try and stop it from bleeding. "Good," says baldy, "now you understand. Is the full thirty thousand there?"

Rageev nods. "But I owe you less than twenty."

"Consider it a fee," says the old man, "a tutoring fee. You would not learn. I had to teach you. Don't ever try and put me on hold for payment again. Now, you're free to go."

I take Geetha. They fetch her stroller, strap her in. The woman pats Geetha's head, making her gurgle. This woman has not said a word nor shown reaction the whole time I've been here.

"You'd better take the stroller," says Rageev. "I think my finge 's broken."

"Such a mess," Rageev moans when we're outside. "Where am I going to get thirty thousand to pay back Muruges's people?"

"I'm glad you got the child back," says Muruges when we get to the car. "So you knew who it was. Tell me, did praying actually help you?" Rageev says nothing. He straps Geetha into her seat. I fold up the stroller, put it in the trunk. "Now you see whom your patron has gotten himself mixed in with," says Muruges as we climb in. Rageev tells me to take the driver's wheel. He's not capable of driving. I say goodbye to downtown and pull us out. Every time we come down here, it gets worse.

"I want to know everything," I say as we go down Bloor. "If I'm helping you, you're telling me everything."

Rageev hikes up his shoulder, holds his hand up, tries to deal with the pain. Even through the pain, you can see how relieved he is to have Geetha back. He plays with her, strokes her face. "I'll tell you what I told Soothy," he says.

"No. I want to know everything."

DANIEL

Halloween fell on a Friday in 2008. When Lynn and I saw all the kids dressed up, walking down side streets as princesses and dragons and superheroes, we talked again about having our own. Many kids wore Iron Man masks that year. I tried to imagine Lynn large bellied, steadying her back with her hand, but couldn't. I tried to imagine myself in those scenes. It felt staged and unreal. Like looking at a movie set through a viewfinde . Lynn in the foreground in some maternity dress, palm against spine for support. In the background, in the back corner of my set, some unknown actor I had hired to play me. Roughly my height, complexion, and build, he'd been outfitted with my plaid shirts and dusty pants. They'd given him a haircut like mine, but he didn't know what to do. I keep yelling into my megaphone, "Act like an expectant father," but what I specifically mean, no one knows

"You have to bring it up when you visit your parents this weekend," said Lynn.

"Why don't you come with me?" I asked. "Strength in numbers."

"Uh-uh," she shook her head, "give them time to let it sink in. Then I'll come over. Better that way."

The ravine had entirely changed colour. Its trees were large, the babbling brook was loud and rowdy, the burdock and reeds were overblown with flu f. Ducks nested there in the winter but it was too early for them now.

The other houses in the neighbourhood had Halloween decorations up. My parents' neighbour with the cherry tree had placed cobwebs and bats around his eaves. A scarecrow, its large pumpkin head ripening, stood watch beside the cherries that had fallen. Flies buzzed around them. As I walked by, the flies rose up and swarmed over the scarecrow and his big toothed leer in one black cloud, then dispersed, settling back onto ripe and crushed fruit. My parents' house was bereft of decoration. They didn't believe in Halloween. When kids came to trick or treat, my parents drew the curtains, turned off the lights, pretended no one was home.

They refused to make concessions to this louche land and its decadent customs.

The Yutani S class stood in the driveway. It turned out only Malathi was there – Mahesh couldn't make it. Since my parents and Napoleon didn't have to put up a front for the in-law, we soon began to act like ourselves. Things devolved quickly. "So you're finally all moved in with her – you've given up your old place for good?" asked my sister over the kitchen table.

"Who knows?" said my mother. "If things don't work with the black woman, you could come back here."

"Her name's Lynn, Amma, not 'black woman'!" I stated. "And things are going to work out. I'm not moving back here."

"We're keeping a room for you," my father stated as if my words could not bear weight. It was not a conversation for him so much as a joint statement of facts. "You're not in a favourable situation. The mortgage is in her name. You should have something too. You should be thinking about property for yourself."

"Actually, my stuff is in that room," mused Napoleon. "Mahesh and I'll move it sometime in the summer. Alright?" I didn't care how long she stored her stuff as I never planned to move into the room. They had a large photo of Malathi and Mahesh – their friends called them M & M – in a gilt frame upon the wall. For all intents and purposes, the room belonged to my sister, though neither of us lived here.

"I can't buy a place of my own," I replied tensely. "I only paid off my student loan a couple of years ago. You know that. You can't really afford this place either, but who wants to talk about that?"

"What's to stop her from just kicking you out if she feels like it?" asked my mother. "You know how these people are."

I put my hands together as if I were praying. "What are you talking about, Amma? What do you know about black people? Remember the time you thought the neighbours across the street were black because they played their music too loud? They were brown like us."

"Not like us. Indian. They park their car in front of other people's lawns."

"Here we go," I groaned. "Anyway, the reason she won't kick me out, as you put it, is because she and I are going to have a baby."

"Really?" gasped Napoleon, her mouth quivering slightly. "She's already pregnant? But you're not married!"

"No, but…"

"Kadavalei," said my father putting his hand to his forehead. He paused in dramatic fashion, then resumed eating in an aggravated manner. He couldn't manage half a mouthful. "You didn't have to get involved with that woman!" he yelled. "Have you lost your mind? What did we do to cause this? You could have been so many things. If you didn't want to be a doctor, you could have gone into science or engineering. Something – anything! Did we try and steer you for our benefit? You're throwing your life away!"

"It's not too late," interrupted my mother. "Maybe it's a good thing his name's not on the mortgage. We can get him away from her and arrange a nice match. Why don't you come to the Sai centre and talk to some people about it?"

"Why? I'm happy where I am. You know what I think of that charlatan Sai Baba. If you want to focus on changing someone, change yourselves. Remember when I agreed to go on that trip with you to Sai Baba's compound in India? You all said it would be good for the family. You twisted my arm. Remember how that turned out? This is why I don't want you anywhere within a hundred feet of my marriage, if it happens."

"You said 'if'," said my mother, clinging to hope. "Why 'if'? Are you not getting married? Worse and worse! Just come and speak to someone first. What do you have to lose?"

"Leave it," said my father, lowering his head. "Can't you see he'll never listen to us? When has he ever listened to us? He's too smart. That's why he went into film and became a teacher. To teach us!"

I searched for a suitable rejoinder while my mother wailed: "How can you do this? Don't you know who we are? We're your parents! Should I go on the road and try to advise and help someone I don't know?"

She did everything but beat her chest.

"Did you hear that?" Napoleon cocked her head. We all strained to listen, the food going dry in our hands. Yes, there it was: an unusual sound, a rustle. Something from outside. Something prowling the perimeter.

Our father raised his head; his eyes sprang open. He walked agitatedly to the closed curtains in the living room. After taking a quick peek, he came back and turned off the light that hung over the kitchen table. With the electric hum gone, I could hear something new. The shuffle, muffled but distinct, of footsteps down the driveway, kicking aside dry leaves in their path. They stopped in front of our door and paused before the doorbell rang.

Our father went back to the curtains to peer out again. I tiptoed behind him. A young man, dark skinned, thin and moustached, wearing sunglasses and a winter jacket, stood in front of our door, clipboard in hand. He pulled at his moustache and checked his clipboard.

I could see the patches of driveway where he'd kicked aside the leaves. Absolute silence as he reached forward with his bony finger to press the doorbell again. "Anna, open up, I know you're in there." My mother and sister sat patiently at the kitchen table in darkness. It was a drill they were used to.

The man balled up a fist and pounded it against the front door. "Open up! We know you're here! The grass has been cut. Your car is here. You must contribute something to the cause – we are fighting for the good of you and your family!" And then after a while, "We'll only come back later – again and again until…"

I'd seen this man once before. He was thin, possessed a wiry moustache; he collected money from people for the LTTE. Sometimes as much as five to seven thousand dollars at a time, I'd heard. He was especially persistent. He and others like him found Tamil names in the phone directory. My father and mother, after the payments that went to the house, had nothing. They stonewalled him as best they could. As he did with the kids that went trick or treating on Halloween, my father closed the curtains, turned off the lights, and pretended no one was home. He did not have any candy for the LTTE either.

We did not move, and the man began ringing the doorbell in jagged stops and starts, extending his bony finger, like death trying to penetrate the home. Finally, he turned to the window as if he could see us through his dark glasses and the drawn curtains and cursed something in Tamil, then turned around and slowly walked down the driveway. He walked by my father's transplanted mums and peonies, glanced at them for a moment, then kicked at them again and again until their stems broke. Petals and stalks lay fragmented on the mud. He took out a key and scratched a streak down the windshield of my sister's Yutani. A horrible jagged squeak of a sound. Immediately, the alarm began to wail, but he didn't care. He just checked his clipboard, chuckled, and walked away. The swish, swish of dry leaves accompanied him.

Shock and anger passed over Napoleon's face. Only fear kept her paralyzed. When we'd had time to calm down, our hearts and breathing slowing to an acceptable rate, I asked my father whether he'd ever opened his door to them.

"Never!" he said. "Why would I? Once they have you hooked…"

"Our car!" gasped Napoleon.

"Believe me, you got off lucky," our father said. "They break windows and other things."

"You usually argue for the Tigers," I reminded him.

"Yes, yes, it's true. They have it bad. Do you know how bad things are right now? They've lost ground. For a long time they ran things up there, but these Rajapaksas have doubled the army. More than doubled. They're giving the Tigers a hard time. Our boys have held the place for years. They've managed somehow. They know what they're doing."

I stared back at him, still in shock.

"Well – who else is standing up for us?" he asked. "Do you know how many soldiers they have? How many people do we have? What other choice is there?"

On such contradictory impulses were his opinions formed. "Do you know what's really happening there?" he asked again, scoffing at our ignorance. "Do you know how people are suffering?"

I could only shake my head. "Don't you ever stop to think how brutal the Tigers are?" I asked.

"The Army's attacking them. They'll try to take Kilinochchi, the capital city. If the Tigers don't do something, you know how bad it'll be for our people? Your mother's relatives too. Sometimes I'm glad my parents are dead already. My brothers, their families, are still there. The Sinhalese don't care. We're like dirt to them, always have been. It's an open air prison, you know. People dying without food, without medicine, bombed and maimed and killed. Ordinary people. Not Tigers. Then you ask me whether it's right for Tigers to kill Sinhalese soldiers. Don't be naive! We're very lucky to live here, you know? You find it so easy to complain.

"So why didn't you let him in and give him money?"

"What money?" asked my mother. "The money that you should be helping us with by living here?"

The wave of fear finally released Napoleon's voice. "He keyed my Yutani!" she yelled.

NIRANJAN

The ravine has completely changed colour, as if the land is growing old. Wind rustles through the tree tops. Branches shiver.

Rageev gets a fire started near the rocks. Beer bottles are around. The shopping cart, in the stream, with the plastic bag still blowing in the breeze. This is where white people light bonfires and drink beer on weekends. Not us. It's the middle of the week. Rageev's got some wood. He uses a lighter, but it won't catch fire. Not dry enough. The wind blows out the fire before it can catch. He brings out the lighter fluid he's brought, and the saucepan. Asks for our passports. Today is not a day for guns. This is stronger than guns.

Soothy hands Rageev his Sri Lankan passport. I do the same. My burgundy Sri Lankan passport: one of the things I carried away, along with my mother's letters, photos of my family, and movies I enjoyed with my dad. Rageev pulls out his passport too, being careful as his broken finge's in a splint. His passport is old and creased and stained. I try to see his photo in there, before his face was burned. When he was young. But I can't. Rageev places all three passports in the saucepan. He pours lighter fluid over them. Next, from his bag, he pulls out a piece of paper. It's got writing on it. In the cold breeze, Rageev reads what he's written. The plastic bag in the river keeps flapping the whole time, like a flag in the wind

"From this moment on, you are my brothers. You are family to me. What I do for you, I'd do for my own family, my daughter. This means that we are of one blood. I will be there for you, just as you will be there for me. From now on, nothing will separate us. This goes beyond blood, beyond culture, beyond family. We unite our souls. We burn our passports to show that we cut our ties to the past, to everything except each other. This our ultimate fealty – the loyalty which goes beyond words. This is a symbol to show we cannot go back. What is truly being pledged, lies in our hearts. We do so with our living souls."

It is a bold statement. Though Rageev has read it in Tamil, it does not sound like something from the old country. He removes a Wilkinson razor blade from its wax wrapper, draws the blade into his palm. The blade is passed on to Soothy, who hesitates. Not wanting to seem scared, he quickly pulls it down his hand, cutting way bigger than necessary, biting his lip. When it's my turn, I tap it against my skin. I've never liked knives or sharp objects. But I close my eyes and slice. In the end, I don't even feel it. We all smoosh our palms together, mixing our blood. The mixed blood is smeared over Rageev's speech. He puts the paper down on top of the passports. Holding the paper down so it doesn't flutter away, he sets the whole thing on fire

We clean our wounds with tissue paper. My passport is the last to burn. The words on Rageev's paper go first. Blood on the paper dries and curls very quickly. Not unlike the ash of the incense at the Tamil shop. Rageev's words are like a priest's pooja, but in Tamil, not Sanskrit. The plastic in the passports smells awful. Melts like liquid poison, toxic. Turns into black wispy smoke. Smells the way insects roasting in Hell might smell, gets in your nostrils and throat. All our photos in there, young, Sri Lanka in the background of our lives and minds, turning into flame. It all burns to one ash in the pan. The fire dies out quickly though Rageev adds lighter fluid to keep it going. A solid black-grey ash is left.

Wind lifts up flakes of ash, swirls it amongst the trees. Rageev takes the saucepan and scatters its ashes into the stream. The ash drifts up in the air, swirls in the water, slaps against the rock. My dried blood is floating in the air with Rageev's and Soothy's. Eventually, the ashes and smell are all gone. That familiar smell of pine needles, wet earth, and cold air takes over.

We all hug, embrace real hard. The only time I have ever had physical contact with Rageev. He ruffles my hair, being careful with his finger that's in a splint. Even clasping Soothy feels strange. I feel openness, a sense of hope. For the first time, I'm more than a little plastic footballer on a foosball table: no arms, turned upside down, yanked this way and that.

Rageev collects the saucepan, washes away the rest of the ash in the water. The pan and lighter fluid go in his bag. We walk up the path, through trees whispering around us. Dry leaves blow against our faces. Their colours are pretty. The sun is still out, but it keeps getting colder.

"Soothy knows," says Rageev, placing a hand on each of our shoulders, "that when my crew went, one by one, either taken away or deported or... the other thing that happens... I thought I'd find nobody else. My heart was broken. I'd given it to Kannan the same way I just gave it to you. So when you guys came, I thought maybe there was hope left, maybe it didn't all go to shit. I thought it was over for me. But you came along."

"What is it you want to do?" I ask.

"I want to build something out here. Make a name. Be somebody. I don't want my daughter to grow up with nothing."

"How is Geetha?" says Soothy.

"Oh, Geetha is fine," smiles Rageev. "Good as gold. But you won't see her no more. I've told Yalini to stay at our other place. Not to go out with the baby."

"Yalini akka is okay with it?" I wonder.

"Oh, yeah. She was mad at me, but she knows it's the best thing."

I still don't know where this other place is. Don't want to. But I do want to know about Muruges and Black Moustache and what Rageev's doing with them. I want to know about the Asian dudes. Professor X and Basketball Jersey and the Identical Suits. I ask him to explain how he's working for the LTTE.

"Okay," he says, scratching his chin with his finger splint. "But you should not tell anybody outside, ever. Got me? These people are serious. They will kill you quick and cold if they feel they can't trust you. I'm helping them, but not officially. They gave us guns before. We helped them with things."

"Like what?"

"Like collecting money, obviously," says Soothy. He gets irritating on the best of days. So what if he knows stuff? I'm new and want to learn it all. "Remember when we took you to that couple with the place on Lawrence?"

"Of course!" I reply.

"We're collecting from them and others, regularly" says Rageev. "Muruges isn't happy I'm dealing with the Asians, but he knows them too. Some of them, anyway. Besides, I've got to make money. Muruges isn't paying my way. Now they've given me thirty thousand dollars though. This is big. If I don't find a way to pay them back... They're not easy to deal with."

"Who's harder to deal with? Tigers or Asians?"

Rageev scratches his chin again. "Tigers of course. They know more about me. The Asians took Geetha, but they eventually gave her back. Shows they're only interested in money."

"Are you going to keep buying drugs off them?" This is what I've been wanting to ask all along. What he says next surprises me.

"Of course. That's why I wanted you to stay in school and do well in your courses. I want you to start selling there, thambi."

DANIEL

Classes ended early before parents' night, and I went down to guidance to talk to Lynn. She kept her office door slightly open, and I could tell she was in there with a student. "Janelle, we've been playing around for two years now. As a black girl with hardly any courses under your belt, you're going to have a very hard time out there in the real world. Sooner or later – it's not all about clothes and make-up and boys, you know – you've got to take the future into your own hands. As a black woman, nobody out there is going to help you."

For just a moment, I glimpsed how ancient and worried and solemn Janelle's face had become. Upon seeing me, the girl smiled, pulled herself together and grinned. They're all so charming when they want to be – such little geniuses and sociopaths. Lynn and I watched Janelle gather her coat. "Bye, miss."

The girl didn't even look at me.

Trying to be nonchalant, Janelle stuck her hand in the bowl of condoms on the secretary's desk and put a whole bunch inside the pocket of her Adidas track top. As if it were free candy, without making it a big thing, she turned around and sauntered away. "See you later, Miss."

How do you like that?

"How can you stand her?" I asked Lynn.

"If you think she's bad, wait till you meet her mom." Lynn shrugged. "You'll almost feel sorry for her then."

"Yeah, but that's no excuse." I closed the door so we could talk privately.

"Dan, she's failed eight out of sixteen courses over the last two years. Not a single teacher will accept any of her excuses. She's given the same sob story about her father dying in grade eight for the last three years. No one's listening. I've talked with her mother about having Janelle assessed. Her reply? 'No way, no how.' The shame of having an IEP and being stigmatized as a potential special needs student."

I tried to lighten the mood. "Maybe we should take a cue from her," I whispered, stroking Lynn's leg, moving to her shoulder, tracing my finger into the crook of her neck. "Maybe we should use up the rest of the condoms in that bowl before they're all gone – what do you say?"

She grabbed her mug of coffee, which had long gone lukewarm, and sipped it, pretended to mull over the proposition. "Why don't we skip the condoms? We should be trying to conceive."

That killed any playful coziness left in the air. "Jesus – not that again."

"Why not? It's always about doing it in some forbidden place for you – camp, here. Why not get serious?"

"I'm worried I'll never make that film if we have a baby now. It'll never happen."

Lynn swivelled around in her chair with a gesture of dissatisfaction. "Don't you think raising a child is creative? Don't you think it's an accomplishment? Are you so selfish, so shortsighted, that you think only a film can have any meaning?"

"Let's not talk about this anymore. What's happening with Raptis and Janelle Rochester?" I asked. "Are they going to do something?"

She cracked her knuckles. "Dan, there's a process in place, and it's a good process – why trouble things that have nothing to do with us? Are you set for parents' night? I got Jayanath to help you."

"Okay," I agreed, relenting, and kissed her goodbye. "Jayanath's good." I felt as if both Janelle and I had come down to see Lynn, and she had been nicer to Janelle.

*　*　*

Parent's night. It has both a sacred and terrifying ring, reeks both of sentiment and sacrifice. Like Valentine's Day or Mother's Day, it evokes something both artificial and heartwarming. The gym had been set up with small tables bearing our names. My last name 'Narayan' is alphabetically close to 'Raptis', and I saw him already there, set up along the west wall of the gym by the time I meandered down. Cram was far away, on the other side. The walls had been festooned with streamers and a giant sign proclaiming 'Welcome Parents!' as if we ourselves were neither parents nor children, but some strange intermediary, arbiters and oracles of other people's youth. There was a feeling of both freedom and formality, the vice-principals strolling the gym, the chairs in front of the tables with their name cards just so, waiting to be filled

Raptis wore his lab coat. He gripped a sheaf of marking and circled items with a red pen. My mind was still on the conversation I'd had with Lynn earlier in her office

I wandered to my spot behind my name card. Raptis seemed filled with vigour. These battles with Badlamenti and the admin kept him going; as hungry as I was for details, I didn't want to ask too much. Once he got going, his tirades and rants were difficult to stop

Jayanath, from Prefects, president of the SAC, had been assigned to me as the prefect to keep appointments running on time, make sure lines were orderly, and parents knew where to go. I remembered him from two years ago at camp – the bottle of Malibu rum. Every time our eyes met, he glanced away and looked down. If he knew what we had done with the bottle, it would have been me who blushed. Small mercies. He was tall and lanky, all bony arms and black hair almost like a bouffant. The LCC red prefect's cardigan only made him look even thinner as it swished around his knees. He was quieter and more serious when he was with me, but that was fine. His work as a student was meticulous and excellent; he was a pleasure to have in the school. He vindicated my decision not to call his parents from camp that night.

I suppose my whole relationship with Lynn was founded upon that decision. In a way, Jayanath and Allan were responsible for bringing us together. Lynn often said, in private, that the Tamil students in our school fell into two distinct groups: thugs and nerds. Those were the names that the students themselves used. Jayanath belonged to the second group. When Lynn asked me, I couldn't tell her why the same culture, the same history, and even the same families sometimes produced such different results. After all, my sister and I had grown up under similar circumstances, but turned out very differently.

Jayanath had been assigned to my table because he could help me translate for the Tamil parents who could not speak English. My spoken Tamil was poor at best, about as good as their English.

There weren't many parents during the day. Most of them were at work. They were shy and polite for the most part, and since traffic was slow I could take my time with them. We took a break before the hordes came in during the evening. I called Jayanath over and give him money to get iced teas for us.

Raptis still sat close by, and I could lean back and mimic taking a couple of flaming skewers and sticking them in my eyes. I twisted them around and he chuckled. Parents' night ended up being a long day.

I shouted over to him. "Hey! What are you marking?"

He looked up from the sheaf of papers. "Biology of the brain. Some kid just answered that the seat of fear and aggression is the hippopotamus."

When I looked at him in blinking incomprehension, he added, "It's the 'hypothalamus'."

"Oh."

"It's funny, the human brain," ruminated Raptis, putting down his marking and placing his hands on his belly. "It's the most complex thing in the universe, the supreme achievement of evolution, yet how many of our students use theirs?"

I could feel a rant coming on, but instead he surprised me. "The brain is a physical thing, it is a machine made of tissue and blood, but what are thoughts – where do they come from? Where do they go?"

"Thoughts and feelings are in the brain of course," I replied.

"They're relayed through the brain, the central nervous system, but what are they? A thought, a reaction, is nothing more than an electrical impulse, I suppose. Your nerves are nothing but electrical relays."

"I know that, John. I took all my Science OAC's."

"Oh yes, I forgot. But yet, you chose to go into film. Why is it that everybody with a few favourite films and a special wish thinks he's Spielberg? But those creative thoughts of yours – what are they exactly? You took your Biology OAC, when we had OAC's, and you presumably did well, so you'll remember activating potential, the pH balance in a nerve, the movement of electricity, and so on. But where is the thought itself?"

"In the neurotransmitters?" I asked, beaming at remembering how the axons and dendrites worked.

"But they're just chemicals – on/off. Do you think that something as supreme as Homer's Odessia can be created by a sequence of on/off chemical triggers? Most of our body is space. Most of you is space. You know that if you took all of your matter and condensed it into a tight ball, there would be less than a handful of molecules dancing around in there? Where do the ideas go when they jump across the synapses?"

I had no idea and mimicked dumbfoundedness. It was strange to think that I had once chosen art over science; it didn't matter anyway, here is where life had brought me.

"You know," he said, waving his arm, gesturing to the grounds and ravine beyond the school's walls, "the space inside us is exactly the same as the space outside us. You know that? That's the greatest secret. If you understand that, you understand everything."

"I suppose our students can't be helped," he continued. "Their brains aren't fully formed. They're swimming in a sea of hypothalamus behaviour. That's all they're surrounded by. Their amygdalas – seat of compassion and love – haven't reined in their baser instincts. But how does that explain their parents? Our admin? How does one explain their behaviour? That fuck, Badlamenti! What warped electrons are bouncing around in that coronary sandwich he calls a brain?"

He had brought it back to Badlamenti after all. When I didn't answer, he continued, "Haven't seen much of you or Pete at lunch lately. Are you avoiding me? Yes, you are. Don't lie. It's because of what happened a couple of weeks ago with that Rochester kid, right? Goddamn, you know it wasn't my fault. They always do this to us, you know that. This is the way they do it. That fucking prick Badlamenti – you know the wops just stole everything from the Greeks, right?"

"Lots of parents?" I asked, attempting to change the subject.

He shook his head and laughed. "Hey, how Italian is Badlamenti?"

"I dunno," I dutifully replied.

"He's so Italian he thinks Obama's a name from the Old Testament."

I looked across the room and saw Lynn, but she didn't see me. I tried to look away quickly, but Raptis had caught my glance and ribbed me further when he saw me uncomfortable. "Hey, look at Lynn in her navy blue blazer, talking to Stevenson. It feels weird to see them so chummy, doesn't it? She's in our union, and Stevenson's in the admin. It's like the goat chatting up the wolf at the fence's edge."

I didn't say anything.

"Did you know that our union rep, Myra, and Stevenson used to teach at the same school?" continued Raptis, pulling at his beard. "Apparently, Stevenson used to teach gym before she became admin. Myra said the girls in her class tried to get out of swimming by saying they had their periods. Stevenson got one of those old scoring calendars that coaches use for keeping track of Varsity teams – those calendars – and started keeping track of the girls who were using this excuse again and again. She recorded the date of their excuse, and if they tried to use it again, she'd refer to the calendar and say it hadn't been four weeks yet. Apparently, if it was legitimate, during a test or whatever, and a girl came up and tried to use her period as an excuse, she'd pull open her desk – she had a whole bunch of pads in there – and give the girl one. 'You've got five minutes to go to the washroom and put it in, honey. Hurry up. I'm timing you!' she'd say – according to Myra anyway."

"Lovely," I murmured.

Lynn and Stevenson were laughing now, chuckling like old hyenas. Would Lynn become like Stevenson in time? Would I become like Raptis? Phlegmatic, irritable, an inflated sense of our own status in such a small pond? God preserve us from becoming like that! There were so many teachers in our school, like the old head of history, who, to hold their own against their students, administration, and colleagues, had become used to never switching off their teacher voices. Mice roaring their way through life, howling their lessons and opinions at the wind. It became their only voice – they no longer had another mode. "Not everything is furze and heath you know," I said to Raptis. "What unholy terrors to their own families some of these teachers must be."

He nodded and went back to marking. Circling in big red. I wondered if it bothered him that he'd never had kids of his own.

Jayanath came back with the iced tea and some food for himself. I made space for him at the table to spread his food out and eat. It was hard not to feel a sense of pride and affection for this scrawny tenacious Tamil boy. I knew I could not take credit for him; his parents had done something right, and since his grades were so high, they wouldn't be coming in this night. I wouldn't even get a chance to tell them how much I appreciated their kid. When Lynn and I had kids of our own, would they turn out like Jayanath? Lynn did spend a significant amount of time with the Prefects and SAC. Perhaps it'd already trickled down into her parenting style. I'd want our kids to be smart, respectful, studious, I suppose. But I'd also want them to be rough around the edges, a bit more individualistic. I'd want them to be the spark that crossed the gap.

But Jayanath would never have said that he wasn't individualistic; he was exactly whom he wished to be. Wasn't he? My father would have loved Jayanath – he was everything as a student that I was not.

Jayanath finished eating, then pointed out the Tamil names on my list for the evening. "Why are Tamil names so long, Mr N?"

"Because Tamils have to make everything as difficult as possible, Jayanath. They're not satisfied unless they've made things as difficult for themselves as they can.

He smiled back at me.

The evening's parents trickled in, and Jayanath lined them up and made them sign in. Almost one in three parents who come to see me were Tamil. As soon as they realized I was Tamil, they began speaking to me in the Tamil language with a barely restrained curiousity and frankness that made me embarrassed: "You speak English so well, you must have been born here. No? Which village is your family from? Oh, it's only been a few years since we got our people over here with nothing. Nothing! Now, everybody's working, we all do our share. It's so unusual to see a Tamil as a teacher, normally they're all white! Why didn't you become a doctor or an engineer? Your English is so good, I'm sure you could have got in if you wanted. Did you not study hard enough? Laziness is the worst crime in the eyes of God, and He's always watching. Don't you agree?"

And then they finally asked, "How is Abirami, Saathuryan, Ganavarshini, Madukrishnan?" And we got down to business. I had to tread carefully, suss out whom I was talking to. If I was the least bit suspicious, the last thing I would do was tell the truth. If Madukrishnan's father was sitting there like a Shiva totem, two hundred pounds of granite stone, tripwired for the first bad words about his son, ready to go into a fury, I knew that Madukrishnan was going to get the living daylights beaten out of him when his parents went home. Talking to a mother, soft spoken and slow, didn't necessarily mean the situation was any better. She might beat her kids just as hard as any man or she might tell her husband, with it being easy and understood that it was the father's job to do the beating. As someone who had been around this for a long time, I could see this was as natural as sleep to them. As routine as drinking their tea. Their parents punished them this way, everybody knew it, and they would think of anybody who didn't discipline their kids as very poor parents indeed. It was their responsibility, no matter how personally unpleasant the task, to mould and turn their children with a severe hand.

In a sense, you could say that to be Tamil was to be beaten. We are born into the worst of situations in a country that is run through avarice, violence, and lies. We are cursed and inured to a condition that has no hope of getting better, and those of us who are lucky enough to escape trade one nightmare for another. The evils that lie in the West (the freedoms to drink, fornicate, and forget obligations) have to be fought with sticks and fists, with words and feelings, as hard and cold as the will necessary to survive. Throw gang crime into the mix, and it was truly a nightmare. If parents did not beat and shame their children, how would their kids ever be able to face the world, where the real abuses were manifold and unending, where the only purpose was to take small pieces out of people, bit by bit, keep wearing them down until they had nothing left, and eventually broke? This was the gist of conversation with some of these parents – they assumed that because I was Tamil, I would agree. It was truly hard to keep my mouth shut and listen. They had no idea how much I hated this line of thinking. I tried my best.

Jayanath helped me keep track of time and made sure that no parents stayed more than twenty minutes. By and large, though pushy, they were not aggressive or violent. They were polite and gentle; here was the befuddling contradiction. The anger and hardness were on the inside. Outside, you would never know what emotions swirled behind those blinking eyes, those withered cheeks, that blistered, peeling dark skin that formed their weatherbeaten faces. That fury jumped across synapses as vast as oceans. As wide and fathomless as the entire universe.

When Niranjan's aunt showed up, I was exhausted and tired from having to deal with more than fifty parents. The surprise of seeing her here perked me right up. She hadn't shown up the year before, and she hadn't told me that she was going to show up this year. I expected an earful.

"Hello, Aunty," I said cautiously. "What brings you here?"

"Have you seen Niranjan?" she asked coldly.

"Only a couple of times. He won't talk to me."

"I asked you to help me. To do one simple thing."

"What can I do if he won't talk to me?" I pleaded. "He isn't any warmer with me than he is with you."

"What am I going to tell his mother?" she asked, her voice sharp, boring into me. Jayanath looked at me, wondering silently if there was going to be trouble, but I shook my head at him. "I know her," I whispered.

"Yes, you know us, except when it's time to deliver on your promises. Then you're nowhere to be found."

Could you believe this? "He's your sister's son," I said. "If you've lost him, what responsibility do you carry in all this?" I thought about all those Tamils, their trips across oceans, their refusal to adapt to the way things were in North America, the problems they brought. Mrs Navaratnam was a living embodiment.

She stared at me with hatred.

"Look," I said. "Mr Raptis over there teaches him. Why don't I take you over, and he can tell you a little more about how Niranjan is performing in his class?" Jayanath and I had to reluctantly lead her over to Raptis, whom I could tell didn't want to talk to her either.

"You must be able to do something," she said to Raptis. "We don't even know where he is. You're his teachers. He's not a child anymore. How can you call yourself teachers if you don't care where your students are?"

"He's over sixteen?" I stammered back. "He's old enough to live on his own now if he chooses. That's just the way it is. There's nothing we can do about it." I was growing angrier myself.

"This myre (shit) country," she said.

Stevenson and Ackerman had heard the agitation now and came over to check the situation. Stevenson held her walkie-talkie, ready to call one of the hall monitors, while Ackerman placed his hands on the back of Mrs Navaratnam's chair, coaxing her to get up and follow him to the office. His voice was gentle and calm; he was good. She got up quietly, cowed by his smooth authoritative manner, and followed. I nodded to Jayanath to follow them so he could translate.

"Please help my nephew. Please!" she pleaded to me in Tamil before she left.

I walked back to our table. It was amazing how all elder Tamils looked like my parents in one way or another. The shape of their beaten and battered frames, the incongruency of their faces (some were stricken with crooked teeth and talked slowly, haltingly), the way they slumped into their chairs and pressed clothes.

Almost the end of the night. Niranjan's aunt had left a strange feeling in me. That old hunchbacked loyalty kicked in. I could not help but feel as if I were responsible for Niranjan now. I don't think I'd seen him since our talk outside Raptis's class. Had I? When was that? The sense of frustration and obligation filled up all the spaces in me. It was a colourless, odourless gas.

"Shut the fuck up!" My aimless thoughts were cut off by the grating sound of John Raptis's voice. At first, so jarring were the words that I thought he was speaking to me.

An immediate cessation of murmuring in the gym. Finally, dead silence. All I could see was a knot of people huddled around John's desk. A middle-aged black lady, short and wearing a blue suede coat, clutched her handbag and tried to get away. Myra, ever present union rep, took her arm and calmed the lady down. The two vice-principals had already left with Mrs Navaratnam. Now a whole bunch of people huddled around John. Cram was there too. Raptis got away, breaking free of their questions. He pushed Myra rudely. She was so flustered, she lost her famous composure.

Cram and I found Lynn on the fringes. "Do you know what happened?" I asked.

"Your friend Raptis just told Janelle Rochester's mom to 'shut the f up'. Then he grabbed her."

"Really?" asked Cram. We were astonished.

"That's what she says anyway. She's a single parent. That woman does not take things lying down."

"Maybe we should go get him?" suggested Cram.

"Your friend is in deep deep trouble. Even Myra's going to have her hands full with this one."

"Okay, let's go, Pete," I said.

We knew we shouldn't have followed him; we should have heeded Lynn's warning. But there we were, in pursuit of his magnetic whereabouts. There was something about his charismatic presence that drew us, even in failure. Cram and I ventured to the science lab. Raptis was hanging up his lab coat and packing his briefcase. He hadn't bothered to turn on the lights, but the sodium glow of the large lamps in the school's parking lot flooded through the lab's wide windows. Raptis looked furtive as if he were burglarizing the place

"What happened?" I asked breathlessly.

He waved his hand in annoyance and sat on a lab bench. "I really fucked up this time, guys."

We waited in the doorway for him to continue but he said nothing, just sat there, life gone out of him, the anger dissipated, finally the old man he was supposed to be. I could see the glints where the sodium light shone off the white streaks in his beard.

"She kept going on about her daughter, you know – that useless Janelle girl. She wants me to pass her just because her dad died a couple years ago."

"Did you grab her?"

"I don't know. Maybe. I didn't mean to. Who can tell for sure in a situation like that? I was pretty pissed. The girl only threw a flask at my head, right? Who remembers or cares about that? The mother spends ten minutes complaining about her daughter, and then she has the nerve to say that I should be trying harder to make her pass."

"So you told her to 'fuck off'?"

"I didn't hurt her. What about what she did? She has the effrontery to go on about what an easy job we teachers have. We do nothing and get taxpayers' money, our union's always striking, we get our summers off, all that bullshit. This stupid bitch doesn't work, her one single task in life is to raise her daughter right, and when she can't even do that, she blames me. So I asked her why she doesn't become a teacher herself if she knows so much about it?"

"What did she say?"

"She said, 'Oh – I couldn't handle teenagers'. Just like that. So that's when I told her to shut the fuck up."

"And grabbed her," whispered Cram. "What were you thinking?"

We looked at each other. I thought of Mrs Navaratnam for a moment, what she had said at my parents' house. Do all people think of teachers this way? Some of them must know the truth, no?

I looked back at Raptis, and I think even he knew what trouble this would bring for him. It wasn't like standing up in a staff meeting and challenging Badlamenti. This was serious.

"What are you going to do now?" asked Cram.

"Go home, what else? I'm not going to wait for those assholes to join their arms together and start sweeping the building for me. If there are no more questions, good sirs, I shall bid you good night." He raised an imaginary hat to us.

His last comment was so affected and impersonal, I knew he could sense what a final blow this was. Last nail in the coffin. There were many reprimands in his file, but this was going to be the straw that broke everything. It was public. The administration would have to do something now. He had given them the salvos to do so.

Cram and I got out of his way so he could walk back down the hallway and climb slowly, lonely, down the stairs. His footfalls echoed in the school's corridor. We both knew he wouldn't be coming back to teach the next day.

NIRANJAN

We take the car downtown, me driving. The destination is an apartment building at Wellesley and Parliament. Soothy's in the back this time. Rageev is riding shotgun, talking to me.

"Remember," he says, "you're new so people will naturally wonder about you. Let them wonder. Just watch. Don't say anything."

"Don't say nothing," echoes Soothy.

Rageev turns around, frowns. "That goes for you and your big mouth too. Double. I don't want what happened last time to repeat again." Soothy puts up his hands. He turns to face outside the window.

It's a pleasure to drive downtown, though it's unfamiliar. Something bad happens every time we come down here. It's still a nice change from Scarborough. Exciting, different, fresher somehow. You take the 401, then the Don Valley. The place we drive to, the apartment complex where Wellesley comes to a dead end at Parliament, reminds me of Tuxedo Court.

Apartment buildings that are old and cracked rise very high. Like tall dominoes, they block off a court. A fortress with gaps. "What's this area called?" I ask Rageev.

"St James Town. Cabbagetown is south of here. Rich white people. But poor ones too, like our people."

"There are a lot of our people here?"

"Oh yes. You could say that. Some of the people at this meeting, they're important. Just stand and watch. Don't say anything. You might recognize one or two. You'll see Muruges. He'll be there. He's high up in the World Tamil Movement. You ever heard of them? WTM?"

"Maybe through my aunt."

"He's only uncle Muruges to you when he visits, but here he's a big man," says Rageev. "You must not annoy or embarrass him. In fact, it's better to pretend you don't know him. You boys are here with me, understand?"

It's understood. It's understood. Now that we're brothers, Rageev is more open with me than before. Soothy too. I'm still in the dark about many things. Some of the things they talk about, I don't really understand. I do understand that Rageev owes Muruges's people thirty thousand dollars. And that is not a debt they will easily forget. He has to attend these meetings to show his allegiance.

We park the car and get out. The apartment towers are huge. Now that I'm in between them, they're much larger than Tuxedo Court. Everything in Toronto is bigger. They're building condos to the west of these towers. "It's like Tuxedo Court on steroids," I say.

"Largest place like this in Canada," mutters Rageev. "Watch out for the dog shit."

They're all gathered in the meeting room in the basement of one of the buildings. A long table, metal legs sagging, a bunch of people in the audience on cheap plastic chairs. All Tamil, like us. Soothy and I have to stand, but Rageev gets to sit down. There are no windows. I can smell the laundry room down the hall. You can taste laundry detergent in the air. It smells dusty and sweaty and soapy everywhere. You can't escape the smell.

There are about twenty guys, all men. Some are young, very casually dressed. Others wear polyester trousers, creased, ironed shirts. Reminds me of back home.

"That's why we have to mobilize the community," says a middle-aged man with large glasses, hair combed over his wide bald head.

"Thank you, Muthu." A white-haired man, very small and very old, wearing a Polo fall jacket and small glasses, stands up, raises his hands. His pants are hiked up onto his belly. "Welcome, everybody. Wannakum. It's been a long time since I've seen some of you." He seems to be a leader – there's space around him. The others treat him with respect. He sits right in front of the long table where the food is. "I have not seen some of you since the summer. Of course, we should try and get together more often. I want to hear from you all. Without your support, the struggle for Eelam would not be possible. We all want what's best for our people. For this reason, we must make sure that all our efforts are coordinated in the same direction." He sticks his hands out, parallel, for emphasis. A lot of muttering, but nobody says anything.

The white-haired man adjusts his spectacles as if he's done this a thousand times. He licks his lips before continuing. "You all know Muruges, what a solid part of the struggle he's been. No one need exaggerate what a fearsome fighter he was. Now, he continues the struggle here, to win hearts and minds for our cause. Muruges will speak now."

Muruges can't get up easily, but he crosses his right leg to keep it from shaking. He runs a hand through his thin hair. "The most important thing," he says, then repeats himself when the murmuring gets louder, "the most important thing is that we keep money flowing. Channels must be open. We've been able to equip our boys with boats, planes, and other tactical gear, which allows them to keep the army at bay. Without continued money flowing in, they have no hope. Remember, they're fighting over there so we don't have to."

"That's what you always say," wheezes a very pudgy man, standing up, glaring at Muruges and Old Guy. "You always say 'more money' but our people are bled dry. Where is this money to come from? From working at McDonald's? People are trying to bring their families over here to escape what's going on back home – you know that. You want money to keep things as they are."

"You've suffered a loss, you've suffered a loss," says Old Guy, "I understand. We've all lost people. But you have to see the long picture. Look at what we've achieved. What can't we do if we only keep trying? Think of all the martyrs who've given their lives to the cause already. Do you want to throw away all they've sacrificed for?"

"You don't know what you're doing. You just do the same old thing. We're not golden geese. There is a different government in Canada now. Since LTTE's been put on their terrorist list, they've hit you hard – that's our money they seized from your bank accounts. And what were you doing, leaving all your accounts and notes lying around? Haven't you learned anything?"

"Be careful," Old Guy says, wagging a finger at the man. "We all know who you are. You're our friend, and I like to respect what you say, but we don't like your tone. The RCMP didn't take anything that's going to stop us long term. We were already moving stuff out. A drop in the bucket, that's all. Do you know how much money we've already sent? Hundreds of millions. They take a few million and feel like heroes. They don't know what they're doing. TV cops. In the meantime, we continue to do what we do and let them feel like they're accomplishing great things."

"But things aren't the same back home either," someone else says. "There's new governments there as well. Double the trouble. These Rajapaksas are mad. We campaigned for them, and then they go and triple their army. They're out for blood. If they push into Jaffna, you know the rest of the country's only going to be happy about it. These guys are motherfuckers. They don't give a damn."

Muruges speaks up. "We'll be waiting for them. How many times has this happened before? We go through a little fighting, then usually some country tries to help us with the peace process. We go along, of course, get more recruits, get more arms – with your help naturally. We have to be strong. Think smart, think long term. This is no different. We've survived attacks on Kilinochchi before. We'll beat them back."

"You're fools. You've been in power so long that you can't see the wolf at the door."

"We all need to be strong," says Muruges calmly, "like these young men over here." He nods to Rageev who still hasn't said anything but sits there silently. None of them react to him; they don't even look quickly away from the burns on his face like others do, so they must know him well. Muruges points his finger at me. "This is the young man I was telling you about. His brother is the one who fought so bravely with us at Elephant Pass." Some nods and smiles come my way. Muruges continues, "He got Rageev's baby back for him. Seems like the same blood that runs in his brother's veins runs in this young man too." Now there are murmurs of surprise and approval. A few turn around and actually look at me closely. Rageev hangs his head in shame. I start to feel uncomfortable, but also proud. Soothy doesn't move at all. Hard to see what he's thinking.

After the meeting, Muruges talks to Rageev and Soothy and me. Dark Moustache is there also, but he never says anything. Just nods, now and then. I've never even heard his name. Have to be honest – I don't like him. Something strange about that man, makes me uneasy. He can tell.

"Machan, good to see you," Muruges uncle puts an arm around my shoulder. Then he turns to Rageev. Dark Moustache sneers. "Brother, you owe us some money, we need it back." His tone is polite, but it's also cold and distant. His voice is low and flat. I realize that I haven't seen him around the apartment. Is he shunning Rageev? Is Rageev avoiding him? "You heard what they were saying. We need that money back."

Rageev looks down, doesn't say anything.

"How's Yalini? The baby?" asks Muruges.

"Good," smiles Rageev, but it's a small 'good'. When he smiles, the line where the burnt white skin meets the dark seems to stretch and strain. It's pulled over his skull, painful almost.

"If everything's good, then get us back the money. We've worked together a long time. But we're not fools, you should know that. Remember who we are. The only reason I have any patience with you is because of Yalini, she's important to me. You know that. Do the right thing – get us back the money you owe us."

Without saying goodbye, Muruges and Dark Moustache turn around and move to talk to others.

DANIEL

November was a tumultuous month. It brought the promise of winter in its maw. If I remember correctly, Barack Obama won the election a few days in, and there was that sense of renewed optimism regarding our neighbours to the south. Despite claims that America would never have a black president, even if he was half-black, and the promises and threats by white supremacists that Obama would be assassinated, Barack did indeed carry the vote. The mighty Bush administration was finally out of office. In a way, Sri Lanka was ramping up its own version of the Bush years; the Rajapaksas and their cronies were stripping rights and freedoms as they moved towards their vision of a police state. Borne on the back of a militaristic agenda, they would eventually put the American chicken hawks to shame. I knew little of such matters then, nor that they'd impact our lives in Canada.

Our economy worsened each month in North America, but Obama seemed level headed and measured. One could believe he'd bring us out of recession with goodwill and humour. Lynn was particularly happy and inspired by the developments stateside. Had we really grown up believing that neither Canada nor America could be ruled by anyone other than an old white man? Lynn decided to throw an Obama victory dinner party for a few friends. I took to calling her 'Michelle' in secret, after Michelle Obama. She said, "Hell, no. I want to be Barack!"

I had to host the party with Lynn. She'd invited her friends Nadine and Mark, who were married, and I supposed trying to conceive. Also coming were Tamara and her oafish boyfriend Darren. Cram was the only friend I'd invited on my side, and he seemed to come more as a favour to me than anything else. I couldn't invite my family of course, as their presence would only rob Lynn of her ease.

Dinner was prepared – jerk fish and sweet bread, corn and potatoes with buttered string beans – my woman was fantastic at everything, even cooking. There were few things she would admit failure at. Nadine and Mark arrived, and I took their coats, made excuses for the boxes that were still in the hallway, got them drinks. Lynn and I sat on one side of the granite kitchen counter like a proper couple, and Nadine and Mark perched on the other. Nadine and Mark had been together a long while; they were married. I was always pleasant with Nadine, whom Lynn knew from university, but Nadine and I had never connected personally. She was probably Lynn's best friend, though they were also rivals, after a fashion. My identity was defined by being Lynn's partner. Nadine and Mark were not really people who connected with others one on one. I suspect they tolerated me because I presented a means for Lynn to move forward in her life, settle down; this made Nadine happy. It was all so complicated, so curiously impersonal; I might as well have been anybody else.

"Your place is beautiful," said Nadine, envy raising her glass into a toast. "You made a really great choice."

"And the harbourfront. No panhandlers a block from your entrance," smiled Mark.

"Plus all our gorgeous southern exposure of water," added Lynn.

"I liked her old view," I offered meekly. "I liked seeing the Fort York troops doing their formations."

We took our wine and walked over to the window. It was stunning! The harbour at night time. We could see the sugar factory and Captain John's boat restaurant, the Gardiner Expressway, all the small people and cars below. In the distance were the murky landforms of the Toronto Islands, lost in dissembling blackness. Lights dotted the water between the harbour and the islands, and sailboats and yachts cruised slowly from one dot to another. Since we were so high, I could not see individual people. I'd been able to see the soldiers from Lynn's old building, the shadows of their rifles across their uniforms as they marched, and I'd liked that. Everything looked so remote here, so lonely despite being filled with light. The elevators had brass panels, the rug pile was rich and luxurious in the hallway, and the people, our neighbours, seemed to gleam. Very few of our neighbours ever replied more than a word or two, resisting my attempts to begin getting-to-know-you conversations.

Just then, the concierge called. I hoped it was Cram because he always smiled, brought cheer to the conversation, but it was Lynn's other friends: Tamara and

Darren. Their small kid Rusty would be with them. Rusty, his delicate half-Asian face full of energy, liked to be chased around the living room. It made me tired just thinking about it. Without realizing I was going into reverie again, I thought of my film, which had stalled for years now. I soon felt guilty. After all, this was what I was putting having our own kids on hold for. My ambitions were grand for a first film, quite untenable. I wished to make something real and gritty like the seventies filmmakers I admired. I wanted to make Apocalypse Now but set it in Sri Lanka. Or something close thereof. A stupid ambition. Without really knowing anything about the war and its politics, I imagined it could be done. The story and its transplantation, images of my father standing on the step of one of those ancient Jaffna trains, hurtling past mangosteen and palmyra trees, all colluded in my mind. It was a wishful fantasy. To let it go would mean having to accept my role as a teacher. Permanent and intractable.

Why couldn't I be like Cram who relished his teaching role? Younger than me, he'd fought tooth and nail to beat out other graduates for one of the scarce Board spots. Lynn, who was committed to her career, had always wanted to get out of the classroom and go into guidance. But Cram didn't seem to want that. Raptis often said that no one, no matter how much they complain, ever leaves guidance to return to teaching. Cram had once talked about becoming a department head, but I couldn't see him leaving the classroom.

"Dan, take her coat – please," Lynn's voice brought me back.

Tamara was the one person amongst Lynn's friends who did value me for myself, and we sometimes had good discussions about movies and art, but today I didn't feel much like chatting with her either. I felt remote. It came from being so high above the ground, I suppose. I missed my film school friends. They had all gone on to other things. A few worked in the film industry; ironically, they envied the stability and benefits that came with my teacher's salary.

Pete Cram finally arrived, bearing a bottle of Crown Royal, and smiled genially at everyone, sorry he was late. He was dressed in a powder blue shirt with a penguin logo, neatly shaven and pressed. Sharp and cheerful as ever. Always so cheery and cheerful. "Why did you take so long?" I asked.

Cram's smile faded. Looking up at me from underneath his yellow curls, his eyelids took on a hooded look. "I had to go visit Raptis," he said, "to see how he's doing? No one's gone to visit him, you know."

I became tense. "Lynn says we should avoid him," I whispered.

"I know, but the guy's miserable. He's not allowed in the school until he has to come in for his hearing. Even then, he knows he has no chance. He asked about you."

"Oh yeah? Tell him hi, if you talk to him again."

"You should talk to him," whispered Cram, the barest hint of annoyance in his voice.

I led Cram to the magnificent view at the window, staring down at the harbour. He made the appropriate motions of admiring the locale. We watched the red and yellow lights of the boats bob on the water.

"How do you like the new place?" asked Cram.

"It doesn't have the culture I liked in the Annex, but it's nice."

"Uh-huh," Cram nodded.

"I can't believe it's me. I'm not used to luxury. My parents live in a tiny bungalow they can't afford. They had to be of retiring age before they could live in a house, and still they can't retire. Somehow, life doesn't seem fair."

"It's the Canadian dream, I guess," stated Cram, staring at the water, hands in his pockets. "Isn't that a good thing?"

"What, to live beyond your means?" I poured Cram some of his Crown Royal on the rocks, lifted Rusty, and carried him around the condo before joining the others. Cram had already realized we were moving away from the other guests, isolating ourselves, and he jumped back towards them, began gabbing away with smiles that were warm, made his conversation glowing. I thought about Raptis. I thought about my parents. Yes, the Canadian dream. But there was also a Tamil dream, was there not, as I had discussed with students many times? The kids in the Tamil Students Association knew all about the Tamil dream.

It's very close to the Canadian dream. One of equal opportunity, civility, service. Where you don't have university or employment quotas just because you happen to be Tamil. It's where you can practice your religion and culture within the safety of your community. Once we'd paid thousands of dollars for an immigration lawyer and spent years hanging by a thread, being passed through the refugee claims process. Now we had a right to own and live in the land, its society, just like anybody else. We had to start from scratch, but at least they didn't drag us from our houses in the middle of the night, at least they didn't tie us to trees and set us on fire. What were the sneers and jeerings of a handful of racists, the taunts of "You're stealing our jobs," and being called 'paki' every day, in comparison to that?

God, those first years in the Tuxedo Court building. And then the Gilder Block for all that time until I moved out and my parents eventually bought their bungalow. Having left our genealogy and family and homes and jewellery behind. Having to share our apartments with the cockroaches that found their way into the fridge and ran all over the vegetables, the butter dish, their long legs becoming stuck in the soft butter. You'd open the fridge, and their legs would go click-click-clicking all over the floo . Yet it was worth it. The cockroaches had been in the apartments longer than we had, said my father – it was worth it – the cockroaches had more right to the place than we did.

My thoughts ran to Thambi and his mother in the Gilder Block. I thought of Niranjan. Where was he now? What was he doing? Was he laying out cockroach traps wherever he was, some mouldy cinder block hole, even while Lynn and I drank Crown Royal and celebrated Obama's victory? There were certainly no cockroaches in this condominium.

Something else beside cockroaches nested in the soft underbelly of the Canadian dream, something hard and determined and Tamil that gradually developed scales, a hard carapace, and dreamt of flight. This was the Tamil dream. It was over for our parents – they had barely survived. Their hopes nested and took root in their children, the next generation. My sister and her husband and their house in the Scarborough Bluffs. It was a crowning achievement. The thing about being a doctor in Canada is that it makes one recession proof. Expectations were passed on and internalized as invisible legacies, replacing patrimonies that no longer existed.

Our students' parents did not want their children to adopt the values and culture of North Americans – definitely not! They wanted them to remain good little Tamils. Tamil on the inside and Canadian on the outside. To blend in, to camouflage, take on the accents and elocutions of success but remain fiercely Tamil, never forget for a moment where they came from. That Eelam, that mythical red blot of nationhood, was being fought over with blood and agony. Canada – this would have to be the new Eelam. This was the Tamil dream. Had my parents done all this so I could be here, having dinner with these people, overlooking this view? Had my parents done it all so that I could come home to Lynn?

I then thought of Raptis rotting away in his house, all alone. Nothing but books to keep him company. It was a shame that Cram had gone and talked to him, but I could not because Lynn had told me not to.

"Daniel, where are you tonight? Earth to Daniel. Earth to Daniel. What do you think of what we're talking about?"

"What?"

"We're talking about the new Obama administration and the sea change it promises for the States," said Lynn, her face taking on that look of annoyance I knew so well. The others looked at me curiously. Her eyes narrowed, and she continued. "We can go visit my cousins in Louisiana again."

"Not me," I said. "They're still going to interrogate my ass at the airport. I'm not interested in politics."

I could feel Lynn's frustration growing as her cheeks darkened. "If only we had the same kind of thing happen up here," she said, forcing her cheek muscles to stop drawing upwards. "Just because you're not interested in politics doesn't mean politics isn't interested in you."

Tamara obliged me, between bouncing Rusty in her lap, by asking me about my interests outside of school – what films I'd seen and enjoyed. She was the only one who remembered what I'd done before teaching. I'd promised the others that they could be extras in my film when I finally got it going. They knew it was all smoke in the air. Lynn was the one who decided things and she was right – she knew what she was doing. I did not. Having tried to make a 35mm short in university, I had really fucked up. My partner took all the money, wrested control of the project, and ran it into the ground. Money that should have gone into paying back my student loan vanished into a project that became an increasingly toxic black hole. The film was a joyless mess. I had been too weak to fight for it. Had proved my father right.

Darren pulled out a joint while Tamara and I played with Rusty. He licked the end. You could see that he was already imagining smoking it. "Anyone want to do a jay?" he asked.

The rest of us were too polite to join in, but also too polite to object. "Put that away," scolded Tamara.

"Why? We're celebrating Obama," said Darren. "He's a cool guy. He'd want us to." Darren looked at Lynn for permission.

"Oh go ahead," she said, good naturedly. "You only live once."

Tamara wasn't happy. "Not around the kid," she said and picked Rusty up to take him out in the hall. "He needs his bottle."

The rest of us were subdued while Darren smoked his jay. We watched him uncomfortably from the couch. Cram grinned at me. I didn't find it all that funny. Darren didn't seem fussed enough to reverse his decision as he wrapped his oafish lips around the joint and took drag after drag. In between puffs, he held out the joint like a curious artifact and stared at it as if he couldn't quite fathom how it'd gotten into his hand. I hated the smell and didn't like it clinging to the carpets and sofa. That skunk smell must have made it out beyond the open door and into the hallway because two minutes later, one of our uptight neighbours came over and asked to speak to Lynn and me.

"We're really really sorry," I said.

Darren wanted to get in an argument with the old Toronto blue-haired blueblood, but she immediately threatened to call down to the concierge and report us to the cops. Lynn and I pacified her some more, reassured her that we'd never do it again.

The victory party broke up after that.

"Rusty's real cute, isn't he?" asked Lynn, after everyone had gone.

"It's strange," I told her as we washed the dishes. Lynn didn't mind doing the cooking, but insisted I clean up the plates. "We're on these tracks moving forward, but they sometimes don't meet."

"What do you mean?"

"Nothing. You bring up children all the time now. We've only just moved into this place. Give it time."

"I'm ready now, baby," she crooned. She was a little drunk. "You're the one having doubts."

"It's not like that," I replied. "I wonder about bringing a child into the world with people like Darren around. I think about my parents and how things turned out. I don't want to become like my old man. I don't want to have the kind of relationship with my kids that he has with me and Malathi. You're an only child. You don't know how it is to have everything fucked up."

"Nonsense. You just overdramatize. It blows over. Why's your sister so angry anyway?"

"Aw, you wouldn't understand," I replied. "You grew up and had a normal Canadian childhood. I'll tell you some other time."

"Alright," she laughed. "I am dead tired. Leave the plates. Let's go to bed."

Always an irresistible proposition. I still found her beautiful, had never imagined anyone such as her would be interested in marrying me. My previous conquests had been artsy types, fellow film junkies and arts majors I met in university: flaky women who could discuss social theory but ended up working in big box bookstores and threw it all away to move to Japan and teach English. Every one of these relationships had sailed under the power of my being able to flatter and prop up their insecurities; once their need for constancy and reassurance faltered, they drifted.

Lynn wasn't one of those women. There was no dissembling or false modesty. She embraced things fully. The sweat just rolled off her forehead as we made love, and her vigour and appetite often exceeded mine. It was that baby thing, I suppose – it gave her hormones a kick.

Trivial matters hung on my brow and always encumbered my stroke. She was hungry, yearning for pregnancy to the very bone, blessedly free of doubt.

Lynn held my hand. She looked me in the eyes. "If I say something to you, promise me you won't get angry?"

"Did I do something wrong?"

"No." She smiled but tightened her fingers, pinching, the clasp painful. "I feel bad. I've been fighting with whether to tell you."

"Lynn, we should be able to say anything to each other by now. It bothers me that you'd even…"

"When I tell you that I struggled with it ethically…" Her eyes searched my face even as her words trailed. Her braids and rows had become undone while we fiddled with each other's clothes. The anticipation of sex, the sweat, caused her hair to become loose and fuzzy. Her skin sweated that smell of linseed oil, intensifying as we hedged around our subjects. "I've known all along where Niranjan's living," she declared.

"What? You're joking. Why didn't you tell me?"

"I'm his guidance counsellor. He's over sixteen. Niranjan specifically asked me to keep his new address private. Specifically from you. I tried to reason with him, but he was very deliberate about it. Don't look at me like that. I'm telling you now." When I didn't say anything but continued to stare at her, slack jawed and accusatory, she whispered, "I want to help you with the problem he's been having with his aunt. That you've been having with his aunt. If there was another way, I'd have preferred that."

It was easy to forgive her because I understood why she'd kept this information. In a way, I didn't know which I minded more – her intransigence, keeping her knowledge secret, or the violation of her ethical principles. "I wish you'd told me that you knew, Lynn. You could have told me that you knew, then said you couldn't reveal the particulars."

"It would only have caused tension."

She was right. Yet I knew that's all that would be on my mind the whole time we made love.

NIRANJAN

"Door! There's somebody at the door!!!"

I'm downloading movies onto my new laptop. Rageev took the laptop from an electronics store that owes him money. I'm grateful.

"Niranjan! How many times do I have to call you?! Somebody here for you!" yells Yalini akka. She's been a lot more shrill lately. Geetha's never with her.

I take out my earbuds slowly, push through the red beads. Out into the living room. You won't believe who's standing there.

Mr Narayan and my cousin Thambi. They're just outside the front door, trying to peer in. Hands in their jackets, looking stiff. I stare at them. They stare back, like I'm lost treasure. Is Mr Narayan shaking? He's definitely rubbing his hands together. Thambi has a scowl on his face.

Yalini akka stands by the front door, arms crossed. Rageev and Soothy look up from the couch. The TV is on mute: some Tamil movie – people in cars, guns shooting in slow motion. The colour's always so overdone in those movies.

"How did you find me?" I finally s .

"It wasn't easy, let me tell you," replies Mr N. "Do you know my father's been worrying about you? Our entire family has."

"Not to mention your own flesh and blood," adds Thambi.

"Why didn't your mom come?" I ask Thambi. "Didn't she want to make a scene? Tell everybody how hard she works for me?"

"She did want to come," says Mr N, rubbing his hands and looking down his nose. "But we persuaded her to let us meet you alone. It wasn't easy."

"I don't want her coming here. You tell her that," I say.

Rageev finally stands up. That's when they get their first full look at him. I get a kick out of seeing people react to his scarred face. So priceless. Like seeing a map of the Tamil parts of Sri Lanka. Bombed red earth. Scares them to pieces.

"Who – are – you?" asks Rageev, each word a stone dropping to the floo . "What do you want with Niranjan?"

"I'm his cousin," says Thambi quietly. Mr N doesn't say anything, but just looks from Rageev to me, back to Rageev again. Soothy hasn't gotten up from the couch yet. He's finding all this pretty funny, trying not to laugh. Probably high. At least I have family. His would never bother looking for him.

Rageev looks at me. "Is this true?"

I nod, a little scared for myself. "This is my cousin I told you about."

Rageev surprises me; his tone's quite gentle. "Well, you should come in. Niranjan's like a little brother to me now. He's family, so that makes you and me family. Right?"

Thambi doesn't like this, and Mr N shakes his head. "We'd like to talk to Niranjan outside."

Rageev looks at me again, and I signal with my eyes that it's okay. He stands aside as I get my jacket. As I'm putting it on, Yalini akka glares at Rageev and juts her chin out. He sighs and looks back to us. "I'd better come with you," he says. "Let's go for a walk outside so the neighbours won't hear us."

"You have nosey neighbours?"

"Yeah, they're Tamil."

We walk out into the courtyard in pairs. Rageev and me, used to this place, all the grit and dirt. We walk behind Mr N and Thambi who go ahead. Once in a while, they look back just to make sure we're still here. That we haven't vanished into the ground.

"You've never been here before, have you?" shouts Rageev to them as Mr N looks over his shoulder. "A bit rough for a teacher, no?"

Mr N laughs, his voice still tense. "Actually, I used to live here – my family and I lived in the thirty building when we came to Canada."

"So you know this place?"

"Oh yes, I know what goes on here. I teach at the school, just over there. I've taught Niranjan before, you know? We're all very worried about him."

"Is that right? Like who?"

Mr N doesn't respond to the sarcasm in Rageev's reply. I don't say anything. We're up at the chain-link fence. The wind whips through its rusted wires, cutting us. "Well, as you can see, Niranjan's well taken care of," says Rageev. "He's not starving. Not cold. Got clothes on his back. Nothing to worry about. Niranjan, take out your athsma inhaler." I take out the orange Flovent puffer, squeeze out a puff, make it look good. "I even buy his medicine for him," says Rageev.

"He should be with family," states Thambi, balling his fists, suddenly upset. "You're not family." Mr N checks him.

"Being the age he is – that's partly our concern," says Mr N. "I know what he gets up to here. That's why we want to talk to him. Get him back on track at school, if nothing else."

"You don't have any idea what happens here," says Rageev threateningly, his voice going all flat. "Let's leave it at that." He digs his hands in his pockets. "Hey, is that guy listening to us? That man behind the building. Watch out – over there!"

I turn around to see some old guy climbing the hill behind the Tamil store. "That's nothing," I say. "Let me go talk to these guys alone. I'll be fine, don't you worry." I put my hand on Rageev's shoulder to reassure him. He stands there, hands in pockets, shaking in the wind as he tries to decide what to say. Finally, he turns to Mr N and asks, "What's your full name?"

"Daniel Narayan."

"Daniel. What kind of Tamil name is that? Which part of yaarl you from?"

"My mother went to a convent school. Outside Jaffna."

"Daniel!" He laughs again.

He watches us walk away, hair blowing in the wind, scars scratched over his face like worn out rust upon metal. I go between the other two, and we walk in the opposite direction from the school. Autumn will soon be gone. Gummy pine needles with it. The hardened mud on the ground pushes against our soles.

We walk past the tennis courts and approach the swings. It's late. I hop into a free swing and sit there swivelling while the other two stand around me on the hard sand. I remember when I sat here with my garbage bag holding everything I own. The day I moved in with Rageev and Soothy. A hundred lifetimes ago!

"What's up with that guy's face?" blurts out Thambi.

The chains holding the swing's saddle are especially cold, but I grip them tight, will the blood to flow into my hands. "You don't know him," I say. "You don't know anything."

"Right!"

Thambi is behind me and starts pushing me gently.

Mr N goes out in front and catches me, pushes me back towards Thambi. For a moment, I feel caught. "There are so many people worried about you," says Mr N. "From Ms Varley to your parents to your aunt."

"My aunt is crazy," I say. "She's got a mental problem."

"You're throwing away all your chances by being here," states Thambi. "You did well in Sri Lanka, didn't you? You going to throw that away?"

"Yeah, I did well back there when I had my family. Here, I've got no chance. You think the teachers give a shit? They don't. No offence, Mr N. Do you think anybody cares how hard it is to do everything differently when you come here, to learn English in a few months just to keep afloat?

They stop pushing the swing – it slows down. I let it. I don't really have any problem with them. Like I said, I just hated being treated with no respect by Thambi's mom. I'm not talking about big respect, just the smallest, tiniest amount of common human decency.

"Let me tell you this joke that a guy called Muruges told me," I say to lighten the tension. "There's this guy, right, and he dies? He goes to that place with the gates, you know, the entrance to Heaven? The guy who reads the book there looks up the guy's name and says, 'You weren't so bad, but you weren't so good either. You could really go either way. Tell you what – you decide whether you want to go to Heaven or Hell.' So the guy is given the chance to check them both out and then he can choose. He spends a week in Hell. He takes a first-class elevator down. In Hell, they're partying all the time, drinking, lots of beautiful women. Sin all around. He has a great time. He then goes back up to Heaven. In Heaven, people just play harps and float around on clouds all day. It's boring. At the end of the week, the guy at the gates asks him. 'So buddy, what's it going to be? Heaven or Hell?' The guy thinks about it and says, 'I choose Hell. More fun there.' Immediately, these demons come and bind him in chains, stab him with knives, cut him and tear him, take him back down where he suffers and suffers in total agony. And he's made to work like a slave. It's roasting, he's sweating all the time, continually tortured and burnt. One day, the Devil comes by to watch him work, and he says to the Devil, 'I don't understand. It wasn't like this before when I visited?' The Devil laughs. 'Well, before you were a tourist,' says the Devil. 'Now you're an immigrant!'"

That gets Thambi and Mr N laughing. It's a good joke. It wouldn't be funny if it weren't true.

"This Muruges sounds like a real wit," laughs Thambi, punching my shoulder. "But are you sure you want to throw it all away? We can't make you come back and live with us, but if you do come back…" He pushes me gently. "If you come back, you just have to finish high school, then you can move away somewhere for university without shame. Right now, it's embarrassing everybody."

Mr N's not saying anything, so I respond. "You sound like real parrots. Throw it all away – throw it all away! That's how it is, is it? She's more worried about being embarrassed than she is about me, isn't that true?"

"You know," says Mr N, "Tamil children always have it hard from their elders. You know that. In my generation, if my father pointed to a white wall in public and said that it was black, I had to agree with him. He once beat me with a bamboo rod mercilessly just because a schoolteacher made a slightly negative comment on parents' night. At least I think that's why he did it. We've never discussed it. He sure as hell didn't take the time to explain it to me. Look at him now – you've met him. He's a tired old man with the fury bled out. And I'm happy living my life. I've moved on. You just have to wait a while."

"Pay your dues," says Thambi.

I don't say anything. I'm not going back.

"When I was a child growing up in Sri Lanka," continues Mr N, filling the painful silence, "I came out of our family house to see somebody driving his kid in front of his cart on the street. In the dirt! He whipped him through the dusty road. With a tree branch, driving him through the public street with his cart. In daytime. Everybody came out to watch. Nobody said a word or lifted a finge . When the kid died, they all went to his funeral and brought food to the family, but they never disapproved. That's the way it was growing up in our village."

"I don't have to put up with that anymore," I say.

"Look, kid," Thambi speaks with frustration, "you don't want to come back, fine, but then whatever happens is on you. We're holding a bed for you, but you don't come back – we're not going to come begging again."

"That's okay with me." I jump off the swing and begin walking back towards the apartments. The sun's almost gone, and the sky's that steel denim colour. The apartment buildings of the court are silhouettes, and lights come on here and there, in units.

"We don't want to close the door on you," says Mr N. "Anytime you want help from me or Ms Varley, you just have to come and ask. We're here for you." He's not a bad guy, I suppose. He's alright. What he and the rest of the school can never understand is that I don't belong there. No more than I belong in this fucked up country. I'm not from here and I hate it. I hate the trees and I don't recognize the bird calls. I hate the people and I hate the ground itself, all hard and cold. I look to my right, through the branches, imagine the water flowing through the dark ravine where Rageev and Soothy and I performed our ceremony.

Brothers, we three.

We walk and walk and reach the chain-link fence. "There's nothing you guys can help me with," I say. They're from a different world and that's that. I'm now in Rageev's world. Part of me wishes I could hang out with Mr N and Thambi, maybe go to the mall, watch a movie. It would be a change from Rageev and Soothy.

I feel the tug and longing for family. So lonely here in this cold land. But this softness isn't for me. "This is where I turn. You guys'd better go the other way. I'll see you around school, Mr N. I'll make more of an effort to come, and try harder, I promise. I promise."

"Is there anything you want me to tell my mother?" asks Thambi.

"Yeah, tell her I'm happy where I am. I'm never coming back, and if I never see her again, I'd be more than happy with that."

"Nice kid," chuckles Thambi.

"We tried," replies Mr N.

They both walk away from the court. Neither looks back.

DANIEL

All the slides of dead people and rifles in the mud and troops in liberation parades washed over the screen. The eleventh hour of the eleventh day of the eleventh month. Lynn had been granted the 'honour' of running the Remembrance Day assembly, now that Raptis was gone. He had affected laziness, but his fingers had been in a lot of things. Remembrance Day was something that he handled, backing up the head of history – Mr Rocking-Chair-Left-Out-in-the-Muskoka-Sun, himself. The head of history didn't want to do it without Raptis, and Badlamenti gave the responsibility to Lynn. She knew very little about the Great War and World War II, but she attacked her new chore with ferocity and vigour. Like a platoon commander, she rallied the student council and the prefects and the music teacher and the choir to help her. And me, of course. The prefects and SAC members who were also part of the Tamil Students Association wanted to include slides about the war in Sri Lanka, the photos of Tamils who had died there, and Lynn had to tread skilfully to retain their support.

On Remembrance Day, the assembly went smoothly. We had a slide show assembled by the prefects showing wars all over the world, past and present, soldiers and affected civilians. Sri Lanka made it in there but it was only one of many places, lost among Iraq and Afghanistan and Palestine and the Sudan. We had a reading of poems that inspired hope. Abirami and Jayanath were the readers. My own students made the slide shows: poppies and mud and grinning veterans interspersed with the odd pile of bodies and torn barbed wire and blood-spattered trenches – mostly cheery, we kept the gore to a minimum. The work could have been more polished, but it was serviceable. I sat behind the projector the whole time during the assembly, and I glanced up at Lynn. She was such a different person in front of lights and an audience. Finally, the chime struck the eleventh hour. We all stood up in silence for the bugle call. The assembly eventually came to an end, and we sang the national anthem:

"O Canada!

My home and native land!"

I had sung the national anthem a million times but rarely thought about it. The lyrics, unlike those belonging to 'The Star Spangled Banner', were generic and benign. We used to have to sing the Canadian anthem every morning when I was in high school. Now they just make you listen to an audio recording. My father often described me as a 'complete Canadian'. He said it with a sarcastic air.

It's true – in many ways I am one – I love thoughtful foreign films, the works of the American brats in the seventies. I detested the Tamil TV shows and movies my parents preferred. To me, they were phony and unsubtle. But I had been in Canada exactly as long as my parents had. I had arrived with them. A full third of my life was spent in Sri Lanka. It was the Jaffna soil that nurtured my formative years. Like Niranjan, I hated it here – at first. But movies and comic books and novels became a second soil to me. Lynn said I was an art nerd, my head lost in the clouds. I told her that I could only gulp at the rarefied atmosphere of Western culture while white people breathed it in. She didn't understand what I meant. In that way, she was like my parents. They had resisted Canadianisms for more than twenty years. Nobody had ever made my father sing the Canadian national anthem. Even when we finally received Canadian citizenship, he mumbled his oath during the ceremony. Though he hated the people who ran the country back home, he was Sri Lankan through and through. He actively resisted being

Canadian, even though he'd fled here and brought us with him.

"Well," said Lynn, coming down off stage and taking me by the arm, "what did you think?"

It was a sombre mood, and the audience was still standing. The formal part continued. Lynn only held me momentarily because we couldn't display physical affection in front of the kids. "It's a feather in your cap," I smiled, "one of many." I really was proud for her – she was the standard bearer for the both of us.

Badlamenti later waddled up and personally acknowledged her hard work. It was her first assembly that year. All of her running around and shouting at the prefects and other students to get everything organized – so worth it, you could see the exuberance on her face. Their faces too. When a senior music student blew the French horn and we all stood in absolute silence, a chill went up my back. This was part of Raptis's old program, and the head of history had insisted it be kept. I think Lynn wanted to change that part, the bugle call. It was tradition: the ghost of Raptis flew out of the French horn and floated above the assembly. "I didn't have any relatives in either world war," she said to me afterwards, "but my ancestors were brought over to the West Indies in chains. It's not so long ago that I can't feel it in my blood. Tell me I don't understand the meaning of the day!"

That Sunday, we went to Lynn's parents' house after church, for lunch. Though she would not go with me to evening dinners at my parents', I still had to accompany her to church on the odd morning. I washed and cleaned up in the Varleys' kitchen, the stacks of dishes quietly crowding the place as if they'd grown out of the counter tops and walls, while Lynn and her mother looked through old photo albums. The potted ferns and spider plants hanging from the ceiling were deliriously overgrown. The house was stuffy, rich in hermetic oxygen. Lynn had lived in that house until she was twenty-four, the year she finished teacher's college. "Look, Mom," she said as she pored through the old photos. "Are these those blue curtains we used to have back in the nineties? I remember those curtains. You used to sew 'em yourself. Whatever happened to them? They were nice."

"You must be fooling," replied her mother warmly. "Those curtains are no good. Even these ones here, they're frayed. I gotta replace them. But you know, child, I'm not as fast as I useta be. Maybe you both oughta help me." I could believe that, what with all the dishes stacked up with dried rice and crumbs. Her dad hadn't lifted a finger to help. He'd stayed in the living room the whole time since we got back, watching TV. Mr Varley kept changing the channel every few seconds, which made me restless.

"I've got no time," exclaimed Lynn. "If I make yoga class, that's an achievement. Dan, you've got to look at these – can you believe this was me in the nineties?" I'd seen those photos many times before. No, I couldn't believe that was Lynn with her afro and neon Nike Airs. Well, not a real afro but pretty big, still. If I'd met her then, I'd never have believed that I'd end up going out with such a person, so different from the crowd I'd grown up with.

"Dan, look at these photos of me and my friends in the caf," she continued. "I'd go into the caf, and the social groups were laid out like a map with different countries. The jocks and popular white girls at the back corner – the cool corner. The nerds at the tables in the wing. The goofballs and skaters close to the service area. The metal guys on the side of the wall. You can see it all. The Asian students, their high-pitched conversations in the middle. And us, the black kids, near the door. That was that. If you didn't know who you were, you didn't belong anywhere. Thank God it's not like that anymore!"

"Thank God, you're not like that anymore!" agreed her mother. "She used to drive us mad. Isn't that right, Lucius?" Her husband grunted, not bothering to look up from the TV, still flipping channels

"We used to battle with teachers and school administrators to wear the clothes we wanted, play dominoes at lunch, hang out in the hallway, and play our music," Lynn continued, waxing nostalgic. "Sometimes the guys would break dance. Right there in the hallway, not caring who walked by. Now I battle with teachers and colleagues to get students identified, tested, and certified. It's all about moving forward I guess. For me and them." I envied her ability to laugh over the past with her parents. They'd grown together, after a fashion. She still seethed resentment about the way her father used her mother, and the way her mother allowed this uncharitable dynamic, but she rarely challenged it. I think that's why she loathed visiting my parents' house so much. In my family, everything from the past was deeply buried, a mutually agreed upon but unvoiced accord, which if it should erupt, none of us could bear to reckon with. My life was like Lynn's mother's current fraying mustard curtains. Something I used to be so sure of, something that felt so strong – an aura so purposeful it possessed a colour – seemed lost and out of place as I grew older. The past only frayed and frayed into threads, the longer I kept battling to move forward. I washed the last plate and stacked it, joined Lynn and her mother at the table. "You know, you're a very nice lady, Mrs Varley" I commented. As I said the words, I realized how formal my relations with Lynn's family still were – I addressed them as Mr and Mrs Varley instead of Lucius and Emma.

And yet, Emma had her own way of wheedling that could turn me into a wreck. "When are you going to get married and have kids?" she asked. "In my day, a man and woman didn't live together unless... Well, you can see where I've left pages of the album open for photos of my grandkids. There's nothing that we old folks like more than hearing the pitter patter of grandchildren's feet. Isn't that right, Mr Varley?"

Lucius grunted.

They weren't old, but Lynn was their only child and they put an undue amount of attention and focus onto her. Bearing up with it had made Lynn the woman she was now.

I scattered some ranch mix into a small bowl and opened a can of beer. When Lynn was a teenager, she knew every line to NWA's 'Fuck Tha Police'. But she also used to volunteer at Caribana. I think she led a complicated teenagehood. Her grades weren't the greatest. In grade thirteen, angered by the way she and her friends were treated, she ran for and became president of the student council out of sheer spite. Somewhere at her old school is a small plaque with her name on it. That's way more than can be said about me. She defeated the cool kids and white privileged groups who couldn't muster a solid candidate. In the process, she rewrote her destiny. Her past was mythologized in these photo albums preserved by her mother. No wonder her father watched TV all day without settling on a channel. He knew how much Lynn resented him.

"It really was a good service today." Her mother smiled, nodding happily, nibbling on a cracker.

"Not as many people as there used to be," said Lynn, absent-mindedly thumbing through more photographs.

"Smaller and smaller every year," added her mom, the smile fading.

I had no idea how to enter this conversation, so I just answered Emma's earlier question. "Don't you ever wonder about the wisdom of bringing children into this world, Mrs Varley? I mean, think about the world they're entering. Is it a surprise they turn out so mean and foul mouthed and filled with hate, so immature and incapable of doing anything constructive with their lives? Is it really such a surprise? Sometimes I think that any child of ours would only be distilled into the worst aspects of me and Lynn combined."

Mrs Varley was a little flustered. "Well, nurture over nature, Daniel. The Lord provides, yes sir, the Good Lord provides. It's our duty to bring children into the world and raise them well."

Lynn's father hadn't said a word. Where did his mind go when he flipped channels? "You know, Mr Raptis told me once that all that nurture versus nature bunk's been settled for a long time, scientifically speaking. DNA prevails. And another thing, Mrs Varley," I admitted as I grabbed more ranch mix, "I don't really believe in God."

"Well, that's not a surprise," sneered Lynn's mother – she would have sucked her teeth had that not been undignified, "growing up Hindu as you did. Weren't you praying to hundreds of Gods?"

"I'm pretty sure my mother believes in one God," I replied.

"Ha ha," chortled Lynn's father from the couch. "Daniel's really in the lion's den now!"

Later, Lynn drove me to my parents' bungalow in her Toyota. She would drop me off there before returning solo to our condo. "What's wrong with you?" she asked. "Provoking my parents like that? They walk around you on eggshells as it is! Do you want more trouble in our lives – is that it?"

"Did you have to get your mother to jump on the baby thing too? Like I don't hear it from you every other day at home?" I countered.

"I didn't say a word to my mother. She brought that up on her own. And I do not talk about it every other day."

I felt deflated before I could really muster up the energy to fight. The light was cold on that pre-winter Sunday. Lynn was still flushed with pride from her Remembrance Day assembly earlier in the week. I didn't want to take that away from her.

"And another thing," she continued, "do you really believe that our child would combine the worst aspects of ourselves? Do you really believe that you wouldn't teach our child to become the best he or she could be? You shouldn't be teaching kids at all if that's what you believe."

"I don't know – it just came out," I said. "Your mother was provoking me. I felt a little threatened. And you did nothing to help me out. You always side with your parents when I'm around. Why do I have to come to church with them but you never come to my parents' house with me?"

"We've gone over this, Dan. Your parents are hostile towards me. At least mine accommodate you. They know I'm serious about you. It's different. And you yourself don't seem to want to go visit your parents very often either – yet, you go whenever you're beckoned. Do they really believe in only one God? I thought you and the Tamils at school worshipped all of Shiva's family, at least."

I asked her to stop the car. We were on Bellamy, heading south towards Lawrence. She parked beside the electrical field. There were not many cars out today, and she did not want to drive up to the bungalow as she would have to encounter my parents' hard stares and opprobrium. Lynn's plan was to drop me near the ravine so I could cross the small bridge and approach my parents' house from the back. I looked at the heavy cables above us, cackling and humming with electricity, their charge flowing over the frozen earth, its hard blades of grass. On the way to some transformer. "They believe in one very demanding, severe God who controls the destinies of animals and men," I said, "but at the same time, my mother prays to everything she can get her hands on. Somehow, the beliefs aren't contradictory to them. I told you about the trip they forced me to make to India when I was in university?"

She nodded. When I'd moved out of the house, gone to film school, and was living on my own, my parents had coerced me into going on a hastily arranged trip with them to Sai Baba's compound in the south of India. I hadn't wanted to go because I was taking credits during the summer and working a full time job – to pay off my loans. I needed both the credits and the job, the money it brought, to survive. Little known to me, my parents had been planning this all along as a way to get me to move back into the house. They got my sister, then only in high school, to call me and coerce me into going with them – she claimed that it was an important trip for the family, that to miss it would doom us forever. It turned out to be a horrible experience and I should have known better, but that misguided sense of loyalty and regret did me in. "What I've never told you before," I said, "is why things are so bad between me and my sister, me and my whole family. What happened before I moved out."

"Well, I know they hit you and their expectations were severe and unrealistic, Dan," she said softly, her hand on my shoulder. "Remember, many of the kids I counsel are Tamil. I know this very well."

I took a deep breath and continued. "What I never told you about was the severity with which my parents beat my sister when she was very small. It had happened to me and then it started happening to her. They beat her almost every day because she was wilful and shouted back. They took a coat hanger to her almost every day – and she was only a little girl in grade school. So I talked to a teacher at school. I'd never done that before for myself, you understand. I was absolutely loyal. But when it came to Malathi, I couldn't bear for her to go through the same thing."

Lynn stared into my eyes, her voice grew soft, and there was an understanding there that her kids at school must have felt every day. No wonder she was such a popular guidance counsellor. I could see her being a good mother. "Well, you did the right thing, Dan. It's what everybody should do in a situation like that."

"No, you don't understand. I told a teacher, but I was terrified of my dad, of my parents, so I asked my teacher not to tell anybody I'd told him. He agreed, and then they got in touch with someone at my sister's school. They called her into the office and examined her for marks. When they found some, they contacted the Children's Aid. Children's Aid came over to our apartment, we were living in the same building as the Navaratnams, and talked to my parents, warned them not to beat my sister."

"Did they stop?"

"Well, they didn't change their attitudes, but they stopped beating her with the hanger. In a way, you could say they were still new-ish to Canada and were terrified of getting into trouble. The problem is that because they pulled my sister out of class, she thought it was her fault for the longest time. She felt guilty. She carried that for many years. It wasn't until after that disastrous trip to India that I told them the truth. My sister's resented me ever since. It's the black river that runs below everything in our family. It's the reason my father hates the fact that I've become a schoolteacher. He spits on Canadian schoolteachers and thinks we're all frauds. And, even beyond the fact you're black, they would never consciously articulate it, but it's probably why they're afraid and resentful of you in the first place.

It took her a long while to absorb what I'd said. She took her fingers from my cheek, then removed her hand from my shoulder completely. The wires above us continued to crackle and hiss. Some kind of tenderness must have fought with revulsion in her breast. "But you said that your sister and father were very close in your family," she said finall . "You say that she's his favourite."

"It's true, no doubt about it. Napoleon is his favourite. He was always softer on her growing up, perhaps because she was a girl. They had a bit more money after I'd moved out and they lavished it on her. She had a different power – she was able to get what she wanted from an earlier age. She fought back and yelled at them, and somehow she eventually had our father wrapped around her finge . Maybe it's what happened with the Children's Aid. And then when she married Mahesh, it was like they were afraid of his family simply because he was a doctor. Or on his way to becoming a doctor. It's all fucked up. That's why I have a lot of reservations about becoming a father. I worry that I'll have the same relationship with our kid that my father had with me. What if I do something? What if I can't make it work? You know I hate when I have to make a call to Children's Aid about a kid at school. I go into a kind of withdrawal."

She cocked her head and stared out the window at the ravine and bridge that lay beyond. The back yard leading up to my parents' bungalow. The smell of ozone in the air from the charged electric wires overhead. We stayed frozen in our individual seats. The car had become cold since she'd turned off the engine. "We're a fine pair, aren't we?" she exclaimed. "You've had a harder life than me, I won't deny that. Until I met you, I always thought black was the worst thing a person could be. Yet it's possible to heal and move on. Your sister's proof of that. She shared your home but it hasn't stopped her becoming successful, marrying, wanting to have kids. I almost have respect for her. Did you call her 'Napoleon' just now?"

I nodded. "Slip of the tongue. Sorry."

"Geez – it's better to be born stupid than complicated, I guess."

NIRANJAN

Christmas break finally comes, bringing a little snow with it – more than a little sometimes, enough to make you wrap your arms tight. My third winter in this frozen country and I know now that it always begins like this – just a small taste, a quick rush of cold air. The snow falls in drifts. Little by little, this place kills you with its coldness. I huddle against the evening wind when I walk home from school. Either it's my turn or Soothy's to make food. We bake fish fingers, fries, microwave frozen food, boil pasta sometimes, or fry up chicken and rice. Money's an issue, and Rageev doesn't want us eating out too much. If he's in a good mood, he might pick up food at a Tamil shop.

On the rare time that Yalini akka comes over, she'll cook, leave something in the fridge. None of us are any good at making real Tamil food. If there's curry in the fridge, she made it. I miss my family and brother just as much as when I left Sri Lanka, maybe more than ever. I remember the smell of my mother's food when I was small, the turmeric and cumin and other spices hanging in the open air. On a hot night, we'd sit outside and eat dinner off a plantain leaf.

It's hard not to think of my mother and home as I try to do homework. Thinking about home will carry me through the whole night. Hours just slip by. There are still words in textbooks that confuse me. Ideas that, if I don't know them already, are hard to understand. I go on the computer, try and look stuff up, see if I can find a translation in Tamil. Then it's real hard to get off the computer. I might check out Tamilnet, then go to another Tamil discussion forum, go on to random Google searches from there. I look for news of my village. Eventually I'm looking up movies. It's impossible not to go on YouTube. Sometimes I just get too tired, sit on the couch beside Soothy. Pretend to join in a conversation with him. My mind's on the other side of the world.

Asking Soothy for help with homework is no good. I've tried. He makes fun of me for sticking in school. If Rageev's not there, Soothy's playing the Wii and pushes me to join in. It's hard to say no. If he knows Rageev won't be home for days, he'll just sit there, surrounded by Cheetos, maybe a pie or ice cream. Smoke weed and play Wii or Xbox for hours. It stinks even when he opens the balcony door. When we get a little money from doing collections, I spend mine on food. His goes to weed.

That's why, when Janelle Rochester asks me to hang out with her friends, I say yes. Some people say she's no good but I don't mind her. Girls aren't like her back home. She's bold. Her moods change without warning; she's interesting. Mr N is dating Ms Varley at school – they even live together. Do girls like Janelle grow up into women like Ms Varley? I don't know.

I wrap up my homework, what little I can do of the science questions. I'd ask Janelle, but she's even less help than Soothy. Since Mr Raptis has been replaced, it's been a little easier on us. The new teacher is younger – an Asian woman, Ms Kim – she explains things really well, uses the digital projector, gives us a lot of handouts that she's made. Ms Kim's more eager and friendly than Mr Raptis was.

Soothy's smoking up, watching TV in the living room. A Simpsons episode. A rerun, where Barney trains to go into space. He looks up as I walk by. I put on my jacket, begin to tie my shoelaces. The shoes are soaked from the slush I waded through coming back from school. Soothy hasn't gone outside yet today.

"Can I borrow your shoes?" I ask. "Just the old Nikes? Mine are drying."

"Where you going?" he asks, mouth full of smoke, hazy eyed.

"Just out. Get some food."

"There's still some pizza from yesterday."

"Nah, that's cold," I reply. "I want something fresh."

Soothy stares at me with bloodshot eyes, then offers his joint. I shake my head. "Want me to come with you?" he asks.

I shake my head again. "Hey, where you goin'?" he yells out, but I've already put on his shoes, am out the door. I've locked it behind me. I know I'll be in the elevator by the time Soothy's managed to climb out of his nest in the couch. In his state, he won't remember the shoes.

Thirty minutes later, I meet Janelle Rochester and two of her friends at the bus terminal of Scarborough Town Centre. It smells of cold wet concrete. The wind and snow whistle through the big hollows. The glass windows can't keep the cold out. "What's up?" I nod to the three girls when I see them waiting at the McCowan bus bay.

Janelle is friends with me, but her friends are not. Sandra and Drea hardly tolerate me.

"Hey – there he is!" smiles Janelle brightly. The other two look the other way as if I stink. I say hi to them anyway.

Quickly give Janelle a half-hug. Sandra and Drea snicker without looking at me. "Drea's cousin's waiting for us in front of the movie theatre," says Janelle, still smiling. "He's got a car."

"You still haven't told me what we're doing," I reply, excited, happy just to be invited. Nice to hang with them outside of school. To get out, spend time with someone other than Soothy.

"Come on, Marcus is waiting!" She grabs two of my fingers and leads me towards the stairs. "We'll tell you everything on the way."

Marcus is a guy I've seen around school, but I've never talked to him. He's a year younger than me, like Janelle. I think he likes Janelle. There are other hallways in the school where the black guys hang out. Janelle doesn't hang there because she has enemies. They find her a little suspect. Marcus is dressed in a black pinstripe Sharks baseball hat; he wears a Brooklyn Nets jacket. He's tall, has muscles. Next to him, my clothes and cheap haircut look like shit.

Thankfully, his cousin is sitting up front with him. I'm in the back with Janelle and Sandra. Marcus drives a Pontiac Solstice – his parents' car – nowhere near as nice as Rageev's Yutani. The Solstice has problems with its transmission. I can tell just by listening to it, feeling its rumble and shake through my leg. Also, there's a leak because I smell gasoline. Can taste it on my tongue. When Sandra's not looking, Janelle strokes my knee with one of her fingers. It's cold outside, but a bead of sweat, heavy and wet, collects in back of my neck, rolls down my shoulders. It's a tight fit, both Sandra and Janelle pressing against me. You can smell their hair products. Too much perfume on their clothes. Marcus smells of oiled steel and cheap jewellery.

"So," he says, "Janelle says you're new to Canada?"

He's never talked to me before when he's seen me. Now he's trying to seem nice in front of Janelle. "I've been here a little more than two years," I reply.

"Man, this place must seem like fucking Disneyworld compared to where you're from, right?"

I look to my right at Sandra. Her coloured curls and fake nails twitch as she watches my face. "Actually, I miss my home and family," I admit truthfully.

They all giggle, even Janelle, making me uncomfortable. They seem to communicate in giggles and sniggers. "Why don't you go back?" laughs Drea from the front seat.

"Too expensive. Besides, it's dangerous for Tamil guys to return to our country. The government…" I stop talking because they're not listening. Nobody here knows anything about the war in Sri Lanka. How lucky they have it here. Spoiled with money and clothes and music. It's hard not to feel jealous sometimes. I lean forward, forcing Janelle to pull her hand back. "You guys haven't told me what you're doing. Why'd you ask me along?"

Nobody answers. It's some big fucking secret lost in the swirling snow. Then Marcus says, as we stall at a red light, his fingers tapping the wheel, smiling his big smile at me through the rear view mirror, "It's a surprise. Janelle says you're cool. We're almost there – why don't you tell him, Janelle?"

I'm worried that we're going somewhere to smoke up and get drunk. It's not the smoking – Soothy does it all the time – but it means there'll be others like them. I feel out of place already. Rageev would not be happy with my lack of discipline. Janelle doesn't say anything. She makes a point of pulling away her legs, trying to cross them. Looks out the window to let me know she's peeved for the way I flicked away her fing .

Marcus pulls into a street off Markham Road. Not too far from Cedarbrae Mall. What are we doing here? It's all residential streets. Small houses, big trees. Marcus brings the car to a stop, turns off the motor.

"Where are we?" I ask.

"You'd better tell him," says Marcus. The others giggle.

Janelle smiles at me. Joy fills her face as her cheeks pull back. She's got dimples. "Down at the end of that street is Raptis's house," she says.

"What?"

"Remember the way he treated us, Niranjan? The way he talked to you – and to me?"

I nod. The others aren't smiling now. Sweat begins to pool up behind my neck again, runs down from my hair to my shoulders. My stomach is suddenly filled with ice. I feel short of breath, fumble for my inhaler. Having a hard time getting it out my pocket.

"Do you want some help?" asks Janelle. She pries my fingers open, takes the orange inhaler. I feel trapped with them. Janelle shakes the inhaler like she's seen me do a hundred times and strokes my head with her other hand. "Come on, Niranjan, open up." They're laughing at me now. I'm sure of it. My chest feels tight, my throat's turned to the size of a raisin. What choice do I have? I open up.

Janelle puts the inhaler in between my lips and presses the button. I suck it in. They all laugh aloud, not bothering to hide it. I snatch the inhaler away from Janelle. Can feel the hot shame all over my face. "What!?" I say and quickly take another puff.

I know what they're thinking.

Marcus pulls out a bag from underneath his seat. He shows me. Empty Snapple bottles are inside. He lifts one up, and I see now they're not empty. Too dark to see before. He shakes the liquid at me, but he doesn't need to. I can smell it. There's no leak in the fuel lines. The smell isn't just coming from the girls' hair. It's what's in the bottles.

Gasoline.

He has rags too.

"No!" I shake my head.

"Look," says Janelle, "when you're with us, you're with us. You want to be our friend?"

"Yeah," I say. It's a little 'yeah'.

"Then you gotta do this. With us. We all take a bottle and throw it through the window. Well, everybody except Drea. She's gonna watch the car."

"Four bottles?" I ask. Are they mad? "That's gonna burn down his house!"

"Hey, he burns down our lives – and other people's. Remember when he caught you searching the lost and found, then reported you? This is what he gets. Do you know what he did to my mom? He told her to shut the fuck up and grabbed her. He was going to hit her!"

"I didn't know that."

"Oh yeah. That's who he is. This is payback."

"Why not key his car?" I ask.

"He doesn't have one," says Janelle, eyes metal slits, like a panther. In the dark car, her face is suddenly cold, made of rock and stone. She has many faces and moods.

Sandra, Marcus, Janelle, and I stand outside the little house at the end of the street. It's dark, but a streetlight from another block throws a pale glow on the house and snow. I shiver. Soothy and Tuxedo Court feel miles away. There's a big window in the living room. The roof comes down at a low angle, making a kind of shed over the driveway. This would be his garage if he owned a car. A small rundown house, different from the others on the street. The others have new lamps, paint, trim, curtains. There are footsteps going up to the doors of other houses, in the snow. None go up to his. As if people avoid him. Almost makes you feel sorry. Almost. At least I have Soothy and Rageev.

It's one thing to hate Raptis at school, but it seems wrong to be standing in front of his house like this. An old curtain is drawn over the living room window. We can sort of see the outline of his furniture. There's a lamp on somewhere. Maybe he's home. Marcus's plan is that we each light the rags (which are in the bottles now) and throw our bottles through the window. Then run. Drea drives us away. I didn't even know that Drea could drive. Marcus says I should go first to show my courage. I don t like it.

"I don't want to," I say again, very quietly.

"Look," says Marcus, "you're the oldest of us, the strongest. We want to see you use that arm of yours, old un. You gotta break through that window for us!"

I don't like Mr Raptis, but this just makes me sick to my stomach. The snow and ice are inside me now. Churning. Acid rises up my throat. I'm more frightened now than when the Koreans ran me all over town to pick up Geetha. I think of my brother and what Muruges said about me – that I have his bravery. Is it true?

"If you're with us, you're with us," says Janelle. She's holding Marcus's hand. Their free hands clutch gasoline-filled bottles. Sandra just hangs behind, keeping lookout down the street, serious expression on her face. For once, no giggling.

Then Marcus bends forward and kisses Janelle full on the lips. She lets him put those big rubbery lips of his around her mouth. They make out for what feels like a whole minute. It's dead quiet, awkward. They make out, knowing we're watching them. Hasn't Janelle said that Marcus deals sometimes? He's taller than her. Her hair covers his face. All I can see is the shark on his pinstripe Sharks hat, its eyes and teeth shining.

Had enough of this. I just want to get it over with. Grab Janelle by the arm, pull her away from her buddy. "Okay, okay, let's do this already," I wheeze. I can feel the inhaler in my pocket, but I won't pull it out again. It's only been a few minutes since the last time.

Marcus takes a lighter out of his Nets jacket, holds it in his fist. For a second, I hope the snow'll snuff out the flame. I raise my bottle, rag hanging out the mouth like a drunk's tongue. "You gotta walk right up to the house, nigga," sneers Marcus. "Know what I mean? Otherwise, this bottle won't go through the window. You gotta throw it so hard it smashes his window. Feel me? Gotta do it right. The girls are watching you. Don't let them down. Don't pussy out. You get it through the window, then we throw ours in there, and we all run. We gotta book fast, so concentrate. You only got a coupla minutes."

I half hear what he says. He must have seen something go over my face because he whispers kindly, even though he's still smiling that shark's smile, "Don't worry. It'll all be over soon, big guy."

I nod.

He lights the rag. The flames blow up on the cloth. Lighting up his face and Janelle's. I feel the warmth just as I realize that I can't read her eyes. Still those dark slits. Shut closed to me even though they're open. Just how well do I know her? I can see the fillings in Marcus's mouth say "Go!"

I walk up to the house, across the fresh snow. The first one to leave a trail up to his door. The smell and mould that comes off the old brick meets me halfway, tries to push me back. I can feel the fierce heat near my fist. The flame roars. Gotta act fast. Almost up to the window. For a second, I try and look through, see if I can spot his tall shape, the gut, the way he walks. I imagine him wearing his lab coat full of food stains like always.

Flame crackles and hisses, crisping my fingers. Heat travels up my arm, begging to be thrown. Even then, I wonder if I can put down the bottle, turn back. The flames are large, destroying the rag, and I know it's too late – it must be launched.

I heave the bottle through the window with as much force as I can. It smashes the glass easily. There's no alarm, nothing. The window breaks so easily. The glass just sort of tinkles, and then the wind's blowing right through the hole, pushing the curtain back. Spiderweb crack made of shards where the glass still stands. The curtains push apart. I see the flames jumping up from the floor of the living room, lighting up the glass from the inside, throwing the curtains on fire.

I signal to the others they should come up and throw their bottles.

Then of course: nobody's there.

They were just here – where are they?

Street's as empty as a beggar's bowl.

Squint through the light thrown by the streetlamp down the street. The sound of the Pontiac's bad transmission starting.

Nothing for it.

Snow and slush have soaked my socks again.

Motherfucking Canadians.

I break and run through the snow for my life.

DANIEL

For Christmas, I got Lynn a puppy. It was not the same as
having a child, I know, but I thought it would make her
happy. I contacted breeders outside the city and finally
drove out to Oakville to pick up a chocolate-coloured
Weimaraner. He and his brothers were very cute with their
sleek coats and wet noses, rolling around on the ground
outside their kennels. There were five or six of the pups
available, but one of them hung back from his brothers
and lounged upon the hay with an inquisitive thoughtful
expression. He had something about him, an aloof calm,
as if he were already fully formed. It threw me off yet
drew me in.

This initial impression changed by the time I got back
to Toronto. Perhaps it was the city that made him hyper.
As soon as we hit that belt on the Gardiner where all the
condos start rising up, he began to whine and scramble in
the carrier beside me. If he were older, he would have
howled.

Christmas was at Lynn's parents' place. My family had
never really celebrated the holiday – I think my mom
occasionally said a sentimental prayer from her convent
school days – but between Sai Baba and Shiva's family,
she had her hands full. Amma called on the phone, we
exchanged Christmas wishes, and she asked me to come
over and help shovel the snow that had piled up. That was
it.

At Lynn's parents', I prepared everybody for the
surprise that was about to drop into their laps. I'd left the
puppy at Cram's place so that I could go fetch him and
deliver the present with maximum anticipation. We'd
finished dinner, and I had to ask to be excused – I said that

I'd forgotten one of my presents back at our condo. When I got back with the dog in his little carrier, Lynn and her mother were already cleaning up and her father had slipped into TV mode. He was flipping channels as usual, not settling on any one channel. They were all broadcasting insipid Christmas specials anyway. Without preamble, I released the pup into the living room. All I'd said was that I'd be picking up a Christmas present – he hadn't been named yet.

He was a gorgeous chocolate pup with energy and affection to spare. Lynn's parents didn't say anything, just looked dismayed as if they couldn't understand what a living breathing happy thing was doing in their orderly, dish abundant, over-oxygenated house. Her father looked at me as if the dog was a disappointment, then went back to the TV soon as he could.

But the dog wouldn't let him. The puppy jumped up onto the couch, then sprang onto Lucius's knees and gut, winding him, knocking the remote out of his hands, and sending it sprawling across the floor. We heard the knock of the plastic shell and its catch spring as the remote's panel came undone and batteries spilled across the floor. Damage done, the dog ran up to the Christmas tree and began attacking its tinsel and branches. It pulled ornaments down and chewed on the boxes that were sprawled on the floo .

"Go to your Mom," I said in that awful baby voice people adopt for their pets. "Go to your Mom!" I pointed at Lynn. The dog understood immediately, and lifting his head, tongue lolling out, bounded towards Lynn and began jumping at her legs. He pawed at her stockings and skirt, and she did something I'd never seen before. Flustered and nervous, she pulled her skirt around her knees, pushed her legs together, as if to withdraw and guard herself.

"Get it away! Get the damn thing away!" cried Lynn's mother. It took effort to get hold of the puppy and lift him up, calm him down. Secretly, I was glad at the havoc he'd caused. It shook up the moribund visit with her parents. As I gently held him and carried him back to his plastic carrier, I pretended to scold him, but secretly I nuzzled his ear and made affectionate sounds at his head.

Lynn liked the dog, I think. She named him Chuck D, after one of her childhood heroes. He became Chuck for short. It was left to me to walk Chuck most of the time. He would quickly grow into a sleek young dog. I called him and he responded, seemed to know when it was time for me to take him out; he was intuitive and excitable. Too excitable sometimes. Legs longer than his body, soft grey brown fur shining, he ran around people and almost knocked them over. His tongue lolled out, and he was like a shadow on the snow – so much energy! His breed was bred to hunt, and he hunted for food in our condo like you wouldn't believe. He would get into the garbage can and the kibble bin, which we locked up, and even found a way of balancing on his hind legs so that he could stand up and steal food from the kitchen counter. At night, if we tried to make love, quietly, he would sit up and howl on the other side of the door until the mood was wrecked. I didn't mind so much – there was a kind of liveliness to our household – obstacles only seemed to lend us greater engagement, drive us further.

Pete Cram's request, in return for looking after Chuck at Christmas, was that I go visit Raptis during the holidays. Apparently, some kids had thrown a firebomb through his window, and there was no one else to visit him. I told Lynn that I was visiting my parents but ended up going over to his house instead.

Raptis actually lived not too far from my parents. His house was near the Cedarbrae library and mall. During my high school days, the Famous Players cinema used to be across the street from the mall, and I had sometimes stolen money from my mother's purse so I could skip school and see double bills there. Cedarbrae Collegiate was nearby. It lay in the lush ravine, the lush green scar. You could see the trees under tufts of snow, their dense undergrowth of roots and branches exposed, from Raptis's living room. They looked like cranial nerves, spindly brains dusted with dandruff.

Cram said I should take something to him, but I didn't know what to buy. Flowers or chocolates would have been laughed at. Books were what he liked, but after all this time I was clueless as to what to buy. What had he not read? It was as if I barely knew him. Yet, only a couple of months ago, we had seen each other every day at LCC.

His house was an old bungalow, packed floor to rafter with piles and piles of books. They overflowed from the shelves, the smell of must and brittle pages permeating the house. It looked as if some of those piles hadn't been moved in years, and were now supporting the walls. The air carried the scent of burnt pages, as well as the the acrid smell of the wood and fabric that had perished in the fire. The toxic fumes had seeped into everything. A large charred area spread from the window to the kitchen. The new window pane, freshly installed, smelled of paint thinner and rubber insulation. It clashed with the charred carpet, which from its charcoal and mocha colour, looked at least a couple of decades old. Powderized paper, atomized words, and ideas that could be tasted coated my tongue when I said "Hello."

Raptis, for once without his lab coat, sat down in an old armchair in front of his largest bookshelf. The muscles in his face sagged, but otherwise he was much the same.

Behind him, rising to the ceiling, were editions of European history, classics, sciences, and philosophy, their spines blackened. A stack sat beside his armchair, some of the books that could be saved. His right forearm was encased in plaster.

"Did you get burned?" I asked.

He shook his head with exasperation. "No, it's nothing. Don't worry about it. Just tripped and fell when it happened, you know? Trying to get out. Jesus. At my age, bones don't heal well."

The white hardness of the plaster shone as sunlight played across it whenever he moved his arm. The only signature on the plaster was that of Pete Cram's.

He lifted the cast in the sunlight and waved it around, "Well, it's a fucking new year, isn't it?"

"Happy 2009," I said. "Do they know who did it?"

"Just some kids. One left a few footprints in the snow. The police think it was kids anyway. There's tracks on the sidewalk where it looks like they ran away. Hard to tell with all the tracks coming and going. Anyway, the tracks on my lawn were from a big Nike shoe, so it might not have been kids."

"A Nike shoe? Not a boot?"

He snorted. "Kids, these days. You can hardly call it a hate crime. More like a crime of stupidity."

The unspoken question that hung in the air, the question that Cram could not bear to broach either was, who would have wanted to do such a thing? Could it have been somebody he knew? Someone he'd taught even, who now carried a grudge? "It must feel good to be retired, no?" I asked.

"It's driving me crazy," he said. He lifted his arm, suddenly wincing. "I have a cousin. She and her kids come by once in a while, but they drive me nuts in another way, I can only stand them for so long." He put his forefinger and thumb together to describe the limit of his patience. "What is it with fucking kids these days? How did we get from the old days to here? I tell you, they did me a favour in retiring me. Gives me more time to read, but you can only do that for so long. You start to go a little crazy. All this time in my head." He lifted up the cast again to block the sunlight, then dropped it. "I go on the computer, but it's hard with this. You know, a lot of people accelerate towards death after they retire. I don't want that."

"I got Lynn a dog. She and I have been talking about having a child."

He paused, staring at me for what seemed like an uncomfortable period. "Yeah, you mentioned it once before. All I can say is that you should think carefully before making such a strong commitment. Maybe the reason you hesitate is because you know it's not right for you."

"Lynn and I are happy," I declared.

"She's Badlamenti's pet. Don't you know that?" He rubbed the side of his nose. "Trust the Raptis sense. Badlamenti and everybody like him who care only for their careers are a particularly nasty form of cancer currently afflicting education. They don't know what they're doing, and it only makes them more jumpy. They move upwards to hide the fact they haven't got a clue. You're not like that. If they want to live the corporate life so much, why don't they work in business?"

Gripping the sides of the couch on which I sat, I savoured the ashy coat of pulp in the air. All those dead books, their decomposed bodies floating. Microparticles of words, words, words. Raptis seemed to delight in my frustration, for he smiled twistedly and said, "You think that I'm an exception, that you're different from me, but you'll see. You'll have to make choices too. They'll sum you up, put you to the test; shake you in a tube and let the emulsion settle. They're always looking. They gauge to see if you're one of them, part of the machine. Some of them go through life wanting nothing else."

We stared at each other. We were similar animals underneath. Even though he was not an artist, there was something similar about the way we approached the world and understood it. I was afraid of turning out like him. Perhaps DVDs lining my shelves instead of books.

"I think of you like my son," he stated. "You can ask me anything you want. Frankly, I was a little hurt you didn't come visit after they let me go."

He wasn't looking for an argument, only acknowledgment. He needed to be acknowledged for what he had striven for and endured. There was something of my father in him, some Greek madness and lightning borne of stubbornness and pride. "Come now, you're being extremely quiet," he declared.

"There was something you said to me once," I admitted. "I've always wondered about it. You pointed in the gym and said that what was on the inside was the same on the outside. There was no difference, you said, between inside and outside." The words had seemed enigmatic to me at the time, cryptic, yet memorable. We were talking of the brain. The statement had been unnerving in its obfuscation. "Do you remember when you said that people are essentially just electricity jumping the gap? What did you mean?"

"Did I say that?" He jostled uncomfortably in his bath robe and moved his plastered arm around in the air, flexed the elbow, then squeezed the right bicep with his left hand. "I probably only meant that your worldview, your neural network, determines what you see. It's a reflection of what you've built over time. Every thought you think, every impression you have, builds a neural link. It's all a mirror. The links in the worldview you construct determine in a very hard practical and definitive way the connections that are made between your neurons. It's an exact mirror image for the way you see the outside world. Inside is outside, outside is inside. No division between the two. The membrane is just an illusion.

"I'll tell you one more thing," he continued. Pointing to his temple, he tapped it twice with his free hand. "If our experiences in life shape us up here, then this also shapes what's out there." He took in the the ravine behind his house with his hand. An infinite gesture. "We're really the same thing inside and out." He moved his hand to the front of his breast. "What's in here is also what's out there. Not a mirror, the same thing. If you understand that, it'll tell you what to do. Death is not death after all – trust the Raptis sense." He stroked the side of his nose and almost winked.

We talked over how the Rajapaksa government in Sri Lanka had deployed tens of thousands of new soldiers, and tired of negotiations had attacked Kilinochchi towards the end of 2008. I was only beginning to learn this stuff, but Raptis knew that Kilinochchi had been the Tiger stronghold, the de facto capital of the Tamil state. Thousands of Tamil villagers had fled their homes. Newspaper photos detailed the long exodus lines. Heavy shelling and mobilization of artillery broke through the Tiger defences, and Sinhalese soldiers attacked the civilians with cluster bombs and other shells. The days of the Tamil Tiger state were gone. My cousins, my mother's brother and sister, and their families were outside Jaffna. These were scary times.

"What are you going to do?" he asked finally. "About the baby, I mean."

"Seems like a fucked up time to bring a child into the world, doesn't it?"

"Yes sir. Anytime is, I suppose. And yet all the ancients tell us one thing: life – it's the greatest gift anyone can have."

NIRANJAN

For days I am frightened there's going to be a knock on the door. Some policeman is going to arrest me for throwing the bottle through Mr Raptis's window. I dream about it. In one of my dreams, Rageev tracks me down to kill me before they can put me on trial. The last thing I see is his patchwork face coming down to meet mine. It's not that different from being back home. There, your nightmares are about Sri Lankan Army soldiers knocking on the door. Knowing that my brother is a fighte . Here, at least I know they won't beat and torture me. I think they won't. Perhaps I say something in my sleep. Soothy never mentions it if I do.

We hardly hear from Rageev during the holidays. Collections are made according to the schedule; he stops by to pick up the money. Rageev and Yalini akka make a point of coming round on Christmas day to have a meal. There are no gifts, but it's nice, a bit of a surprise, a good gesture. We didn't know they were coming. If I'd known, I would have bought a present for the baby. But they don't bring Geetha with them anyway. Who's looking after her, I have no idea. I don't dare to ask.

The holiday is over. Our money runs low. We have to be careful what we eat.

Still nothing from the police. I go back to classes, but hear nothing about Mr Raptis at school. I start to relax a little, feel almost normal, throw myself into studying for final exams. I'm going to fail all my courses – I know that. But I've been here before. I go through the motions of at least pretending to care.

I see Janelle and her friends beside her locker but don't speak to them. I don't sit next to her in class. Avoid her locker, but it's near our science lab. When she sees me, she smiles that dimply smile. Eyes dance wickedly. She only smiles, doesn't say anything. Her friends know – they're laughing at me. What did I see in her? Why did I think we were friends? Better to stick with your own people after all, as Soothy tells me. I blush with shame when we cross paths. Still, hard to believe she enjoyed setting me up more than wanting to throw a firebomb through Raptis's window herself.

After school, I hang by myself. It's lonely.

One Friday, I'm at Scarborough Town Centre, just walking around because I can't afford to buy nothing. I spot Soothy coming out of Sears. He's got his hands around the shoulders of a girl. I'm pretty sure that's a girl. They're wearing winter jackets so it's hard to see their faces, but I would recognize Soothy's red jacket and ponytail and Nike Jordan high tops a mile away. She's got a light blue puffy coat, long black hair, and a backpack. I follow them but hang back. They don't see me.

They stop at a display selling jewellery. He picks up a long gold earring like a chain and holds it to the girl's ear. Now that I can see her face, she's familiar. Where have I seen that sharp nose and thin face before? At LCC – my school – but where? Soothy puts the earring back down. Can't afford it. They laugh. When the guy running the stand comes up to them and begins talking, they shake their heads and move away.

At the food court, I walk up. Confront them directly.

Soothy sees me, immediately becomes uncomfortable, sits right up. His ponytail swishes back and forth. Nervous I guess. I've caught him in something. Usually, he's all condescending with me, but now he's nervous and shy.

"Soothy, how's it going?"

He looks all around, like he's expecting other people we know. "What you doing here?" he asks. Fear in his voice.

"I'm just walking around. Who's this?"

The girl looks surprised. Wearing a dress that's brown with stitching on it that's kind of old fashioned. "You're Niranjan, right? He hasn't told you about me?" I wait for her to continue. "Well, it's a bit of a secret. He's told me a lot about you!" I can tell she's nice, not like Janelle. "You had some trouble with your aunt, right? Now, you're living with him? We've met before. You were at Albion Hills – the camping trip? Two years ago?"

Her sentences spoken like questions. Hits me where I know her from! She's on the Tamil Students Association, Prefects too, I think. At school. I saw her read during the Remembrance Day assembly. I never really talked to her on that camping trip, but she was there. I nod my head and shake her hand. Her name's Abirami, goes by Abi for short.

"What are you two doing here?" I ask. "Are you Soothy's girlfriend?"

They get embarrassed, look away. Then Abi does something daring – she takes Soothy's hand. Big tough guy that he is, this embarrasses him even more. He's a totally different guy around her. Sensitive, vulnerable. "It's amazing," I tell them, "the secrets this guy can keep. He's never said anything about you. I thought all he did every day was play video games and smoke weed."

She frowns and pulls away. "Are you still doing that? You told me you'd stopped."

Soothy gives me a look – I've ratted him out – not that I knew. Now that I look at Abi, the picture fills in. She's with the nerds at school. Heavy backpack full of books at her feet. What's she doing with Soothy?

"How did you two meet?"

Soothy's reluctant to talk, so Abi says, "Come on, sit up. You're being rude. Tell him how we met."

Soothy quietly tells me, "One of those meetings in St James Town. Downtown. She came with her dad. I was there with Rageev. Before you came along with us."

She takes his hand again, rubs his fingers. "We started chatting on Facebook, and then he told me how he felt. He's very sweet."

Very sweet? I don't know. But it's nice he has somebody. Wish I had somebody. Makes me feel even lonelier than before.

"You can't say anything about this to Rageev!" Soothy grabs my arms. "I mean it!"

Abi nods her head. "He's right. If my father finds out…" A flash of fear jumps across her face. "Anyway, my appa and amma will be home soon – I should get home. It was nice meeting you."

"Oh, come on, can't you stay a while?" whines Soothy. I've never seen him like this.

"Come to the meeting on Monday" is her reply. Awkwardly, they hug. "It's important." He shrugs a little, stiffl . Agrees, although he'd rather hang with her outside of meetings, I suppose. She turns to me, "You should come to the meeting too. It's important. You do know what's happening in our country, right? This is serious? Worse than it's ever been."

"No, it's always been like this," I tell her. "War is all we've ever known."

"No. It's really bad now. An emergency. Everybody knows it."

"Nice!" says Soothy after she leaves. "You scared her away, you fucking idiot!"

* * *

The smell of soap from the washers in the laundry room hits me full force as I enter the basement of the Winnipeg Tower in St James Town on Monday. A very different scene from the last time I was here. The room is packed wall to wall with people. All ages. Women as well as men, but still more men. At first, I look around for Rageev, thinking he might be here. He is not. I do see Muruges uncle up at the front. The only seats in the room are behind the long table. Everybody else is standing. No room for extra chairs. The man called Muthu, bald, who was speaking the last time I was here, is beside Muruges. Old Guy, white hair and small trousers hiked up way above his waist, is there as well. I finally spot Soothy and Abi, but they're on the other side of the room. No way I'm gonna get over to them through all these bodies. Near them, I see another familiar face: the man Soothy and I call Dark Moustache. Still wearing sunglasses indoors. Skinny and silent and mean as fuck. Arms folded, he stands apart from everyone else, even in a crowded room. A room like this.

Lots of talking, lots of shouting. Things are noisy. People talk over each other. Old Guy tries to keep people from shouting. "What's going on?" I ask the guy standing beside me. Dressed in blue check shirt and black pants – don't think I've seen him before.

He looks me up and down, takes his time replying. "They're trying to decide on a strategy to do a peaceful protest."

"Peaceful?"

"Yes, nonviolent but dramatic, striking hearts of Canadians everywhere."

"You can't all talk at once!" roars Old Guy. People gradually quieten. It happens in waves and murmurs, like people talking softer and softer, not really wanting to but forced to do it. After waiting forever for people to reluctantly stop shouting, Old Guy asks them, "What do you want to do? We have to make a decision."

First, there's only more murmurs. Then someone says, "Human chain." Somebody else echoes him. Another person says, "Human chain." It builds into a chant: "Human chain, human chain!" A guy near the front steps forward, speaks boldly in an accent that's Tamil, but not the Tamil I know. More like Indian Tamil. "We want to do a human chain tomorrow."

People nod. Murmurs turn into agreements. They take it up and chant. They want to do it tomorrow. It's kind of a small room. Might explode from the energy. Soothy and Abi are into it too, rocking back and forth, almost jumping. Fists in the air and chanting.

Muthu gets up to talk in his reasonable, amused voice. "Tomorrow? Better we do it on Friday, people. Give us time to prepare."

You can feel the anger and resistance to his words. "No – we want it tomorrow!" the guy from India shouts. There's shouting again, people backing him up. Fists in the air. Rage hovering above their heads. "No! No! No!"

"What do you mean no, no, no?"

Old Guy is about to try to quiet them down, but Muthu puts a hand on his shoulder, gently pushes him back. Muruges never says anything, but he's spotted me. He makes eye contact. Hard to tell whether the feeling is friendly or not. His mouth is a tight slit. Then his attention goes back to Muthu who puts his fists on the table, leans forward, almost chuckles as he speaks. "This is Monday night, and you want it Tuesday morning? How many thousands of people do you want to come?"

Somebody yells back, "Fifty thousand!"

"Okay," says Muthu. "Fifty thousand. Then you all need to go to everybody's home, knock on their doors, and let those people know that they are going to come to the streets tomorrow instead of going to work. You said fifty thousand people, right? At least one out of five of them's got to carry a placard. That means ten thousand placards. Right? So a group of people need to take responsibility for writing the slogans on ten thousand placards. Another bunch of you have to go to the printers' houses, get them, and bring them in to start printing flyers. We've got to have something to give to the Canadians passing by so they know why we're doing it, right? How many millions of people are going to be moving through the downtown area? More than a million? Then we need at least a hundred thousand flyers. Before we print the flyers, somebody needs to write the material that goes on the flye . Get what I'm saying? Who's going to do that?"

The crowd quiets down.

Muthu continues, "So who's going to take responsibility for all these things? You want the protest tomorrow, right?"

Dead silence.

"Okay," says Muthu, "we'd better plan for Friday then."

There are murmurs and nods.

Later, Muruges finds me. "Hello Muruges uncle," I say respectfully.

He's different with me, kinda cagey. "Where's Rageev?" he asks, very quiet but shaking just a little, his right leg wobbling. Dark Moustache, as usual, stands behind him, arms folded. Might as well be a ghost. A very dark ghost.

I shake my head, look down at the floo .

"Didn't you come with him?" asks Muruges.

"I don't know where he is," I shrug. "We hardly see him at the apartment. He just comes by to pick up the money Soothy and I collect. That's it."

Muruges grabs me by the shoulder, stares at me. Searches out my face. I can feel the shake from his leg, all the way through his arm, down my left shoulder. "That's good," he says finall , "at least he's doing that. Tell him… tell him this is his last chance to get our money back. He's been hiding. From us! Can you believe it? Very, very disappointing. Very insulting. We can find him anytime we want to. After this, our friendship will be broken. Seriously. Tell him this is a final warning."

I say nothing.

Muruges softens. "Anyway, good to see you here, thambi. You going to go knock on doors and get people to come out for us?" I nod my head. Dark Moustache follows us both, never unfolding his arms. "There's one place in particular I want you to go," continues Muruges smiling, "a family that I'm told you know. We've found it very hard to talk to them in the past. Anyway, you do this for us, and I'll put you in touch with your brother like I promised. Okay. Chariyo?"

I look for Soothy. He's nowhere to be found.

I nod again, and a smile trembles on my lips.

DANIEL

The snow continued to fall during the exam period. It covered cars and heaped itself onto SUV's as I rolled into Scarborough on the subway. The RT train ran by the petrochemical sheds, the rusty railway tanks that always reminded me of my father. Long defunct carriages stood beside factories with white snow graffitied against their walls. Exhaust from chimney stacks hung like frozen clouds, the smoke brittle and solid, stark against blue sky.

Petrochemical pollution clearly visible in the dark underbellies of their clouds.

Lynn was working from home, and there would be few teachers in school that day. The end of semester emptiness.

An early morning glow lit the twisted spikes of a chain-link fence as they poked their sharp ends through the settling snow. A plastic bag whipped in the wind, caught in a tree, gathering snowflakes as my RT train rushed by, metal wheels spinning, kicking up powdery chuffs of snow.

It was an unusual day. Though it was no Sunday, I had been summoned to my parents' house. My father had told me on the phone the night before that Niranjan had reached out to him. It was a great surprise. Niranjan wished to come by to talk to us, and only us. The express wish was that his aunt should not be present. That part was not so surprising.

Niranjan came alone. He was already sitting with my father on the plastic sheeted couch. The boy had yet to remove his coat and leaned forward worriedly while my father sipped his tea. My father seemed comfortable and quiet. Niranjan's beard had grown in, and I doubt he was much taller, only that he seemed so as he perched there in his winter jacket, long legs sticking out, seriousness clouding his brow. Was this the boy whom I had talked to only recently? The one who had told me to go screw myself outside of Raptis's classroom that day, the one whom I had pushed on the swings with Thambi? He had grown in just a few months, seemed that much older. A wolfish adulthood hung over him. I felt as if I were talking to some older brother he had.

"Wannakum," said my father, "sit down. Do you want tea?"

I shook my head no from the entrance. I took off my coat, and as I hung it up I noticed Niranjan's shoes sitting on the mat by the door. The treads were turned up and they were Nikes. Still, a lot of kids wore Nikes, didn't they?

"We were talking about you. I was asking Niranjan how he's doing in school," said my father.

"I'm not teaching him this semester," I replied, removing my coat and gloves, then stamping my boots and removing them also.

"I'm going to fail all my classes. Yet again." Niranjan spoke solemnly. "I don't know what to say. I have no excuse."

"We must get you a tutor," my father sighed in a tired and unhurried manner. He had just finished work himself. I waited for the other shoe to drop, but nobody said anything. Where was the yelling, the violent recrimination? With me, he had been so stern and demanding, but with others something resembling softness sometimes poked its way out.

"I'm sorry to hear that," I said. "What are you going to do?"

Niranjan shook his head and brought his hand up to his face. His nails were ragged. "Ms Varley says they're going to have to send me to another school. A Section 23, something like that. I'm not sure."

"What's that?" my father enquired.

"The sad answer is that it's a last chance kind of school. Not a regular school. They're very strict," I replied.

"Maybe that's what he needs?"

"It's not the kind of school that breeds successful people. It's like a gulag. They just want him out of sight. If he can't manage our school, he'll die in there. There are some real hard cases."

My father put his tea down and sat straight up. "Can you do something? Niranjan's almost family, no? The boy's reaching out. They were our neighbours for many years – we helped bring him over. We must do something."

194

"It's not really my department," I said, a tone of defeat entering my voice. "Where's Amma?"

"Your mother went to pick up some DVDs at the Tamil store."

We sat like that, each contemplating Niranjan's future. The young man in question rubbed his hands. "Actually, that's just the side news," he said. "I came to talk to you about something else. It's important."

My father motioned for him to continue.

"I've fallen in with some people. Mr N, I told you about them before. They're organizing some protests about... you know, what's happening back home." He jerked his head involuntarily towards the window.

"Have you called your parents?" my father asked. "They're worried about you. You must consider moving back to your aunt's. Just for their sake, allow them to stop worrying."

"It's hard to get hold of my parents with everything that's happening," said Niranjan. "They don't have their own phone. Anyway, these people... they know your house. They've tried to make collections here."

My father immediately became rigid. The white hair stood in wisps off his dome. "Oh, I know those useless people. You're in with them? Be careful. One drop of ink poisons all the milk, you know. That guy with the sunglasses. Mr Movie Star? He's been coming here since we bought the house!"

Niranjan nodded. "Anyway, the money's one thing. They really need help now. Anything you can do? They're organizing a mass protest – downtown – this Friday. They're linking hands. You know – like a human chain. They want as many people out there as possible. What about you?"

"My father can't go," I said, immediately becoming defensive. "Look at his age. How can he stand outside in the cold all day? Absolutely not!"

"Well, I thought you would say that. Anyway, just think about it," said Niranjan. "They wanted me to spread the word. You could go too, Mr N. I'll be there."

"You should be spending your time on your studies, not this rubbish!" exclaimed my father with a disgusted air.

I didn't go. I had no idea what to think of the protest. Neither did my father – he had to work.

At the end of the week, I looked up from my computer at the school. The exams were over, and it was only left for me to assign my students their marks and enter their report card comments. It was a shame about Niranjan. His own fault – he had stopped trying a long time ago. After our last conversation, he had seemed so riled and agitated about the Section 23 school that I felt badly for him, problems and all.

I remembered Seelan and how I had to check MarkBook after he'd died to see whether I'd failed him or not. I suppose I had failed him in more ways than one.

To distract myself, I checked the CBC website to see if the Tamil thing Niranjan spoke of had actually panned out. If anything, it would be a blip on their news feed, nothing more.

The computers were slow, and while the page loaded I looked out the window and saw the snow-covered fields and parking lot. The slush was streaked with brown slime where cars had left, the other teachers having finished their report cards hours ago. The small hill upon which I had stood to watch Niranjan walk home that day, the hill between the playground and the Tuxedo Court, was covered, as white as a blank sheet of paper.

Finally, the CBC news page finished loading, and I was shocked at what I saw.

Not a local blip in relation to the war back home, but a line of agitated Tamils right here. In Toronto. A veritable army of protesters.

Photos of the slush and snow blanketing the streets of downtown Toronto where across Front Street and up University tens of thousands of local Tamil protesters formed a human chain to draw attention to the Sri Lankan Army's taking of Elephant Pass and push into Jaffna.

Thousands and thousands of Tamils in cold downtown Toronto, tramping back and forth repeating the words 'We Want Justice', beating on toy drums and holding placards. A mother gasped in one video clip, holding up a photo of her child, maimed and bleeding, spreadeagled on a dirt floor. She was wailing. Could that really be her child?

I saw the word 'genocide'. It was there in bright red letters on hundreds upon hundreds of placards. 'Stop the Genocide in Sri Lanka'. I'd never heard the word in association with Sri Lanka before. I was stunned.

Thousands and thousands of Tamils linked to stop traffic and passersby, stretching across one major thoroughfare and up another.

How did this happen? I thought it would be something small. A group of demonstrators walking in a circle, perhaps.

Would Lynn have gotten through the cordon safe when she drove home from yoga? She had left hours ago.

The horrific pictures on the placards

For once, I was grateful my father had gotten us out of the country and settled us here, in Canada. I thought all these things while I sat in front of the school computer, waiting for my inconsequential grades to load. I massaged the glut in the middle towards their technical fifties while bodies upon bodies dropped from shrapnel and white phosphorous in and around the Tamil areas of Sri Lanka.

SEMESTER TWO

DANIEL

I fed Chuck while Lynn brewed coffee. The Weimaraner pup, all gangly limbs and chocolate suede coat, was too much for Lynn sometimes, too much for our condo. If you don't know what a Weimaraner's like, you're lucky. He slobbered and ran circles around Lynn, turning around to let his haunches be patted for a millisecond before buzzing off again. A demanding dog – he had to be exercised regularly or he barked and became insane. It was a good thing he was so high energy. He distracted us from some of the other things that were especially difficult in those days.

Like Niranjan.

I cornered Lynn about him while she and Joyce sifted through the failure reports during the last days of semester one. Seeing the photos of Tamils blockading Front Street and University Avenue had really put the hook in me. Once I saw them chanting, holding their placards in the ice and snow, I couldn't un-see them. Niranjan was in that crowd somewhere, worried about his family back home.

Lynn and Joyce were running the last batch of alpha timetables for semester two. The students would come in the next day to pick them up and find out their final marks from semester one. Oh, to be so young and free again! I pulled Lynn aside, away from Joyce.

"It's going to take me a while to finish up here," she said. "Do you want a ride home? Joyce and I still have to get through this bunch of reports, Dan. Badlamenti's waiting for them."

"It's not about the ride," I replied. "Excuse us, Joyce. Please?"

Joyce didn't have much choice. She was visibly annoyed at being interrupted. She cursed under her breath as she and Lynn were forced to stop halfway. What must Joyce think of me, Lynn's choice for a partner? Shirt untucked, I was almost sweaty, agitated – I'd been going round and round in my classroom thinking about this.

"What's this about, Dan? What couldn't wait?" We stood in her office; the door was locked

"I've got to talk to you about Niranjan. I want you to give him another chance."

"Oh, no. Why?"

"He knows he's being expelled. Look, I know how difficult he's been and believe me, if it were anybody else, I'd say you were in the right – I'd tell you to go ahead – but he's different." I didn't let go of her arm. "You've got to give him another chance. For me."

"You can't do this," she replied, shrugging. "You can't let your family push you around. There's no good reason to keep him here. He's flunked more than ten credits in two years. The ones that he's passed are technical fifties. I think the teachers gave him a fifty to get him out of their rooms. I'm all for generousity when it comes to grades, you know that, but this is an open and shut case. He's only going to damage the school's standing."

I pushed her away more roughly than I'd planned. The hair on my arms stood up with frustration. "People make those decisions" – I could feel my eyes glaring at her as I spoke – "people make the decision to expel him, and they can make the decision to pull him back."

"Yes, but only with good reason. Paperwork has to be done. When there's a chance to turn the kid's future around, we do what we can. Niranjan's shown no potential at this point. Frankly, I'm sick of him. I'm sick of all the time and aggravation he's cost me."

"Well, I don't see it that way. What are schools for if we can't be there for everybody?" My voice rose to a naive flourish. "Especially for the kids who need it the most? Normally, I'd agree with you, you know that, but he does need our guidance and help."

I could see tiredness and impatience in her face. "Dan, put your energy into the kids who give back. Those who actually do something for the school and its reputation. Or – and you're going to hate my saying this – let's have a kid of our own. Pour your energy into being a new dad. That's where it needs to go. That's what this is really about."

Her condescension! I could feel my jaws grind. As if my lips couldn't decide which way to go. "Look," I stated, firmly as I could, "we start classes in two days. We're halfway through the year. It's possible, it's more than possible, for you to put him in a timetable for the rest of the school year. Put him in my Media 11 class. Yes, I know he's failed it before! He fucks up, and it's on me. You can tell me 'I told you so' and send him wherever you want. Anywhere. But just once… do it for me."

"Lower your voice, Dan. Why him?"

"I don't know why him." The anger left me. "Hard to explain. It's not just what my family wants. Well, I admit it's what my father wants. He did help Niranjan's aunt to do the paperwork and bring him over here, but this time I feel something. He's not all bad. Look at what happened with Seelan. It was my fault that I didn't do anything. My sister too – I told you about us as kids – I couldn't help her. Whenever I turn on the news or see all the homeless people downtown freezing to death… it gets to me."

"I didn't know you felt so strongly, Dan. It's okay, I understand." She reassuringly took my shoulder. "But you need to pour your passion into someone new. You're going to have ninety new kids looking up to you in a couple of days, and they're going to need every ounce of your attention. Let Niranjan go. We can't help him, and he can't help us. It's up to Niranjan to help himself."

They were the wrong words. My anger, like thunder, flared right up again. That horrible chasm fell between us, a feeling I hated. How different we truly were.

"Look, Lynn – you owe me."

"For what?"

"For all the things I do. Putting up with your parents' ridicule of me, for one example. The fact you won't appease my parents just once. The fact that I walk on eggshells, bending my life around you. Maybe I'd like to have a say one time. I want you to go into Joyce's office and convince her that Niranjan stays one more semester. Or… we're through. There might as well be no point in talking about anything. After this."

She stared at me, startled. I had to explain myself.

"Oh, we could get married. And in time, maybe even have kids. But beneath that, beneath everything we do together will be the memory of this day. When you wouldn't budge and help me just this once. I'll remember it, and even if, in time, I push it down, very far down, try to forget, I'll resent you, and there's nothing we'll be able to do to change that."

She regarded me coldly. I could hear the emotional calculations clicking inside her head. "It's not like you to take a stand, Dan," she stated. "I do do things for you. But this isn't for you, is it? It's a gust of pushiness from your parents – not easy. The apple doesn't fall far from the tree. The famous Tamil pushiness you go on about – are you at least going to give me twenty-four hours to think it over?"

"If I wait, Niranjan goes. I think we both know that. And don't talk about my family when you know nothing about them. Don't throw my identity in my face. How could I expect you to understand? You're black."

"I'm Canadian," she hissed between clenched teeth. I'm sure Joyce heard some of our words. What must she have thought was going on? Not just the garden variety frustration we usually threw at each other, but real palpable fury. It made me tired just to stand here. "Okay, I'll do what you want," she said. "But remember, you owe me now. You hear? Big time. You hear me, motherfucker? I'm doing this for you, and I'm never going to forgive the way you made me do it."

"Oh, so now you can do it?"

We had spats all the time. Just like anyone else. And this was one of those times, right? We'd bounce back. Life would go on.

NIRANJAN

Dark Moustache and Muruges sit in the front of a grey sedan. I'm in the back with construction supplies. Power drills, paint trays, rollers, hammers, tools, that kind of stuff. Whenever Dark Moustache makes a turn, this tied-up wood rattles, pushes against me. It sends up a sawdusty smell. My inhaler is within reach.

Today is the day I get to speak to my brother. Finally. At last.

I have no idea where they're driving. We're in Scarborough somewhere. It can't be St James Town, or anywhere else downtown.

"Turn here," says Muruges. I can feel his right leg shaking against the passenger door.

We're on a residential street, a bit like Mr. Raptis's. But not his, thank God.

They park the sedan and tell me to get out. Muruges checks his clipboard one more time, then throws it back in through the car's window. I wait by the sedan and trace its rust pattern with the tip of my finger as Muruges limps up the driveway. Dark Moustache follows him. It's a small house, a little bigger than the one owned by Mr N's parents. The lights are on. Muruges knocks on the door a couple of times, then Dark Moustache bangs on the window. Finally, they open up. A surprised guy stands inside the door. Obviously, we weren't expected. I wonder if the guy's a dad.

Muruges and Dark Moustache talk to the guy. He argues back. I don't hear what they say. Finally, the guy hangs his head, goes back inside. Soon, the whole family's putting on their coats and coming out. There's the man, his wife, their two kids – a boy and a girl. Both the kids are young. They make me think of the couple from the Tamil shop, in a few years time. The kids look down; they don't make eye contact, but the mom glares at me.

"What's going on?" I ask, once we're inside.

Muruges and Dark Moustache check the house thoroughly, make sure no one's hidden, lurking behind. "If we need to have a meeting," Muruges tells me, "sometimes we pick a house at random where Tamil people live. We ask them to leave the house for a couple of hours. This way, we know the phones aren't bugged."

"You think your lines are bugged?" I wonder.

The other two laugh at my innocence. Dark Moustache comes over to me. He presses on my shoulders, forces me to sit down. "There's a lot you don't know. Yes, these

RCMP jokers – even in a country like Canada, it's no paradise."

It feels strange to be in somebody else's house. Like I said, I don't know what neighbourhood we're in. I look at the photos of the kids in the display case. Other photos of their relatives back home. A newspaper lies messed up on the table. The mother was cooking dinner. The food, half cooked, just idles on the burner. Curry stains all over the stove. Probably, the food'll go bad. And of course, the kids' homework is all opened and laid out in the living room. My family back home in Sri Lanka: does their house look like this when the shells fall and they have to run?

"Don't they mind? These people?" I ask.

"It's not up to them to mind or not mind," states Muruges. "There are some things that must be done. You want to talk to your brother, don't you?"

I nod.

"Then what do you care what they think?"

Dark Moustache sits beside me. He watches my face as Muruges fishes out his glasses and a piece of paper. Muruges pulls a chair up to the kitchen phone. Once he's finally rested, his leg stops shaking. He peers over his glasses at the paper, then slowly dials a number.

Can't believe my brother is going to be on the other end!

Muruges waits a long time. Finally, someone answers. Muruges barks in Tamil down the line. He seems like someone else for a second; he's never raised his voice above a quiet, friendly tone before. He has to repeat himself often, asks for my brother by his fighter's name: Prabhu. Just hearing those syllables, the 'pra' and the 'bhu', makes me want to cry. Gotta pull myself together. Just when I think Muruges will give me the phone, he hangs up.

"Sorry, thambi," he tells me, "they're sleeping. Hard to find people now. The boy's going to try and get him though. Don't worry. Going to be another hour, I'd say."

Air whooshes out my lungs. What disappointment! I know it's nine and a half hours later there. Still, I thought this was going to be it. Karuna, my elder brother, my anna!

We sit around the kitchen table and wait.

Muruges asks me, "Thambi, what is it you want at the end of all this?"

"What do you mean?" I ask.

"The question is simple. I've known you for a few months. I asked you before. You seem like a good boy: honest, loyal, people seem to like you. I know your brother, so I know that you're also smart. The village your parents come from – they raised you well. But what are you hoping to get from Rageev? What do you hope to find, living there?"

I have to think a while. I'm so used to people questioning me about my decision, and me in one way or another telling them to mind their business. But that won't do for Muruges. I come up with something: "I want the same thing that you want. Freedom. The same thing you fight for is also what I wish in my own life, my own small life. To be my own person. Aren't we fighting for the same thing?"

He sighs and leans back to straighten out his poor leg. "Yes, but I'm prepared to kill for it. Can you say the same? I became used to this a long time ago. Your brother became used to it, but I don't think it's in you. You may find yourself in that situation, thambi, if you follow Rageev.

"Freedom's a slippery business. I've been fighting for our freedom in one way or another since the late seventies. That's thirty years. First we fought for rights, then we fought for land, now we fight for global perception. Life has moved me very far from the village in which I was born. You might not think it to look at me, but I've been all over the world: India, Palestine, Malaysia, Singapore, the Netherlands. You know, in all those years, war, talks, negotiations, more war, I've never had a family. Thalivar married, but I did not. I feel less free now than I did when I started. This country is not bad, better than some, but I'm too old to start again. You on the other hand, thambi, are a young man."

"Don't tell me you think I should become a doctor too." I cross my arms.

"Well, they say you used to be quite good in school when you were younger. But no, I wouldn't say doctor. A businessman maybe. A lawyer. Politician. Don't laugh! We need Tamils who can work their way into Canadian society and have influence. No good if everybody becomes doctors and computer engineers, no?"

"We need lawmakers, not doctors," laughs Dark Moustache.

I see. They believe their jobs as opinion shapers will never end. They're already planning for ten years down the road, fifteen: the next generation and the generation after that. The current tensions are only a hiccup to them. "I'm tied to Rageev and Soothy," I say. "They're my brothers now. I can't only think of myself."

"Don't be stupid!" Muruges slams his palm on the table and laughs, sending newspaper pages flying. He stops just as a twinge of pain shoots across his face. When he recovers, he asks Dark Moustache to make us some tea while we wait. "Check around and see what they have in the cupboards, Karthik. Maybe they'll have some of those lemon cream biscuits we like?" Dark Moustache rises and finds a saucepan to boil the water like an obedient cadet

"What were they cooking?" Muruges asks after a while.

Dark Moustache checks, lifts the lids on the pots already on the stove, sticks his nose down, takes a couple of sniffs. "Looks like chicken briyani and lamb curry. Special!"

"Oh, well." Muruges turns back to me and sighs. "Don't worry about Rageev. He's a muttal (fool). What did he tell you? That you're brothers until the end of time? It's just for show. You know that, right? Did he tell you about Seelan, the boy living there before you?"

Seelan, the same Seelan from school I'd heard about so often? The one who'd been shot? "He lived there?"

"Oh, yes. And you can be sure that Rageev performed the same ritual with him." I think of that day in the ravine, the piece of paper with the oath, cutting ourselves until the blood flowed together, burning until matter became energy, dust and smoke to be carried in the wind. "Has Rageev told you anything about his past?" continues Muruges. "He has his uses, but you mustn't believe everything he says. He's a drunk, good for nothing, just like the other boy living with him." This is Rageev and Soothy he's talking about! "Some people tell you stories. You have to be careful not to get wrapped up in them. If it weren't for Yalini, who worked very hard for me in Sri Lanka, poor girl, I wouldn't have given him a chance. But..." he sucks his lips regretfully for a moment, "she fell into a bad time and became involved with him. What can one do? Still, she's a good girl, and here we are. Did they ever tell you about his 'gang' that he was involved with?"

I shake my head. "Not really. He mentions Kannan sometimes."

"They used to hate the LTTE back then. Where are they now – vanished!" chuckles Dark Moustache. The saucepan holding the water, milk, and sugar with three tea bags swirling in it begins to boil on the stove.

"Don't make fun of him," chuckles Muruges, then he too begins laughing. "We can't help it. What a joke. They used to fight the VVT who we were close to. They were trashed by them. They brought in a few rifles and guns, got one of our guys to train them. Useless. They did some random robberies, got involved in drugs and liquor. Any surprise all of them are gone?"

"But Rageev's hard," I say disbelievingly. "Look at his face. What about that attack on the highway he fought his way out of?"

"He makes a big deal out of that," laughs Muruges. "It's just superficial wounds. Burns are easy to heal from. Those of us with guts got our wounds back home. Yalini has a wound, but she's never told you, has she? Of course not. She's like your brother. They're real soldiers. Karuna's your real brother, not Rageev. Rageev is only using you. Karthik, come show thambi your eye."

Dark Moustache takes a little time finding mugs and pouring the tea, more time than necessary. He dips the tea bags a few times, takes his time getting rid of them. Says nothing. He pours each tea and brings the mugs over to the table, places them on the newspaper. Wet rings form on the pages the guy was reading. Dark Moustache returns to the sink, places the foamy saucepan in the sink, runs cold water into it. And then, he looks through the cupboards.

Eventually, he comes over and sits down beside us, puts a packet of biscuits on the table. "They don't have lemon cream, only these pink wafers. Want one?" Muruges takes one and bites into it without excitement.

Dark Mustache swirls his tea with a wafer. Without saying anything, he removes his glasses, and I finally understand why he wears them all the time. The left eye is completely blown out. There's an eyeball in the socket, but the pupil has become completely misshapen, as if it had imploded. It's a funny wavy star-shaped thing, almost a black hole. The eyeball floats there in the eye, completely uncoordinated with what the rest of his face is doing. The right eye is normal, but the left is filled with burst vessels and rage, a bloody red.

Dark Moustache puts his glasses back on.

Nobody says anything for a while.

We just blow on our tea.

"You said his name's Karthik?" I ask, sipping my hot tea quietly.

"Karthik Sivananthan," says Muruges proudly, as if talking about a favourite son. Dark Moustache says nothing. "He's another one who fought with me. He has the fury of Shiva, it's in his name. That's why they sent him here. To help me."

"What do you mean, by Rageev using me?" I ask.

"You must have realized that they've deported or imprisoned everybody in his gang," says Muruges quietly. "Don't you wonder why he's still here? Can he have really been so fierce if they've left him on the street? He has a weakness for the drugs. He and his buddies thought they could be like the blacks, but they don't know what they're doing. He uses kids because when the police crack down, he can insulate himself through you guys. Your punishments will not be so severe. He's a coward. He gets you and Soothy to do all the collections for him now, doesn't he? See, that's right. He'll say it's because Yalini is worried about him, but don't trust anything he says. He's crafty. Did you enjoy being used to get his baby back?"

I shake my head. "But you were there, you let him do that," I point out.

"You belonged to him," says Muruges. "Not my place to interfere. I was only there to help with the money. But now we know each other a little better."

"You can see what a fuck up he is even with the drug business," says Karthik. "He ended up owing money, and now he's in trouble with us. Whatever use he once had is quickly running out."

Muruges shakes his head and drinks his tea. "You can't say you weren't warned."

We drink in silence after that.

They finish their mugs long before me. When I'm done, Muruges takes out his piece of paper and dials.

This time, they get hold of him. Muruges passes the phone over. I can't believe Karuna's on the other end. I have to sit here between Muruges and Karthik and have the conversation with them there. No such thing as privacy.

"Anna, is that you?"

His voice comes back with a delay. It's hard to hear him because the connection's weak. He sounds very far away. "Niranjan? Am I talking to Niranjan?"

"Yes, Anna, it's me! I can't believe it. How are you? How many years has it been?"

"How do you know Muruges uncle?" he asks. I knew he was going to ask me this, and yet I haven't prepared a good answer. "He knows somebody that I know here," I say cautiously. "He's very important."

"I know he's very important." Karuna is a bit short with me. I'm surprised he's not as excited as I am. "I've known him here. Since his injury, they've sent him to your country. Don't think he's harmless. Be very careful around him and do as he says."

My country? "Have you heard from Amma and Appa," I ask. "How's our sister?"

"Don't you know? You should tell me. I haven't seen them in more than three months."

"Well, I was wondering if you'd known... I moved out from Aunty's apartment. It was impossible to live with her. Listen, you're not listening to me. Let me talk..." He's cursing me, calling me an idiot, a good-for-nothing.

A supreme fuck up, that's what I am, according to him. I thought it'd be nice talking to him. He's become a lot meaner than I remember.

"Listen, idiot," he says, "don't make my blood boil." He sounds exactly like our father. "I left university and went to fight so you wouldn't have to. The whole reason we got you over there was so you could do well and bring Appa and Amma over. Now you've gone and thrown that away!" I've started to hyperventilate. I need my inhaler. While I fumble with the orange inhaler, he continues to yell at me. "You have no idea how much this kills me! Our family had to move three times in the last two months, I've heard. It's not easy to find good information on them. And now you go missing! You're playing the fool! Do you know how bad the barrages are over here? What kind of life people are living? And you're over there – playing the fool?"

I finally manage to take two puffs on the inhaler. It does nothing. My throat feels like a twisted sock. Muruges and Karthik watch me curiously. "I'm still in school," I finally gasp. "I'm still in school."

Karuna stops for a while on the other side, and there's just silence. I think I can hear the crickets in Sri Lanka. He comes back and asks, "What marks did you get on your last report?"

I have to tell him the truth. "I failed all my courses."

"Motherfucker!" I hear him cursing and banging the phone against his head. "Aiyo!!! What have I done to deserve such an idiot brother?"

"I'll try harder, I promise," I plead. "It's difficult, but I'll try harder. Please don't be angry at me!"

"If you don't start changing your habits right now, I promise you I'll find some way to come over there myself and beat the hide off you. I will make you bleed! You understand?"

I am terrified. I say nothing. "Do you understand?" he screams at me.

"Yes, anna," I say. "I will do anything you say. Please don't worry. Just look after yourself and our family. Please don't worry about me."

"What are you going to do?" he asks.

"Turn my life around," I reply.

Silence. "Succeed in school."

He makes me give him the contact information on the new iPhone I've got. It is one of the things we took from the Tamil electronics store on Kennedy Road, where we got my laptop.

Karuna hangs up without even saying goodbye.

"I was telling you. You've got to figure out what you want. Sometimes it's better we don't get what we long for," says Muruges quietly.

Dark Moustache puts our cups in the sink without washing them, leaves the pink wafers on the table. He shuts off the lights, and then they drive me back to Rageev's apartment.

DANIEL

The library at school had papier mâché planets and styrofoam models of molecules swinging from the ceiling. Yet another reminder of Raptis's involvement at the school. He had worked on this as a cross-curricular assignment between the science and art departments before I'd gotten here. It made the library an inviting place. Many students came and went, were on computers or hung out in groups, smuggled in food, stuck gum under the tables, and tore attractive ads out of magazines. That we even still had magazines was due to John Raptis's fights with Badlamenti. If Badlamenti had had his way, most of the books would have been replaced by computers and databases.

It takes a different type of mind, a keener investment, to look things up in books, cross reference and read, instead of simply Googling and copying information. Issues of Scientific American and National Geographic and Time stood their place beside GQ and Esquire and Cosmopolitan. Principal Badlamenti's strategy was to technologize all aspects of teaching – 'the connected teacher' being his catchphrase – and I was guilty of sometimes thriving off his agenda.

I had my Grade 11 Media students in the library to work on an assignment where they had to research famous films. I had gotten through the advertising and music video assignments as quickly as possible. For me, film was where it was at. I structured my course through sustained study of rich and relevant films. My brain was made of celluloid, and silver nitrate bubbled in my blood.

Niranjan had been placed in this class by Lynn, at my request. I could see why she'd been reluctant about retaining Niranjan in general, and making him retake this course specificall . He had already failed it once, but I wanted him close to keep an eye on him.

I had put him in a group with three other Tamil guys: Raj, Kumar, and Nadesan. Niranjan was definitely the odd one out as the other three knew each other. It was only through my pushing them that they accepted him. Niranjan was aware that he was unwanted. He was more than a year older than the others. Just like camp all over again. They were supposed to research films by Martin Scorsese, but all they did was goof off, huddled around a computer watching clips on YouTube.

"What are you doing?" I asked, coming up behind them.

They tried to minimize the screen, but it was obvious what was happening. They were looking at Batman clips. The Dark Knight movie, along with Iron Man, had been big blockbusters the previous summer. "What is it with kids and comic book movies these days?" I asked. "They used to have real movies when I was young."

"They don't have any books on the director you asked us to look up," said Nadesan. He was obviously the leader of the group.

"Did you look in the encyclopedias? Did you look in the indexes at the backs of the books they do have on film?" I replied. "He was a prominent filmmaker in the seventies, one of the American 'brats'. There are other things you can do, you know."

"If you let us use the computer," shrugged Kumar, "we could find a whole lot."

"Why do we have to do the older films?" asked Raj. "Why can't we watch a superhero movie? That's media, right?"

Niranjan didn't say anything.

"Well, it depends on how you analyze them, I suppose," I conceded. "If we just watch them to be entertained and do no work, we're not really doing media studies, are we?

"Look, I grew up with superheroes too, but they're only recycling stuff for the movies. It doesn't tell you anything about real life, about what it means to be human. Superheroes are great, but they work better as comics, not film. If Hollywood wanted to do something original, they could actually look into why people like the superhero myths. Take Superman for example. He's basically an immigrant," I continued. "He's assimilated, but an immigrant nonetheless. He's a living God who's emigrated from another world, who could shape or affect our world in any way he wants. Instead, he chooses to serve, why? Why does he choose to please the authorities and uphold the rule of law? Because he's an immigrant – that's why. That's the classic immigrant mentality. And that's why the last Superman movie failed – they haven't made any more. Batman and Iron Man are renegades: independent, childish, get whatever they want – that's why they're popular with all you kids."

"Maybe." Kumar leaned back just enough to make the back of his plastic chair stretch and squeak.

"Think about it," I pressed. "Spiderman too. Those movies are old hat – why? Because Spiderman's a nerd who's poor. He tried to act for himself when he first got his powers and was immediately punished for it. His uncle was killed. He's wracked with guilt for the rest of his life. The emotional harness is on. He's beholden and smothered by his auntie, and he's a nerd who has no clue how to talk to girls. He's neurotic and an undergraduate in the sciences who is desperate for a scholarship to get him through school. He's practically Tamil. That's not what people want these days – a superhero who's practically Tamil."

"So what's Batman?" asked Nadesan, getting into it.

"Batman?" I floundered. "He s... Eurotrash!"

They laughed, even though they probably didn't get what I meant by Eurotrash.

It was one of those moments when I forgot what I should be saying as a teacher and tried to ride their laughter. I'm not proud, but I'm human. From time to time, I ride applause when it comes. "Batman's a jerk!" I whispered over the boys' heads. "He gets all the chicks, has all the cars. 'Oh my parents were killed and left me a billionaire' – poor baby! Our entire culture's been killed and raped and enslaved in Sri Lanka. Whole Tamil families are killed or forced into camps – try that on for size, Batman, you self-involved jerk. Instead of brooding and running around in Gothic costume, try working for a living. It might do you some good."

I had gone over the edge, stepped too far. The humour had backfired. The boys became rigid and quiet. It was not right to make fun of what happened in Sri Lanka, especially given recent events.

"Anyway," I said, straightening myself. "Research online if you have to, but make sure you check the reliability of your sources. You're presenting what you find, and I want an evaluation of the sources you use.

I walked away to go check on other groups and oversee how they were mismanaging their time. It wasn't the kids' faults, really. If adults couldn't keep away from their electronic distractions, how could we expect teenagers to focus? Badlamenti practically encouraged this direction with the new computer lab, and I would take advantage of it when I got my students to make their own digital films

I gazed at the styrofoam planets and molecules. "Fuck you and your superheroes!" Raptis would have laughed, as he once did. "You want superheroes, go back to classical Greece where everything started. The Gods and the Heroes: Achilles and Hector, those were our superheroes. We had Homer and Herodotus. Pythagoras and Plato. We invented civilization. The wops just stole everything," he would have exclaimed, making one final dig at Badlamenti.

Lunch hour was not the same without him. As you might imagine, Cram and I didn't make the effort to have lunch together anymore. Perhaps we worried that we would be targeted next. Raptis had been our charismatic glue. He used to sit there, picking at his lunch behind a lab bench, not caring one whit how tenuous his standing had been. Food slowly disintegrating and being decimated by his formidable colon and gastric acids, lab coat unbuttoned freely. He was Greek and came from a culture where the Gods had no shame. They expressed their violent darkness and passionate urges upon each other, on family, on animals, without shame. I come from a culture where our Gods are like Superman – they know their place in the order of things. They respect their familial obligations and duties. Like Shiva or the many incarnations of Vishnu.

Raptis was not the only one who fought Badlamenti. The parents' council wanted to use the school's meagre budget to fix up the building. The problem was that the contracts were often given to known associates, friends of friends of the Toronto Board of Education, who charged three times the going rate and took a long time getting things done. Last year, Badlamenti had wrangled things and gotten council's approval to abrogate a room that had been earmarked as a music rehearsal space, and turned it into the media computer lab. Yutani donated the computers and hardware, and Badlamenti was going to have a large mural featuring the Yutani logo – a crab grasping the world in its pincers – painted upon the walls. The teachers got very upset about the proposed commercialization of the walls, and Badlamenti and Yutani had to settle for simply painting the walls in company colours. But the media lab had gone ahead. Cram and I had been very glad about this development at the time, though Raptis detested it. Now that Raptis was no longer here, I wondered what had really been accomplished. Was the need to make student digital videos more necessary than a space to practice classical music? Which was more beneficial to the human soul, the development of a teenage child's mind?

What good were my courses? I was a teacher who coasted along, faking it just like my students were, sitting in front of those computers, watching YouTube clips on the sly, thinking of joe answers to weak, joe assignments.

NIRANJAN

Mr Narayan tries to get me out for some of the clubs as a way of socializing with the other students. Says it'll be good for post secondary. I can't see myself on the Debate Club. I don't really like to talk, anyway. I'm no good at sports. Could you see me in the Prefects? They'd never take me. He tries to steer me towards Math League and the Tamil Students Association. My group members from media class, Kumar, Nadesan, and Raj, belong to both. With everything going on at home, while trying to hold onto my courses this time, I can't do it. But Mr N sometimes coaches driver's ed. I like driving Rageev's Yutani, so I ask if he'll help me get my G2. This seems to make him happy.

During our first driving lesson, Mr N and I sit in one of the driver's ed Toyota Echoes they have on the lot behind LCC. It's nowhere near as nice as Rageev's Yutani Quantum, but it's okay. A nice little car. I'll definitel feel the wind resistance on it. Mr N's scarf is bundled around his neck. He warms his hands in it from time to time. I know I'm a nose hair from being expelled. I know that. If I don't pull my school grades out of the gutter, I'm gone. I'm supposed to check in with Ms Varley once in a while, even though we don't like each other.

    I've got my hands at ten and two on the steering wheel.

    Mr N gets me to start the Echo. I turn the ignition, put the car into reverse, edge out, circle around the lot. I pump the gas gently, only when necessary, emphasize all my motions.

    He gets me to do three point turns and parallel parks for a full hour. I move the car slowly in the slush. Just to show how careful I am. I line my mirror with the mirror of a car parked behind me, put the Echo in reverse, turn the wheel all the way to the left, turn back to the right, line up the car, and so on. Again and again. Can't wait till I get my licence. Then Rageev will let me take the black Quantum out onto the 401, racing. No stopping or parking then. Only speeding up and passing. That speeding air. That sense of freedom. Something to hold onto. Something really fine, really freeing about managing a ton and a half of steel and glass. So adult.

"Yes, that's it. Make it a smooth turn. You're coming along nicely." Mr N sniffles into his scarf, tugs his seat belt. I know it digs against his shoulder because some of my turns are sharp.

"When did you learn to drive, Mr N?"

"Well, let's see – not until university. My family didn't have a car, you see. You're very fortunate. My sister learned when she was in high school, like you. She got my parents to pay for driving lessons – that would have been unthinkable when I was her age. She was spoiled. Anyway, I had to learn how to drive if I was going to work in film. Ha – I learned to drive and ended up being a teacher instead!"

"You've never talked about her," I say curiously, "your sister, I mean. I've never seen her when I visited your parents. Just the photo of her and her husband. What does she do?"

"She works for the federal government now. Citizenship and Immigration, which is a laugh, a pure irony if you ask me."

"Someone was saying to me that we need more Tamils in positions like that," I tell him. "It's probably a good thing she's in the government."

"All Malathi cares about is money, believe you me. She doesn't care about the plight of Tamil people. We had so little growing up that she found someone as far different from us as possible. They live for shoes and vacations. What about your brother? He's probably happy that you made it out here."

"Brothers are another thing," I say. "You know how they are. Maybe not. Maybe you got lucky there. Anyway, thanks for the lesson."

The snow's really coming down as we leave the car.

DANIEL

After I said goodbye to Niranjan, I saw how heavily it had started to snow. The snow really came down in those bran-sized flakes they only have in the suburbs. I was at school, not that far from my parents' house, so I decided to visit them to help my father shovel his driveway.

He had already been shovelling for a while by the time I got there. Appa had finished half the driveway by himself. He strained heavily and needed a rest; my arrival furnished an excuse.

Inside, my mother brewed tea while my father went to the bathroom and ran hot water over his arthritic hands.

His lordship returned to the kitchen, fingers trembling. Water glistened on his face, or was that sweat? I could see he'd taken the trouble to comb his hair, and the white fringe flowed down from his dark bald head. My father's reaction to pain had always been to ignore it, suck it up as best he could. As his eldest and a son, he expected nothing less from me. Suck up the pain from the beatings, suck up the pain of growing up, and suck up the pain of general life, a malaise he couldn't verbalize. Yet the pain ran through him and also ran through me. If every culture has a darkness, this was ours. We'd never had the power to articulate it.

The fact my father and I had never talked intimately negated the hope of having a normal relationship. We'd never been a proper father and son. He wasn't unintelligent. Did he not love me? Why did he not understand the need for closeness, for bonding?

My father drank his tea too quickly to taste. It must have burned his tongue and throat going down. Quickly lacing up his shoes, he put on his gloves and was already heading out to reach for his shovel while I finished my cup.

"Go out and join him – his heart!" urged my mother.

If his heart was so bad, why did he have to push things? But these were not conversations we could have in this household. They would simply have been words evaporating in the air, going nowhere, strands of hair swirling in the bathtub, clunky stones dropped from my lips, unanswered, worse than rhetorical questions. His shovelling the driveway, despite his heart condition, was a firm 'fuck you' to the life that had brought him here.

After we finished, the snow still continued to descend in bran-like flakes. Lynn and I were spared that. My father and I paused to admire our handiwork, which was already being eradicated as we stood there, the flakes leaving a wet and woolly coating over the shovelled tarmac.

"What's happening now in Sri Lanka is incredible." My father shook his head – his smile was rueful.

"It seems really bad," I nodded. "But Jaffna's seen tough times before, no?"

"Your mother's father and sister are there. She is very worried. We couldn't bring them over. She feels as if she's at fault. Still, we managed to bring Niranjan over. You must help him get on his feet. He's been through a lot."

"I know that," I said against the cold, scraping the shovel against the frozen tarmac. "I'm trying my best."

"Be gentle with your mother. Go along with her if she asks you to pray."

"Why the insistence on praying?" I asked, putting up my hands. "Wouldn't it be better to make preparations to adapt to our lives here? We're never going back, are we? You might as well accept you're Canadian now, adapt to it."

"Yes, how could I forget?" he asked. "This wonderful country. You've become such a complete Canadian. Your Tamil is almost gone, you know that? If somebody had told me when I was young that this is how we would end up... Who can know what God has in store?"

How could anyone rational and intelligent believe in an omniscient, omnipotent God? Especially someone as hardy and durable in temperament as my father? It befuddled me. If such a Being existed, he must be a monster. My father's parents had passed away long ago. My grandparents died, never having ventured far from their village near Jaffna where they'd been born. For them, the universe was their village, and God had ruled their dust ridden lives. But at least they'd been allowed natural deaths. My mom felt guilty about not being able to bring any of her relatives over. Did she resent us for it? Her family had not possessed the foresight of my father. Amma prayed to whatever deities she could to assuage her guilt, but why did my father go along with her? Was it all a charade to live up to some Tamil mark of reputation? There were other Tamil houses on this street, and inside I was sure they were happy to buy cars and flat screen TVs and furniture sets on instalment, get on with the business of living, move on with their lives. Trying to be happy with the little time they had left.

"Go inside and pray with her," said my father with a tight expression on his face, looking at his flower beds, now stripped and laid bare by the snow. "What does it cost you?"

To lie? I thought. With you two, it costs me my soul. One asks to play up to the other. In between, you both drive me crazy.

The history of Sri Lanka was little more than misery and bloodshed. It seemed wise to leave it behind.

"The snow's coming down. We'd better start shovelling again," my father said, bringing me back to reality.

"I'm sick of this," I replied. "I'm tired."

"Go in if you like. Spend some time with your mother. I'll keep working."

It was a guilt thing, not a love thing. I remembered those unendurable hours in his presence as a child, sitting at his feet, watching the second hand on his watch's dial go round. His weak heart beat control, not love. I had sworn to myself that I'd get away, as far as possible, but here I was.

Because he had worked so hard to bring us over and keep us safe, I picked up my shovel and fell in line beside him.

NIRANJAN

Soothy says he's going to place chopsticks in the guy's ear, then light them on fire

We're back downtown. Rageev has decided to act. He could tell I didn't want to do it. He yelled at me, "So they told you I'm soft? That I can't take care of obligations? I'll show you who I am tonight!"

We're in Korean town. The old guy – Professor X with his wheelchair and his puzzles – is nowhere to be seen. But the casually dressed guys – Basketball Jersey and Tracksuit Top – are here.

Tracksuit Top lies on the ground, cold, gash across his jaw and forehead. Blood on the ground. Basketball Jersey is tied to a chair. They'd been alone, eating Chinese takeout. One set of chopsticks had been unused, lying in their paper sleeve. Soothy uses them now.

There have been troubles between Soothy and Abirami. I think she's dropping him. Her father is that guy, Muthu. He saw them together at the meetings. They don't hold hands or anything – but he knew. Besides, she was never going to be okay with his lifestyle. He's taking it pretty hard. I've heard him yell at her on the phone. He's crushed inside. She brought out a nicer side to him. His frustration at not getting what he wants works itself out in other ways. Makes him mean and creative.

Rageev tried to question the first Asian guy. That didn't go so well. They broke his nose, then his jaw. Now he's lying face down on the floo , beaten to a pulp. Dark blood drains across the floorboards. The blood has slowed to a trickle, turns into pools of rust on the floo . The pools are wide, have bits of scrambled egg and fried noodle and greasy broccoli in them. His jaw, half of it sunk in that pool of blood, is pulped, the forehead so mashed it looks like it's rising out of the fast food goo. Smell of oil and iron in the air – blood and won tons and mashed eggs.

We are here because Rageev owes the LTTE thirty thousand dollars. I realize this is a problem. He owes them thirty thousand dollars because they fronted him the money to get back his baby. The Koreans took his baby because he owed them thirty thousand dollars. He says they were unfair to demand that, he owed a lot less, but I don't know all the details. Now he wants revenge. When I heard the plan last night, I went into the bathroom and threw up.

"Listen," Soothy says to me, "where's your balls? You should be doing this stuff too."

"Seelan was our boy," says Rageev in a menacing voice. "We know you shot him. We know you had something to do with that."

"I... don't know... anything," says Basketball Jersey weakly.

Soothy looks at him like he's a raw insect. I remember the time he had taken his stance, cocked his safety, and demolished those bottles in the ravine. "The point is territory," he says in a whispery voice. "The point is revenge."

Rageev nods his head. They have an understanding. Do it.

Soothy rips apart the chopsticks' paper sleeve with his mouth. One tear. The guy hangs his head, tries to nestle his ears and shoulders into his neck. Like a turtle. The wire tying his hands cuts into his wrists. How old is he? Where are his brothers and sisters? His parents? Rageev leans against the wall, gun in hand, coldly watching. The gun already has blood on its muzzle. Tracksuit's blood. Where Rageev beat him with it. Soothy exaggerates each act, like he's doing a performance. He rolls the paper sleeve into a tight ball, throws it at the guy's face. The guy snaps his head up, stares back with pure hatred. Sweat runs down his scrunched forehead. He twists side to side, flicks away sweat from his eyelids

I look at Rageev, questioningly. "It won't kill him," says Rageev in Tamil.

Soothy, holding the guy's jaw firmly in his fingers, inserts the pointed end of one chopstick into the left ear.

As the guy struggles, the other chopstick gets lodged in the guy's right ear. The boy screams. Soothy jams them in tight.

"Sshh. Shh... What if I slammed the chopsticks together?" asks Soothy. "Do you think they'd go right into your brain or would they just break your eardrums?" Soothy claps his palms together loudly. "One way or another, what's in here," Soothy taps the guy's forehead, "is going to come out."

Soothy looks up at us and smiles, like he's seeking approval. "Hey, did you know – I saw on TV that woodpeckers have a tongue that wraps all the way around their brain. Think I can wrap these chopsticks around this guy's brain? What do you think?"

"Just get on with it," says Rageev, his face cold. Like he's almost bored, leaning against the wall, holding his gun, lazily fingering the trigger. Me, I'm ready to puke again. I hold my automatic. It's clean, blood free. Only thing that's on it is sweat. Mine. I'm sweating more than the guy in the chair. How much sweat is in that basketball jersey? I can probably beat it.

Soothy flicks open his lighter and brings the handle of the flame close to the right chopstick. The boy can feel the burn of the flame close to his cheek. I can feel him feeling the flame. Dry hairs on his cheek crisp, then smoke into little puddles of liquid as they singe his roasting skin. He pulls his head as far back as he can – tendons on his neck stretch against skin. His face looks like it's going to burst. He moans. He doesn't scream. He moans. The smell of his burned skin and Korean hair fill the small kitchen.

The chopstick takes a while to light and burn. Puke rises in my throat. Burnt wood smells like roasting bugs. Somewhere, I can hear cockroaches click-click-clicking small legs along the floor. Can almost feel them scampering up my leg and chest. Into my mouth. Burned cockroaches. I throw up what little I have left.

"Shit!" cries Rageev, disgusted. "Get a grip. When you going to toughen up? You're not a child anymore."

"Hey, we should have used incense," jokes Soothy.

Rageev is annoyed. Some of the puke has splashed on his shoes and jeans. He yells, "Just get on with it!" Somehow I hold my gun steady.

"Oh God!" There's a dry raspy trickle. Korean guy's wet his leg. The smell of piss combines with puke and blood. The other two laugh.

He's older than me, I think. This is the end of his life. Soothy will let him live, but he'll never be the same. I remember throwing that firebomb through Raptis's window for Janelle... and also for me. Am I so different? Was Raptis okay afterwards? It never bothered Janelle or the others, far as I could tell. Why doesn't this bother Soothy and Rageev? They are like the LTTE. Like the AK Kannans. AKK doesn't exist anymore. Yet we are like them. As if we are ghosts already. Part of me knows I will never go back to those early days with my brother and family again – the good days. Watching the Korean burn is like watching my own self burn. He tries to protect what little information he has. If it were three Koreans against me, I would be the one in the chair. My hairs and clothes would be burning to a crisp. My skin would be melting. This is the way it works.

These Koreans had been extra bold when we came in. Seelan's death was somehow linked to this? Wasn't it a rival Tamil gang? "This boy and his raggedy crew are not only going to give their money but also their stash to us," says Rageev. "If his bosses have any problem with this, they'll have to settle with me." I know now Rageev is out of options. Muruges may say that he's a fool, but Rageev's not so different from the LTTE. He's desperate. This is what being Tamil means. It means doing anything you can to survive. There is no wisdom, no strategy to what we're doing. At best we're buying a few more days. Revenge beatings and hits. That's all it is. Rageev talks about it like it was some glory days, but it was just stealing and a little dealing. Short tempers and long grudges. I know I don't belong here.

The guy with the burning chopsticks begins talking. When he talks, the words come pouring out. He cries for his mother. Soothy twists the chopsticks in harder. Rageev calms Soothy down, restrains him. Soothy writes down the combination for the safe that they keep in Professor X's bedroom. We will methodically ransack the apartment. In the bedroom, a puzzle lies half finished on the table. In a garbage bag behind the washing machine, we will find smaller bags of weed, vials of heroin and coke. I don't know how much. More than I've ever seen. My mind goes to ten different places at once. There will also be heroin in dark smears on plastic strips. Baseball Jersey says it's for smuggling into prison, on the backs of books, inside food. There's a bag holding bottles and baggies with assorted pills. We're not talking bricks or anything but still... and then the safe. The safe in the bedroom. Near the puzzle of a bald eagle in its nest. The safe has money in it. More than enough to pay Muruges, and then some.

Before the fire reaches his eardrums, Baseball Jersey gives everything. His body evacuates piss, shit, and tears. His mind evacuates information. He gives up friends, numbers, routines. His tongue doesn't work normally afterwards. He talks about prostitutes he's slept with. His head sags loosely to the side so that one charred chopstick sticks into his shoulder. Soothy takes the burnt chopsticks out of the boy's ears and forces them into his mouth to shut him up. Rageev watches while Soothy hits the boy in the face, splintering the chopsticks.

"Go on," says Rageev to me kindly, "hit him in the face."

I can't! I shake my head and open my mouth but no words come.

Go on, mimes Rageev and gently takes my gun away from me. He smiles a warm smile. The burned and unburned skin on his face stretches apart. My will breaks down.

I sniffle, and slap the guy with my palm. Blood and splinters come out his mouth.

"Harder," says Rageev.

With the back of my hand, I beat him again and again against the side of his face. Like my father did to me. Like his father did to him. "Stop crying," I hiss. "Stop crying, you bastard."

Again.

Again.

Finally, my hand is rawboned. I can see bruises, cuts around my knuckles. Inflamed pink breaks through my dark skin. Rageev takes me by the shoulder, gives me back my gun. It feels extra heavy, butt pushed against my limp wrist.

Soothy and I have to go around the apartment, pick up the various bags and vials, stuff it all up. Rageev bundles the cash. "Hey, want me to take the food as well?" Soothy asks jokingly. He has a sick sense of humour.

"Stop playing around," replies Rageev, curt, all business. I carry a mixture of pills in my hand. They're heavier than I'd thought. Some of the pills are big, almost like what I'd imagine horse pills to look like.

The poor guy is sobbing silently. My hand still hurts. Tied to his chair, broken chopstick splinters in his mouth, his life in this organization over.

"Remember," says Rageev. "We know where to find you. You make sure to tell them it was just some rival brothers."

DANIEL

We took Chuck for a walk by the harbour front. Snow had left the grass a wet, muddy, slush-ruled world. Everywhere were forgotten drifts of snow, now brown. Drizzle in the air wet our clothes. A Saturday; Lynn and I had gotten through the first weeks of the new semester. Luckily, we both had immense piles of work at home. It helped us avoid the subject of Niranjan. She was still angry at me for making the demand, but she'd smoothed everything out for him at school. Niranjan could stay at LCC one further semester.

In gratitude, I almost exclusively looked after Chuck. I walked him by the harbour front as soon as I came home, cleaned up the messes he made as he progressed through house training. I picked up his feces and washed him. Chuck had grown large in the month that we'd had him, although he'd already been a big puppy when I picked him up at the breeders. He was almost as large as a dalmation, but sleeker, much more agile. It was getting harder for Lynn to handle him. Chuck's fur began to turn colour. It was still brown, but there was a trace of grey, even dusky blue, in his hide. He whipped around, a streak of dusk, a strange demanding animal yet enjoyable to have in our lives.

Perhaps I was guilty of using him to fill up the spaces which existed in our relationship.Now, Lynn walked ahead of us to the dog park in her black MEC winter coat.

Her hood was drawn over her head, so I could not see her face. From the back, she looked like a wraith or an executioner, a snow queen with that fringe of fake fur trimming around her face. Her irritated footsteps kicked puddles of dirty water aside.

Chuck, on the other hand, was much less restrained. He loved to run at people, making them lose their balance. He would veer away at the last moment, run back without actually hitting them, like a game of chicken that gave him sadistic mirth. Tongue wagging and jaws salivating, he bore down on people's dogs when we weren't looking, and plundered their toys. Before anybody could do anything, he would leave the dog or toy, run circles around the owner, then come back to me, tongue lolling out, before bounding off again. A hefty bribe, a handful of dog treats, brought him back to the leash. The regulars in the dog park began to know and hate us.

We walked him the long way back to the condo. "You going to visit your parents on Sunday?" Lynn asked by the time I'd settled Chuck into a trot and caught up with her.

"I think we should visit them together," I suggested. "If they get used to seeing you around, maybe they'll accept you."

"Why can't they come here? They've never even seen our place."

"They won't visit. They don't have a car, and they'll say they won't know how to take the TTC downtown. Really, it's just pride. They won't deign to do it. For them, it'd be admitting defeat. But if you go, they'll have to deal with you. They can't insult you from afar. They can't think of you in the abstract," I ruminated. "They'll be forced to contend with you as a real person, not somebody they sarcastically call 'the fiancee'. I'll tell them that I won't visit anymore unless they show you some respect."

She scratched her head worriedly. "But it's not a good time now, Dan. We should wait until you and I have a wedding date set, all our ducks in a row. I work with Tamil parents, remember. I know how they think."

Chuck became tense and sat on his haunches, looking at us. I seized the moment and took her by the arms. "We have to get along and stand together. Otherwise we'll do their job for them. At one point or another, they've taken the opportunity to wreck any chance I might have at a normal life. We can't let them defeat us." She strained a little but finally her elbows went slack as if sick of resisting.

"I don't know," she said. "Working with Tamils at school is one thing. Dealing with your parents is another. Sometimes I think the best thing would be to stay as far away as possible. Know what I mean? Thinking about everything you've said, I don't know if I can maintain composure. It's not what they think of me that upsets me so much," she admitted. "It's everything you've told me about them, the way you were brought up. I can't get what you said about you and your sister out of my mind. I keep picturing it."

I let her go. "God, I know it. There was some fucked up stuff there. They felt they owned our bodies. Because they produced us, they had the right to do whatever they pleased. Just try to be your amazing self around them – they'll have no choice but to accept you."

"Okay," she said, "but we should also try to set a date for the wedding. For real. If they know we're getting married, they'll have to accept me into their lives. If they don't, well…"

I agreed so we could discuss other things. I didn't want an all out war between Lynn and my parents. On the other hand, I didn't know which made me more uncomfortable: talk about having a baby or setting plans for a wedding.

Why was I so hesitant to move forward and grasp these things, steps that my sister easily accomplished in her twenties? Like her clothes, like their cars, their house, Malathi's wedding had not been done in halves. It had been a large excruciatingly painful wedding that bore many new embarrassments and crushing reminders of my status in the hierarchy.

I knew that it had something to do with my great unfinished film, the film that in my heart of hearts I knew would never be made. Getting married, having a kid, this would only make that defeat, the compact with the future that could never be, manifest.

NIRANJAN

I fall into Rageev's plan to sell the drugs with a heavy heart. At first, I even say what I think. "Not that I have anything against them, or what you do, you understand? But I don't want to go door to door, handing this stuff to people."

"You think I want to be doing this?" asks Rageev, scar twisting to a sneer. "You think I enjoy it? You think this is what I thought my life was going to be like when I came over here? This is what Canada has left me. All my friends are gone, and I'm the last one standing. But why am I telling you? You live in this apartment. You eat my food – well, don't you? You don't want to sell this product, fine. You have a better way of earning money to cover the bills? Nothing comes for free, machan. Driving a car's not gonna cut it. Feel me? I'd go out and do it myself, but you should pull your weight. Be a man. Go out and do your part."

I'm scared to look up at him. He continues, "Look, it's not for a long time, anyway. Just so that we can get some money together, you know? Every bit helps. This is going to help your brother and everybody else back home. This is the only way I can help Muruges and his people, pay back the money and interest I owe them. Understand?"

Interest? I don't know what to believe. If it's only for a short while – maybe I can handle it. I can grind down, get through the days or weeks that are necessary. After all, my brother's had it much worse.

"But what if there's trouble?" I ask.

"That's what this is for." Soothy points to the handle of his .45. It gleams, poking out the waistband of his jeans. It's a big gun against his skinny waist. Looks like Abirami's left him for good, now. Way he's throwing himself into this.

Rageev makes us pray in front of God one last time before we begin the enterprise. Before we begin slinging. I'm no good as a shooter. Obviously. I'm not carrying anything except pills and drugs. Soothy is muscle, but I'm doing the counting, the deals. Putting math to use, you know. Am I being used because I'll only go to a juvenile home or detention centre? Don't know. Is seventeen old enough for them to lock you up?

I still go to school, still do the odd driving session with Mr N. My one condition to Rageev is that I will not sell at the school. No way. They can call me soft, but I won't do it. Rageev makes more appearances at the apartment now. Occasionally, I ferry him back and forth to various locations, this meeting, that meeting. Soothy does things without me, but I am only Rageev's driver. I don't mind. Rageev lets us know when he's going to swing by. He drops off small batches of vials and dime bags, then picks up the money we bring back. We're still doing collections. On top of everything else. Rageev counts the money carefully.

Nothing stays in the apartment very long. There's a small stash for emergencies: some weed, some pills. Soothy raids the weed regularly. He's smoking more than ever before. Rageev overlooks it – cost of doing business, I suppose. The weed and bravado go to Soothy's head. Soon starts acting like a different person. That small sweetness, which made him human, flickers away. No longer plays Wii with me. All his free time is spent smoking weed in the bedroom or on the balcony. He loves the balcony, despite it being frozen outside. Watches everybody coming and going to the Court like he's waiting for something.

A dry bit of curly fluff grows into a wispy beard on his chin. When he raises his hood on the balcony, all you can see is his chin, the wispy beard jutting out, steam blowing from his mouth. Something final and dark about the gesture.

Though Soothy takes his .45, sometimes an additional .38, I never go strapped. I carry the product – the vials, the glassine bags, the rolled-up joints, the tablets – all in my backpack. Soothy walks with me into the buildings, but never talks. He hangs back with his hands in his coat pockets, hood on, watching everybody. Paranoia makes him silent. Soothy never handles the cash, I never handle a gun. Better that way. My hands shake when I count the cash, give it over to Rageev for the pick up.

I hate selling to Tamils in the Court. I feel bad about this. Rageev has other ideas. Because I can drive, he sends us to other parts of Scarborough. We go to apartment buildings on Warden, Finch, Eglinton. Always apartments, never houses. There's a mix: Tamils, Asians, different kinds of white people. Contacts and customers from before. Each building holds that musty old carpet smell, despair. I try my best to put people at ease. To not be a thug. Soothy's always standing there, behind me, like a bad thought.

Once, Rageev gets me to deliver to an apartment building near Victoria Park, where we haven't been before. It's swarming with Tamil guys. I don't think it's a good idea, but Soothy says nothing. He just stands behind me, hood up, as I press the button for the sixteenth floor. As the doors begin to close, one of the Tamil guys leaning against the wall in the lobby pushes himself forward and jumps into the elevator. He jams the door open, then lets it close. It's an old, heavy elevator. Brown panelling with scratches. The grimy smell of dirt and urine caked onto the floor. The elevator moves up slowly. You can hear the grinding of its winch.

"You my six o' clock?" asks the guy, in Tamil. His voice scratchy like paper.

I shake my head.

"What you want on the sixteenth floor?"

"Seeing a friend," I reply. Soothy says nothing. Elevator continues to climb.

"You want a stereo? Forty bucks."

I shake my head again.

"Come on, man – forty bucks."

"He said he doesn't want it," says Soothy, hissing the words 'said' and 'it'. There is that very distinct racking sound as Soothy reaches his right hand underneath his shirt and pulls the slide of the .45. I don't turn around. The slide can be heard above the elevator winch. After that, the guy doesn't say anything. We just watch each other as the elevator comes to a stop. The doors bang open. He watches us leave to walk down the hall, but stays in the elevator. Doesn't seem to flinch

"You think motherfucker finally got the point?" asks Soothy.

"What if he gets some guys?" I whisper. "What if they get some weapons and wait for us downstairs?"

"Be cool," says Soothy, flicking his ponytail. "Do your business and we'll go."

Loud, riotous rap music belts from at least two different apartments. 1616. I knock on the door and wait. The light through the peephole goes dark a long time, then an old man answers. A Tamil in saram and filthy banian. He hasn't shaved in days. He moves slowly, and the smell of sweat, dust, mould, and curry come washing out the door. All these apartments smell like rot and spice. Unnatural winds in the middle of winter. Door creaks. He opens it all the way. We go in.

Inside, two spider plants are dying from lack of water. A large flat screen TV plays Who Wants To Be a Millionaire? The wife comes out from the kitchen, wiping a plate with a towel. She is grey haired, short and stocky like my amma, plaited hair hanging over a shoulder.

"What can I do for you, Amma?" I ask.

"He needs painkillers," she answers, pointing to her husband.

I open the bag and take out the packets I have. Small codeine tablets. Yellow morphines. The Percocets are large and white – the 'horse pills'.

"For him, only," she says. "Needs ten Percocets." I'm curious. Why does he need them?

She is open, matter of fact with us about it. "He was taken by the Sinhalese Army and beaten. They used razor wire on his back. We did not see him for three weeks. Then they dropped him outside our house, near death. My nephew brought us here, but we don't have health cards so there's nothing we can do." The man says nothing. He continues to watch Millionaire from the ratty couch.

I take her money, want to give her a discount on the pills. But if I do, Rageev might hit me. Soothy says nothing.

"What do they do?" I ask the woman as I hand her the large pills.

"Do?" she asks, blinking as if I've asked a stupid question. She palms two pills, hands them with a glass of water to her husband. He moves very slowly to take them. Ignores us. He even swallows with difficult .

"They take away the pain of course," says the woman, making sure he swallows properly.

"Have you ever tried them yourself?" I ask.

Soothy becomes impatient, but I want to hear the answer.

"No," whispers the woman. Her plait swishes against her back. She shows us the door. "You don't take it unless you have to."

No one in the hallway. We walk to the elevator and press the button. I can tell Soothy's as nervous as I am. His hand stays on the handle of his gun. Mine grips my backpack. The elevator takes forever to roll up to our floo . Maybe we should take the stairs. I think of the Korean house downtown. Taste of burned cockroaches in my mouth.

In the lobby, the young guys are there, talking in papery voices. Their legs propped against walls. They have their hoods on now, hands balled into fists. They look just like Soothy, noses sticking out, their chins and wisps of hair. Everything freezes as we exit. I swear their lips stop moving. Their mouths stop talking.

Am I getting paranoid too?

They watch us leave the lobby. I think of Rageev's stories – the time the VVT ambushed him in front of the apartment building.

We walk to the Yutani Quantum, not slowly, but without hurrying. The black beast starts. Motor turns over. Exhaust coughs up fumes. I want to throw up. Soothy whispers, "Drive, asshole!"

Fingers tremble as I weave the car out the parking lot.

"At least you didn't pull out your inhaler this time."

DANIEL

My mother became hysterical about the prospect of Lynn coming over. "What are you doing to me, mahan?" she screamed over the phone. "How do you expect me to pretend to like this black woman? I don't know what she eats! How can I know what she'll eat? Are you trying to humiliate me? You're much too good for her. Haven't you realized that? Stop this nonsense. Come back here and live with us. I'll drop everything and find you a good girl. No one will ever know. Think of it as a simple mistake."

"Amma, calm down," I said. "For one thing, she's going to come over and that's not going to change, is it? You might as well accept her. For another thing, you can't always tell me to stop everything and let you find me a bride. That's not going to happen, so stop saying it. Who I marry is the biggest, most important choice in my life. Why would I let you handle it, when you've done nothing but destroy my life in the past? You couldn't ask me to do anything more suddenly life changing than what you're asking me to do right now. The only way you could ask me to do something more drastic is if you asked me to get a sex change."

My mother continued to sob hysterically. She didn't like my cavalier attitude. I don't know if she even understood my point. The hysterical sighs permitted these conversations to be suitably one-sided. "Amma, get hold of yourself. If you spend time with her, you'll be impressed by what a wonderful person she is. Don't believe me if you don't want to – just wait and see."

Her sobs choked out, "She'll want all different kinds of meat, I suppose? I don't know what to cook!"

My father came to the phone and took it away from her.

"Your mother is having a hard time," he said in a tired voice. "Are you sure this is a good idea?"

There was some vague anger at the back of his voice. It was a tired anger – something different about it. It took me a moment to realize what was so different. Usually, he would never ask my opinion on anything. But now he was asking me whether it was a good idea.

"We have to go ahead," I heard myself reciting slowly. "Everything's all set up."

Lynn made cupcakes and grilled vegetables to take over, but I suggested we leave the vegetables. I knew my parents wouldn't eat them. Even the cupcakes were dubious at best. Lynn was sore, but she heeded my advice. The staples of my parents' diet consisted of rice, lentils, and other vegetable curries. I refrigerated the grilled vegetables, and we took off.

The fog and rain of downtown dissipated as we drove in to Scarbrough. Shadows became longer, and the light slid into the earth. We did not talk much as Lynn drove – we listened to talk radio. When we got there, my sister's car was already parked in my parents' small driveway. Lynn and I had to look for parking on the street.

"I didn't know your sister was going to be here," muttered Lynn.

"Yeah, if I know her, Napoleon weaselled her way in," I replied, annoyed. "She's obviously curious about you. I wonder if she brought Mahesh with her?"

"You weren't kidding about her tastes. That is a very nice car. I think it's the model Badlamenti bought for his wife."

It was a long walk after we found parking. We shuffled inside the house before removing our boots. There was a cold that swept in during March, an exhaustion of the bones. Slowly, the warmth of the house, held by its postwar brick exterior, seeped into our bodies. The nineties era carpet felt soft beneath our feet. Napoleon was sitting on the plastic-covered couch, confabbing with Mahesh, who stood up when we entered. As he turned towards us, his profile filled out and an embarrassed smile crossed his lips. He knew my sister had roped him into coming without telling us.

You might almost feel sorry for my parents as they stood by the window, waiting for us. The snow fell steadily, cascading upon heavy sheets of cold air. The light from other houses served to illuminate the flakes against a stark winter sky. People trudged by, kicking aside the drifts.

"Here, Lynn brought you some cupcakes," I said, handing my mother the tray. She placed it in the fridge with a solemn face.

"You found it okay," said my father to Lynn, as if I were not there. "Come, let's eat."

Lynn was careful about what she ate, so she only took a little onto her plate. Napoleon and Mahesh dug in. Lynn and Napoleon made small talk as they passed around the dishes.

"How did you and Daniel meet?" asked my sister.

"We work together obviously," replied Lynn, perhaps a little abruptly, then caught herself. "What I mean to say is that we were working together when Dan volunteered to help me take kids to camp. We bonded."

"You like working with teenagers so much that you take them away?" asked Napoleon, her words measured, eyes and smile beaming at ten times magnification

"Oh yes," replied Lynn. "They have great team building exercises at Albion Hills. There's a predator and prey game where they take on the roles of different animals and learn about the environment and its habitats. Really good food. Beautiful silver birches and a soft pine needle floo ."

Lynn was beginning to ramble because she could tell that none of this was registering. "We've been to Europe and India, the Caribbean of course," said Mahesh, flipping his palm back and forth. The clasps on his gold watch rattled. "If you're travelling somewhere, wouldn't you want to get as far away as possible? I've never understood the Canadian romance for camping. It's cold and wet and dirty and hard. There's a reason most of the population lives close to the forty-ninth parallel."

Conversation fell after that. At some point Lynn pretended to go to the bathroom. On her way, she sneaked one of the cupcakes from the fridge that she had brought over, as if to compensate for my mother's cooking. There were still crumbs on her sleeve and lips when she returned. My mother was furious. Why not make a McDonald's run while you're at it? I thought.

"I'm sorry the food is not to your liking," said my mother tersely.

"No, it was fine," smiled Lynn. "I just have to be careful of eating too much that's oil fried and spicy. It's hard on my stomach afterwards... sometimes."

"Well, that's the problem when people mix out of their culture," said my father, his eyes piercing her apology. "Don't you think so?"

She swallowed. "Our country is the most multicultural in the world. It was made by mixing people together."

"That might be the fairy story you tell children and stupid people," he countered, "but we all know the truth. I remember when we came here in the eighties. The white people definitely thought it was their country and resented us being here. A long-haired type almost drove his car into me while I crossed the street. Here in Scarborough. He was parked at the red light, then he just drove into me. They called us 'paki' almost every day. That was a normal day. They thought so little of us that they couldn't even bother to put effort into their racist comments. Sri Lanka is nowhere close to Pakistan."

"Still," said Lynn, "you must be happy that things have progressed in twenty years. Look at how well Dan's done, how well your daughter's done. You succeeded in your dreams to build a life here."

"Have we?" he sighed, moving into his sad performance. "Daniel could have been anything he wanted: a doctor, an engineer, a scientist. He picked something with the least amount of work required – it's just like him. Did we do the right thing in coming here? You tell me. Seems like it wasn't worth the trouble of killing myself every day."

"Here you die a slow death," added my mother. "At least back home, we would have died quickly."

"Don't say that, Amma," said Napoleon. "How can you say that with all that's going on?"

Lynn retrieved the cupcakes from the fridge. Plates and dishes were cleared away. Tea was brewed. My sister was the first to try one of the chocolate swirls. The devil frosting, soft and creamy, yielded to her touch.

My father shot her a look of disapproval. "The sugar content," he said. "Take half."

"No, no, take as many as you'd like," cajoled Lynn, smiling. She could be very persuasive when warm, and she and Malathi seemed to enjoy regarding each other, despite their initial reservations. "So Dan's happy with you?" asked Napoleon. "His life used to be so unstable when he was younger – moving out, then moving back in. Telling everybody that he was going to be a filmmake , then giving it all up suddenly."

"He works very hard. He has a warmth and genuine connection with the kids that I don't have." Lynn rubbed my back as she spoke. The gesture, though small, was startlingly intimate in my parents' strict Tamil home. Even Napoleon and her husband, despite their success, did not stroke each other in public. My mother curled her lip, but my father frowned embarrassedly and picked up a cupcake, his arm crossing across our closeness. Lynn handed him a saucer so he had something to put it on. It was doubtful she realized how uncomfortable she made them feel. She might as well have discussed our sex life. Not all the cupcakes and all the frosting in the world would have sweetened the waters.

"Are you thinking of having children?" asked my father.

"Absolutely," replied Lynn.

"Appa! That's not something to bring up!" I sputtered, but Lynn was in her element now.

"We'll have to get a small house," she said. "Maybe something in Scarborough. It's become too expensive to buy anything downtown. With both our salaries, we should be able to carry it." This was news to me. Lynn had led me to believe that she'd always wanted to live in the city.

"You want to be closer to work?" asked my father.

"I want to become a principal, eventually," she replied. "When I get posted as a vice-principal, which I hope will be sooner than later, I don't know where I'll be sent. If it's somewhere in Scarborough, that's fine. In the meantime, I want Dan and me to have at least one child. It'll be harder once I'm promoted." The conversation was spiralling too close to home for my comfort, and I nudged Lynn underneath the table, but she pretended not to notice.

"You don't believe in getting married first?" asked my father. I could tell he wasn't sure what to make of her; she certainly didn't conform to what he'd been expecting. He'd probably expected her to act like someone out of a hip-hop video.

"That would be nice," replied my Lynn regretfully, "but what does it matter the order in which you do the important things, as long as you do them? Right? I'm not getting any younger, am I? A person has to be practical sometimes."

My father leaned back, trying to take it all in. His mind had to zoom out to find a perspective that fit. Lynn's skin glowed, her hair was done up, and she was dressed in a burgundy jacket and blouse that oozed softness and confidence. Especially when she smiled. "You're practical and ambitious," he finally said. "Qualities I wish my son had more of." Lynn took the compliment graciously.

"We parents get to a certain age," said my mother, now on her second cupcake, "and we need to hear the voices of little children again. We're waiting for grandchildren – that's the only thing that will bring us comfort in old age." She sounded like Emma.

"What about you, Malathi?" asked Lynn. "Don't you and Mahesh want to have children?"

"We're trying," admitted Napoleon, "but we wanted to see what you were doing first. Mahesh and I waited as long as we could to get married, out of respect to Daniel here. He's always done things in his own time, different from everybody else."

"What do you mean?"

"When a woman marries, she goes to her husband's family," replied my mother, as if this was the most basic known fact. "It's always a son that a mother leans on. The girl goes off to be in someone else's family. Don't worry. We saved up and provided for Malathi, gave them the best start possible. My husband paid for the wedding and bought them a car. But now we're worried about him." Her finger darted towards me. "Besides, my daughter and son-in-law are only in their twenties. Daniel's getting older, and it's been difficult to find someone for him

"You say that as if you have any say in the matter," I stated, annoyed.

My father shook his head. I supposed it was a good thing they didn't drink – I could only imagine what would come out of their mouths then. My mother continued as if she could do no wrong. "The woman goes and lives with the man's family. He still lives with his parents and takes care of them because they've spent all their efforts providing for the children. Isn't that right, mahan? Only with Daniel, he pretends he's white. He wants to be a big shot. So he rejected everything his father and I did for him. Isn't that right?"

For once, Lynn was unsure what to say and turned to me for guidance.

"Look," I said finally. "I've told Lynn all about us. She knows what happened."

"What do you mean?" asked Napoleon, suddenly tense.

"There's no need to pretend. There's no need to preserve the illusion that we're a normal family. She knows – about the Children's Aid, the hitting, all of it."

My parents looked worriedly from Lynn to me, from me to Lynn, from my sister and Mahesh back to us again. "In this country, they give children too much power." My father looked away as he spoke, as if the matter was beneath him. "How was I to raise you both? Should I have just let you make mistakes and not corrected you?"

"There's a difference between a spanking and terrorizing someone with a coat hanger. You enjoyed what you did. There was an air of cruelty and vengeance in your actions. If I needed to be disciplined, tell me why. Tell me what I did that was so bad. I dare you to come up with a single thing."

"You stole," declared my mother triumphantly.

"Only because you didn't give me any money. You gave Malathi money. You gave her whatever she wanted.

You bent your lives around her, but me, you treated like shit."

"You were the eldest. You were a boy. You were supposed to be setting an example for her." My father shrugged his shoulders and looked at Lynn as if she would also think I was spouting gibberish. "We had a little more money by the time she came along. Why are you always comparing?"

"Yes, why are you always going to the past? Can't you look forward?" chimed in my mother.

"Once, I came into the living room to find you bowing down in front of Malathi theatrically," I said, remembering with disgust – Malathi must have been an adolescent then. My father crossed his arms. "If I hadn't said anything when she was small, you would have just kept beating her and beating her into submission."

"I didn't do that. Where do you get these things?"

Napoleon had been quiet all this time, a state of shock had momentarily descended upon her, but she quickly found her fury again. "What is wrong with you? You were no angel yourself. You used to throw me on the sofa, or have you forgotten that? You used to beat me up!"

"Every older brother beats up his younger sibling!" I snapped back. "But I did what was right when I was a teenager. If I hadn't said anything, they would have just kept beating you."

"You just do what's to your advantage," she countered. "Why did you come back if you were going to leave us all like you said?"

"You think it was easy for me to go talk to someone? The only reason you're the way you are now – the confidence, the brassiness – is because my reporting it gave you a chance to grow into that. Do you think you would ever have found your voice or strength if you'd grown up with them beating you every day, the way they beat me? They already were beating you every day. I had it ten times harder than you, easily. They treated me like shit, and they would have done the same to you. You never had to deal with all the moving around they put us through. They let you drive, they gave you spending money. I suffered, and you profited. You have a great life because I was broken a thousand times over."

Mahesh looked very uncomfortable. We all were, but he seemed the most affected. He squeezed his neck with his hand and didn't say anything. What were things like for him in his household?

"Maybe I wanted to be hit," Malathi replied weakly. "Did you ever think of that?"

"Sometimes we wish we'd never come here," my father reluctantly added. His glum tone did not waver. "You do everything for children and for what? For what? So they can forget you and say bad things about you. Every family has problems. Your mother and I were hit in our day, sometimes very harshly. It was a fact of life. We didn't love our parents any less. Sometimes I wonder why we ever came. If not for the war, then…"

"You don't know anything about love," I said. "Your idea of love is shouting at us and telling us what to do. You'd just be happy to invade my body, to possess it, to pour yourself into me and inhabit my life. You're not happy unless everybody else is miserable. Everything you did from leaving Sri Lanka to where and how we went, you did. It was your choice. You never asked me or cared what I thought."

"You were a child!!! Don't you understand that?!" He lifted his arms and took in the walls of the house, as if they might understand him.

"Why did you have children if you didn't want to care for them?" I asked. "All you do is complain about how hard you have it, how hard you have it and what little gratitude you get."

"I'm going to die soon."

"You've been saying that for twenty years," I sneered. "Go ahead and do it already, then."

"How can you say that?" gasped my mother. Even Lynn seemed ready to defect after those words. I regretted them somewhat.

"They're going to have it very hard in the last stages of their lives," added Napoleon, "and Mahesh and I are the ones who are going to carry the burden. You're not here, and we're obviously going to have to shoulder the costs."

"Everything here is about the money," sighed my father. "They say one thing to your face, do another without caring. All a big nothing. Family is everything back home. Here, you're supposed to marry the person you love. Isn't that right, Ms Varley? Where we come from, you love the person you marry. You might as well see what you're marrying into. Now you've seen the way things really are in our family."

"What do your parents think about this match?" asked my mother boldly. "Wouldn't they rather that you find someone from your own background? That way, your values will connect. You would only end up fighting, and I guarantee it won't be easy for the little ones if you marry Daniel."

"I'm Canadian," she replied, flushed. "So's he. We're both Canadian."

My father's mouth fell open slightly; his eyes widened in delight as if he had just heard the funniest thing, as if a chimpanzee had gotten onto a stool and sung a song. I could read his face as plainly as a book. Who're you kidding? You're black! was what it said. You're worse off than we are.

"Anyway," he said to stop himself from laughing – already the mirth had spread across his characteristically stern face, "I'd better shovel the snow. You stay inside and talk. I don't have anything else to say."

We watched him roll on his socks and lace up his boots, go through the ritual of donning his coat.

"What are you waiting for?" my mother hissed. "Go out there and help him!"

I felt exhausted. All the fight in me flooded ou

"All right," I said.

He was already out the door by the time I was bending down to find my boots in the pile

"Hey!" I yelled at Napoleon who was sitting there smug, spoilt, used to having everybody else do the work for her. "Aren't you going to help us? It's your car we're digging out, you know!"

NIRANJAN

"It's a good thing you're back at school," says Rageev. "We need that money coming in."

"I told you – I don't want to deal at school," I reply.

"You wouldn't have talked to me like that before Muruges took an interest in you. You'd better remember who's paying the rent here."

I pull out my inhaler after he leaves. Couple of puffs hardly make a difference anymore. I need something stronger.

I have my own reasons for making an effort at school. He can't understand. It's not only that Mr N is a nice guy – I want to make something of myself. I don't want to be a fat fucking zero. Rageev may be happy coasting in the gutter, but I could do something. I was good at school – once. There are no customers at school I want to deal with.

Soothy continues to smoke free weed. He goes further inside himself. Acts punch drunk, and I let him. Slinging drugs is not how I pictured life in Canada. One day I'll get out of this, be normal. There are still many pills in the Ziploc bag we boosted. I pick them up from time to time, almost roll them round with my fingers through the plastic. They helped that lady's husband. He was in worse pain than me.

Rageev gets me to drive him downtown again. Another meeting with Muruges and Karthik.

"So, what you going to take?" asks Rageev.

"What?"

"What you going to take after high school, if you do graduate?"

"Maybe a film program. York's got one. Ryerson too."

"Film? What? You're going to Bollywood?"

"Mr N's been encouraging me. I'd like to make something that tells what it really is like. To be Tamil in Sri Lanka. Real. For our people, you know?"

"Our people don't need movies. They need guns and money. Teacher's just filling your head with bullshit. You think there's a chance a Tamil like you is going to make it to Hollywood?"

"No…" I reply reluctantly. It's not about money. I just want to live a normal, happy life. My whole life, it's been Tiger this, Army that. War over here, shelling over there. Now it's slinging. Just once, I want to be normal: have an apartment, a job, a dog, a boring life. A girlfriend maybe. And yeah, I know I'm not Hollywood, but I'd like to make a movie. Something about what life is like for us. Invisible people who walk through streets to save bus fare and clean people's dishes when they've finished eating

Mr N says it's important to have vision. For art, you need vision. You need to pull truth out of your life.

Sometimes I cry myself to sleep to stop from thinking. So quietly Soothy can't hear. No, it's not great to pull things from my life, but if other people can relate, maybe it's okay.

"I know your school," chuckles Rageev. "If you're a Tamil, you're either a nerd or a thug, isn't that right? No artists or filmmakers come out of there. Where you gonna get money? You think it's cheap to make movies? Why not be a rock musician? Ha ha. How many courses you got to finish before you graduate high school?

"More than twenty," I say.

"There you go. There you go. Concentrate on that. Gonna take three years at least. You won't be a teenager no more when you graduate. University isn't for you, man, better think of college. A filmmaker!

We are almost downtown. We can see the big bridge and exit the DVP. "Look – take a left here – onto Parliament – take it slow." He directs me, even though I know the way. "You know, your driving's bad today," he continues. "You made that turn like you were going round a mountain." He taps his fingers against the dashboard in a nervous rhythm. "You know I need you to stay focused. What we're doing is no joke."

"I know that," I say.

"I'm not talking about driving no damn car… talking 'bout this meeting. I've got big plans. They're not going to give us no trouble, but I don't want no surprises either. Got your glock?"

"It's in the bag."

"What's it doing in there? You think they're gonna give you time to reach into your bag and find it?" He slaps his head. "What's wrong with this boy?"

I pull into the underground parking lot.

"They shouldn't make any trouble because I paid them back their money," he says.

"Then why are you worried?"

"If we carry ourselves with confidence, they'll know everything's okay. Back to normal."

"Are things not normal?" Should I be worried?

Rageev catches my gaze in the rear view mirror, wills me to look up at him. He takes my chin in his hand. For a rare moment, I remember the old Rageev. The electricity I used to feel when I first met him. How fearsome he must have been when he was young.

"Stay sharp," he says.

Inside the building, they're having a meeting. The usual suspects. Not as packed as when Soothy and I came by ourselves, but there's discussion. People are not happy. They're talking about strategies to get Canadians' attention.

"We have to do the chain again," says the guy from Tamil Nadu.

"The chain didn't work," says Old Guy. "All it did was create a news story."

"Some politicians are listening to us," says a young woman in the back. I recognize the voice. It's Abirami. Good thing we didn't bring Soothy. Try and hang in the doorway so she won't see me. "We just need to keep pressing them," she continues. "They'll see our situation." I don't see her father.

"Politicians won't do anything!" someone else shouts from the front. "They're too slow. Everybody'll be dead. All they'll do is wring their hands. We need to act now!"

Muruges sees us from the front. He excuses himself quietly, picks up his stiff shaking leg, comes to join us. Karthik, Mr Dark Moustache, separates himself from the back wall, silent as a shadow, falls behind Muruges. I was looking straight at him when I saw Abirami. Didn't even see him. That's how still he is. I imagine that imploded blob in his left eye behind the glasses, the black hole. Shivers down my back.

In the hallway, Muruges and Rageev stare each other up and down. Both cross their arms.

"Well, you've done it, you've really done it now. You're a first-class genius," says Muruges

"What do you mean?" asks Rageev. "We paid you your money." He's leaning in too far. His words come like spit at Muruges. Karthik puts a hand between them, pushes Rageev back.

"Who asked you to do that?" barks Muruges after a while. Half turning away from Rageev, looking at the room down the hall. The door is closed. We can hear arguing through the thick door. The voices mesh with the sound of washing machines, the smell of laundry detergent and mould. "Now you're in worse trouble than before, machan. We can't help you. We can't be seen to get involved."

"What do you mean?" asks Rageev, words almost becoming a whine. "I've worked very hard for you."

"Yes, but you're stupid. I don't care anymore if you are the father of Yalini's child. I asked you to get back the money, but not in such a way that it'll come back to us! Don't you think we have enough trouble already with everything back home? You're going to ruin us faster than the army. I don't have time to clean up and smooth over your messes!"

"They've been in contact with you?" asks Rageev edgily.

Karthik and I look at each other. Just the barest hint of a nod. A smile never touches his lips.

"Of course, of course! Are you a complete fool? Did you think you were just going to walk away? You haven't paid us back – you've created such a problem for yourself that we've got to distance ourselves from you."

"I thought you'd protect me. Think of all the work I've done for you."

"And now you're useless. You're a liability."

"You're just going to cut me off like that?"

"You think the end of a gun can solve everything. They have connections more powerful than guns, more powerful than us. We are stretched too thin now. Our partnership is not worth it."

"Well, set up a meeting for me to speak to them at least," pleads Rageev. "Tell them I'm willing to atone – they can bill me for what I've done, extra points – I don't care. Whatever it is, I'll pay it off."

Muruges takes me in also with his glance before answering. "This is right where you were when I lent you the money in the first place, only worse. I'll think about it. Don't call me in the meanwhile."

He turns and hobbles back into the meeting. Karthik joins him.

* * *

Another driving lesson with Mr N. I pull the Toyota Echo out of the school's cold parking lot. Feel my foot's weight hover over the brake, know he's doing the same thing over the instructor's brake. For an hour we act in tandem. I'm allowed to pull the car out of the parking lot now, take it round the neighbourhood. The school's in a residential area. Lots of stops. A lot of 40 km/h speed signs and pedestrians. I feel the urge to move my foot from the brake to the gas pedal. Just gun it. But my foot stays frozen. Mr N looks at me sternly as we pull out. He has no idea that I've driven beyond a parking lot.

"You know you're getting good, Niranjan" he says, relaxing. "Watch that stop line. Stop before the line. No rolling stops!"

I let go of the brake pedal, begin driving again. "I can go for my G2 soon?"

"I think so," he replies. "You've been doing really well in class too. You're coming, working with your group members. I liked what you did with your Scorsese presentation."

"You liked the presentation video I made about his movies?"

He slaps my shoulder, startling me. "It was good, except you didn't mention your sources. You've got to mention your sources." He reminds me to check my mirrors every seven seconds. Not get distracted. "Besides, you really like those movies, don't you?" He continues to smile. "You weren't just doing it for the grade – you were passionate about your presentation."

"Yeah, some of the other guys think it's an easy class," I reply, not looking away from my mirrors. "I like what he does with the gangster movies. They're not like Godfather or Scarface. Something real that he does, the way they talk. He connects scenes through emotion. You feel them."

"Yes, that's right. I like his ostentatious camera movements, the way it kinetically comes together. It's euphoric."

Not sure what he means by 'kinetic movements'. Or 'euphoric'. I just concentrate on driving. "You've gotten really good!" he continues. "Whomever you're learning from, it's not me. Just keep it up. You handle turns well, you accelerate and decelerate to posted limits.

"Look, pull over here," he says, pointing to the side. "Turn on the heat."

I do what he says. He rubs his gloved hands together and looks at me. "What is it?" I ask.

"Well…" He opens his mouth as if he's going to say something, then thinks better of it. He picks it up again, rumbles ahead cautiously. "I want to talk to you again about where your life's headed. Now wait a minute, wait a minute. I have to ask – did you have anything to do with what happened at Mr Raptis's house a while ago?"

"What happened at Mr. Raptis's house?"

"Oh come on – you know!" He turns around and stares at me. "Everybody knows. Some kids threw a firebomb through his front window."

"I didn't know it was kids. Anyway, he wasn't a nice guy to people. Maybe he deserved it."

"He could have died, Niranjan. His house could have burned down. I hope you didn't do it. Maybe he was difficult, but we can t go around beating people up."

"Why are you telling me this?"

"Because of the people you hang around. I know some of what goes on in that apartment building. Those are the kinds of Tamils that give us a bad name. They go around assaulting and killing people without thinking. Our own people too – doesn't that make you sick?"

"What do you care?" I ask angrily. "You don't care about us Tamils."

He pulls back. "What do you mean?"

I regret saying it, but it's already too late. "You're just like Mr Raptis and Ms Varley. You're one of them. Not like us. You're part of the school – you just want to push us through, then forget us."

"Are you upset about something? You can't be telling me that the gang you hang around cares more about you than we do, at school?"

I try to eyefuck him, but I can't do it. I don't have the meanness. He was right about Janelle Rochester, and he's probably right about Rageev and Soothy. But it's too late now, isn't it? I made a pact. They're my brothers, and I can't put them down. "It's all gangs, Mr N. Don't you realize that? We're all living in gangs. Your school, or the Tigers, or the army, or the country you belong to. The family you're in. It's all gangs, anyway. The one that wins just happens to decide what's right."

"Okay, how about this?" he says. "I won't say anything. You do the talking. Tell me what it is you see for yourself. In five years. Seven. Where do you see yourself with this mentality?" I don't say anything. I've said too much. He goes real quiet, then asks, "Do you even see yourself alive in five years? The way you're going?"

What a question! "Maybe not!" I blurt, hands on the wheel. He can tell I'm upset. He makes sure the parking handbrake is on. He reaches over and slowly turns off the ignition. "I can't see nothin," I say.

"Shouldn't it matter?" he asks carefully. "It would matter if it were my life."

"That's because you have a future," I say, gesturing with my hands. That's something Rageev sometimes says to me. "You have parents. You have a career," I continue. "You have a girlfriend. You have something to be proud of and look forward to. You don't know how lucky you are."

"And you have time," he replies. "You can have all those things too. You have time – the ability to make choices. So what if everybody else is a little younger than you in college? In a few years, it won't matter. I'll never be able to make those choices again. You could really become a filmmaker if you wanted. Do it right, not like me. Maybe it's a good thing you don't have parents telling you what to do – you're free from all that."

"I don't know if I have time," I sigh. "What matters is how you live your life right now. Isn't it? What your values are in the moment."

"Okay, well, tell me. What values do you live by? What do you want?"

"I don't know. A nice girlfriend maybe. Somebody who'll really love me."

"Okay," he says real slow, like he's humouring me. Makes me angry. Then he says, "I care where you'll be at in five years. Whether you're dead or alive. We both came here with little on our backs from a country where land mines and falling shells kill people at any moment. It doesn't make sense to come from a country like that, and then kill each other."

You couldn't really argue with that.

"It doesn't make sense to come to this country and just copy another culture," he adds. "Why would you want to do that?"

"Black people? The gangster stuff? But you're dating a black woman yourself!"

"We're engaged, more or less." He looks out the windshield and nods his head. "You know, my father used to beat me too. So what if your aunt was harsh? Don't go throwing it all away now, just because you can."

"Mr N, why couldn't you adopt me? I could be a son to you." I'm surprised to find there are tears in my eyes as I ask the question. He freezes. His easy condescension is gone. The words sucked right out of him. "I would be a good son to you," I continue, my throat going tight. "Most of the hard work would be done – you wouldn't have to clean up after me. I'd just live with you for a few years. You could help me get into college, and then I'd be off your hands! Promise!" I rush through the last part before I lose my nerve.

He looks like the blood's been drained out of him – he doesn't want a child. Know I should never have asked him. What a stupid question! Stupid, stupid me! Rageev and Soothy's problems. Has me tied up in knots. Can't get out.

Finally, Mr N says in a broken voice, "You know we can't. I can't! We're trying to have a child of our own. Ms Varley would never go for it."

"Congratulations."

We both sit there for a couple of minutes.

"Besides," he continues, "you can't adopt someone after they're sixteen. That's when you're no longer a dependent in this country."

It's an awful conversation.

"Niranjan, you've got to get out of there," he rambles on. "You don't know what you're mixed up in. That older guy who runs with you – he went to our school. I've heard some stories about him. You're not of the same cloth. Trust me. You should get yourself out of their company. I don't want you to end up like Seelan." He feels very far away now.

"Yo, man, Seelan was stupid." I'm trying to regain my toughness.

"Fine," he sighs and looks out the windshield. In that sigh, I can hear a thousand judgements.

I've had enough of driving. All the backseat drivers in my life. I get out of the car. He can drive it back himself. You're lucky Soothy or Rageev aren't here, I think to myself. They'd have smacked you for just opening your mouth. But whether it's him I'm talking to… or myself… I'm not sure. The cold air whooshes in as I open the door. Our breath becomes hard like ice. Snow is supposed to fall tomorrow. It's ramping up to that.

"Wait," he whispers, but I'm already walking away.

Cold air surrounds us. "Later," I say.

I don't wait to hear his reply.

DANIEL

The anger over the night Lynn and I visited my parents had to recede eventually. Like all things, it ebbed with a gradual dissatisfaction. My father went to work, made his rounds, more morose and self-pitying than usual. They had probably convinced themselves that they had been the perfect hosts, and it was me who had dealt injury simply by foisting Lynn upon them.

When my mother called as if nothing had happened and asked me to help my father shovel the snow, because he, as she put it, "was killing himself out there, day after day," what could I do? What could I do?

I sat quietly on their plastic-covered couch. My mother served tea. The cup stood on its saucer, growing cold, as we sat in uncomfortable silence. My father stared out the window, and my mother silently worked on her sewing, her head down. The anger in me still buzzed inside my chest and around my head. I couldn't resist saying my piece.

When they asked why I hadn't called since then, I replied, "You really treated us like shit. That's why. It's all you ever do. No matter how old I get, you treat me like shit."

My father looked startled, then turned away again to stare at an angle through the large window. Was monitoring the snowfall more important than what I said? Was he keeping a lookout for the Tamils and their clipboards? What went on inside that grizzled old head of his? After all these years, I still didn't know him. My mother smirked, without raising her head from her sewing.

"You think this is funny?" I asked. It bothered me – on a good day, I could deal with a class of difficult and rowdy students with calm efficienc , but these two could always get under my skin in minutes. They seemed to live for it.

"She's black," pronounced my father finall , as if it were some great revelation. "Do you know the values these people have? Do you? The way they drink and smoke drugs. Do they think about their responsibilities? Open the paper and take a look – that's the kind of people she comes from."

"I'm going to marry her," I said, less sure than ever that I would. After all these years, my parents still had the power to make me doubt my convictions.

"You think anybody will come to your wedding?" laughed my father.

"You're trying to hurt us, but you're only hurting yourself," added my mother, now looking up. "Your sister's married, and she's part of someone else's family. We only have you left. We want to help you – we care about you."

"You want to control me." I emphasized the words, allowing each to derisively roll off my tongue. "You want to live inside my body, inhabit my brain. That's all you ever wanted. Your hearts beat control, not love."

"We did everything for you children," my mother said simply. To her, it was a universal truth, well known. "All we expected was that you'd listen to us once in a while. For your own good."

"You shouldn't have had children if you didn't want to put in the work to build bonds. Building a family takes effort, you know. You don't have children and then blame them for the work it takes to raise a family."

"What do you know about it? You left as soon as it was convenient. You only think of yourself." My father had made out that he was taking everything lightly by grinning sarcastically, but the moody oppressiveness of his manner could be heard in his grinding teeth. The clouds around his brow had been darkening for some time. His hands plunged into fists in his lap as his body bent forward, focusing its anger on me. "If you didn't want to take my advice and become a doctor, it's your loss. I gave up everything – my position, my standing – to come here, and for what? For what? You think I worked in a factory, you think I work as a security guard, because that's what I wanted? I did it all for you and to make your mother happy. She kept pushing me, and I gave up everything."

My mother looked down when he said this. I couldn't see her face. My father continued, "If you and your sister had become doctors, you would have reaped the benefits of what we sacrificed. You had chances and chances – opportunities I never had. Everything I did was a waste. Ultimately it didn't benefit you or me.

This pushed upon my last inch of forbearance. What bullshit! I wanted to vomit. "You came here on your own choice, your own recognizance!" I screamed. "We never had any say in it! When did you ever ask me? When did you ever ask me what I wanted? You didn't like what was going on in Sri Lanka – you helped yourselves by coming here! When did you ask what I thought?"

He gazed at me with wearied patience. "Again? We've gone over this. You were a child. Why would I have asked you? You were still a child when you said you wanted to go into film. What happened to that? What did you make of yourself? You only threw away money on a student loan. You should have helped us with that money. You should have stayed at home and helped your sister get into medical school. If you knew what you were doing, you would have done something with your life by now." I didn't have a response to this. I wanted to tell him that he'd abused me, abused us, had manipulated and controlled us. But the words wouldn't come. To that day, I couldn't tell him what I really thought. The thoughts pressed like boulders against my chest. They weighed me down with insistent pressure, but I just couldn't let go. As if, by letting those particular words go, my very identity would disperse and float away. Not just a fear that I'd cry or emotionally implode, but that I'd be nothing at all. All I could do was talk and talk around the thing. These thoughts, these circumlocutions, had no effect against him at all.

"You hit us, but you never hit Amma," I said. "Why is that?"

"You're joking," he began. My mother snorted but only continued sewing her cloth. "You were my children," he continued finally, "my flesh and blood. She wasn't." He managed a dignity that I could only envy. I didn't agree with him, and I thought he was crazy, but he possessed a dignity that I just couldn't penetrate with questions and statements.

"Well, I don't want to marry someone you pick out for me," I retorted. "I'm going to marry Lynn – sooner or later. I don't want to be part of this culture you think is so great if this is what it is. I don't want to be part of this. I'm happy to have children with her, and I'll never force them to do anything, let alone be this fucked up idea of what you think it is to be Tamil. You'll never even meet them."

My father's eyes shrivelled, and his cheeks tightened in a rictus of anger. The impact of my words was finally beginning to show on his face. He began to wheeze lightly, and my mother got up, abandoned her sewing, and walked over, stroked his shoulder and calmed him down. "There, there," she said, ignoring me completely.

"See how he talks to me," wheezed my father.

My chest was straining too, lungs heaving.

"That's the way they all talk nowadays," soothed my mother in calming tones, pretending I was not there, that they were talking about me in my absence.

"You cause me nothing but pain and trouble," she muttered, finally glancing at me

"You act as if you're the ones who are pained and suffering," I said. "You're monsters." This was not a typical fight. Usually, our conversations were brusque and filled with residual tension. I only ever carped about one or two things at a time. I held off. But now I was dangerously close to forcing everything open. I was emptying my gall. It felt briefly empowering – there was a fleeting sense of power that came. My head felt dizz .

"At least we tried," he finally spat. "We tried and helped you two. And when you weren't grateful, we tried to help others."

"You tried to help others too?" I asked. "This I have to hear – who did you try and help?"

"We helped Niranjan, didn't we?"

"Niranjan?" I laughed. "Niranjan he's a criminal. He joined a gang. Did you know that? Oh yes, I'm pretty sure of it. He's living with criminals. That's how much your help fucked him up. But you should be used to that. There's no saving him! He's committed. I think he firebombed another teacher's house. Oh yes. How do you like that?"

I picked up my tea and blew on it for effect, but it had long gone cold.

My father got up from under my mother's hands and jutted his body towards the doorway. As he put on his winter coat and boots, we understood that he meant to go out and shovel, despite it being late. He didn't wish to talk.

"Leave it, leave it until the morning," said my mother.

The rage and frustration simmered off his body. "Nobody's asking you to come help me," he hissed. "When did any of you lift a finger to help me?" He looked at me expectantly. I stared at the teacup, then put it down.

When I didn't move, he immediately went back to the closet and pulled on his gloves, wrapped his scarf. I stayed on the plastic-covered couch and even squared my shoulders to prove he could not emotionally manipulate me with his antics. He slammed the door shut with a dramatic clang and went out there. We could hear the wind howl as the door briefly opened

My mother became hysterical now. "What are you doing? What are you doing?" she shouted. "Put on your boots and go outside – help him!"

I refused and stood, or rather sat, my ground.

"Why should I?" I asked. "When did you ever think about me or do something because I asked you to? All you ever did was serve me to that man on a platter. You let him beat me and beat me, and you never said a word or lifted a finger. You're supposed to be my mother, but all you ever do is let me down. You'd sell me out at the drop of a hat."

She placed her bony hands to the sides of her face, hair unravelling and coming down in wisps, crying without tears in one of those rare moments of vulnerability she never exhibited to me or my sister. "All we ever do is think about you," she said. "All we ever do is worry about you."

We stared out the window to watch him methodically, slowly, chipping away at the snow. He was a dark blur against the icy, cold night. No one else was out there. He was crazy – my parents didn't even own a car. It was all borne out of some irrational fear that someone would slip on the ice and sue them.

My father was oblivious to our glances as he continued to shovel. Even through the window, I could feel his icy contempt for me radiate upon the wind. Something howled that was not wind itself but frozen waves of water surrounding him, something tidal carrying him away. We had never connected. Not once in all our lives had we bonded or shared a moment of warmth. For someone who avowed himself so much of his sacrifices, I'd never once heard him say that he was glad he'd had a family, that he was thankful he had children.

"What are you doing? What are you doing?" cried my mother. "Why don't you go out there and help him?"

We stood in the living room and watched my father through the large picture window. We watched as he shovelled, chipping away at the ice and sleet where it was hard, pushing the small shovelful of snow one row, then the next, panting, his body heaving as he worked. He could have been a worker ploughing the field in our village back home.

He was almost done as my mother finally began putting on her own winter clothes to go out and help. She glared at me, and I glared back.

By the time she made it outside, it didn't matter.

He collapsed, not falling, just crumpling down sideways, not letting go of the shovel until the very end. He didn't clutch his chest so much as his side, and it was still hard to see through the dark and snow. Though I couldn't hear him, I could see him mouth the words through the window, "See, I finished!" His face began twitching. The only sounds that came out of his throat after that were gurgles.

All that time, I watched and didn't move a muscle. Though it was winter, I could smell the smashed cherries in their neighbour's back yard. I saw flies gathering in a large cloud at the base of the tree. They feasted on the rotten pulped cherries that were no longer there.

The flies rose from the ground, as if one being, one force. It couldn't be possible, but the flies descended upon my father.

He had that heart attack we were all worried about right there on the driveway.

NIRANJAN

"I don't think I can teach class today," says Mr N in a tired voice. It's scratchy and it cracks. He hasn't shaved. He gets us to put on our coats and grab garbage bags from the caretaker. "We're going to walk through the fields in the back and pick up litter."

Nobody says anything.

We're in the middle of working on our storyboards for our school PSA's. I was trying to be serious about it.

We all realize there's something wrong when he puts on his own coat, hanging in the corner, and boots. He then begins shutting down the classroom lights. He doesn't talk or even look at us. Usually, he has to shout three or four times to get us all to listen. Now, nobody says a thing.

We go to our lockers, grab our coats, then get garbage bags – one bag for each group. I'm with Nadesan, Raj, and Kumar, as usual.

It's winter, but it's not a bad day. Actually pretty, although cold.

I see the Tuxedo Court in the distance. For a second, walking with Nadesan and Raj and Kumar, I almost feel like one of them, like somebody looking at the Court from outside. As we pick up pop cans and candy bar wrappers, the odd sheet of student homework, a styrofoam cup, and put these in the bag, I feel like I'm looking at the grounds through new eyes. Their eyes. Without the dirt and grime, things look almost fresh.

The school sits pleasantly on the edge of the fields. The hills roll and run into the ravine. Everything else is normal Scarborough – strip malls and apartment buildings and electrical towers – but this one part is beautiful. "The soil's eroding," says Mr N, walking beside us. "The soil is rich in minerals and ions. When I was young and lived around here, the water trickled more strongly. It seemed alive then. A musical burble. The notes of thinning brook, slapping rock, were counterpoint to the moss and sand. One shaped the other so that matter became liquid, and liquid evaporated into air."

"Are you talking about this land?" asks Nadesan.

"No, no, not just this land. At one time, that's what we believed. In the eighties when I got here, the environmental movement was strong. We were led to believe that the Canadian dream of multiculturalism was a corollary to that. Immigrants and white Canadians all mixing in, one mosaic."

"By the time we got here, most of the white people had left," says Kumar.

"Yeah, those that had a little money moved to better areas."

"Mr Raptis told me that at one time," begins Raj, "the Seneca Indians populated Scarborough. They fought the Mohawk, and archeologists find shards and pottery remains from both tribes. Is that true? He says it's hard to tell which is which."

Mr N glances at me when Raptis comes up, then looks away quickly as though he's embarrassed. I look away too. If the other guys pick up on it, they don't say.

"Mr N, is it true?"

"I don't know." He walks away, picks up a broken hair clip with his gloved hand, comes back to put it in the garbage bag.

"How many postage stamps can you fit on a football field?" he asks, pointing at LCC s football field

"What?" asks Raj.

"It was a thought problem designed by Enrico Fermi. Mr Raptis told it to me once. How many postage stamps would it take to cover a football field?

"Too many – it's impossible."

"No, it's not," he replies, jutting his chin towards the snow-covered field. "You can figure out the dimensions of a standard football field and measure the edges of a local postage stamp. After that, it's just plain arithmetic."

Not long ago, it had been fall. My life had been carefree. Relatively carefree. I remember the red track mostly lost in the dirt and dust, overgrown grass, and dry leaves. The spines and veins of the leaves that had been ground into flakes and powder by runners and football players. Everything beautiful in the golden light and cool air. Me sitting on that swing in the park with Mr N and Thambi. How can that only have been months ago?

Now the trees are nude, as Mr N might say. We can hear his thinning brook, if we listen closely, through the denuded trees and icy wind. The air broken by the cries of birds. The water slaps against rock. Sounds like the ghostly footfalls of the native Indians. The ones that once ran through these fields. In front of the hill, where we stand, you can see the Tuxedo Court buildings where people without hope struggle to live their lives.

Mr N looks like he's going to cry. I step back. Whatever is in him, the core holding him together, breaks. I feel it hover above my own head. The river from the ravine runs through my body and his. We are linked. I feel his molecules and particles break apart in front of me, on that hill halfway between the school and the Court. I do not want to be caught up in the forces that rip him.

"My father died," he says, "of a heart attack. I wish I could have given him something of my own life to bring him back, but he died at the hospital... and it's all my fault."

One of the guys clears his throat.

"When's the funeral?" asks Kumar.

"This weekend."

"Are you ready?"

"No. I have no idea what I'm doing."

The sun is high in the sky now. We can see activity on the balconies of the distant Tuxedo towers. It's sad, I suppose. One death in this snow-covered country in which we have exiled ourselves. One death standing crisply against the tide crashing into the East and North of Sri Lanka. A whole tide of death that is to sweep over us, sweep over the Tamil people.

Somehow I know we're all thinking this.

When it is done, there will be no counting the casualties. Mr N's father is like a preview from fate, a relief of the coming attractions. There will be more deaths than postage stamps on a Fermi football field. Counting bodies will be impossible. My parents will probably suffer too. And what will I be able to do to save them? Nothing. In this way, Mr N and I are alike. Death will ride his horse thick through the bodies, and the Grim Reaper will work harder than a single mom with a thousand mouths to feed.

The bodies will pile so high that if they form a tower out of them, they'll fill up the Tuxedo buildings in a day. Climb so high towards the heavens, even the Gods might have to look down and take notice.

DANIEL

A vision of my father laid out in the snow haunted my dreams. Not his body but a substitute: a series of clay canisters, lying out in the cold, sundered and lifeless. Made of red Jaffna earth, the clay vessels lay quartered, each quarter pointing in a different angle. The snow comes down and settles on the shards, fills the cavities, slowly piles up until there is more snow than clay. The flies from the smashed cherry tree hover above the shards.

Apparently, my father had suffered from an embolism. He should not have been shovelling snow. But maybe, just maybe, I should not have told him the news about Niranjan. Should not have thrown it in his face like that. I was just so sick of him comparing me to everybody else, and finding me wanting. I never had a chance. If I were to compare him to the parents out there – the happy, balanced, functional parents of the world – how would he fare? Surely, he would have been lacking himself. Severely so. He could not express honest emotion or love. Let alone find fulfilment in simple pleasures. But I should not have said the thing about Niranjan. I should have let him preserve his illusions. I'd been loyal for many Sundays up until then. I should not have exaggerated Niranjan's situation like that. I did not know how he lived.

But my father should not have always put me down. They should not have treated Lynn as they had. Not if they were people who could honestly appraise themselves and others. But which of us can? Did I have a hand in killing him or was Niranjan responsible for getting himself into the trouble that he did? Who was most responsible for my father's death: Niranjan, my father, or myself?

The memory of him shovelling the snow and collapsing without a sound came back to me. I always thought I would instantly know when he was ready to die, would feel a cold absence within me, freedom perhaps. Instead, it had been sudden. It couldn't be true, I told myself. My mother just stood there pushing me to go out. The final message from her was a whimper, her throat hoarse, telling me that she was going to call my sister. She would call Napoleon before she called an ambulance. That's how unreal it was.

I had stood in the freshly shovelled driveway, willing my energy to flow into him, bring him back to life. If I could have used some ancient yogic technique to transfer my life energy into his, I would have done it. I even mumbled a prayer to that effect. But all that came out of me was frozen air.

I could not touch him. Even in death, he scared me.

* * *

Napoleon and my mother made arrangements to hold the services at a funeral home west of my parents' house on Lawrence Avenue, close to Morningside. My mother wanted to get the Sai Baba people involved, but Napoleon and I convinced her against it. They could attend but would not be running the show. We settled on a pseudo-Hindu ceremony combined with a Christian viewing at the funeral home's chapel, followed, of course, by an instant cremation of the body as Hindu custom required.

Lynn was supportive and understanding. We decided I should go alone so as not to upset my mother. My sister and Mahesh graciously paid the costs of the funeral and cremation.

That image of the four clay canisters lying on the ground, cracked and irreparably broken, came to me again as I viewed him in the casket. The snow filling up the canisters' cracks and cavities. He'd climb out the coffin any moment now and hector us for the poor job we'd made of the funeral arrangements.

I did not recognize him in that casket, shrunken, in a suit that was not his security uniform. Even the hair that had always seemed so wild and unruly, a white shock of flame around his withered head, the bone seeping out in tendrils from his cranium, now seemed lifeless. It was neatly combed and lay flat against the pillow. Fanned out around his cheeks. The undertakers had dressed him in a suit that seemed too large for his body. Was this the terror that had held sway over my life? His body had been turned and composed, smothered in formaldehyde, embalming fluid, and ointments. He would never say an angry word again. However, despite the formaldehyde, the ointments, the smell of mustiness and stricture still hung over his body like a dry cloud.

The ceremony began with the priest and his assistant chanting. People from the Sai Centre went up in ones and twos to pay their respects to the man who lay dark and still, withered, with garlands around his neck. There was oil in his hair, rouge on his lips. They had only tolerated him when he lived – my mother was the zealous one.

Mahesh and I greeted people. Thambi and his older brother Roshan and their mother came by with lowered heads. Roshan and Mrs Navaratnam smiled at me distantly. Thambi seemed very embarrassed. He was the only one who knew how I felt, I suppose, this terrible confusion and numbness. He sensed it.

"Look, I'm real sorry," he said. "I'm so sorry for what happened, man."

My hand shook, but I was able to place it very lightly on the padded shoulder of his jacket and smile.

Amma sat in the first pew of the chapel, crying her heart out for the both of us. She wailed as it was customary for Tamil women to do, supported by her Sai Baba friends. Napoleon sat at the front too, and shook mourners' hands as they filed past. All the women who had come wore saris under their winter coats. The men wore white shirts and neatly pressed black pants.

The priest went to the end of the coffin and lowered a flame over my father's head. His assistant handed him a tumbler of water, which followed the flame. The tumbler held large green leaves in it, and the priest took water out with the tips of his fingers, sprinkling it over my father's body. They washed him with a sponge and strewed flowers over him. The flowers fell with a muffled clumping that I imagined would annoy him no end. I imagined his body heaving to shrug them off. They were nothing compared to the fresh flowers he would have planted on his postage stamp of a lawn this spring. His eyes, closed, simply seemed to stare up from beneath the lids at whomever passed by.

Amma and Napoleon stood up with sticks of incense to recite a bhajan song he had supposedly liked.

Finally, the priest got me to circle around the coffin counter clockwise, carrying a small metal pot with a coconut in it perched on my left shoulder. I did this three times, and each time the priest hit the coconut with a machete. I felt the shudder run up my arms and realized how alone, how utterly lost I was. I had no idea what any of these rituals meant, and if the priest had not directed me, I would have stood there like a simpleton. A pleasurable rivulet of pain shot through my palms every time he struck the coconut, juddering my wrist and shoulder. It was nice to feel something. The assistant sprinkled the coconut water that fell from the coconut, the final showering of ritual.

The casket was closed.

My mother looked at her husband, disappearing from view as the lid closed upon the coffin, as elegant and simple and final a goodbye as she would ever get. Her head bent to the side as far as she could go to see him disappear, the lid closing shut. Gales of tears broke from her anew.

And then I supported her as best I could to the room next door, where it was my job to push the button. Where we would watch him burn. It was a small red button beside the window through which we could see the casket, and people had followed us there to witness the final stage

I felt conflicted. Part of me wanted to watch him burn. I wanted to destroy his corpse completely so that he would have no more hold over our lives. I wanted to eradicate all trace of his existence with flame. I thought that with his incineration all the bitterness and misery which had run its course could finally evaporate. The other part of me was scared of losing him forever. The impressions and presence of him in my life.

Could he really be dead? Somehow, I had thought he would live to gloat and make a final analysis over how thoroughly I'd messed things up. It must be some trick, some test, some final summing up. I imagined being at his knee, staring at the second hand make its way around the dial of his watch one final time as he assessed my performance as an adult. If I were in Sri Lanka, I would have had to lay him out on a pyre in some field and set the torch to kindling, everything so magnificent and immediate.

"Go ahead and do it," whispered my sister, a cold edge to her voice.

When she saw that I couldn't, small as she was, she reached up over my shoulder, grabbed my right index finge , and pressed it to the red button.

The flames roared to life, and we watched the casket burn. My mother wailed quietly.

Afterwards, Napoleon, Mahesh, my mother, and I stood outside in the hard cold sunshine, watching cars pull away. The last of the mourners were finding their coats, murmuring to each other. When the urn was ready, we would retrieve it and bury it in the bungalow's front garden beside the flowers and mulch my father so loved. We would have to wait for the ground to lose its hardness.

The time between the cremation of those embers and our progress to the top of the stairs outside gathered epochs. His death, like the opening of some play, now behind us, was an assured fact. The last of the attendees proved it. My mother looked at us and said, "There's barely any money. Did you know that? How will we pay for the house?"

I felt a dry heave come up.

"What's wrong?" asked Mahesh.

"I didn't have lunch today. My stomach's all tied up."

Napoleon who had been strangely silent until now said, "I suppose you'd better come live with us. Daniel's not going to support you."

"She doesn't accept Lynn," I said weakly. I could see that Napoleon still possessed her youthful looks, even now, but her cheeks drooped and her hips sagged. Her profile was tired. The tight line of her smile, which normally expressed displeasure, curled downwards. She looked more and more like our mother. Her shoulders were still pulled back underneath her coat though – there was still a glimmer of anger in her voice as she laughed.

"We haven't talked about it," replied Napoleon, turning to face me. "What exactly happened that day?"

"Let's discuss it some other time," said Mahesh.

"No, let's talk about it now. Amma says you two got in an argument."

"They're the ones who caused it," I defended myself. "They were horrible to Lynn when they met her."

"Um-hmm." Her smile tightened into a straight line again. "You know, there's a lot you don't know since you moved out. Sometimes he'd fall asleep on the couch and talk about going over the hill and seeing his village. He thought he was in Sri Lanka. He was a sick man."

"He just played that up," I said. "He had no awareness about what he did or the way he talked, but not in the way that you mean. He thought everybody was wrong, and he was always right."

"So do you," countered Napoleon. "No one can talk to you either." In the absence of our father, she argued with me and pulled my chain. She seemed to stand in for him.

"He just died," whispered my mother, trying to hush us both. "Let his memory rest."

"Yeah, your tone's certainly changed since the person you used to gang up with is no longer here," I responded bitterly.

"You know, you people really are something else," said Mahesh, smugness exuding from his stick insect voice.

"Shut up!" snapped my sister. He became quiet.

I remembered the time I had come into the living room to see our father prostrate himself in front of her in mock obeisance, acknowledging her superior will.

As if reading my mind, Napoleon said, "I just used my head and made some practical decisions. It's called thinking ahead. If you want to be a filmmake, be a filmmake. Why do you have to talk and talk and do things in the most difficult way?

"You used to say that you were doing everything for them, that you were becoming a doctor, so it was okay. That's how you rationalized the fact that they poured so much money and effort into you, remember? Remember the path you picked? Well, you didn't become a doctor, did you? You just married one."

At this, her face fell again, and the angry stars in her eyes dimmed a little. We both remembered her deep depression upon graduation when her husband was still in medical school and she didn't know what to do. The only one living at home with our parents. When I did visit, she resented me being there. If she had gotten into medical school herself, perhaps she could have held her own against them.

"Remember all that Sai Baba stuff you did?" I said, continuing to rub it in. "All that character education? Where is it now? It just seems to me that you sold out, got as much money as you could, and ran. You always said that I was selfish for moving away and leaving you, but what does that make you?"

"Do we have to fight today?" she asked in a sad, tired, tone.

"I'm sorry," I replied.

Her head nodded slightly. In the past, she would have replied with something like, "You're always sorry." Perhaps something else to cut me down. Now she stood there alone, diminished by our father's absence. Almost as if our mother and Mahesh were floating elsewhere. It was just the two of us with our painful history.

"Appa had a very tough time growing up," she said. "There's trauma there. Appapa and Appuchi sound like they were very demanding parents."

"I remember them," I replied, nodding sympathetically. "You were too young, but I knew them before they died. It seems like we Tamils are always paying it backward instead of forward."

"Why do we act like this?" Malathi whispered, looking me in the eyes.

I didn't know if she meant us two or our whole family or what.

"Because we were hit," I said finall . "It's at the root of everything."

She nodded again. She understood. It was why we fought. It was why we couldn't love in the first place. We had more anger and recrimination towards each other than love. My father's heart beat control, and we adjusted ourselves accordingly. It was why I dated Lynn and hoped to make things work with her. It was why I couldn't marry a Tamil girl. This was at the heart of all that pain and madness. It was why my sister was sucked into her husband's family, but could do nothing about it. She used to worry, before she married him, that once he saw the mean side of her, it would be over. Now they knew each other too well.

We said goodbye to the last person who waved from afar, and then we all walked down the steps. Mahesh held my sister's hand. She was so small that a winter coat inevitably looked huge on her. She disappeared into it and her winter boots, and became nothing more than a short glimpse of black sari, skinny leggings, and long hair.

Napoleon had once told me, firml , declaratively, that we were not friends. Worse than that, we did not even feel like family. I remembered the time my father had taken us to the supermarket and asked us to pick out the canes for our corporal punishment. The blue or the red. All we had to link us together was pain. Not love, but pain. We were barely family – I was closer to some of my students than I was to her.

NIRANJAN

"It's okay, don't worry – there's a process here," says Rageev. How many times have I heard this before?

We are sitting in our car at a stop sign. This is the meeting Muruges and Karthik have set up. They've brokered this meeting so that Rageev can figure out a way to repay the Koreans. And get us out from under this mess.

Rageev's cellphone screen flashes. He checks it. He'd allowed me to program the ring tone for him, and I'd chosen the howling flute notes from the soundtrack to The Good, The Bad, and The Ugly. I've got the DVD, but haven't watched it in more than a year. I wonder where my father is tonight. Wish I'd picked a different ring tone. Every time Rageev's phone rings, it makes me sad.

He reads the text, and then touches his burned skin thoughtfully. "Soothy's already there," he says, stroking his chin. "Muruges set up this meeting personally. Hopefully, he talked to them right. It's better for them to settle up with us quickly. They don't want their business interrupted any more than we do." He clasps my shoulder, tells me to get the glock out of my bag.

"Do I have to?"

"I don't think anything's gonna happen, but just in case. Put it inside your pants – remember what we taught you," he says.

"Okay." I remember the time Karthik gave us guns, then ordered us to shoot bottles in the ravine. Fire into the centre of mass. Strike a blow, defend myself. Didn't feel right then. I wasn't built for this.

Rageev has me drive to a Chinese restaurant on Painted Post. I realize with a sinking feeling it's the same restaurant the takeout came from. The takeout the boy had been eating until Soothy jammed chopsticks into his ears. Then set them on fire. I had slapped his face. Sticky blood and greasy lo mein. Something in my mind begins screaming.

Inside the restaurant, it's dark. Daytime, but snowing outside. Not much light comes in. Blinds are drawn, but not shut. Rays enter through slits. You can see all the dust dancing in the air like specks of eternity.

No one's in the restaurant. Just a middle-aged guy eating noodles in the far corner. An Asian-looking grandma eating dumplings, her back closer to us. A couple of large rubber plants with big purple blooms. Between the plants sits a tall thin waiter in a red and gold waistcoat. He's talking to Soothy across a table.

Soothy seems happy yet jumpy all at once. Haven't seen him this excited in a long time. Hands fluttering jerkily. I'm assuming the big .45's tucked in his waistband. Just like my glock. Hope I'm not the only one strapped. Soothy looks childish without his hood.

Rageev whistles.

They stop conversation. We hear the old people eating, those slow mushy sounds created by people who eat without closing their mouths.

The waiter leads us to the back, down the stairs. I expect the place to look like a shithole, a whole bunch of people drinking Tsingtsao beer, playing mahjong or something. It's nothing like that. Just a cold dark basement with no windows. A lot of vegetables and other food in cans and bottles, bending the sides of their waxed boxes with weight. Bottles of items like pickled bamboo shoots, tinned pork. Lots of Chinese labels.

There's a large pool table in the corner. Coloured balls and two cues lie on the felt, a game suddenly forgotten. Beside the pool table is a smaller card table. A drink and ashtray on it. A woman sits at the card table. She wears a cream suit with a green handkerchief in her breast pocket. I recognize her. She rocked the baby that time, held Geetha. Never talked.

She smokes now, holds her cigarette high as we walk in. Beside her are the two guys we stole from. One looks really bad. Signs of the beating still on his face. Much the same, frightened, shaking a little. His jaw has some kind of wire and padding around it that hooks onto his head. I freeze. I can't look at this guy. But I can't not look either. Rageev takes my shoulder as if to say easy.

The Asian lady watches us, hardly moving. Smoke from her cigarette drifts up. She has a severe updo. The two guys in shirts and suits from the first time we went downtown stand behind her. They don't move either.

She motions Rageev to sit down. There are no chairs for Soothy or myself.

The first guy we beat up, Mr Blood-and-Lo-Mein, has bruises all over his face. He's dressed in black jeans and black shirt, thick braid of gold resting on his chest. He flashes a smile at us. What does he know that we don't? Guy beside him, with the stuff all over his face, just shakes, shivering with fury. Twitching with fear and rage, spit slides out his mouth, falls onto the wire around his jaw.

Soothy and I hang back. Again, I'm reminded of a mirror reflection. The Asian guys. Only they don't move, while we keep fidgeting. The guys in suits are built, ready to rumble.

The woman and Rageev assess each other. I can feel their personalities through the dark haze. Sort of the same way I could feel the river flowing through Mr N. Something happening, but what? Her personality ripples out like a steel ribbon. It flicks the air.

I look at Soothy nervously. He holds his hands behind his back, close to where his gun should be.

I cough. Can't help it. The guy with stuff around his face. After living around Rageev and Muruges and Karthik, you'd think I'd be used to deformities.

"You brought guns?" the woman asks, staring hard, tapping her cigarette in the ashtray. "Why would you do that?"

"You tell me," replies Rageev, leaning back in his chair.

"Your people got in contact with us, so talk," commands the lady quietly, inhaling smoke and blowing it out. The smoke moves into her guards' faces, but they don't budge an inch. I remember her rocking the baby. She's a totally different person now.

"Where's the old man?" asks Rageev. "I came here to deal."

"Money isn't going to make right what he did to my boy," says the guy in black, speaking for the first time. He hasn't shaved. His voice is nasal. When he talks, his whole body jumps. Shoulders rack up and down. We really did a job on him.

"You want to get even?" asks Rageev, chuckling.

"We'll talk about them in a minute," says the woman. She brings her cigarette down and taps the ash into the gold-cubed ashtray. Something hypnotic about her. The gesture of bringing the cigarette down. Everything graceful, poised like a performance. Preplanned. She slows time down with her words. Maybe it's just me. Do others lose focus?

"You want to talk even?" asks Rageev. "Even doesn't come close to what I've paid. Seelan's gone, and I'm not even gonna mention what you did to my daughter." Seelan again. What is it with that name?

"What a big fool!" laughs the guy in black. The gold braid bounces up and down on his chest. "You're the guy they shot up on the highway? Big deal! Weren't you supposed to die?"

Soothy becomes even more agitated than me. "This bastard…" he whispers under his breath.

"Enough!" hisses the woman. The temperature in the room drops ten degrees.

Rageev scratches an itch.

Soothy starts to lose his cool. "Hey," he blurts, "are you guys Chinese or… North Korean?"

"Shut up, Soothy," says Rageev.

I know Soothy is hurt. As different as we are, I do live with him. His anguish comes clear through these emotional wires that seem laid between us.

Everybody can see Soothy fidget. His hands hover around the waistband of his jeans. The woman answers Rageev's previous question. "I'm in charge now. Why? You have problems dealing with a woman?"

Rageev shakes his head. Now I can taste his fear. Almost tastes like alcohol, like concentrated lemon. He starts to lean forward instead of back. I can no longer see his face, but I can imagine it. A bead of sweat, perhaps, runs down that groove where his skin divides. His tension all hunched in his back.

Soothy shoves his hand to the back of his jeans. The waiter who'd been calmly sitting down all this time, the one who'd been laughing and chatting so friendly with him upstairs, gets up. In a smooth motion, without stress or fuss, he places his hand on Soothy's forearm, locking his arm at the joint. All too fast for me to catch. The waiter has Soothy's arm twisted behind him by the time I look. Takes away Soothy's weapon as if Soothy's in slow motion. Soothy's beloved silver .45 now pointed at him. Panic in his eyes. The goons behind her haven't moved yet.

"Wait a minute," says Rageev. "We're here to do business with you. Look, I'm putting my hands up. I'm not touching my gun!" He puts his hands up to show good faith. Not sure that's a good idea. "There's more than enough for all of us to share. I give up any bad feelings I had from before. It won't interfere again." He gestures with an empty palm to the guy in black across from him. "We should be working together. There's no point – no profi – in carrying a feud."

"I don't care about profit anymore," says the guy in black.

"You heard him," says the lady. "I'm not my father. I don't have a soft spot for you. You understand what's going on? When you take something that belongs to somebody, you must pay for it. That's business. There is no aspect to life that does not work this way." She brings the cigarette down in a final flourish. Flattens it in the ashtray. The suits finally move, as if it's a signal. They come around either side of the lady and pull out their own guns. One is trained on Rageev. The other on me.

It all happens faster than I can understand. Sweat is pumped out my body. Adrenaline races through my heart. It knows before I do.

"You don't have to do this," says Rageev. "We're here to do business with you. I have money... I can get money..."

"You Tamils are so stupid," says the woman. Her words slap Rageev in the face. "Don't you think we've been watching you? The men you've been leaning on have given you up. They're finished. They know it.

"We know what's going on in your part of the world. In two months, three, do you think there'll be anyone left? You're a freak, an aberration. You have no organization, no discipline. It's because of people like us that you've been permitted to live. You shoot each other and take money from weak shopkeepers and small businesses. Are you proud of that?

"You come in here and tell me you're going to make more money. You don't feel sorry for what you've done, for the damage you've caused? And you think I'm just going to go along with it, because of your arrogance? You shouldn't have come in here."

Instead of buckling, though fury and desperation swim in his eyes, Rageev pulls on something. Something I haven't seen since the first few times I met him. Something different from me or Soothy. Something real that we never had. It got lost in the deals and the schemes with Muruges, his fears and hopes to have a family, a child.

It comes out now. He could plead, he could beg, he could tell them he has a girlfriend and child waiting for him. Instead, he says, "We're nothing like you." Then he looks at the two guys we beat up and spits on the floor. "I could have killed you, but I let you go. Remember that." Everyone waits to see what happens next. Rageev turns his attention back to the woman. "When you're gone and rotting, the Tamil dream will survive. I may be flawed, I may be weak, but we're fighting for something. Others will come after me. We will succeed. We produce doctors and engineers and scientists. We're the best. And we're determined. I fell into this, but I don't regret what I did because I did it with honour. Maybe even my child will understand, though you won't. She may go on and do something to change the world. She's Tamil. That's what's inside us."

Silence.

The woman chuckles. She looks around the room. People slowly begin to laugh. Rageev's words might have been brave or utterly foolish. I don't know. The laughter carries on, then dies out. "You're special," she smiles. "Just for you, I'm going to show you what's really inside of you."

I've been standing here so silently all this time. I have a gun. Even now, I can't bring myself to reach for it. I hear myself saying, from far away, "Please... he has a girlfriend and a daughter."

The lady finally turns her sharp eyes on me. She bores through me. I stare at her green handkerchief. This cannot be the same woman who cradled Geetha. The baby hadn't even cried. She knows I won't go for my gun. "If he were Korean, we would also have his girlfriend and daughter. We would make sure no one was left, you understand?

That would be the final message. But you're not Korean, are you? Just a bunch of pakis whose grasp extends further than your reach.

"A gun is a powerful weapon – not meant for children like you. Give it to me."

Before I know what I'm doing, my hand reaches for the glock, hands it over. Already in her hand before I realize. Something commanding and hypnotic about her voice. Gives me pleasure to obey.

Soothy scowls.

"I just want you to watch," she says to me. "And you…" she turns to Soothy, "you'd probably kill me if you could. Young and crazy. But this man is in charge of you, isn't he? He's the elder of your little family. Why should I punish the cubs when the tiger should have known better?"

Rageev finally goes for his gun. He knows all hope is lost. He has nothing to negotiate with now. His right arm reaches across his body. Unfortunately, it's all too slow. The goon closest to him has grabbed his arm, pinning it against the table. Rageev's fingers curl into a grip. The crack in his knuckles is drowned out by Rageev's head slamming down. I've never heard Rageev wince before. The muscles of his face stretch. An emotion I don't recognize.

Rageev is pinned. Soothy has a gun pointed against him. I am the only one free.

What a joke I am. Why did they ever take me in?

"You took our money and drugs," says the lady, coldly, now pointing dramatically with her cigarette-less fingers, "but I'm not going to insist you pay them back. I'm going to give you a lesson. You probably never had mothers to take care of you, to show you what was what – so I'm going to make up their shortfall. This is what happens in the real world."

She claps her hands and a couple more guys come down the stairs. More Asians. They're dressed in pale green scrubs. Doctor's masks on their faces, paper caps over their hair. Paper booties over their shoes. The one with the glasses carries a case. The other one has a huge plastic sheet. They go over to the pool table and, dropping what they're carrying, quickly clear the pool table of cues and balls.

"You see, for what you did, I should put those pool sticks in your ears and set them on fire," says the woman to Soothy, "but I'm going to teach you all a lesson instead."

The goons force Rageev over to the pool table. He struggles. Up until the end he struggles. A jungle heart or a fear-filled heart is all the same in the end. It's not enough. They have him on the pool table, and the Asian in the scrubs with glasses opens his case. He lays out things on a towel. He has syringes and bottles, needles, scalpels, even a small motorized circular saw. It's one of those times when I wish I didn't have an eye for detail. There are other things I don't recognize. I retch but only air comes out. I feel faint.

"Stay awake!" commands the woman. "You're going to see this! You think you Tamils are the only ones who can do things, become doctors and engineers?" She laughs. "You think you're the smartest people in the world? These two of mine could have gone into medicine, couldn't you?" She winks at me and Soothy. "You know, they're almost surgeons!"

Her trills of laughter hug the air.

I look at Soothy. He still has the gun trained against his head. He watches without saying a word. All the nervousness and bravado gone out of him. He looks on, helpless as I am.

They pump Rageev so full of dope they could have put an elephant to sleep. They just hold him, pull up his shirt, mainline it into a vein so fast I'm sure his heart will stop. His eyeballs roll upward. The eyelids flutter. Body stops struggling.

The lady looks on while her 'doctors' take the small circular saw to Rageev's head. They cut away his scalp. Go round his head. Scalp him like a Seneca warrior.

The sound of the saw, that motorized whirr, kills me. I can feel the saw blade scrape against bone. Rageev's bone. Cuts into my ears. The saw keeps cutting. All I can do is stare forward. Blood and gore fly onto the walls, the tables. Can't even see the cut anymore. Too much blood. Can feel it in my ears and my bones.

They keep cutting until they peel away his scalp. The one without glasses grabs the flesh behind Rageev's ears, pulls it down across his face. I expect it to split down the line between his burned and unburned skin, but I can hardly see clearly anymore.

What used to be Rageev's face is turned inside out. He doesn't move. He has to be dead. He has to be. The legs kicked a little, but even that's stopped. His body seems slightly smaller, less personal, than I remember him.

The Korean pulls the flesh back from the skull as if it is a superhero mask, as if Rageev has been doing nothing more than wearing a costume all this time. Underneath the blood and gore that had been his face, lies what's left. His boot soles point out at me, and I look at the ridges of snow and salt caught in their tread. Just half an hour ago, we had been sitting, talking in his car.

Now the skull peeks out, the eyes nestled in the whitish yellow bone. I thought they were going to bring their fists down, smash his skull into smithereens. Instead, the 'surgeon' with the glasses takes a lever that lies beside the scalpels and tools. He uses it to pop the top of Rageev's skull off. The pop of the skull plate – it's the last straw – I'm crying and falling onto the floo .

"Pick yourself up," says the woman harshly. She comes over. Picks me up herself and slaps me. Surprising how much strength she has in her small body. No strength of my own. She gives me her green handkerchief. I gratefully take it. While I mop the sweat, the tiny bit of vomit, on my face, she walks me over to the pool table. I try to resist but do not have whatever it is that Rageev did.

"Look at your friend," she says, "your leader. You know, I came from Korea years ago because they didn't really let you expand your business. They were anti-capitalist, which is just a way of saying that they wanted to keep the money for themselves." The 'doctors' have cut Rageev's brain from the stem. They hold it in front of me – a grey yellow lump that seems much smaller than I expected.

"This is your friend," she continues. "This is what he is on the inside. Greasy lo mein, you said? Now you see – it can go the other way. I don't have to tell you this is a warning. The only reason we're letting you go is because you're young, you're children. If you want, you can come work for us. Take a couple of days. Think about it. Or don't work at all. I don't care. There are no other options." I look at Soothy, just as shocked as I am. This is not a dream.

"There's nothing special about you Tamils," finishes the woman. "There's nothing that makes you different from anyone else."

With that, they let us go.

I am a mess and cannot drive. I can no longer feel the gears, the axles, the old familiarity of the car. The ghost of Rageev still hovers in it.

I am in shock.

I have to switch seats with Soothy. Somehow he takes control of the Quantum and gets us out of there. His hands are sloppy. The car swerves around the parking lot before he pulls out.

I don't care.

DANIEL

After the funeral, I went home and curled up on Lynn's striped black and white loveseat. It was small and she hated people lying down on it, but I didn't want to climb into bed. I was hunched up in that fetal position, my head uncomfortably upon the armrest, when she came home.

"Weren't you supposed to go to yoga today?" I asked.

"I left early," she replied and said no more. I didn't press. "How was the funeral? Wasn't there a reception afterwards?"

"I couldn't go," I answered. "It's at my sister's place in the Bluffs. I couldn't stand it, to hear everybody forced to come up with something nice to say about him. I had another argument with my mother and sister on the steps outside the funeral home."

"Oh yeah? What else is new? What did you argue about?"

"Guess."

She rolled her eyes. I didn't need that, but she was right. I had behaved shamefully.

"Come here." She put her bag down and came to the loveseat and sat beside me. Gently, she pushed my curled up legs onto the floor, forcing me to lean against her. Then, after stroking my head, she lowered it into her lap.

"You can't go to pieces every time you see them," she told me, running her fingers through my hair. "You have to be stronger. Think about the future. Think of our own children, our family that we'll have. There's nothing you could have done with your father. He shouldn't have shovelled the snow. He knew that." She gave my palm a squeeze. I didn't have the strength to squeeze back. "You take your three bereavement days that you're allowed and then you soldier on. That's all any of us can do."

I wasn't going to pieces, but I felt hazy. Conversation made me dizzy.

"I was there, Lynn. I keep thinking of what I could have done differently. Even the smallest things. I could have called him more. Gone over more often."

"He had your mother," she said firmly. "It's normal for people in this culture to move away from their parents. You know that."

"It's normal for you. My mother's left all alone in that house by herself. She'll have to sell it."

"She's going to live with your sister. It's not the end of the world. Your sister has a lot of space. You've said so yourself."

Chuck D got up off the floor and came over to nuzzle between me and Lynn. We had to pull our hands apart and pet him. He was a good presence in the awkwardness of our lives. I was grateful he wasn't hyper and begging us to take him for a walk.

"Remember the low ropes?" said Lynn. "At camp? The kids had to stand on a see-saw and balance out the plank? We set a record last time – ten minutes."

I nodded my head.

"Good food, clean living, everybody nice to each other. I miss the hike," she continued. "The hoots of the owls, the rustle of foxes and racoons in the tall grass. Once, with the girls, I came face to face with a fox."

I missed the trees. The gentle roll of Ontario land in the summer. The quiet rustle of birch and poplar trees. The hum that sang from their leaves. It made me almost believe that I had grown up here. As I thought of the memory, some of the knots in my shoulder began to loosen. Lynn gently turned Chuck over onto his back. His legs were wonky and splayed everywhere. We rubbed him on his ribbed belly. His tongue lolled out, and he began shaking his hind paw, then his front ones. We tried to get all the paws and tongue going at once. "Look," I said. "You can see down here, on the side of his belly where the fur's still brown like it was before. It becomes blue on the sides and his back."

She bent over and stroked the dog's side, followed the line, nodded her head.

"Daniel," she whispered, "he treated you horribly. Trauma's always difficult for the people involved. What's the point in beating yourself over it now?"

"He wasn't worse than any other Tamil dad. Better than most. He never drank, never left his wife and kids to fend for ourselves. He sacrificed himself till the day he died."

"Dan, when we start giving our parents awards for not being worse than they were, we're just making deals with ourselves. It's okay. We're all beaten or taken advantage of some way in our lives. There's no point in holding onto half a lie and imagining it better. He was hard on you, for you, and you survived him. Now he's gone, but you're alive, and you have to go on, just like you've been doing all this time."

"I don't know," I curled up in the little space that I had, rested my head against the armrest.

The dog began to bark and jump up and down now that our attention had drifted away from him. Lynn was annoyed at the slobber that flew from Chuck's jaws onto the floor and the love seat s upholstery.

"I'll take him for a walk," I said. "I need to get outside."

"Okay. I need to change."

After she'd gone into the bedroom, my body slumped. I could feel lactic acid building in my shoulders. From the periphery of my vision, I sensed Chuck rouse. I could hear that streamlined frame lifting itself off the floor, those loping footsteps padding towards the kitchen and dining room. His shadows stretched against the wall as he searched for food. As if front lit from two different light sources, I could see two shadows behind Chuck: a dark one, but also something lighter, spry and free, as if it were shadow to his spirit. It flickered and threw itself in the opposite direction. Both shadows wavered and lengthened so that his legs became pointed and eight feet tall. I could sense hostility and weight in the gloom. The body of the dog vanished round the corner, but the shadows remained, as massive as a table. They even seemed now to be made of soft fur flushed with blue, electricity in the room charged like a thunderbolt. I imagined the power of his haunches, jaws that snapped, and the goofy tongue that rippled outward like a forked whip.

What was he doing?

I got up and followed him to the dining area. The shadows were all wrong. There was something wrong about their perspective, their shape. I turned on a lamp and rubbed my eyes. There was the dog, Chuck D, padding up the wall until his paws made silent footfalls on the ceiling. He stood upside down, on the ceiling, his toenails scraping the stucco pattern that had been speckled there. His legs were straight, defying gravity, and his furious red eyes, upside down and unblinking, stared back at me. Flakes of plaster floated down through the air.

It was too much to look at. There was something wrong with my mind and imagination. I shut off the lamp, turned my cheek, and watched out the corner of my eye as he loped across the ceiling, towards the kitchen, and then nonchalantly padded down the wall.

NIRANJAN

Shit, shit, shit! Damn, damn, damn! Fuck, fuck, fuck! What are we going to do now that Rageev is gone? How could something like this happen to us? To him? I knew something like this would happen! Why didn't I stop it? I've crossed two years and multiple continents. Ended up even worse than when I started.

Soothy hasn't said a word.

When we get home, he pulls a can of bug spray and walks around the whole apartment spraying it underneath the cupboards and trims. There are so many fumes you can't escape them. Poison hangs in the air. "What are you doing?" I ask, holding my T-shirt over my nose.

He doesn't answer. The whole apartment soon smells of dried bugs. I can taste them in my mouth, burning and crackling up. The poison coats our tongues, gets in our eyes. The cockroaches come swarming out. They're everywhere, driven by the spray. He waits, and then stomps on them with his shoes. He stomps and stomps and stomps – there are hoardes and hoardes of cockroaches. How do we live side by side with so many? Herds of them. Cockroaches, big cockroaches with their feelers waving all over the place, little beady ones that look like drops of oil, medium-sized bugs with the gross disgusting brown-shelled backs. They come out, scurrying all over. I knew there were a lot, but I didn't know there were this many. The entire building is nothing more than one big roach motel. We're just the latest cockroaches to set up and live here. The newest cockroaches in the tower, that's all.

Soothy stomps and stomps and stomps. He's struggling and sweating and exerting himself. He's going to tear out his shoulder. He keeps going. Afterwards, there are hundreds of broken bodies, loose feelers, heads with eyes squashed flat, all over the flo .

I get a cloth and hold it to my face. "Why'd you do that?" I ask. "Now we won't be able to eat in here." I begin opening the windows, but he still says nothing. There's a twinge in my leg. I imagine it wiggling like one of those broken feelers on the floo . Are we all cockroaches just waiting for our fates? Like Rageev?

After I open all the windows, he rips open the weed, rolls himself a joint. We have to stand outside on the balcony because of the fumes.

I was growing unsure of Rageev. Now he's permanently gone.

Forever!

Every single thing in the apartment is basically his. The pictures of his girlfriend and daughter in their green and gold frames. The God pictures, the little statue of Ganesha – even the little line of incense ash from the last time he'd made us pray just before driving to the restaurant – was caused by him. The curtain of red beads in the hallway. His goddamn fucking toothbrush in the bathroom cabinet. The cologne he used. I would have to clean his hairs out of the bathroom sink after he shaved.

No more.

"We've got to figure out what to do. We've been sitting here doing nothing for too long! What would Rageev want us to do?" asks Soothy.

"Get a grip," I say. "Our bigger problem's money. What are we going to do? We've got some of the pills and drugs left, but after that, what then?"

Already, the smell of reefer is flooding the balcony. It competes with the roach spray. Soothy and I have never been too close, but I've grown used to him. He helped me get out from under my aunt, and for that I owe him, but he's not a good thinker. We've become roommates, not friends. But right now he can feel my pain, and I can feel his. I can understand his need to lash out.

I decide to join him – I'll try one of the white pills from our stash. The big one, like a horse pill. The old woman – she said they were for pain. I swallow one dry. It's chalky, bitter, tastes the way the cockroach fumes smell. Tastes like cockroaches on my tongue. It takes a while, but then I feel it. Warm sort of, like I'm in a bath. Dulls the pain. Slows down my mind and feelings, makes me not want to move. Take a codeine to put me over the top.

What a perfect temperature. The last few hours become soup in my mind. Don't want to eat or do anything – just sit here. Pills don't just take away the pain – they make memory remote. As if it isn't real. Just a movie I'm watching. I can pause the DVD at any time. I can turn off the sound. My mouth hangs open, my throat chokes, my mouth is chalky.

"What should we do?" mutters Soothy again. "You know that Muruges sold us out. We have to hit him back."

"Why?"

"We can't go after the Koreans. We have to do something. Rageev was our brother."

"It was Rageev paying for the apartment," I say, looking at my hands. "He was paying for everything."

"I know that," says Soothy. "Don't you think I know that?"

"He looked after us," I go on. "Where are we gonna get money?"

Soothy laughs, "The funny thing was that we were goin' to let you go!"

"What do you mean?"

"Rageev and I talked about how you just weren't fittin in. We were goin' to give it a couple of weeks – then try to get someone else, if you didn't work out."

"Where was I supposed to go?"

"Who knows? You were supposed to find people to sell to at school. You never did. Your heart wasn't in it. We were just carrying you."

"Maybe you're right." I feel the words through my calm. They hurt.

He strokes his lip. "Maybe you owe us. Owe Rageev. Maybe you ought to stop thinking about money just this once."

"What do you mean?"

"We can find Muruges and get him for what he's done. We can do that much right."

"Listen moron," I say slowly. "We don't know the whole story. Maybe they had reasons to do what they did. Maybe more than one reason." The image of the tread on Rageev's boots enters my mind. His body lying flat on the pool table after it had finished kicking. Bits of bone and flesh flying from his skull. The sound of that motorized saw. "And we can't get to Muruges without getting to Karthik. He's a monster."

"Who?"

"Dark Moustache," I tell him. "His name's Karthik."

"I'm scared too," admits Soothy reluctantly. "But I can't go back to selling. The Koreans won't allow it. They want us to join them – you heard the lady. You're in school, but I don't know nothin' else."

"You could go to school too. What do you want to do with your life?"

Soothy makes a fuck if I know face, throws his hands in the air. We are a couple of losers, all right. Well and truly fucked.

Eventually, we try to get into Rageev's room, see if we can find some money. The fumes are still bad, and we have to hold cloths over our faces. Rageev's room is the only one in the apartment with a lock. Soothy gets a wire coat hanger and strips the end. He uses a knife. Sticking the tip of the hanger into the top of the lock, he jimmies the tumblers with the knife. We crouch in silence. I hold a rag over his face while he works. The scrapes of his knife ring out in the apartment. He fiddles. Feels like a forbidden act.

When the tumblers click and the door swings open, we are surprised at how small the room is. He gave us the bigger one. There's not much here besides the shells of cockroaches that have crawled in to die. His bedspread and thin comforter are still on the bed, perfectly neat and tidy the way he liked. All his jeans and shirts hang straight in the closet. A small desk and a light stand are the only other things. Envelopes on the desk are stacked in a straight pile. His pens are lined up. Even three stacks of coins stand perfectly straight. They are ranked by size: quarters first, then nickels, then dimes.

Counting the change, Soothy says, "Great, man. There's three dollars and change here."

"Shut up and look around," I reply.

We search through all the drawers. Comb every inch of the closet. Underneath the mattress is a small .22 calibre pistol. It has a loaded clip.

"Even I know this is tiny and useless," I say.

Soothy shakes his head. "No, we can use this. I've heard some stories where .22's do real damage. The bullets are small so they pancake and bounce around inside the skull, don't exit like a .45 will."

I find some photos of his girlfriend and child, a copy of Rageev's refugee claim, and a box with some jewellery. It's nothing fancy. Probably Yalini akka's. I wonder where she is now. Imagine her cradling Geetha, not even knowing that the baby's father is dead.

We look through the refugee claim and see an old photo and signature. Standing straight, looking dead centre at the camera without smiling, a real FOB. There's no scar, no burned flesh. Rageev looks much younger, a new person, as if time has moved backwards and his soul is purged clean.

Rageev is younger than I am.

DANIEL

There's a lethargy about the middle of second semester that's difficult to shake. It's different from the first. For one thing, the weather continues to be cold and miserable. Layers of frozen ice have melted, but rain and snow abound. All the hope and joy from the end of summer has dried up. After March break, all that we have to look forward to are the longer days at the end of the term.

The drudgery of work. Oppressive late winter blues. Then my father's death. Shouldn't I have been forgiven for not being more in touch with what was happening in the Tamil community? I hadn't noticed at first when students began missing class. It wasn't just my class either. It was all classes. First, it was one or two, here and there. Then a few a week. Eventually they were gone for long stretches, days at a time. The whole school reverberated with the Tamils' absence. Tumbleweeds almost blew through the cafeteria. Tamils formed a majority at our school. As I mentioned before, grades and performance in school mattered highly to many of them, rank being a source of prestige.

Other teachers could not understand what was happening. The kids just vanished mid course. Pete Cram, who was so popular that students always went to his classes, was befuddled. Lynn, who had to deal with the very real problem of enrolment, was mystified. The administration was livid. We did not have to wonder long as to what was going on because the local news told us. There were mass demonstrations in front of the US consulate on University Avenue. Tamil protesters, wearing red T-shirts emblazoned with the Eelam tiger's head, mounted protests on that busiest of downtown thoroughfares, holding aloft placards and demanding intervention. They stood there, shown by the daily news, day after day, occupying University, between Dundas and Queen, demanding that Barack Obama and Stephen Harper intercede to stop the wholesale slaughter of Tamils in Sri Lanka. Again the word 'Genocide!' was scrawled large across placards. Again, they were out in great numbers. Again, they shouted their demands. How long could it continue? There was one difference this time. Many kids and youth were with them.

We held staff meetings. We tried to phone home. But it was impossible to get hold of anyone. If we did, the language barrier made it hard to communicate. What had happened? How had things gotten to this? It was as if the Pied Piper had blown through our school and only picked up the Tamil kids.

I phoned my mother and asked if she knew what was going on? She did – Thambi and his mother had joined the protests on University Avenue – but she herself did not feel strong enough to accompany them. Amma still reeled over the death of my father, so the Navaratnams understood.

But did I understand them?

When a stronger complement than usual of my media class was present, I tried to discuss the matter.

"There are more of you here today than usual," I said gently. "What's going on?" They were all tired, their heads on their desks, as if they hadn't slept.

"There's a protest at the Board of Education offices," said Nadesan without raising his head. "A whole bunch of us are going."

"The Board of Education offices? Don't you mean protesting on University Avenue? Or Queen's Park?"

"No, sir," said Kumar, twirling a pencil. "The Board of Education won't let us go down to protest at Queen's Park during the day, so we have to go at night. If we're going to come to school. But they need people during the day because that's when our parents work, right? At least some of them. And we've gotta replace them. We've got to keep the protests going 24/7 downtown. The Tamil Student Associations from different high schools have organized us to protest in front of the Board of Education offices. We need them to let us leave class to go protest with the others downtown. It's not like we're just skipping school, right? It's important – I know you understand?"

"The classes have been very thin lately," I said, looking around. It was the most lethargic class I'd had in years. "I've been preoccupied with what happened to my father. I'm sorry. I didn't know about the protests. I don't know anybody in them."

"Yes, you do," said Raj, jumping in. "You know us. Everybody's going out there. I mean, people who didn't give a damn before are going out there now. They know this is the Tamils' last chance to be saved. Sinhalese are slaughtering them. There won't be nobody left."

"He's right," said Nadesan. "Half our school's going to be gone in the next few weeks. The protest in front of the Board offices is just the beginning. We just don't want them to cut our grades while we support our community. But even if they don't give us that right, we're still going. We'll keep going as long as we have to. This is our families, our people, sir – they can't expect us not to care."

"Hmm," I put my fingers to my chin. "And you're all going to protest in front of the Board offices this afternoon? I wish we could arrange it as a school trip."

"To let us protest the TBE?" asked Athirvu. "You must be joking!"

"I guess I must be," I replied. I looked at Niranjan who hadn't said a word this whole time. "Niranjan, don't use this as an excuse to start skipping again."

"Oh, he's not going," replied Raj, flashing his teeth. "He ain't with us."

NIRANJAN

Soothy and I go about our lives almost as if nothing happened. Sometimes I feel like I can hear Rageev's footsteps behind me in the school stairwell. The smell of his hair oil and aftershave sticks around the bathroom at home. We tried to clean everything, get rid of everything that had been his, but the smell just mixed in with the cockroach fumes that were left. The smell had even sunk into the sofa cushions. More and more, the taste of dead cockroaches becomes a nagging thing under my tongue. I remember the tread of Rageev's sole. With the snow and grit in it. Pointing at me, accusingly, from the table. Sometimes I wake up, and the cockroaches' spindly legs and feelers are stuffed in my throat. Is this what the brown streaks on the apartment's walls come from? Dead cockroaches? Their burnt smell lies in my nostrils. It stays there chalky, sickening, for hours. The Percocets help with that some. The pain becomes a little less torn up, a little less jagged.

I go to class every day, try to attend every class. Even when the others don't. I just can't face going to the protests right now. The Percocets and other pills are quickly running out, so I only take a half of one, maybe a full one if I really need to get going in the morning. I worry the nod is written all over my face, all over my body. I just want to appear normal. Don't say anything.

Mr N looks at me after Raj says I'm not with them, and smiles. "You've really grown, Niranjan, you know that? You were already shooting last year. But the way you speak, man. You're more expressive, you communicate in discussions a lot better than last semester, know what I mean?"

I blush a little, hate him singling me out. Nadesan and Raj prick up their ears, lift their heads off their desks, watch us talk. "How're you dealing with your dad's death?" I ask.

He straightens and folds his arms, "I'm just trying to throw myself back into work. You know how it goes."

Nadesan and Raj and Kumar are now watching us closely. It's like we're performing for them.

"How's your driving going?" asks Mr N. "You must be getting a lot of practice, getting ready to do your G2 soon, right?"

"I've been driving a little," I say, trying to keep it vague.

"You should register for your test. Get it over with."

I nod my head. Try to keep that dopey look out of my eyes.

DANIEL

The problem took another turn the following week. Lynn was summoned down to Badlamenti's office. I wasn't there, but she told me what happened.

The room was commandeered by Badlamenti and Ackerman. Lynn Robards, our local school trustee whom Lynn had never met, was there. So was MPP Paisley, our Liberal representative. He was seated right in the centre, in front of Badlamenti's large desk. The Liberal provincial government had a representative sitting in our school.

Lynn shook hands nervously. She said Paisley was slow moving and blustery in person. He cleared his throat after each sentence. She described him as "white as they come – pasty freckled skin and large framed glasses." The type of white man that always made me uneasy as a kid. He doesn't look you in the eye. He doesn't try to look good because he doesn't have to – these are the white men who have the world in their pocket. There was nowhere for Lynn to sit. She had to stand in the corner.

Badlamenti began talking. "The drop in numbers started earlier in the year of course, but we were too busy with exams and finalizing report cards to catch on. You know how it is. It took us a while to tally the numbers and connect the dots. It's a particular segment of our students who have disappeared." He paused and leaned back, dramatically emphasizing the point, light bouncing off his bifocals.

Ackerman, who sat on the window ledge, an angel on Badlamenti's shoulder, leaned forward. "It's the Tamils. At first, we had to be sure. There's always a drop in attendance in the middle of the school year. The weather, final report cards from first semester, apathy – the usual drill. But as we know, this school has a higher percentage of Tamil students. In a school of just over twelve hundred, two thirds are Tamil. We have difficult cases. No doubt. The ones who cause trouble, get into fights, swear at teachers, keep us awake at night. The difficult Tamils. But it's not just these students the recent rash of absences applies to. It's the others as well. The Tamils who work hard and earn A's. The ones who serve as prefects and run the student council with Ms Varley. In short, the ones who get scholarships and give our school a good name."

"What have you done to stop this?" asked Robards, shifting in her chair. Lynn described her as a heavyset white woman, wearing a tan suit and woollen shawl. She's a forceful, commanding woman and had Badlamenti on a string. Though they shared the same name, Robards made Lynn nervous,

Once again, Ackerman leaned forward. "Phone calls home and letters and tracking sheets and things like that are not going to work in this case. A lot of parents have difficulty with English. For another thing, the parents are quite aware. They've approved these absences. In fact, the kids are standing right beside them."

"Where?" asked Robards.

"You want to see them?" asked Ackerman. "Turn on your news feed and look at the CBC home page. The Tamil protests downtown. All those people who are lined up University and across Front Street trying to block people going to work. Well, maybe only a few of our students were involved in that back in January. Now, they're staging protests in front of the US Consulate. So that's where our students are going. With their parents. Their friends. Their relatives."

"It took you a whole month to realize that?" asked Paisley, crossing a leg, cushions creaking.

"How could we know what was going on?" smiled Badlamenti. I could just imagine him apologetically turning his palms up – what can I do?

"Something must be done and quickly," emphasized Robards.

"This is why I've brought Ms Varley in here to meet you," grinned Badlamenti. "She's a whiz with these Tamils. Knows all the overachievers. She'll be able to get a handle on them, won't you Lynn?"

Lynn had to back pedal. "I barely knew the problem existed until last week," she explained. "Still fairly early in the semester. We haven't had any student council meetings. Truth to tell, Joyce and I were trying to iron out other issues."

"Well, this has been moved right to the top of your plate," said Badlamenti.

"We must do something," repeated Robards.

Nobody knew what to suggest.

Finally, Paisley coughed into his hand, then smoothed his tie and patted down his belly. "I've been talking to Dalton on this, and he's talking to Ottawa, off the record of course."

He looked around to make sure everybody understood. Lynn said they all nodded.

"What do the Tamils want?" Robards asked Lynn.

"They want us – in Canada, the United States – to step in and intercede for them. Their war back home."

"Hasn't the war been going on for a long time?"

"Almost twenty-five years," she acknowledged

"Then why are they deserting school in droves now?"

"It's not just us," explained Badlamenti shrugging his shoulders again. "It's schools all over the GTA. Leonard Cohen's hit particularly hard because we've got such a high Tamil population."

Ackerman picked up the thread. "University students are skipping their undergrad classes. People are leaving work."

"They're showing up on Parliament Hill in Ottawa too," said Paisley.

"We can't just have people leaving their jobs and responsibilities! Why not go the regular route and hire lobbyists or other professionals to meet with politicians?" asked Robards. She didn't have a clue. None of them did.

"They're desperate," admitted Paisley.

"They don't have the patience," Lynn informed them. "They feel like their relatives are dying now, in their country. In my experience working with Tamils, they're an intense, driven bunch. That's why they make such good student leaders. That's why they win the math and chemistry medals at the Olympiads. Our school's done very well by them."

"We can't be seen siding with terrorists," Paisley stated, looking everyone in the eye. "There's the problem," he continued. "We don't have any jurisdiction in that part of the world. We try to communicate with their government. We sent over funds when the tsunami hit, and we've dialogued about some of the human rights issues, but this is different. The government's got the LTTE on the run. They're probably going to crush them once and for all – all this might be finally over. Who's to say? The Tamil Tigers are a listed terrorist organization. No Western government's going to side with them. Especially the United States and Britain. Maybe it's in Canada's interest to just wait and watch."

"Are they insane?"

"What can Canada do on its own?"

"But much of our own community and our school is Tamil," Lynn countered. "We should do something."

"That's where you come in, my dear," smiled Badlamenti, leaning forward and glancing at her over his bifocals in his creepy way.

"Yes, I suppose we must do something." Paisley coughed into his fist. "We can't just have the school hemorrhaging students."

"You did such a magnificent job with the Remembrance Day assembly," smiled Badlamenti. "We want you to do it again."

"But this time for the situation affecting the Tamils," added Paisley, stating the obvious.

They all nodded their heads.

"We want you to organize the best assembly ever – we're going to invite the press and the whole community!" finished Badlamenti with a flouris

When she told me, I didn't know what to say. It all seemed a bit loose and impractical. They thought that by creating an assembly for the community, they could somehow counter the protests. But Lynn could not escape. She had the responsibility thrust on her. If there was one thing about Lynn I knew, it was that she did not take responsibility lightly.

NIRANJAN

We run out of pills and weed. We run out of money. No money to pay the rent, no money to buy food, no money to pay our phone bill. Nothing.

I can feel that I've only got a few more puffs in my inhaler.

"We're going to have to do something!" says Soothy.

"No shit!" I reply, irritably.

"Don't talk to me like that! You should be thankful you've got me here – on your own, you can't do nothing!"

"It's because of you I'm in this situation to begin with!"

We don't have any solutions. All our conversations are screaming matches.

"Why don't you go back to your aunt if you don't like it here?" asks Soothy.

That's the ultimate card he can play, and he knows it. "You know I can't do that," I reply, throwing my hands up. "You're the older one – so smart – think of something!"

Out of desperation, he decides we should go collect money from one of the Tamil places we know. The takeout on Lawrence Avenue. It's too early in the month to collect payments, but he figures we can bluff them a little. Front them. Pretend everything's normal. We still have the car and the little .22.

"I don't think it's a good idea," I tell him.

"Why?"

"Because they'll know something's wrong. Rageev always sets up the time with them on the phone when we collect. Rageev always did, I mean."

"Well, I don't hear any ideas coming from you!" After a while, neither of us say anything. I have to admit I can't think of anything better.

"What worries me most," I state, "is that we haven't heard anything from Muruges or Dark Moustache. They must know about Rageev by now."

"They think we'll keep quiet because we're scared," mutters Soothy, "but they're wrong. We just need to get some money, then figure out what to do.

That's just great, I think. I keep my mouth shut.

The next evening we park the car on Lawrence. We enter the takeout place. Immediately, I can tell something's wrong. I don't know what. It's the way they look at us when we enter. I see the cast iron figure of Shiva as Nataraja, dancing upon the spine of the world, flames all around him. It makes me cold. The picture of Krishna's still there, with his flute, smiling his slightly wicked smile, looking at us out the side of his eyes. His eyes seem to follow us as we move from door to counter.

The woman with the limp stands talking to a customer, handkerchief tied over her head, greasy apron around her waist. She turns her head to look at us, away from the customer she's serving. Glowers. Just a slight narrowing of the eyes. Nostrils flare. I can feel the hostility. I constantly get the sweats now, itch all the time. Pills are gone. I become nervous very quickly. At first I thought I could tough it out. But my whole body cramps on me. I become sick. On top of that, my bowels have started to move again. They make my legs real shaky, as if I've forgotten how to walk.

The hot fluorescent lighting throws itself out through the window onto the street. A cold evening. All the animals in the grass and undergrowth around the plaza stalk loudly. The rain in the April air. You can smell dry pollen. My nose itches. I want to sneeze but cannot. "What do you want?" barks the woman. "It's not time – we've paid up already. What are you doing here?"

The customer she's talking to is kind of old, bent over with age. I feel uncomfortable in front of him. Can see the frayed cuffs on his winter coat, splashes of mud on the hem.

"Amma, why are you talking to us like that?" asks Soothy, trying to be charming. He only freaks everybody out even more. How'd she get that limp? Everybody I know is scarred or broken in some way.

Soothy's charm makes the woman less friendly. She calls her husband. He comes out from the back, also wearing a grimy apron, wipes his hands against it. Face shows surprise.

"Thambi, why are you here?"

The use of the word 'thambi', just like the way Muruges says it. It pisses Soothy off. "Why do you think I'm here?" he asks angrily. "To look at your beautiful face? Time for your contribution – what else?"

"There must be a mistake," says the man. "We've paid already. You take more than we can afford as it is. Now you're asking for more?"

"There's no mistake," says his wife, bitterness dripping from her cold mouth. "They know exactly what they're doing. They want more." After a moment, when nobody speaks, she continues. "Isn't it enough you took my good leg? You took our children. You took our earnings. Our lives. We came here to get away from people like you."

"Be careful what you say, you old karuppi," Soothy grits his teeth. His hand reaches down to pull out the .22. He rearranges his sweatshirt and stands with the gun in his downstretched hands, meeting at a V, as if the gun is a cane to lean on.

We hear him release the safety. Then, after a while, he scratches his nose with one hand and places the gun on top of the counter, sideways. It points at the woman.

I can feel Shiva's cold purplish hand press against my abdomen.

The tall skinny man, constantly drying his sweaty arms against the apron, twitches his moustache, says, "Come back in two days, thambi. We don't have anything today. But come back in two days, and we'll get your money for you. Please?"

"Goddamn it!" shouts Soothy. Bangs his palm against the counter. The gun rattles.

His shoulders begin shaking.

"Stop it," I say and put my hand on Soothy's back. Soothy looks at me for a moment. Somehow, mentally, I step up and calm him down. I do that thing with my face and eyes that Rageev used to. For the first time ever, I am able to dominate Soothy. His body does something, adjusts its posture and balance. He stops shaking. It's that thing I've been feeling growing in me over the last few months. A sense of control.

Just like that, Soothy's mood is gone.

He calmly takes the pistol off the counter, puts it away. I have pulled Soothy back from something. Everybody knows it. We demand some food from them, for free, then walk across the road, shivering, not saying a word.

I drive us home.

DANIEL

Lynn informed me over lunch in her office that Badlamenti wished to see us.

"What does Badlamenti want to see us about?" I asked, peeling the foil lid off my yogurt and licking the yogurt caked on the bottom.

Lynn hated me doing that. "The kids skipping. What else?" she replied tiredly. "Stop that."

"The big show he wants you to put on?"

"He's going to want you in on it too," she said, picking up my quiche crust, which I hadn't touched. Then she put her fork down, remembering that she was supposed to be on a diet. Or maybe she was stressed. I dropped my yogurt foil by accident, spilling pink drops across her file folders and our hands

I grimaced. "What does he want me to do? I know as much as you do."

"You are our Tamil teacher, after all."

"Well, the joke's on them. I no longer speak the language."

Badlamenti squatted behind the desk in his office, overweight and rheumy eyed. Clogged arteries behind that smiling face and designer bifocals. Blood vessels rimming the nose. That could be me if I don't take care and exercise, I thought. I'm overweight, but I'm not that far gone. Yet. He sat there and didn't care. As if he knew he had the whole world on a string. His wardrobe told the tale: silk shirts, navy blue vests shimmering like chameleon skins, shoes so pointed he could cut someone with the tips. It was hot in his office, and he'd taken off his vest, sitting there with the suspenders down. Ackerman sat on the ledge behind him. As always. Badlamenti peered at us over his bifocals. "You make a lovely couple, yes you do." He and Ackerman smiled in unison.

"What's this about?" I asked, perhaps a little too abruptly. Badlamenti straightened and looked at Ackerman. I couldn't help but stare at the Italian duelling pistols that rested in their red trimmed case, a reminder of Badlamenti's ancestry. The light glowed upon the burnished copper, which reminded me of the doorknobs and fixtures in our condo building

My attention came back to the spray of burst blood vessels across Badlamenti's nose, like he was some sort of prizefighter, alive and standing only because so many others had their faces bashed in. Ackerman the wise manager.

There was something in their smiles I didn't like. "There are a lot of Tamils…" began Badlamenti.

"And you're our Tamil teacher," continued Ackerman. "So we thought we'd come to you to help Ms Varley. After all, you're close, and you did a fine job with that Remembrance Day assembly."

"Yes," agreed Badlamenti. "We need your help again. We've talked with Ms Varley." He turned to me. "You know what's at stake?"

I nodded vaguely.

"Yes, of course. Now, our MPP, Mr Paisley, is caught in the middle. There are a lot of Tamils in his riding. A lot of angry Tamils. And Tamils vote, yes they do. But they're going around shouting all kinds of things, waving red flags with terrorist symbols on them and throwing around words, like the 'G' word."

"Genocide," said Ackerman, frowning across the desk. "And now our students are protesting at the Board of Education offices. The TBE doesn't need more bad press – they haven't done anything. The kids can't go around saying these things, waving their flags. Like a, like a…"

"Bunch of mad bulls," stepped in Badlamenti. Ackerman drew back to the window ledge. "And we need to stop the stampede. It's no good. Too many of our students – too many of our prize students – have been missing classes, whole days of school actually, to join these protests."

"Have you looked at your attendance reports?" spat out Ackerman.

"Yes, yes, he has – they know all about it," continued Badlamenti, throwing up his hands, "But it's not just the burnouts and troublemakers – the prefects and the student council, who should know better, are ditching classes too. To go to these… demonstrations? Why? What do they do there? Why can't they do it here? We have to do something to nip it now."

"It's their families," I said, stating the obvious. "They're suffering back home. They don't know what's happening to them."

"I understand that, I understand that," nodded Badlamenti, folding his arms. "But a school is a kind of family too. And we must do something, no? Something to show we care. We can't just go around waving red Tiger flags, can we?

"Yeah, that's not our students," I agreed. "It's a certain group of people who wave those flags, wear those T-shirts. They've sort of brought it into the crowd. It shows up on photos, but it's a minor element."

"That's not what we've heard," interjected Ackerman. "They're a terrorist organization, and everybody obeys them. It doesn't look good, Dan. For them or us."

"They look like terrorists, they use terrorist tactics, they block up major avenues " Badlamenti shook his head and chuckled.

"We know it's bad," I agreed. "It's affected our morning and afternoon drive."

Badlamenti took a mint out of the tin on his desk, then offered us the tin as an afterthought. I shook my head, but Lynn took one. "Suit yourself," continued Badlamenti. "You're wondering how you fit into all of this.

Silence.

"Well, it occurs to us that you have no small measure of involvement with these kids' lives, Dan. I need you to use that computer lab I've provided for your classes and turn out videos that we can use for the upcoming presentation, even better than the ones you did for Remembrance Day."

I hung my head.

"We know you've got a lot on your plate," continued Badlamenti, "with the passing of your father, but the Liberals are a force of nature that has to be contended with in this province. They've taken the last two elections, and they'll probably take the next one too. They've done more for the Board of Education and its people than the Conservatives ever would. And I'm not just saying that because Paisley is a personal friend. Oh no. They've had this riding for more than a decade."

"Lynn assures us that you're a team player," said Ackerman, "and you need to get on board. This goes well, and it could be good for all of us."

I looked around to see how Lynn was taking this – the suffering of the Tamils could play out well for us – but she only gave me a be patient look.

"It's no secret that I'm being considered for the next superintendent position to open up," whispered Badlamenti, leaning over his desk, straining somewhat with the effort, peering at us over his glasses so that his eyes went large with anticipation. "Ackerman's done his time and will probably get his principalship soon at another school. There's going to be a real shake-up at LCC over the next few years. Lynn has shown some real leadership, and she knows I'll back her. She'll get Ackerman's old spot. If not that, a vice-principalship somewhere else. And she's only thirty-one. Amazing how fast you can move with a little effort."

I was stunned. Badlamenti'd never been this direct in my presence. Of course, Lynn being there put the varicosed one at ease. He depended on her.

"Which leaves you." Ackerman took down a folder from a shelf and held it in his hand. "It's a good thing you're friendly with the kids, but that'll only take you so far. Understand? You have to understand the way things work here. You've been here long enough. We need you to step up, and this is your chance. Our friend Raptis left a hole that we've got to fill. We've got a few candidates, but this could also be a chance to shake things up. How about it? Do you understand what we're saying?"

I didn't, and I looked at Lynn. She touched my arm and said quietly, "They're not going to renew Janarius's term as head of the department. They want to give it to you."

I was shocked. The other two nodded their heads, peering at me closely. "But Mr Brent has been there forever," I said, "since way before I got here."

"He's useless," said Badlamenti coldly. "He doesn't know what he's doing and uses other people, claiming credit for their work. You know that. We all know that. Any usefulness he served is long gone. He's not reliable."

I didn't know what to say. It seemed conversations had been had, and some of those conversations had included Lynn. Perhaps she had not told me the whole truth regarding her meeting with Robards and Paisley. I didn't know. I did know that if somebody wanted to become administration, 'management' so to speak, they either became a CL – department head – or went Lynn's route: through guidance. I bore no love for Janarius Brent – everybody would have been happy to get rid of him – but I knew Pete Cram wanted the job. And he deserved it too, much more than me. After football practice, he could be found putting in long hours preparing notes and PowerPoints for the next day's classes, long after I'd gone.

I didn't know what to make of the proffer. I sort of knew the way these guys worked, but it had never directly involved me. Raptis said that the proffer always comes when they're having bad luck and they need you. I looked at those pistols, gleaming in their case, lowered my head. This was the kind of task my father would have had no problem accepting.

"Are you bothered about Brent?" asked Ackerman. "Don't be. He'd rat out one of his own family if it worked to his advantage. If he was sitting in your place, he wouldn't think twice. You know, he won his CLship by reporting on union meetings? He's proud of that."

"That position should go to Cram," I said. "He's been working at it for a long time. He coaches football. Does a lot of other stuff. He has all his professional certifications. I think he's been waiting to apply."

"And we'll give him a fair interview," said Ackerman. "But promotion's more of an art than a science. Take our friend, Mr Paisley, for instance." He threw a file folder onto Badlamenti's desk.

I reluctantly opened the folder and looked inside. Lynn peered over my shoulder. Inside were a bunch of email printouts. From what I could tell, Paisley and Badlamenti had been communicating for a couple of weeks. A sentence or two, checking in with each other regularly. The heading of the email thread: What to do with the Tamils?

Now, Badlamenti looked over his glasses and held me with his stare. Despite the spray of blood vessels, despite the corpulence, despite the silly blue suspenders with the drifting clouds, there was definitely something hawk-like about him. Something predatory in the veins around his eyes.

"Our friend Paisley," stated Badlamenti, "wants us to hold an assembly in our auditorium. For the community. Not an assembly exactly, but a performance. He can't support their flag waving downtown, nor can we. Their flag waving, the chanting – they've pretty much alienated themselves from any politicians worth their salt."

"But he needs their votes, he needs their confidence," admitted Ackerman.

"What he wants is an assembly, but one run by us, not the flag bearers. To take control of the situation. To address the concerns and worries of the Tamil people. They must know that we Canadians care and are doing everything we can. But we're going to be positive about it. We're not going to be negative, oh no. And this is where you come in. We're going to have classical dances and music, the usual.

But we need something modern, something new to show that we're thinking about what's going on over there in the homeland of many of our voters. Your students need to come up with some videos showing the positive aspects of being Tamil. Because we've had enough of the negatives."

"No flag waving, no burning anything, no shouting and accusations," said Ackerman.

"How long do we have?" I asked.

"A little more than a week."

"Just over a week!"

"Now that they're protesting in front of the TBE offices, we need to step things up."

I shook my head, leaned forward, and clasped my hands. My fingers were trembling

"Do you see what's happening out there?" asked Ackerman. "Do you? Our school's falling apart. We need to get them off the streets and back in class. Where will it all end? Is this anarchy? What do you think will happen if half our students drop out? If our best students fail? You do realize the funding to the school is determined, wait – your very position – is determined by how many students we have, don't you?"

"A little more than a week," said Badlamenti. "And Ms Varley's going to coordinate the show with whichever students she has left on Student Council. She's got it even worse than you, okay? A week and a half, more or less, and we've got to show the community something. Or we'll all have hell to pay next year. Work with Lynn on this one. You've got no choice."

NIRANJAN

We drive back to the Tamil place on Lawrence. I know something's very wrong. I knew it last time. But it's no good talking to Soothy. My bowels squirm against the .22 tucked into my pants. The little gun. Soothy said I should carry it this time. Just to mix things up. Does he also feel what I'm feeling? That sense of my insides turning to glass?

The woman and man are there at the counter, but no customers. We go in quietly, without making fuss. When they see us, they look at us differently. It's dark. Hot fluorescents are turned off. Just a small lamp behind the counter to shed some light. Incense has been lit. Nataraja dances his dance of iron on the spine of the world. Krishna smiles from behind his flute. What's wrong?

After we go in, they say a curt 'wannakum'. The man goes to lock the door. The woman limps to the back.

Muruges and Karthik come out, replacing the woman. We stare at them. They stare back at us. This is the bad thing my gut's been writhing about. Muruges seems amused. Karthik wears his sunglasses, as usual. Hard to tell what he's thinking.

"Thambi, what's going on?" asks Muruges, crossing his arms. "These people say you're trying to take money that doesn't belong to you."

Soothy's in front of me. His body stiffens up. "You sold Rageev out," he says quietly.

Karthik indicates, silently, with a turn of his head that the shop owner, in his greasy apron, should leave. Join his wife in the back. The guy nervously wipes his hands on his apron, hurries away.

"Rageev screwed up one time too many. There was nothing we could do for him," says Muruges, shaking his head sadly. "He made a lot of enemies."

"If it wasn't the Koreans, it would have been somebody else," mutters Karthik dryly.

"He worked for you," stresses Soothy. "He was one of us."

"No, he went his own way." Muruges clicks his tongue regretfully. "He didn't listen to anybody. Lost his sense." Then, placing his hands on the glass counter, he stares at us. "Have you lost your sense? To be honest, I'm amazed you survived, thambi. I thought they would have killed you along with your leader."

"They asked us to work for them," I say slowly. "They don't want to kill children."

"Weakness," laughs Karthik. "If it were us, we would have killed all of you," He smiles. I remember what they did to Rageev on the pool table. Didn't seem weak to me.

"You're not going to work for them," Muruges adds after a pause. Strokes his beard. "Nobody works for us, then goes to work for someone else. You know that."

"We don't know anything."

"That's not the point. No one leaves us. Ever."

Soothy looks at me, looks back to Muruges. He leans into Muruges so far his spit lands on the glass counter when he speaks. "You don't own us."

Muruges grins and lifts up his hands. "No? Who do you think supported Rageev when he needed help? Without us, he would have been gone a long time ago. Of course we own you. Everything is made possible by us." His leg begins to shake, the only telltale sign he's going to do something, before grabbing Soothy by the neck. Muruges slams Soothy's head onto the glass. The counter cracks but does not break. The cash register rattles. Soothy's staring at the vaddais, cheek squashed against the glass. Muruges uses all his weight to hold him there.

Soothy's lips are flattened, but he croaks out the words, "Now – you idiot – pull out the gun." The gleaming .22 is out of the waistband, in my hand, before I know it.

I remember what happened to Rageev. Helpless, not being able to do anything with my gun. Handing it over without will.

"Shoot!" cries Soothy.

Safety is off. But can I do it? Actually put a bullet through someone's head?

I've seen those YouTube videos of bullets going through a series of wooden blocks. The wood splinters, pushed in by the impact, the explosion as the bullet passes through. Nothing left but a raggedy hole – completely shocking how such a small thing can punch so much force.

Karthik's gun is already out, in his hand, pointed at me. Didn't even hear or see him.

My own little .22 is pointed right back at him. Imagine that spot where neck and cranium meet. There's a hinge there, a space or something, we learned about it in Mr Raptis's class. A space between bones, between life and death. Imagine firing at Dark Moustache. The shock of the bullet entering his body, making him jump. The ejection of the cartridge, the smell of barium and lead. Burning hissing cockroaches.

"Do it!!" screams Soothy.

Muruges pushes even harder on his neck and twists it. Soothy gasps. "Are you watching closely?" asks Muruges, looking at me. "You know, I can't lie to you. I'm too fond of you, thambi. The Koreans paid us good money for Rageev. It was too good an offer."

I point the gun back at Muruges. He grips Soothy's neck, and the muscles strain in my roommate's face. Sweat pours down Muruges's forehead through his balding hair.

Soothy grits his teeth and almost yells. Muruges squeezes and twists, crushing Soothy's windpipe so that he cannot talk any more, snaps his neck. A wrenching sound as Soothy's head goes one way, his body another. The ponytail swishes widely. That long skinny body thuds against the glass, crumples to the floor. Eyes look up, without life. Drool, coming out his mouth, falls onto his scrubbed Air Jordans.

Muruges, almost wild, panting. Wills his leg and body to stop shaking. Stands up straight and looks at me through a curtain of sweat. My own breath coming out in sawed-off rasps. Wish my inhaler wasn't empty.

"Did you see?" asks Muruges. "You, too, will die. I'm not going to start pretending or lying to you now. You will die. But if you put the gun down, we can do it quickly, without pain."

He's not as hypnotic as the Asian woman. Keep the gun up. Know it's the only hope of getting out alive. Hold it with both hands now, steady myself. Remember the lesson in the ravine. Practice my stance. Shoot for the centre of mass, said Dark Moustache. Strike a blow, defend myself.

"Think about what you're doing, thambi," says Muruges, panting. "I hold the life of your brother in my hands. Your whole family, even. I will make sure every single one of them is dead before all this is over. Mark my words. Every one of them will die in agony, unless you put that gun down."

"Put it down," says Karthik. He hasn't moved a hair. Smells like oil and electricity.

I point the gun at Karthik, then back at Muruges. I know that my brother, my family will never be safe with these people. They will always carry a grudge. That is their nature. It doesn't matter – all my brother's done for them. All he will do. Nothing matters. If I don't strike now, they will always have a hold on me and my family.

I think it's his use of 'thambi' – little brother – that takes me to the final point, the one where I can't come back. This is what I will tell myself later. Not even crushing Soothy's windpipe is as cruel as calling me 'little brother'. There is only one person in the world who has a right to call me 'little brother'. The gun kicks as it goes off in my hand. Don't even hear it. I didn't aim for centre of mass – I aimed for the centre of Muruges's face. That face of superiority and resignation. Like he knows me. I want to smash his features. Want to make him stop shaking. "I'm going to free you."

There's a bullet hole in his forehead – looks like a crooked pottu. Like something the priest put on him at the temple. A look of surprise in his eyes. I wait for the back of his head to shatter, but it does not. Muruges just falls. The bullet lodged in his skull.

Now I'm pointing the gun at Dark Moustache. Familiar smell of barium and lead in the air.

"Don't even try it," I say. "I don't have to be a good shot. Just have to squeeze the trigger again. I'll put a bullet through your eye right where that blob is. I'll put it right through the hole. Just watch me."

A twitch passes across his face. His hand doesn't move. Can feel him calculating. "I'm going to find you, and kill you," he says flatly. "You know that, don't you?"

Longer I wait in here, worse it gets. I'll lose my nerve. Already, I can feel my throat tighten. Stress making me tight. Sandpaper in my throat. Holding my gun level, I back up to the door. Have to hold my gun with one hand while I open the door with the other. Fumble a few times, okay, finally got it open

We keep our guns levelled at each other while I jam my foot against the door. Back away. Still keep the gun level. Don't shake.

I back out and away slowly, slowly, never putting the gun down. Car keys in my pocket. Thank god I drove. Ejected cartridge in the store. Forgot to pick up. Don't worry – couldn't do it. I back away until I cannot see him anymore through the window. Back away. Back away.

Then run for the car.

DANIEL

I told my students, whenever someone showed up, about the assembly. Mr Badlamenti's agenda was revealed to them in full. They groaned at the idea, but were too tired to rail against it. It was just another thing in the school's long program of making something of them that they weren't.

From then on, all our classes were in the computer lab. It still had the smell of fresh paint upon the walls. The slightly heady, nauseous smell hung over a defenestrated grey and white and brown room. The windows had been boarded up and painted over with company colours, like the rest of the lab. It had been rewired. Even the banks of computers lining the walls were pristine and grey, clearly worked into the corporate colour scheme from Yutani Corp. However, graffiti had already appeared in the corner farthest away from the door, near the teacher's desk. A few tags in black marker, almost indecipherable, a large scribble that was little more than a caveman's pictograph. One said 'Mr N is a fag'. I guess some people took the video mandate harder than others.

The Tamil students working on Badlamenti's assembly toiled away on their videos in the lab while non-Tamil kids did their regular assignments. I was to supervise the production and editing of the videos that would be shown at the assembly. The videos were supposed to be exactly the kind of positive superficial expressions that would reinforce the Canadian dream and make everybody happy. Paisley would reassure the Tamil base that he had their concerns at heart. That the government was in touch.

Nadesan, Raj, and all the other students knew the government wasn't in touch. They got an earful about it from their parents every day. On the federal and provincial and municipal levels, politicians had some vague idea that the Tamils were unhappy. How could they not? The Tamils continued to protest vigorously. In front of Queen's Park, cops on horses had rushed into them. Now, in front of the American Consulate on University Avenue, their red T-shirts and their red flags were everywhere. The words 'Justice' and 'Genocide' painted in letters three feet tall. They occupied the major avenue in throngs, shouting their slogans around the clock.

These loud desperate moves could not convey their real concerns, the reason why so many Tamils were in tears. The reason why so many had left their jobs, livelihoods that hung by a thread, to come to Toronto, to Ottawa, to New York, to London, and other cities around the world to protest and sit-in. Mothers wailed and beat their heads over pictures of mangled bodies and shell-struck children.

How could Canadians understand? The events were so remote from their lives. All they understood was that these dark-skinned people blocked their roads. They sat down and would not go. Despite all Canada had given them, they clamoured for some type of justice. What that 'justice' meant, what it entailed, no one cared. They had neither time nor inclination to pause their busy lives and listen.

Though the hallways of Leonard Cohen Collegiate were desolate, half our students gone, Paisley and Robards only understood that the red flag of the Tigers had invaded and coloured the whole protest with a splash of dye. Ink had polluted the milk. Never mind that the colour was the same as that of Paisley's Liberal party. It wasn't a flag he or anybody wanted to be associated with. He found himself currying the favour of his Tamil voters, while trying to avoid having to eat Tiger curry.

Raj, Nadesan, and Kumar needed their credits and marks. I guess that's what kept them coming back. Others too. I took anyone who was willing. Jayanath and Gowri were making a short about being new to Canada. It was a cliché-ridden mess filmed in and around the Tuxedo towers. The guy, played by Jayanath, walked around in a saram and flip flops, went to the convenience store but was not able to communicate what he wanted: hot mix, coconuts, and jaggery. He wanted some milk to do a puja and then tried to pay in rupees, making the clerk angry at him. He went into McDonald's and tried to order vegetarian food, but couldn't and got mad when he realized they were serving cow meat. And so on – you get the idea. I had to say no to that one.

Kumar, Nadesan, and Raj had plans to get their friends who were girls to film a brown version of Cinderella. The wicked stepmother and sisters would wear saris. Instead of a ball, they planned to do a bharatanatyam dance thing, where Cinderella would leave one of her bangles behind. Bharatanatyam again. I hated the oversaturated simple-minded lack of originality or innovation that was celebrated every time the Tamil community put on a bharatanatyam performance! I asked the boys if their friends were reliable, now that so many students were going to the protests. Nadesan said that some were still working with Lynn, so they were around somewhere I guess.

It was all pathetic and hopeless, if you want my opinion. Those students who did show up only did so sporadically. Even those who weren't going to the protests could see the tumbleweeds blowing through the school halls. They saw no point in doing anything above the bare minimum. The life of the school had been sucked out. Our school spirit was on life support.

Niranjan had disappeared yet again. He had been doing so well, working on a project with his group, doing the lion's share of storyboarding and prep for once. I knew I shouldn't have been that surprised, but part of me felt wounded, stung that he would fail us once again.

Lynn had told me that it would only be a matter of time. This is what I would receive for pushing her to keep Niranjan at our school. I avoided mentioning his absence to her – she would only have gloated. When he had skipped in the past, the absences would increase, but there would still be some attendances thrown in, hasty excuses and rushed attempts to catch things up. I wondered if he might show up again in time for the assembly. Only to have his performance taper again into a crescendo of absences that finally became a hopeless flailing in regards to credits and marks. Well, if he did that, I would not cave in and give him the credit out of pity. I was not there to be taken advantage of. I would not continue playing the fool because he promised this, that, and everything under the sun.

NIRANJAN

I'm on the street. This is where things are now.

Getting used to sleeping in the Quantum is no piece of cake. It's a little roomier than your average sedan, I guess. My body cramps. It takes me longer and longer to stretch myself out in the morning. I cough a lot because it's cold. My inhaler ran out a while ago, and I don't have money to refill the prescription. Phlegm fills my mouth and my throat closes. I have to find public bathrooms. I try to park in out-of-the-way places like those small streets around the hospitals, so cops won't spot me. Sometimes, I walk down to the protests on University Avenue, but don't get too close. I'd join in if Karthik and others weren't there. Something mesmerizing about those protests. All the Tamils, the poor and broken hearted, coming out. Normally, they're hidden away in kitchens and factories. Now they make themselves heard, all night, all day.

My people.

Some of them still in work clothes when they come down, do a protest shift, go to their jobs, come back wearing the same thing. That's commitment.

Just can't do it. As much as I hate my life, I like being alive. Still got the .22. I don't think they'd try anything out there in the open in that crowd. But who can be sure? In a way, the protest's safer than being where no one would see me at all. Who am I kidding? All those red flags and shirts. The tiger snarling inside its circle, trying to claw out. They do have food sometimes. When I'm really hungry, I swoop in, grab a couple of samosas, vaddais, sandwiches – whatever's available.

Mr N called me on my cell. Didn't answer the call. Can't talk to him just yet. Don't know what to say. Haven't heard from my brother or family in a long time either. Feel very scared. Very worried.

One day I get a video text. Sent to my iPhone.

Karuna had been a good brother when he'd been at home. Now I don't know where he is. Can Karthik and the LTTE target my brother just to strike back at me? My family? Or do they have too many problems of their own? Karuna gave them many years of his life. But anything's possible where they're concerned. They have no flex. Don't forget or forgive.

I try to remember my brother as a kind, serious young man who thought of others – his face always had a serious expression, his voice polite and firm. He was thinking and weighing things all the time. You could see that even while you sat there talking to him – his eyes would drift to the side, and he'd brush hair away from his forehead – he was thinking about something else and would never tell you what. Like he was embarrassed to be caught thinking.

Earlier this year, when I heard him yell, angry and mean, it was hard to believe I was talking to the same person. What would he think of what I've done? No, don't think of it.

The video text I get on my phone. It's from him, or at least I think it's him. There's no written message with it.

The video is painful and shocking to watch. Either from my brother or my parents using my brother's phone. Can't tell which. Probably my brother. It shows grainy footage of people running between houses in the village where my parents now live. The village is on the coast, where fishermen push off to cast out their nets. I can't recognize where it is exactly – somewhere in our district. There is something familiar about the surroundings. The dark green trees and yellow stone buildings. It is the village, I think. Pretty sure. I can hear the boom of shells going off in the background. The earth is kicked up in large clouds of dust and sand that hover in the air, trying to swallow people and their houses. Where are my parents? I can hear shrieks in the air. "Get inside. Get inside the bunker! Turn off the camera and get inside!" The person carrying the camera is running too because everything is shaky. I can see things from his point of view. If it's not my parents or my brother, is it somebody using my brother's phone? His video camera? The video cuts off.

I watch it again and again.

It is their village, I think… It stings me that so much time has passed that I can't be sure. If someone from my family is passing it on, what do they want me to do with it? Just know what happened? Spread it somehow?

The video raises more questions than it answers. The footage tells me very little. The village is in danger. I knew this was going to happen. The video only gives some shape to my nightmares. The people who have survived, they will be moving on. But where are they moving to? I can barely make out the voices from the running footsteps, the shelling. Why did they send it to me? Why no message?

A message comes a few hours later. My father writes, "Our village has been shelled heavily, but we wanted to let you know we're okay. We're trying to run and hide as best we can." Another one comes after that: "No food anywhere. Thank God you are safe! Your brother is dead – I'm sorry to tell you. We are all very sad, especially your little sister."

Karuna!

How can this have happened? So suddenly? Another body to rack up with the dead – how did he die? Doesn't sound like it was Karthik and his crew. Too soon. Doesn't matter. They're responsible anyway. I'm furious they threatened my family in the first place

We all knew this might be Karuna's fate. Why did it have to happen now, after all these years? Another martyr for the fucking Tigers. Both he and Muruges are dead. Everything I touch turns to shit. To death.

I have been slow to check up on the news, have been avoiding it even. With all the protest stuff, all the agitation, the fact that Canadians don't gave a shit, it's depressing. I feel the weight inside my body. I get headaches. Mood is slow and sluggish.

But maybe this is where I care. The thing to distract me from Rageev and Soothy's deaths. Here is the thing to bring me back to reality. Who's to say that bags of shit like Karthik and Muruges get to decide what happens to us?

I reply to the message but hear nothing. My father isn't a big talker by nature. I miss him deeply. I miss everyone in the village: the kids I went to school with, our stern headmaster, the old women who would scold me at the drop of a hat. Where are they all now? The school closed down. I miss the stray dogs that hung around the schoolyard until the teachers shooed them away.

My parents sold their jewellery to send me here because they cared about my safety, my welfare. Now I've almost ruined it, almost ruined the chance. But I can get back. I can get back on the dream. I watch the video again. I can almost hear the whole village's voice being pulled and squeezed into the video, as if the sound waves coming from my phone are being rattled, stretched apart. The emotion, the hollow rasps between quickly rushed words, as if they are blowing their last breaths into my ear. Strange, chilling sounds. What am I supposed to do with this? Nothing makes sense.

A day later, I send the video to Nadesan at school. He sends me a link to another video on Tamilnet. The quality is similar to my own.

I can see people with children huddle inside the 'walls' of a man-made bunker. They're not real walls but bags of sand. Some of the sandbags are made out of pillows that have been filled up with sand, taken from whatever beach is nearby. The low roof of the bunker is made of palm leaves and branches. These girls, washed, scrubbed clean, wearing pretty pink and yellow dresses, lean out of their bunker and scream, "Amma! Amma! Ammaaa!" As they wail, their pigtails, their long braided hair, jumps up and down from their sobbing faces. They scream and scream. I can hear the report and boom as another shell falls in the background, although all I can see is the girls' faces.

Then the camera pulls out. It's no longer a close-up. I can see where they are leaning out, and the ground... the ground is a complete mess. Broken bits of houses and bricks and wood and smoke and... and dark stuff, which I can only assume is blood. The shaky hand of the camera pans to the right to see a body in pieces on the ground, mixed in with stones and thatch and rubble, the arms of the woman twisted away from her head. Even in the grainy video, you can see her head, her white hair still combed tight though there is a large hole in her cheek. The body is extremely still, but her sari is blown to shreds. A man bends over the woman, raising his hands to his temples and clutching his hair. I try to make out his words, but I can't. His hair glistens with coconut oil, and he has a moustache like most Tamil men. He squats on the ground beside the woman, saram hoisted above his knees, tied over his striped shirt. Then I hear the report again, that deadly whistling sound. The boom, as the place I have just been looking at erupts in smoke and dust, the man and woman obliterated. I do not see their bodies fly apart. One moment they are there, and the next they are gone. There is a cloud of smoke and debris so thick you can't see anything except what is at the very edges of the cloud. The sound of explosions everywhere.

The video cuts out. Who are these people, and who has shot this video?

Nadesan asks me what I've been up to – why I haven't been to school.

I guess there's no avoiding it. I'm already starting to feel lonely. I can't shun them and Mr N forever.

DANIEL

The afternoon had that drowsy feel. I wanted to get home, walk Chuck, and laze on the sofa. The sun shone brightly on the hills and wet grass outside my classroom's window. I would have walked him there if I could.

Checking my messages after class, I was surprised to find a voicemail from Niranjan. I was wondering when I'd hear from him again.

Of course I called him back to find out where he was. "Where have you been?" I exclaimed. "Where are you?"

"Listen, Mr N." His voice, which normally alternated between shyness and a kind of scattershot hurried quality, was now distant, cautious. "I need to see you – when can we talk?"

"You're no longer in your apartment, are you? We've called and called. Nobody's seen you around for a while."

"That's what I'd like to talk to you about," he said. "Can I come by your place?"

That worried me. He whispered his words so faintly, I wondered if he was high.

Lynn found me later. She was busy preparing for the assembly, going over the bharatanatyam dances, setups, other nonsense like that. I would stay with students too, supervising their videos. I told her, "Niranjan just called me."

"What? When?"

"Just now. A few minutes ago."

"I can't worry about him now. Got a list of things to do before we go home," she said.

"He wants to meet with us, at our building."

"I hope you didn't give him our address, Dan."

"I certainly did." I said. "He's coming over for dinner."

She shook her head slowly. "Dan, that kid's trouble – he's going to drag you down, and me with you. I'm not cooking dinner for him."

When he came over, Niranjan looked like he'd aged ten years. He was gaunt, his face drawn so tight over his skull that he had worry creases in his cheeks and forehead. His body was hunched over and looked sucked dry like a pulped fruit. The eyes, which I always remembered as alert and observant, seemed hollow and far away. Something had been taken out of him. Any remaining urge I had to yell at him for skipping class soon disappeared. Even Lynn was shocked by the transformation.

I asked him if he wanted to eat or drink. He shook his head.

"What do you need?" I asked

"To sleep," he replied. "I just want to sleep in a proper bed for once."

"He can sleep here, can't he?" I asked, turning to Lynn.

She shook her head furiously, "Dan, we don't have another bed."

Before I could counter, she folded her arms and whispered to me, "Dan, remember what I told you? Teachers can't take in students, especially not those who're as much trouble as he is."

A part of me had sort of pushed my father's death to the back of my mind, but when I saw Lynn's folded arms, it reminded me of the misplaced hopes my father had in Niranjan. With all the stress over the assembly and then Niranjan suddenly contacting us out of the blue – it was a sign.

"Niranjan," I queried slowly. "Are you in trouble? Has something happened to you?"

Niranjan raised his head. "Have you heard something?"

"Answer our questions first," said Lynn. "What trouble have you gotten into?"

Niranjan looked down and away.

"You're not living in that apartment anymore, are you – why?" Lynn pressed him.

He shivered and eyed us warily. A glimmer of something flickered in his eyes. A suspicion, a deadly hostility. Something reared its head before hiding itself. He lowered those hollow eyes and looked away.

"If the police are looking for you," continued Lynn, her voice growing louder, "you know you'd better turn yourself in." Even then, she had more intuition than I did.

I was afraid he'd bolt – he'd hardly spoken. What little energy he possessed made his body clench in a defensive attitude, as if he might spring for the door any second. "Lynn, can I have a moment alone with him – please?" I asked. "Just a moment – let me talk to Niranjan."

"Fine!" She balled up her fists and stormed out. "I'll be in the kitchen – do what you want!"

Niranjan eased up a little once she had gone. "I'm sorry," he whispered, "if I've caused trouble for you."

I made an impassive gesture. After all our time together, I had very little control over Lynn. It took all my patience to accede to her demands. A state of affairs we had become used to. I turned my attention back to Niranjan, saying, "Where have you been?"

"Different places. I've been sleeping in the car."

Studying his distraught face, I chose to believe him. "Why have you been doing that?"

"Did you hear what happened at the Tamil shop on Lawrence?"

I searched my mind and nodded my head. There had been something in the news, but the details were vague. The police had no names. "You were involved in that?"

He nodded his head.

I spoke softly to reassure him I meant no harm. It made no sense to press him on something that might have traumatized him. What was he hiding? "Did you harm somebody?"

He put his hands up to his face and scraped his cheeks. "I didn't mean to, Mr N. They hurt my friend. I didn't know what to do – it just happened. I'm telling you the honest truth."

"Why not go to the police if they started it?" I asked. I didn't even know who they were.

"What? You think they're going to believe me? Come on, Mr N, I know you're not that naive."

I could see that the hope of recovering the ground he had lost at school was soon vanishing. He was only one of many students in this situation, but his predicament was far worse. "What do you want from us?" I asked. "How can we help you?"

"I don't know."

"Do you want money?"

"No!"

I could hear in his voice and tell from his appearance that he did. We sat like that for a while, the dog watching us, his fur shimmering bluebottle, the sun fading away by degrees. The sunsets were spectacular at that time of year. The sky was all pink and aglow with warm light. The rays reflected golden along the lake and tops of sails, shining upon the people out for strolls far below us. The dusk slowly melted through the window; the warmth and afterglow would burn away very slowly.

"I don't know," Niranjan said again in defeat. "I could use some money for an inhaler, some food. Mostly, I want to show you this video sent to my phone. Nadesan says there are other ones like it on Tamilnet."

I didn't know what he was talking about, so I asked him to explain. After he showed me the horrifying transmissions, I asked him to send them to my email.

Saying I would be back in a moment, I asked Niranjan to excuse me.

Lynn was pouring hot water on top of ginger cinnamon tea bags when I entered. She stood in the small alcove that she'd decorated with preserve jars, hurt that I hadn't listened to her earlier. I didn't have time for an argument. "We've got to let him stay here, Lynn."

I could feel her blood steam, just like the water in the kettle. She was shrill. "Have you gone crazy? What is wrong with you? Can't you see that's completely impossible?"

"He's got nowhere to go, Lynn."

"That's not our problem! That's not your problem. Don't you see what can happen to us if we just take in a kid from school without telling anybody? We're teachers, and we have a legal obligation to do things properly. He should go back to his guardians, his aunt."

I pushed myself away from the door and went towards her with open arms, head bent forward. "Shh. Be quiet. We don't want him to hear us. You know he can't go back to her – she's the reason he moved in with that boy in the first place."

"Like I said, that's not our problem. I heard you talking. He's involved in a crime!"

"It's not his fault. I believe him." I tried to hold her, but she pushed away miserably. "Lynn, my father cared about this boy, he helped his people bring him over. I'd like to help Niranjan for my father's sake – you know he and I were never close."

The smell of cinnamon and ginger flooded the kitchen. It seemed to calm her down, but not enough. "Dan, think what you're doing. You do this – bend the rules and take Niranjan in – and you'll ruin everything we've been working for, everything I've been working for. Badlamenti sure as promised I'd become a VP – I've been in guidance three years – that's an amazing opportunity for me. He offered you CLship of your own department. Your interview would only be a formality. Think about what that means. You do something that could get us both in trouble, and we ruin everything."

"I'm not saying that we shouldn't let them know at school," I explained patiently – I wasn't really thinking. "I just mean we should take care of the boy until he can get to some place better."

"But what about what I just said?" she replied, frustrated. "You're not even listening to me."

"I heard you, but I don't want any of those things. I want to help this boy."

I could tell – she wanted to fling the tea in my face. But she forced herself to speak calmly. "We should be thinking of having kids of our own," she said, taking deep breaths. "He's just a student, not your kin. You need to let him go. It's not professional. We're not getting any younger, Dan, but good things are coming our way. Let's use this time to plan our first kid.

"I don't want to do that now." The words came out before I could stop them. "Let's take Niranjan in and see how that goes."

At that moment Chuck entered the kitchen and began to whine. He stood between us, shaking agitatedly and splaying his feet. The dog was such a deep indigo suede now, I only vaguely remembered that soft brown mocha-chocolate coat he'd once possessed. It seemed a long time ago. When he had been a Christmas present for Lynn.

"What is it?" I asked, and followed the dog back to the living room.

It was empty. Niranjan must have been listening because he'd flown the coop. For a few minutes, we looked around our place – in the bathroom, the bedrooms – but there was no sign of him. As if he was never there. I tried to get him on the phone, but there was no answer.

Lynn was happy to have her way after all.

NIRANJAN

I show up to media class next day because Nadesan asks me to – he says it's important.

It's the last big meeting before the assembly. Mr N seems surprised to see me, but he's got other things to deal with. I can see the stress on his face. The class is a disaster. Those who show up come late. They trickle in as if they don't want to be there. The mood is like lead. I notice the graffiti on the wall in the computer lab. It's grown. Someone has stencilled 'Fuck This School' in black marker right at the bottom. Chaos rules the school.

Most of the videos are unfinished, including my own group's. Those that are close to being done are unwatchable. Mr N tries to proceed as if it's any other meeting. "This is the most important project I've ever been entrusted with at this school," he says. "It matters." Kids look at him, aggravated by his words. Some of them are running on less sleep than I am.

The grey computers, hardly any of them turned on, line the long tables. The graffiti now even tattoos the monitors. This lab used to be brand spanking new.

"Have any of you finished the work I asked you to do?" Mr N's voice rings out in silence.

Nothing. They just sit there, doing the Tamil scowl, some hanging their heads. Hands in their laps, twiddling their thumbs, not able to meet his eye.

"Come on, guys! What did I tell you? If we don't have anything to show for ourselves, you know what that's going to look like? With all the money that's been sunk into this thing, the preparations that have gone into it? Distinguished guests are coming – you remember MPP Paisley – this is the guy who represents you in legislature, right?"

"We didn't ask for this," Nadesan licks his lips and shakes his head. The others murmur, agreeing. Nadesan, bold, keeps going. "You're the one who told us we should do this. You and the principal. We didn't sign up for this when we took the course."

His tone is accusing. The others take it up. "He's right," agrees Kumar. "It's all for you. Don't you realize that? You're the ones who want your video festival. We're just trying to make you happy." Others in the class agree.

Mr N seems genuinely surprised. "Are you serious? Why would we be doing this except for you?" Hearing the words come out, he seems even more surprised that he's said them. Perhaps he hears himself sound like his father? His mother? "It's because so many of your friends are ditching school to go to the protests that Badlamenti set up this assembly," he adds lamely.

Me, I say nothing – just watch. My body aches and I'm tired. I'd like to sleep on a regular bed. I'd like to use an inhaler. I'd like a nice fat Percocet or two. Hopefully, pretty soon, I'll be through the withdrawal, not miss the painkillers so much.

Raj speaks up, "Mr N, we know you've been going through a hard time with your father and all... but we can't finish our videos.

"Why not?"

"A lot of us have family or friends who are suffering back home. A lot of them have already been injured... or even killed. They're running and hiding. The army's bombing them every day. That's why we haven't been able to work on the videos. The things we hear. The things we see. They're lying bleeding to death on blankets in open air buildings. There's nobody to help them."

"Wait a minute," asks Mr N. "You said the things you see. What do you mean by that? What do you mean – see?"

Some of them murmur among themselves. The whispers are fierce. At one point, they actually get up out of their seats to talk and conference. Much of it in Tamil. They speak fast, and Mr N tries to catch what they say. They are like an aged huddle of men, like our aiyahs.

"Tell him, tell him," says one of the boys, breaking the discussion.

"Tell me what?" asks Mr N.

Instead of telling, they show him. I get up to see over their shoulders.

Grainy images of destruction transmitted in short little video clips on Nadesan's iPhone. Old women, their hair wavering in the wind, reaching their hands up to the videographer, begging for food and water. Not being able to move because their legs don't work. Men in coloured sarams kneeling on the floor over twisted and mangled bodies, weeping and wailing, exposing themselves to the air strikes that must surely follow. Hulks of vacant vans and bombed-out automobiles on fire. A child with his right arm twisted off, the arm lying beside him in impossible contortion, the only thing connecting the two a mess of what looks like spaghetti. And the blood. Blood everywhere. It's amazing how real the wounds look, the colour of blood bright scarlet, even in the desaturated grainy videos.

It's not like in the movies where the squibs explode precisely in pomegranate bursts. Here, the spilt ruby blood is everywhere and on everything. It flows through the grooves of corrugated tin that covers a man's body and seeps into the pools of water in the ground.

"How can we make our stupid shit videos after this?" asks Nadesan.

Mr N is in shock and looks at me as if to say, "Where have these videos come from?" The same expression flashed across his face when I showed him mine last night. He really doesn't know. He looks at Nadesan's phone like it's something to be feared.

"Look," jumps in Kumar. In an exasperated voice, he breaks down what everyone seems to know. "The Sri Lankan Army has been designating safe zones, right? Right?"

"Yes," Mr N answers. He's probably thinking about the heavy shelling and warfare and the thousands of casualties of Tamil civilians caught in the areas between the army and the LTTE. The army has blocked out a stretch of the coast to be designated as a refugee safe zone. Tamil civilians can flee there, set up camp, tend to their wounded, or so the Army says. A demilitarized haven for Tamil refugees is what they call it – to escape from the bombing.

"It's no safe zone!" Kumar froths as he tells Mr N, like he's an idiot. The others are out of their seats, urging him on. "They're using it to herd people in there and then they bomb them. Don't you see? The Sri Lankan Army's bombing the civilians. That was their plan all along. They've bombed like sixty times. They've bombed the medical tents. Don't you know anything?"

Mr. N looks from them to me. I shrug my shoulders. His throat sounds as dry, as rough as sandpaper. "But why?"

"Why else? To kill them, of course!"

DANIEL

Lynn went to sleep before I did, not talking, like the previous night. Much was on our minds – the assembly was this weekend. I'm sure that's all Lynn thought about, but I also ruminated about the boys who refused to cooperate with Badlamenti. I thought about Niranjan's situation and worried about him. Where was he sleeping that night? I had asked him to come to the assembly to support us all, but I wasn't even sure the other boys would show up. Would I see him again? I also thought of my mother and to a lesser extent my sister – how were they coping with my father's death? One of Amma's Sai Baba friends would stay over and help her sell the house, but it was not a good time, economically speaking. Would her friend use my mother in the process?

Chuck slept peacefully. His large slumbering body twitched, sending soft ripples of electric blue across his hide. He almost shimmered in the moonlight. There was still food from dinner left on the table, some chicken and rice, which I'd promised Lynn I would clean up. But I was exhausted. The prospect of doing those dishes seemed to suck the last ounce of life from me.

Instead, I wandered into the bedroom, very softly, to watch Lynn sleep. For the last few nights, we had not touched. She thought I was a fool to sympathize with Niranjan. It was difficult not to think of the boy, especially when relations with my own family were so poor. That was partly Lynn's fault, was it not? Or was I only putting blame onto her that squarely belonged with me?

I saw my mother and me a year from now in the house. The very same house. A year has passed since the death of my father, and we sit at the table in his memory. We are joined by my sister and her husband. My brother-in-law conspicuously snaps the golden links of his wristwatch, a phantom impatient gesture that reminds me obscurely of my father. The watch is large and shiny, meant to inspire awe and confidence, ticking off the rising dollars in their bank account.

A small amount of food is dolloped on each plate. A plate for each person plus an empty one for the absent man. There are curd rice, dahl, spinach, and eggplant curries, fried vaddais with dried chilies. Incense burns in front of the hallowed photo of my father. He smiles from a gilded frame, gallant in the dark suit we buried him in, one of the rare times he smiled, evidently forced under duress to flash his teeth for the camera. Propped up against the frame is my father's Canadian citizenship card, laminated and small. We stand in front of the photo, our hands clasped in prayer as the glowing end of the incense burns, the ash listlessly droops. We sing my father's favourite thervarums. My mother prefers Sathya Sai bhajans.

After the prayers, Amma picks up a little food from the plate set aside for my father and, as is the custom, dips it into a glass of water and throws it out the door onto their postage stamp of a garden, over my father's flowers. It is foggy and damp outside. Hyacinths and tulips in the garden, in honour of my father, wave their heads in the wind. The starlings flit around

We start to eat. Conversation begins in cautious whispers.

"The food is excellent," says my sister.

"Where did you get the money to make the mortgage payments?" I interject.

"Here and there," my mother waves me off.

"I should have given you money," I whisper.

"No point talking of the past now."

Suddenly, a knock on the door. Who could it be?

"Daniel, go see who that is."

The door swings open, slamming against the wall; the wind blows a lament of pain and longing. We all strain to see what's going on. A hand of white bone and dark flapping skin emerges from the darkness and mist. White cuffed, dark suit in tatters, moist flesh falling off the bones.

In the palm of the bony rotting hand is the speck of food thrown out earlier in the ritual, rescued from the birds. Attached to the hand, if this state of horrific grisly decomposition can be called attachment, is my father.

He looks different now – one eye and a portion of his scalp gone. Brittle teeth poke out from stripped, bleeding gums. His sharp nose has fallen off, leaving a spade-shaped cavity. Rolling flesh has been stripped away, leaving him tired and excavated. Shoulder blades hold up what is left of a sagging body. One could house a pet bird in his rib cage. A few strands of white hair, wild as dry grass, still grow out the follicles in his head.

"You've set a plate for me," he says. He sits uncomfortably, creaking, with much grinding of the bones. His lungs and alveoli have withered. He has no voice box to speak from. He doesn't speak so much as allow the wind to rattle through him. His flesh emits the light of a thousand photochemical changes. I can see the internal cava of his body: the tired, disintegrating lungs are joined to the stomach and colon in a network of bleeding capillaries. A heart, engorged, pushed beyond its power, beats furiously above his spleen.

He stares at his plate, then scoops a small morsel of food and swallows it. His teeth make an unsettling clacking sound. The grains of food fall out through the holes in the ulcerous esophagus, into his ribcage and guts.

My brother-in-law nervously snaps the links of his gold wristwatch and checks the time. Looks for the slow progress of the second hand round the dial. Suddenly his pupils dilate. His mouth flops open. He takes off the wristwatch and shows it to us. I look closely. On the jewel-encrusted dial, there are no numbers or hands.

Father then turns to me. The stripped-back, tired and excavated face, one eyeball lunging out of its socket, is terrifying. Excruciatingly, he breaks off one of the exposed ribs from his chest. Pops it like a wishbone. Holding the rib, he brings it down like a lever against the palm of his bony hand. He tests its soundness and weight. An instrument of discipline and punishment. When his words come, they wheeze right into my face. "So what did you do with your life?" he wheezes. "Did you become a filmmaker?

"Sometimes I think I wanted that too much," I say, staring into his face. "Too painful. Too much sacrifice. Know what I mean?"

"I felt that way about my family," is his hollow reply.

"You'll never get out from under me," he continues. "From under my shadow. May you have a life even worse than mine. May you live and die alone, a man without a home. A man without a country. May you die unloved, unmourned, unremembered."

I woke up from the dream, sweat running down my body. My clammy body lay on the bed beside Lynn. She roused slowly.

"What is it?" she asked. I was still sweating, and my heart raced a mile a minute. I could see and smell and taste my father's decomposing corpse, even though we had cremated him. The smell of the burned insects he had brought back flooded the room. The spectre of him separating one of the wobbly ribs from his decalcified body and then beating me with it to vent his disappointment.

"What is it, Dan?" she asked again, taking my shoulder. "Do you want to…"

Chuck whined in his sleep in the next room.

I shook my head and sat there staring into the gloom gathering in front of my eyes. She was being especially kind, given how we'd gone to sleep, how we'd gone to sleep the past two nights. Ever since Niranjan had driven a wedge between us – again. I guess there was still sexual attraction there, although we hadn't acted on it. You can fuck and hate a person at the same time. Usually, not having sex for a few days made things exciting. It recharged the batteries. But now I felt nothing. My whole body was wax. It bent to the times. I was cold and rubbery and melting.

The essence of my father still hovered in the room. His dying, his crossing over to the other side. The memory of those long evenings, sitting by his side, staring at the dial of his watch as time crawled by while he checked my sums seemed closer than that of his old age, his months of failing health and attempts to make untimely mortgage payments. The flash of anger that would sometimes come upon him, the heat of his actions, the rage in his eyes. The rigidity of his bearing and conduct. Somehow I missed these things. I hate to admit it, but some part of me missed him, longed for him even. I did not know how I could go on and live the rest of my life without him there to scream at me, to drive me through the wind and furze. He had never realized the impact he had upon my life. The damage he had done. How he haunted me.

I needed him to beat me again. The only contact that I had received from either of my parents was this one.

So this was what drew me to Lynn. I finally understood. Freud said that we attempt to find a woman to replace our mother. Lynn did not resemble my mother in the least. They were like chalk and cheese. It was my father whom she reminded me of: his demanding nature, the force with which he pressed himself through life, upon others. I remembered the weight of her foot upon my neck, the ball and toe with the tendons straining, the sole inches away from my lips.

Had her foot not been on my neck this whole time?

"Lynn," I said, "I'm going to sleep in the living room. So I don't wake you up."

She seemed worried. I could hear her short breaths in the dark. For once, she seemed as adrift as I was. We didn't know what was happening to us. If each of us is just countless bundles of neurons and electricity, who can say when one neuron will join to another, spark off this movement, or that reaction? The whys and wherefores. Who can say?

I must have been really tired as I fetched a blanket and pillow and walked out into the living room that night. I sensed something behind me. In the dim dining space, Chuck, who'd been laid out on the floor for the last hour, tired and asleep, suddenly stretched out those spade-like paws of his and yawned a large halitosis yawn. He then lifted himself up on hind legs and walked over to the dinner table. Not leapt up and placed his paws, like he did on the kitchen counter, but walked. It was a strange thing to see, because most of his weight resided in his front carriage and head. There must have been tremendous strain on his haunches as he ambled forward like a man. Yet he managed the feat without trouble, as if I were not there and could not see him slide into a chair.

It must have been the dreams. It must have been the stress. It must have been a thousand other things. By the time he clasped his paws around the leftover chicken and began lifting it to his jaws, I was ready to fall down.

NIRANJAN

By the time I arrive at the assembly, I see I'm the only guy from the class here. Everybody else must be at the protests. To be honest with you, free food is the main reason I've come. Gut's been rumbling and tight. You can get a free shower, but free food is a little trickier. Plus – I'm curious. I watch people get ready in the halls: the dancers in their costumes. They fuss over their gold jewellery, which takes more time to put on than the actual saris.

I take a seat in the audience near the front. There aren't many people here, but everybody's so busy, they don't notice me. Already, the performance is running late. They haven't even begun.

Ms Varley's checking on the sound system. It's a lot of work to set that up and rehearse the lighting cues. She's talking to Mr N in the pit, and I can hear her say, "God, Dan, anyone who hasn't worked on organizing a stage performance will not understand!" He tries to say something and reassure her. "Do not talk to me about lighting," she replies. "I swear, they must have to fail an IQ test to be part of the stage crew at this school." Wonder if anyone else can hear her? I look up at the kid in the booth doing the lighting. He's tall, skinny, long haired, white. I've seen him around. If I'd sold weed at the school, I bet he'd have been a regular customer. If your ambition in life is to get high all day, why cloud it by taking on responsibilities like stage crew?

The set design is a bit strange. The shop teacher's made these fake wooden pillars for both sides of the stage – they're supposed to represent temple pillars, I guess, with lotus leaves and Indian designs. I shouldn't poke fun at what Ms Varley's doing, even if I don't like her. The assembly's not her idea. She's been working really hard. Mr N has told us that this is all Mr Badlamenti's idea – working for him must almost be as bad as the situation I'm in.

Some more people arrive. I can't be sure, but I think I hear Ms Varley whisper to Mr N, "Am I just another stupid nigger girl who sold herself down the river or what?"

Mr Ackerman, one of our vice-principals, shuffles down the aisle and goes up to Ms Varley. He apologizes and tells her that the media are here. He says she has to go greet them. She nods her head. For a second, that head looks so heavy it might just roll off her shoulders onto the floo . Imagine her picking up her head in her hands, then greeting the press. A good movie image.

Mr Ackerman gives her a glance and smiles. She forces herself to smile back. Mr N just watches. What's going on in his mind? Ms Varley smooths down her skirt and burgundy blazer and tells everybody that she'll be back soon. She follows Mr Ackerman up the aisle.

Watching them, I see that what she thought would be a full press corps is just a couple of local reporters. Somebody from the Scarborough Mirror, maybe. Or maybe The Toronto Star. There's a young guy from OMNI with a pen and pad in his hand – no cameras whatsoever.

I strain my ears to listen.

"Hey, I'm sorry," says the OMNI guy as he shakes her hand. "We didn't have any cameramen to spare."

"But the dances and the singing and the prayers…" she says. "How are you going to report on any of that without pictures?"

"Actually, we were hoping you'd take pictures of your own and mail them in to us," says the other reporter. Ms Varley looks even more unhappy when she hears that.

"I'm hoping that someone might be able to come down to take photos for us," says the woman reporter. She's from

The Star. "I'm waiting on a call from him. Today's been a pretty busy day."

Ms Varley takes her by the hand and leads her away. She's practically begging. I'm glad I came here after all. "My principal is going to go ballistic if he comes down here and sees not a single cameraman among you," says Ms Varley. "He needs you to show people how much we care about the plight of the Tamils. All of this, everything I did, will have been for nothing if…"

"I'm sorry, I'm trying to get the photographer but he's also got to swing by the protests," replies the reporter.

"Forget the protests!" Mr Badlamenti suddenly makes his entrance, bringing that politician guy Paisley with him. Paisley smiles his pasty smile. "This is where the real expression of sympathy for Sri Lanka lies!" announces Mr Badlamenti, waving his arms. Other people have turned their heads and are listening. This'll be more entertaining than the actual show.

Finally, things start.

The girls have all their make-up on, their dancing saris are tucked and folded in all the right places. The musicians, a tabla player, a harmonium organist, and a flautist with his Indian reed flute, have taken places on the stage. Things will begin. Something's wrong with the lights so Ms Varley goes up to the booth to yell at that stoner again.

Finally, we're forced to stand up and sing the national anthem:
"O Canada! Our home and native land!
True patriot love in all thy sons command."

I stand up without singing. It's not my native land.

Badlamenti gets up and introduces the evening in his goofy manner. He talks about the school and what a great community it is, and blah, blah, blah. His gut strains against the podium. His weight sways over weak ankles and knobby knees. I don't think he'd be able to 'stand on guard' for anything except baked pastries. MPP Paisley gets up and talks about how we're standing on land that rightfully belongs to the native Indians. If politicians really believe it was stolen from natives, why don't they give it back? He then talks about Tamil people and all the good values they've brought with them to Canada and their hard work ethic and how driven they are in school, blah, blah, blah. What a load of bullshit. I know that with each word, he's thinking of suicide bombers and militant groups and executions. Mr N has all his technology set up in the pit: the projector on the cart and the laptop and the speakers. Nobody's with him though.

The music and dancing are okay – nothing we haven't seen hundreds of times before. The girls are honed and practised as usual. I see Abirami leading them and wonder if she knows what happened to Soothy. How would she react? Would she care? The dancers' bare feet hit the old wooden floorboards. The waves of sound from the harmonium's organ synthesize with the shaky notes from the flute. Everything pulls along.

And then it's time for the videos.

Mr N doesn't introduce the videos. He goes up to the microphone. There's dead silence. I almost expect the feedback to squawk like it would in a movie, but there's just dead silence and the shaft of light coming down in front of the curtains. Dust swirling in the spotlight's glare. He mumbles something about their original ideas to make videos being upended by what's going on in Sri Lanka.

And that's it. While the crowd waits for him to say more, he turns down the microphone and leaves the stage as the projector screen comes down in front of the curtains. The lights also go down. What happens next is a series of images that I have seen. I know some of the Tamils in the audience have seen it too. But what about the others?

The camera is so shaky, the images so grainy and discoloured that blowing them up on the big screen only seems to add to their incoherence. Sand, hot dust, smoke swirling in the blue air. Straight from Sri Lanka. The footage is all haphazard, not edited. I can see others in the audience strain to understand what's happening. Can't understand anything that's being said. Some of this footage is recorded with a cellphone. People running for their lives. Agitated elderly and disabled. Trying to carry a bag of something. Always the sound of thunder and volleys of shells in the background. Bodies in the water. Bodies lying on plastic sheets, bodies on the ground, bodies with gashes in their legs and torsos, bodies with blood bleeding out.

Non-Tamils are like, What's going on here?

The wailing, the constant wailing and the keening that come from the people stretched out in shelters, in ditches, on the sand. The misery and poverty. This is the norm, people, not the exception. Devastation everywhere. The final video is different from all the rest. In it, you can see army soldiers. They wear green uniforms. Some carry rifles. It looks like the camera person is in the bushes, shooting on the fl . Bodies are laid out in rows like sardines, like tuna in Japanese fisheries. Many have been stripped, some of them women, and the soldiers are throwing them onto the back of a truck.

Is this real? they think. How could it be real? How could a person have gotten hold of it?

Gasps go through the crowd. Then a hush as we all see the exposed breasts and privates of female victims, now dead. Their heads and eyes loll back. You can tell what people are thinking: Have they been raped and tortured?

What balls on Mr N! Wait till the guys hear about this. The lights come up.

I can see Mr Badlamenti fuming.

The photographer from The Star has arrived. He's snapping away while the reporters scribble in their pads.

This can't be good.

THE PROTESTS

DANIEL

Badlamenti hauled both me and Lynn into his office. Never had I seen him so angry. People were still trickling out of the assembly hall – Lynn had to leave the prefects and other students to fend for themselves.

"What the hell was that?" shrieked Badlamenti. He hadn't even bothered to sit down. Instead, he pounded his fist like a pestle into the mortar of his palm

I didn't say anything. I couldn't. Everything I had to say was projected up on that screen. Lynn stared at me, trying to reach me with her eyes. She was tense, alert, constantly checked the bun in her hair with her fingertips. I felt the opposite: deflated, my shoulders rolled forward.

"Well, don't you have anything to say?" screamed Badlamenti, spittle careening out his mouth. "Ms Varley, could you please indicate to our friend here what is going on!"

"Daniel," she said gently, as gently as anything I've ever heard. "If you don't tell us what you were thinking… allowing the kids to show those videos, well…something's got to be very wrong."

"This is your one chance," said Badlamenti, thrusting his finger in my face. "Your one chance! You'd better speak up!"

"I don't know…" I said, "I don't know what you want me to say."

Badlamenti looked at me once more as if he was making it clear that he was giving both of us a final chance. I felt badly for Lynn. This wasn't what she wanted. Yet, at the same time, part of me was a little glad also. "If you were so concerned," I asked, "why didn't you look at the videos before we screened them? If you weren't so worried about the way you looked to reporters…"

"What did you say?" shouted Badlamenti. "What did you say to me? You little shit! You think you're funny? Keep laughing! I could have your job like that!" He snapped his fingers. Lynn, terrified, stared straight ahead. I just glanced at the Goodfellas poster mounted on the wall. Three decades of life in the mafia, damn straight

"If I could figure out what just happened here, if I could understand what the hell it is that you think you're doing, I'd bury you so far, teaching some correctional school program – you'd never see the light of day! So help me, you'll never come within a hundred yards of a regular school again!"

"If it's clarity you're looking for," I said, "that's easy. Those were real videos taken by real Tamils in the real Sri Lanka. That's what's happening now. That's what's really going on. They're being massacred – mothers, fathers, children, normal people – not the fighters, not just the terrorists. That's why my students couldn't work on their films. You want to address the Tamil problem? Address that!"

At that point, Bud Ackerman and Myra Solikowski walked in. I could see concern in their eyes. Ackerman walked behind Badlamenti's desk and placed a hand on his shoulder, but Badlamenti shrugged it off. "What?" he said in a whisper. "You think I didn't struggle against the mangiacakes and all the other bastards running this country? My father worked construction! Go back a couple of generations and look at where the Italians were in this country – look at what they did! Good enough only to fix your toilets and work as bricklayers, but did we complain?"

"What Principal Badlamenti is saying," began Ackerman.

"No! What I'm saying is that you're hanging by a very thin thread, my young friends," cut in Badlamenti. "You exist here because I say so." He pounded his fist again, then just ran out of steam and wound down, finally collapsing in his chair. He swivelled round to look out his window. He sighed, "You think I'm not going to get it from Paisley? What the hell happened here?"

This was Myra's cue and drunk or not, she acted. "He's just lost his father. He's obviously going through grief. Daniel, why don't you take time off and deal with things? It's obvious you're not fit to teach."

"That's putting it mildly," stated Badlamenti.

"Wait a minute," I said.

"Not so fast!" Ackerman talked over me. "There's going to be disciplinary action on this one. What Mr Narayan did was unacceptable. He sabotaged our school and its reputation in front of a large audience."

"You're calling that a large audience?" asked Myra. "They were here for the free food. You put on a two-ring circus – you forced these two overworked teachers to put on a show for you with no time or help, and you're surprised it backfired on you? Believe me, the union will fight this. No, Daniel's going on leave until he clears his head and can come back to teach again. Isn't that right?"

I stared at her, bewildered.

Badlamenti was hushed for a while. Finally, he said, "Get out – all of you."

We drove home in silence, Lynn doing the driving. She wouldn't let me touch the wheel. Or allow me to start a conversation. She simply ignored me and looked ahead if I uttered anything.

We had to avoid the major intersections downtown and take a roundabout way, going down Jarvis. Everything was diverted, affected, slowed down by the protests.

When we finally got home, we stood apart in the elevator as it rode up, each staring at our own reflection in the brassy panels.

Even when we got inside, she refused to talk at first. Only stood at the window and stared out at the small points of light in the harbour. Her back squared, strong shoulder blades raised. Back of her head thrown at me. Chuck had been sitting up, preening and wagging his tail, ready to be taken out when we got in. Now, he lowered his head and whimpered.

"It's over, isn't it?" she asked.

She turned around, and I stopped in the middle of removing my left shoe and looked at her in the dark moonlight filtering in through the big window of the dining room, highlighting the few grey hairs that were beginning to show, the displeasure in her tired face. All her fault lines and dried pores were brought into relief by the tiredness in her eyes. She wasn't visibly angry, but there was a coldness emanating from the tight drum of her skin. Lynn unloosened the bun and shook her hair over her shoulders. She had straightened her hair for the assembly; since it was thick and dry, much of it now stood in wisps, radiating cold fury from her body. Her jaw clenched and her shoulders tightened. I could read her gestures only too well.

"What do you want me to say?" I replied. "Do you want me to say that I ruined your career, that I did it all to give you a hard time? I know that's what you're thinking."

"It amazes me," she said, affecting puzzlement and curiousity, "that we continued as long as we did. I really tried with you. Do you think that all we care about is our careers, that we're out to get you? Myra helped you today, and it's because of her you still have a job. You never did want to have a child, did you?"

I shook my head. "I couldn't take it. I couldn't take doing to someone else what was done to me." But then I stopped. I began to feel guilty and laughed. I couldn't help it. "You asked me earlier tonight whether you'd sold out. You have – you have. You're Badlamenti's pet. Remember who you were in those photos you showed me at your mother's? What would that person think of whom you've become? The way you talk, the way you dress, the people you suck up to? What have you become?"

"You're one to talk," she shot back. "Look at the movies you had postered up on the wall before I met you. The films you espouse and feed to those kids you call students. Those films are white, made by white directors – every single one of them. You're nothing but whitewashed, feeding others the colonized garbage you've internalized. You feed it to kids who don't know any better, try to make them the same. Isn't that so?"

"No, that's not true –"

"You're a child, and you're not fit to work with children. That's why you can't be a father. Because, inside, you're no older than they are. I kept quiet all this time, thinking I could change you. That it would only be a matter of time. But you're not going to change. You don't want to hear what I have to say – what I truly think. It would destroy you!"

"Okay, Lynn. Okay," I admitted. "I hate things at our school. I hate our country and how nobody gives a fuck about anybody else unless it benefits them. Unless they have to. I'm not a terrorist and never will be – I'll never be a Tiger sympathizer – but I can understand their rage and frustration. This was my one act of sabotage, my one act of will in this whole shitty career we call teaching. My attempt at something genuine."

She recoiled. "It doesn't matter now – it's over for us."

What could I say in response? The dog, who had been watching all this time, got up with a low quizzical growl. He came and sat between us. His short tail wiped the dust back and forth on the floor as he watched one, then the other, expecting us to take him for his walk. His stare unnerved me, but Lynn hardly seemed to notice.

"Listen, those videos we played weren't an excuse to piss you and Badlamenti off," I tried to explain. "It's the real stuff that's happening in Sri Lanka. The kids are getting emailed these videos from people suffering over there. How could you ask them to make politically correct lukewarm videos after seeing that?"

"What business do you have going and putting that up on the screen, traumatizing us, traumatizing the kids?"

"They've already been traumatized by what they've seen and heard."

She withdrew, planting herself on a chair, leaning over the kitchen counter. "What will you do?" she asked, clasping her hands. "We can't live together any longer."

She was correct. We both knew it. She folded her arms tightly and raised her posture, flinging her shoulders back, her back straight as a steel rod. You're worse than the kids you deal with because they at least have the excuse of being children, her posture seemed to say. What's your excuse?

Just like that, everything was over. All in the past. Had been for months. Maybe it had never been correct. The realization of that, more than anything, was painful. That we possessed the ability to lie to ourselves for so long. That we had simply wasted our lives.

First my father, now this. I had gotten used to her presence in my life. For two years, I had cared for her. Without loyalty, what does one have?

But she was right. We did not belong together. I suppose this had always been the case. What amazed me was what little fury remained after the acknowledgement. That would come later. And animosity – yes, animosity. But right then, we were exhausted, and it was a relief to admit the truth. There just wasn't enough feeling left between us to fight over. We were like that scrap of verse, scribbled on a napkin, attributed to Leonard Cohen, framed in the foyer of our school. Everyone must know it's a fake, mustn't they? Couldn't possibly be his writing. But it looks good. A handsome prop. A plausible and pleasant fake.

"What're you going to do now?" she asked.

"I'll go to a motel," I replied.

"You could go to your mother's."

I shook my head. "My mother's got plenty to worry about already. She's trying to get stuff out of there, get it ready to sell. I'd only be in her way."

"Well, you can stay the night." She relaxed her arms, made a generous gesture. "We can figure this out in the morning."

I was exhausted, but my pride forced me to refuse. "No, it's okay. I'll gather a few things now. I've done enough damage to your life. I've got a little money in the bank. I'll come back for my stuff later."

Lynn nodded and turned away. At the kitchen counter, chin against her palm, thinking. Silent. She remained like that.

My muscles ached, my heart beat fast, my nerves were shot, I could feel myself beginning a fever. I was burned out. I had been running on empty so long that I could only begin to sense the edges of the large aching hole within my heart.

The dog growled and circled us both. Sweat started to roll down my temples. I thought of the time the ball of her foot rested against my throat, and I began to feel angry. I wanted to go to her and trace the lines around her mouth. I wanted to say, "You know what I see when I look at you now?

369

"I don't see the dynamic person I was moved by, the one I volunteered for. That was just the mask. All I see are the cracks. Here, around your mouth, the awareness and indifference. The way your lips pull upward. The lust for power, need for validation. You still have your looks, it's true. But no matter how much I squint my eyes, I can no longer ignore the insolence or the cold hard mean-spiritedness." But of course, I only thought those words, went into the bedroom to load essentials into a suitcase instead.

The dog growled again.

"And take your dog with you," she hissed.

That was her way of saying she rejected everything I had given her. All the warmth and kindness. The support.

It's not that I don't want kids, I thought to myself dully. I just don't want them with you. I couldn't bear to see you as their mother. We're like rum and Coke. We should never have mixed. It's ruined the both of us.

NIRANJAN

Mr N calls to say he's no longer living with Ms Varley. Now he can help me. He's moved out with the dog and sublets a one bedroom apartment in the Annex. "I'm back where I started a year ago," he says, "except I've got you and Chuck to worry about."

There's a lightness in his voice, besides worry and uncertainty. I'm sleeping in the Yutani. How can I say no to his offer? We go pick up a mattress and pillow and sheets for me to crash on the living room floor of his new place. There's even a place in back of the apartment to park the car.

We go down to the protests sometimes, but never properly join in. He likes to walk through. We listen to the sweep and murmur of voices:

"They told us to put down the flag. I ain't putting down the fla – they're going to have to deal with it."

* * *

"Don't know where they come from or where they're going."

* * *

"It's our identity, man."

* * *

"… think we're a joke… covering us in morning traffic reports…"

* * *

"This is your country – we're here for one cause!"

* * *

"… they tried to block off that side street… they're watching us…"

* * *

"Either you're with us or against us… What are you afraid of?"

* * *

"It's public perception… They don't understand…"

* * *

"… like World War II all over again."

* * *

"Idiot! Get your dog away from the food!"

I haven't heard from my family since those videos. Yes, it worries me. The cops all around don't make me happy either. I don't think they know who shot Muruges, but can one be sure? I kept the gun and don't think I left any prints. Karthik and the couple who run the place wouldn't have told. They're involved too.

Thought I saw Karthik once, wearing a hat and shades, when we drove by. That bristly reed of his moustache. He was wearing a dark green shirt that hung loosely over his bony chest, no coat. I turned my face away. Soon we were gone. I don't know if it was him – he was a face in the crowd – a green shirt in a sea of red.

To pass time, Mr N offers to give me driving lessons again. Still only have a G1. He says we should definitely set up a road test.

He sets it up that very night. He's already paying for the gas and food – I have no money to give him for the apartment. Feel vaguely guilty. People have taken care of me ever since I got here: my aunt, Rageev, now him. He seems to be the best of them, but what can I give him in return? He even buys me another inhaler. I don't have anything. Probably never will have anything. Am I even worth it? What do these people want from me?

He's lost his father, and I've lost Rageev, Soothy, my brother, maybe my whole family. Even if we don't talk about this, there's a common feeling – a numbness. I drive, and he sits there, gives me pointers. We go to movies. It's okay. About all we can handle, really. I can handle communicating with the car. He can handle communicating with the dog. Neither of them talk back. I feel gears turning, the axle spinning, pistons pumping. That's it. I can see the mechanics of this car, but not the world we live in. When I was on pills, they blocked things out comfortably. I lost all care for the world. But now, slowly, now that the pills are gone, the feelings begin to return. The confusion and worry.

As we sit in the car, me driving, him correcting my bad habits, that feeling jumps from my fingertips into the engine and back again. Eyes and brain work together. We drive around, feeling the wheels on the ground, getting a feel for the surface of roads, circling the fringes of the protests, avoiding cops that hang around. We drive west to the Annex or east to the Don Valley. That's about all I can handle. The rest of this world is shit.

"I don't care about Lynn anymore or my career or making a movie," he says. "None of it. All I care about is you and the dog. How was I going to make a film about Sri Lanka anyway? I know nothing about nothing about Sri Lanka. Keep your eyes on the road. There! Turn on your indicator."

I switch on the indicator, make the turn smoothly. "It's never too late," I reply. "Isn't that what you always told us? That being a doctor or an engineer isn't all there is in life – can't you say the same thing about being a teacher? Creativity and dreams are important, aren't they?"

"You're young. You don't understand. You've got to strike early. Before you know better. When you're full of feeling. Once you're old, the world just sucks it out of you. You're the one that should be making a movie. It's your time. You can do anything you want."

He looks out the front window at the university buildings and says, "All we have to do is get through this. I'll help you, I promise. You're not like the others, Niranjan. You're not a walking zombie, just looking for approval and status."

I don't say anything. It sounds good I guess – like something a teacher might say. I signal and slowly turn onto Bloor, heading east. The traffic is backed up. It's slow going as we head towards the Bata Shoe Museum. So strange – to be driving here. At one time, all I had known was Scarborough.

"I mean it," says Mr N, talking to himself. "When I sort a proper place out, you can live with me. You're too old to be adopted, but I'll help you. We'll send you to film school, or write a film together and get it made. I promise. Whatever you want."

"That's really nice of you," I reply. I try to imagine what my future will be. Film school doesn't seem like it. Perhaps it's far too late for me to get into any university.

DANIEL

Glad to help Niranjan out. I was even more glad of his company.

We drove around, and I saw the old homeless men and women sleeping on steam vents at night, lying right on top of the grates. Once, during the day, as we drove west along Queen Street in front of City Hall, I saw the man who used to camp in front of Lynn's old building. With his Inuit face and long moustache and straggly beard, his face shattered in pieces and his eyes scrunched tight, he huddled on the concrete flagstones of Nathan Phillips Square with his woman. They weren't lying on a grate or anything, just huddling together as if it were the end of the world, alcohol in their veins, bodies falling apart, nothing happening to them. Just life itself. They huddled there, and people gave them a wide berth. Still, they seemed to accept their lot, were resigned to it in a way that nobody else was. So this was where he'd moved to after leaving Lynn's old neighbourhood. This was what he'd abandoned Fort York's atmospheric troop formations for. We were equal now, he and I. No, he was better off. At least he had a woman who loved him and clutched him in her arms. And he clutched her back.

I walked through the streets on my own, just me and the dog, before Niranjan's driving test. He was at the apartment, getting a good night's rest.

During the night, hundreds of people sat down on University Avenue, between Dundas and Queen Streets. They sat underneath the crabapple trees, in the shadow of the American Consulate and the other large buildings that flanked the avenue. During the day, there were thousands of protesters, as similar and individual as the decaying crabapple blossoms that lay trampled and strewn along University Avenue. The trees' heady pungency wafted on the springtime air. The dark faced, red T-shirt–wearing protesters sat in clusters, young with young, old with old, waiting out their time. During the day, protest leaders with bullhorns rallied the throngs of agitated Tamils, and they all yelled, "What do we want?"

"Justice!"

"What do we want?"

"Justice!!!"

"When do we want it?"

"We want it now!!"

Now, they sat under the sodium streetlights and shared the vaddais and rice and thermoses of tea that had been delivered from two or three different Tamil restaurants in Scarborough.

Police in uniform and a few plainclothesmen shifted uneasily on the fringes. They were there to make sure the protests didn't become ugly. This had not happened – for the most part, the protests were without incident.

Police chief Bill Blair would later say that we were model protesters, that we came, we protested, we cleaned up after ourselves and left things the way we found them. Others would not be so sure. I can only imagine what it would be like for a white person to come by during the evening, when all the people who had gone home to sleep right then, or were at work, would come out full mass. The carnage and death back home in Sri Lanka continued, so the vigil here, in Toronto, must also continue.

The evening before, Chuck and I ran into Thambi and his mother, Mrs Navaratnam. Her son Roshan could not leave his job, but she and Thambi were here. Thambi's father was stuck in Sri Lanka, much like Niranjan's family. They were talking animatedly with a middle-aged couple. Since it was early evening, the protesters were in full force, and one argument hardly stood out against the throng.

I thought of my own mother as Chuck and I got closer, and wished we had had a rapport. My parents tried the best they could, in their own way. Connecting and bonding were not their strong suits. I could see the stains and soot on Mrs Navaratnam's old sari, the faded red and green. It was one of those practical work saris women wore underneath their coats. She argued with the Tamil couple who stood off to the side – they did not want to be included in the masses demonstrating. The man wore one of those knockoff Ralph Lauren spring jackets and pleated work pants; his wife stood by him, silent but quite visibly upset.

"She has to come home, she has to come home, she has a degree to finish!" said the man

"You should be proud of her," replied Mrs Navaratnam.

Thambi stood sheepishly to the side.

Only then did I realize an argument was in progress. The 'she' in question stood nearby, wearing one of the red T-shirts with the tiger's snarling face on it, her placard angled down against the tarmac as if to steady herself. Her arms bent uncertainly, she looked like she would sway, then fall. She was all of nineteen years old. Obviously a baby to her parents, and still living at home.

"She's learning about her history," said Mrs Navaratnam quietly. "How many youngsters can claim that?"

The young girl raised her head. She became defiant. "I'm never coming home, until we get justice."

Chuck and I joined Thambi and his mother, and stood beside the girl. "Need any help?" I asked.

The parents saw our assembled ranks. Chuck snarled. They backed off.

The girl's defiance slumped out of her, and a sad look fell on her face, but she picked up her placard and joined the throng.

There were many cases like that, uneasy changes in people's lives and personalities that were no less dramatic than if the war were actually taking place here, in Toronto. It was a war fought with anger and chants and recrimination. The old became protest parents to the young. The girl's actual mother and father were forced to wait nearby, worried for their child.

Thambi and his mother avoided bringing up my troubles, and for this, I was grateful. The smell of fried snacks and crabapple blossoms hung in the air as we talked about the situation in Sri Lanka. It was early May and the Tigers had been beaten badly. They'd had their asses handed to them. It was, of course, worse for all the civilians and evacuees who'd been shelled relentlessly. Their lives entailed fleeing from field to ditch, from village to sea. They'd all been pushed towards the East, near a small spit of sand close to the Nandikadal Lagoon. The army used advanced drones to give them precise satellite imagery of what was going on: they knew very well that they were hitting civilians and hospitals and aid workers. That was their plan. The LTTE would not let any of the Tamil civilians, on the run, cross over to the Army's side. We learned later that the Tigers were using the civilians as human shields. The poor Tamils never had a chance, one way or the other. The LTTE cried wolf and had Tamils out there protesting for them for days and days, months and months, and these people hardly knew what was going on. When all was said and done, they shot any Tamils who tried to leave and surrender to Army camps.

People were hysterical. They screamed and chanted themselves hoarse, and the world neglected to listen. It would later be described as the first major failure of the Obama administration.

We had yet to see the other videos that would really take the scalp off and force our nerves to stand on end. The summary executions of Tamil fighters, tied to trees and bleeding all over, their bodies being cut as army officers took trophy videos. The hacked and mutilated and raped bodies of naked women who had once tended to the Tamils. The photos of Prabhakaran's adolescent son being given candy before suffering execution, point blank. The video of Prabhakaran lying in the mud with the gaping red wound, still tender and fresh and bloody, an open portal into his head.

Prabhakaran was still very much alive and present in those days at the protests. 'Thalivar,' or 'Leader,' as they called him was represented in the many garlanded placards, the chants like hymns that kept the protesters on their feet. He was like a very God to some who had known nothing about his existence a few months ago. Like the look in my father's eyes, that distant wistful belief in a future and leader that seemed beyond the hazy visibility of reality itself, the crowd swayed to his dicta until the very end. Even the T-shirts they wore carried his essence, red like the blood spilt on the battlefield

I argued with Thambi about Prabhakaran. "It's building up to something," he said as we shared the food. "I feel it – all of this is going somewhere."

I pulled the chilies out of a vaddai and gave the crushed-up fried dough to Chuck. He licked the oil off my fingers. "If you say so," I replied, noncommittedly.

"They've got to take notice," said Thambi with that gleam in his eyes, that gleam I'd seen too often at the protests. "Governments have got to sit up and take notice now. The way the Sinhalese have refused any aid agencies access to the war zone. The Red Cross and the UN. They've got to do something now!"

"I hate to break your bubble," I said, placing my hand on Thambi's shoulder gently, "but governments stopped caring when we lifted up the Tiger flag, started wearing it on our T-shirts."

"The Eelam flag!

"There's hardly any difference between the two. The Eelam flag is just the Tiger flag without rifles on it. Anybody can see that."

His mother didn't say anything. Her mouth turned down, she followed the conversation by looking from person to person, fished out paper towels from her bag, and got us to wipe crumbs from our lips. Somehow, Thambi seemed more affected by his father's absence and plight than she was, and I didn't know why.

Thambi lowered his head, looked around with theatrical caution, then said, "Something's going to happen in a couple of days."

"What?" I asked.

"What? Something big, something that will draw attention in a way that nothing else has done so far."

"What are you talking about?"

He sounded like a fanatic, but wouldn't tell me more. "You're going to be here the next few days, aren't you?" he asked. "You're going to find out.

I ran into Nadesan, Kumar, and Raj shortly after that. They walked in a larger group, while I was with Chuck by the AGO. I was slightly mortified. How could I forget that moment in class when they threw my ignorance in my face? They all wore red T-shirts. I was still supposed to be, at least nominally, their teacher.

"Mr N, we heard what happened with the assembly!" said Nadesan, a curious smile playing across his lips. The others said nothing. I didn't know what to reply.

"Is it true that you lost your job?" asked Raj.

"I took a sick leave," I said, pulling on Chuck's leash. He strained to run into the group.

Abirami, who was in the middle, bent down to pet Chuck, and he let her.

A boy called Jagan said, "I think you did a good thing there. But why don't you join the protests?"

It was obvious I was on the fringes, in my regular clothes. I didn't know what to say. I certainly didn't want to reveal that I'd left Lynn, and was now holed up with Niranjan. It was a pleasure to be on the same level with Niranjan, to buddy around, but with these guys in their red T-shirts proudly bearing the snarling tiger, I felt odd and uncomfortable. There was something imposing in their mien, their swagger.

"You should definitely come two days from now," stated Nadesan. "Mother's Day. We have something important planned."

What was going on? Did they all know, but me?

If we were in the hallways at school, I would have reminded them to get their assignments in, as they were now overdue. Now, I just nodded and kept Chuck close, for protection.

They fell back to talking amongst themselves and moved on.

NIRANJAN

On the day of the road test, we feed Chuck well and give him a walk before leaving him at the apartment. He moans and whines the whole time. Mr N takes me and the Yutani to a garage to get everything checked out. The engine, the wires, the brake lights. He gets it all looked over before the test.

"Sorry you have to do this with me," I say. "You must really be missing Ms Varley."

"Nonsense. Not at all," he trails his hand outside the window. "We were only together for the sex. Me for the sex, and her for a baby." As soon as the words come out, he knows he shouldn't have said them. He looks at me, apologetic, tries to blink back the words with his eyes.

"Don't worry about it, Mr N," I reply, scanning the traffic in front of me. "You're allowed. It must be hard. I never had a girlfriend myself. I'd really like one. Someone nice and pretty. Soothy – my friend – had one, but things didn't work out for him." Find myself thinking about Soothy and that night at the Tamil store. Something coughs deep inside my chest, threatening to run up my ribcage, ruin our perfect day. When Mr N doesn't speak, I ask him the thing I'd always wanted to ask him. The thing I could never ask Soothy or Rageev. "Mr N, what is sex really like? I mean, is it like… you know?"

He buckles forward in his seat. "Let's talk about this after your driving test," he says. "Okay? Jesus, you ask some difficult questions."

His face is red, but he continues, "An important question, Niranjan. An important thing. It's not that I don't want to talk about it. But I shouldn't have said what I said earlier – about Ms Varley. That was unprofessional and uncool. I shouldn't insult her like that. Sex is many things. Bonding and closeness, building a life together, respect. It's hard to talk about – something you experience.

"It's why we live and die. The only reason we're born in the first place.

At the garage, the greasy mechanic with oil over his mouth and teeth looks under the car's hood.

"These Yutanis last a long time – microchips and satellite controlled –" says the mechanic. "What are you? Guyanese?"

"Tamil," replies Mr N, "and we're not rich, so give us a fair price, huh?"

"Shit!" says the mechanic. "Some father and son!"

The father-and-son comment hovers uneasily in the air.

We don't talk about it as I take the highway, the 401 out to Port Union. Mr N is not old, though he does look like he's aged. We don't look similar. What made that mechanic so sure we were father and son?

When we get to the test centre, we switch places. He drives me around the neighbourhood. Gets me to spot the speed limit changes so I won't exceed them during the test. He shows me the streets nearby. I'm made to practice a three point turn, a couple of parallel parks.

Finally, we go register at the test centre. We're told to wait by our car for the tester. I say nothing the whole time. Shaking again. Just like Muruges. Something I just can't push down. Need to tell him about it.

"What's the matter, Niranjan?" he asks. "Are you nervous?"

"Mr N, I've got to tell you…"

He looks at me funny.

"About what happened in the Tamil store. I must tell you."

No, his eyes say to me, don't bring it up now!

"You've been good to me. Maybe I don't deserve your kindness. If you knew, you might not like me anymore. I must tell you or I'll go mad."

He shakes his head. "Tell me later," he says. "There's plenty of time."

Before I can respond, the tester comes out. Mr N tells me to get in the car and buckle myself in. Looks at me anxiously.

Get in the car and buckle myself in. The tester tells me to start the car. I do it. Then I'm told to turn on the front lights, the back lights. He checks them off on his sheet.

The tester gets in, and we pull away from the parking lot. I try to look at Mr N's face through the side view mirror, but I cannot. Maybe I hear him say 'good luck'.

The tester directs me to turn right onto Rylander. The churning still happening in my chest. It feels as if I hear the tester from far away, through a very long tunnel.

So I turn at the last minute onto Rylander, almost forget to put my indicator on. The turn is very sharp – I can feel our bodies lurch against the seats. He shifts and readjusts his seat belt. "How long have you been driving?" he asks, looking ahead at the road, all impersonal.

"I don't know. A year maybe."

"That was a very sharp turn," he says, as if I don't know it, then scribbles something onto the paper on his clipboard. That can't be good. "When it's safe, make a right turn onto Kingston," he says, not giving anything away.

I have this. I know that we're still in a residential zone and keep my limit near forty. There is a lane for cars taking right turns onto Kingston Road. Once again, my turn is sharp. I almost go onto the sidewalk as I pull into the lane. All I can think about is that day at the Tamil store. Soothy's death, then Muruges's death, behind both of them, Rageev. Beyond all those things… what I have done.

Tomorrow is Mother's Day. And where is my own mother? My father? My sister? My brother? All dead in a ditch somewhere? On Karthik's orders?

That little .22's ejected cartridge flying like a pin tossed in the air. The bullet never leaving Muruges's head. Pancaking around, just like Soothy said.

"Goddamn it, what is wrong with you!" The test instructor takes the wheel and jerks it sharply back to the left. I slam on the brakes. "You didn't even put the signal on that time! How long have you been taking lessons?!"

My heart takes a few seconds to slow down. "Long enough," I say.

"How long?"

"Look," I say, "I'm sorry. I'm just nervous. Usually, I'm a good driver."

"There's nervous and there's this!" he spits. "You seem like you've hardly ever driven a car in your life – you have no control over what you're doing. If this is the way you drive, I can't pass you. I'm going to fail you right here."

He looks me in the face. I look back – he's about Mr N's age, a black man but with light skin and a great scowl. He isn't my friend. I can see that I'm going to have to beg him to give me another chance. I feel mixed up inside. Can hardly concentrate on the driving. We are at the place just around the corner off Kingston, where Mr N made me do a three point turn.

I look back to Kingston. Cars behind me honk their horns – apparently my turn to go. A grey sedan flashes by, and it looks vaguely familiar. I see the rust and dirt around its mud flaps. I know it. Dark Moustache in the passenger seat. I am sure of it. Karthik. He looked at me. Now they are gone.

Are they following me? Is he really here? Only a glimpse of his thin face and dark glasses as he flashes by. It is enough. The sun shines a harsh glare through my Yutani's window.

"Get out," I say.

"What?" The test instructor's eyes bug out, but I can hardly see them because I'm looking ahead.

"Get the fuck out of my car!"

Hurriedly unclasps his seat belt – takes forever – then gives me one last look, opens his side door, gets out of there. I think he's writing on his clipboard when I pull out and turn the corner.

Remember to signal this time. I have no choice but to turn onto Kingston – Rylander ends here. Even if it didn't – I can't stop myself. Not now. Cannot withhold my curiousity. Things fit neatly again; my fingers take over the driving. Wheel feels natural in my hands. The Yutani responds to my control, my will. I can almost sense the ghost of Rageev sitting in the passenger seat, egging me on. The skin folded down over his skull so that his words come out slurred and indistinct. His hair hangs to the side where his ear should be. Soothy and Mr N's dad and Muruges in the backseat.

It's a full car.

Surprisingly, I do some of my best driving. The test instructor should be here now, although there isn't any room, what with all the dead bodies. My chest feels great. Breath comes in and out. No need for an inhaler. Fingers feel the wheel, the wiring, that incredible and famous Japanese wiring extending from the steering wheel to the axle to the wheels. I feel the road underneath the wheels flip b .

The grey sedan is waiting for me ahead, at the side of the road. They've pulled over. Waiting for me to catch up.

Not really a surprise, is it? See the sedan's emergency stop lights, waiting for me there. They want me dead – of that I'm sure.

So I jam the accelerator and speed past them. Around them. I see the westbound on-ramp for the 401. I take it. There are hardly any cars – it's easy to pull on to the ramp – my hands go to the indicator and turn it up. Looking in my rear view mirror, I see the sedan turn off its stop lights and pull out after me. It follows me up to the 401.

We're on the highway. Traffic is light. I am able to easily merge with the westbound cars. It's a glorious May day, full of sun, no clouds. Perfect weather. I'd dreamed of driving down the highway like this, with my licence. I had come so close. But that test instructor will make sure I'll never drive again. I'll be hauled in front of a judge. They'll find a way to connect me with everything that's happened. The .22 is in my bag at the apartment. Maybe they'll find that too. They'll squash me like a bug.

I think of all those cockroaches crawling across our linoleum floor. Soothy trying to squash as many as he could. The glee in his face at the number of scurrying victims. I curse the white people for making us scurry and kill each other like cockroaches in a pit. Not just white people – everybody. We're all in a pit, aren't we, just scurrying through our lives? I tried to tell this to Mr N once. It was no use saying I was in a gang. We're all in gangs. The school is a gang. Being white is a gang. The cops are a gang. This country is a gang. Being Tamil or Sinhalese – well, that's a gang too, isn't it? We're all in gangs, one way or another, Mr N.

My mind turns in overdrive, faster than the axles spinning below the Yutani. No matter the speed I pick up, the grey sedan picks up speed too. Continues to dog me. If anything, it's faster.

I race forward until I get to a stretch of highway where there are no cars. No cars around us. Not between us or beside us. I have a few seconds until the sedan is upon me, and I turn the Yutani around.

Well, I like this black car of yours, Rageev. Your present to me. But I guess I always knew, somehow, it would be a coffin. I should never have taken it from you. Should never have had anything to do with you. I wanted to live and be a free man. That's all. Thanks for allowing me the illusion. It was all I had, and then it too was gone.

How many deaths are these people responsible for? Do they feel anything for the future I may have had?

I keep the car in park, gun the accelerator, flooding the engine with as much gas as it can take. I just keep gunning and gunning this thing. I've been coming to this moment my whole life and didn't know it. Instead of gas filling the car, I can smell the fumes of burning cockroaches. Everything I've done, everything I've experienced, leads to this. Now it's here – I don't mind so much. Where else is there for me to go?

The grey sedan gets closer, and I move the gear into drive. The engine leaps forward, but the brakes stay on. Why? I turn the key in the ignition, but the car still won't move. Feels like a hot kettle, ready to explode. "It's the Yutani," whispers Rageev's ghost next to me. "The online navigation control pad – it knows you're facing the wrong way."

It's the car – it doesn't want to destroy itself – its onboard computer is smarter than I am. I can clearly feel what's going on underneath. Signals are running through its electrical wires, its nerves, bumping up through the air to satellites, satellites that bounce frantic frequencies back down to lock the car's gears into place. I imagine Shiva up there in space with his trident. Shiva, the keeper of the cosmos. Creator and destroyer of worlds, he holds fire in his outstretched palm.

What does Shiva know of us? What does Shiva know of me? I imagine him in the Heavens, his mighty purple and black hand outstretched towards me as I solemnly grind the car's gears. I imagine myself on that hand, a hand the colour of thunder, sinews jointed by magic, each knuckle a black sun, fingers that contain worlds within them, an entire constellation across his palm. What could I matter to a being like that?

Coax the gears and nudge the car. Not caring anymore about anything, I slam my fist through the computer's LCD console. The screen cracks, and the LCD liquid goes all wet and black behind the plastic. I have to punch through a couple more times before I can get to the wires. My fist hurts, and of course there is blood, but when is there not? I pull out the wires and soothe it and shut it down so that it slowly returns to manual control. Crossing the appropriate leads, the ignition turns. It's like boosting a car. This car, my car.

The engine kicks into gear, unleashing the combustive force of all the gas that has built up inside it. It growls forward, the nose of the car heavy against the macadam and asphalt, eating up the ground. The grey sedan is almost here now. I imagine the explosion as the hood of the Yutani folds into the hood of the sedan, the frames crumpling into each other like twisted paper clips, metal and glass everywhere. Our bodies flying through the air. The shrapnel twisting itself permanently into our flesh and bones and hair, the mess so bloody that all the DNA tests and forensics they have won't be able to separate my arms from Dark Moustache's body. The car leaps forward.

I think again of Mr N and that awkward conversation about sex we had. I suppose I'd imagined sex to be like this. Something as powerful as this moment right here.

Look away now. Look away. I don't want you to see what happens next. I don't want you to see me like this.

Leave me alone.

DANIEL

I swear I can feel his absence. Right inside my chest.

A surge of electricity crosses the gap.

I feel it long before we get news of the collision. Somebody pulls him from the burning wreck, but of course Niranjan is dead by then. The Yutani protects his body to some degree. The others are barely recognizable. He keeps his body intact, head stays on his shoulders. The whiplash and the broken glass do the most damage. He has contusions and cuts all over. And the heat. Of course, the heat. His own gas tank holds, but the heat sears and melts flesh right off the bones. The test instructor files a report with the police, and it's easy for them to connect up the car and licence plate. I am on the paperwork at the test centre – they contact me.

No, I have no answers.

No, I didn't know it was going to happen.

No, I have no idea who the others in the crash were.

It feels like an abrupt sundering, a sudden jarring that knocks into my brain. My eyes feel as if they've been pulled out of their sockets. The test instructor returns in a very disagreeable mood, his grey shirt rumpled and hanging out, doesn't even talk to me. He goes straight into the office to call the police. There is also a grainy photo in The Toronto Star the following day. All you see is burning glass and twisted metal on the highway. A crime of passion – two automobiles inextricably fused. No people are visible.

A wave of death surged around us that winter and spring. None of us are prepared for it. Death stands in line with us as we chant on Toronto's streets. He waits under shady bombed-out clusters of trees in Sri Lanka for the maimed to bleed their lives away. Niranjan's fate seems to embody everything that's wrong with the Tamil dream.

Everything seemed sudden and bright when I could help him, give him a place to stay. The ultimate wandering Tamil, the eternal refugee. Life had given us a reprieve, a chance to do something right. He and Chuck and I were an authentic bonded family. Even mundane things like getting food or going to the movies were filled with hope. I felt alive.

A very early memory came back to me as I mourned his death, staring at the grainy photo in The Star, with Chuck beside me. I was a child when I visited the Vallipuram temple with my mother. The temple is devoted to Krishna. In the main courtyard, a stocky man hung on chains planted into his back and legs. I couldn't tell what his penance was for. Wasn't this the permanent condition of us Tamils – so much rage and pain compressed within us? The man swung like a gentle pendulum in the hot sun. We were so serious but kind, yet also harsh. We were devoted but angry, our lives trapped within the bars and clock springs of our regret and recrimination. The Seiko watch of duties and obligations. The interminable progress of the second hand around the dial.

Niranjan had freed himself of that.

* * *

I go to the protests in the morning as promised. Chuck accompanies me. When Thambi comes to find me, I say nothing of Niranjan. "Have you heard about your father?" I ask.

"No, but today's going to be an important day."

I hadn't told him that Niranjan was living with me. Thambi and I are more acquaintances than friends now, known and yet unknown to each other. We talk but do not quite believe our own conversation, as if it is a script and we are simply players in someone else's movie. He knows his father is alive (knows it!), but does not have him here to hold. I, on the other hand, have grown up with my father, too close, too close. He still holds a terrible grip upon me, even after death, though I have never properly known him. I would exchange lives with Thambi in a heartbeat, despite all the pain that absence allows.

He stares at me as if I am lost in space. "Hello? Where'd you go – did you hear what I just said?"

I shake my head.

Trying not to let disgust show in his face, he repeats himself. "We're going to do something important this morning." His thin blue jacket rustles in the breeze. The sun is strong and shines upon his face. "We're going to give them something they won't expect. It's Mother's Day. We're going to use a commercial holiday to make them think about something serious and real. We're going to give them a Mother's Day they won't forget for a long long time. They're going to wish to their mothers they'd done something sooner now!"

I don't know what he's talking about. In his boundless energy, his feverish zeal, there is something of the Tiger supporter's otherworldliness, the Tamil capacity to believe in the most ardent ideals. Scary yet thrilling at the same time.

"Are you with us?"

I can't know what will come next. I can't possibly know what they have planned. I can't know that this is the end for the Tigers, that Death has the hours and minutes, their very microseconds notched upon his staff. The Tigers' decimation and the killing of Prabhakaran and all the senior command are just around the corner. All I am told is the plan to march up the ramp to the Gardiner Expressway in full force, red T-shirts and flags waving, and occupy the highway, refuse to leave until something is done by America or Canada or England or any of the other nations that carry the fate of the world in their hands. The newpenny zeal that seems to flash through Thambi's eyes flashes through the whole idea, refusing to accept that after all these months, it is obvious that others, that Canadians, just do not care.

I pull on Chuck's leash unconsciously. He jerks up from the ground and growls in irritation. I let the leash go slack, and Thambi and I watch him settle back down, eyeing us both in that half-lidded sleepy way he deploys when little happens. Nodding my head, I let Thambi know I will join them. He clasps my shoulder, smile beaming.

There is a recklessness and uncustomary lack of caution on my part. Usually, I prefer to hang back and observe. I have a hard time throwing myself into things like this. Why am I doing it? I've been lucky so far, but this can cause me to end up in jail or worse. But the hordes of dead who have died in Mullaitaivu, the corpses that float in the Nandikadal Lagoon – these matter too, don't they? The hordes of homeless and wretched slowly dying of starvation and neglect, their inner organs turning to black powder and their blood vessels rupturing around us on the downtown streets. They matter too, don't they?

DANIEL

Just as there are some families who cannot take care of their children, there are nations who do not take care of their citizens.

We have all streamed onto the Gardiner Expressway, downtown Toronto. Mother's Day, 2009. Chuck and I stand here with Thambi and his mother. Chuck is irritable and sits down at the end of my leash, tongue lolling out, panting in the midday sun. He is bothered but excited by all the people around us. And there are a lot of people. The sun is high in the sky now. We all wear red T-shirts, me included. We would be conspicuous without them, though I personally will not wave the Tiger flag. Despite all the people, all the action, there is still that latter spring chill in the air. We rock back and forth, making banners out of our bodies.

Thambi's mother wears a coat, but other aunties simply wear their T-shirts over their old saris, pleats bunching out underneath, dropping to their shoes. Some even wear sandals in this weather. Everybody's animated and excited. For most on the expressway, that seems warmth enough.

"Where's your mother?" asks Mrs Navaratnam. "Have you gone to visit her yet?"

"I'm not sure." I hang my head, feeling out of place and forlorn.

"She cares for you, you know," replies Mrs Navaratnam. "If you don't have family, you don't have anything." She echoes a line from The Godfather, Part II, spoken by Morgana King, but is it true?

"We come here and break our backs working, and this is what happens," adds Thambi's mother. She expresses a particular Tamil sentiment. I can feel Thambi's irritation mounting, and it sets off my own. The dog picks up on both of us, and he shifts about, straining against his leash. "Here, Chuck," I call, forcing him to settle back down by pressing on his head.

"Do you know that joke about Tamils in Hell?" I ask Thambi.

"The one where the guy can visit Heaven or Hell?" Thambi asks. "Niranjan told it to us that day – the time we visited him."

"This is another one," I explain. "A visitor's being given a tour of Hell by the Devil. They come to a huge pit of people. The people are chained to the walls inside the pit. Their withered limbs manacled while flames lick their scarred and torn torsos. 'Who are these people?' asks the visitor.

'They're tyrants and people who enslaved, took away other people's freedoms,' answers the Devil.

They come across another pit of writhing people impaled on spikes, their guts and intestines spilling out. 'And who are they?' asks the visitor.

The Devil replies, 'They're all people who tortured and maimed and hurt others, and this is their just reward.'

Then they come across a pit where poor souls are just sitting around, shell-shocked, glazy eyed and sad, hardly moving. 'And who are these?' enquires the visitor. 'Why are there no restraints or devices of any kind to prevent them from escaping?'

'Oh, these,' grunts the Devil. 'They're just poor suffering Tamils. Every time one of them tries to climb out, another one just drags him back in.'"

Mrs Navaratnam clearly does not like the joke. "Why are you dragging that dirty dog around?" she asks. "Chi – leave it somewhere!"

Chuck growls, but before I can answer, we are surprised by the call of my name. "Mr Narayan! Mr Narayan!"

My students. And I look worse than the last time – the embarrassment is overwhelming. Kumar and Nadesan come towards me holding placards. Raj and the others are with them. They all smile, seeming to take things in stride. They're having great fun. Unlike Niranjan, they have their whole lives ahead of them.

"Mr Narayan, have you joined us?"

"So, will you quit teaching for good?"

"You quit your job?" asks Thambi's mother.

"No, no, I just took some sick leave is all." I'm sick of repeating myself.

"Anyway, this is kind of like school, right?" asks Raj.

"What do you mean?"

"Kind of like being at camp – you know, before the school year started?"

I pause and think. It is a little like being at Albion Hills – out in the fresh air, trying to work in a group and balance the see-saw. The bonding and collegiality that happens here at night, when we are far from normal society, on an 'island' of our own. It is like camp in a way. "Call me Dan," I say. "We're not at school anymore."

Abirami leans forward to pet the dog, and Chuck recognizes her, closing his eyes, stretching his back, tail wagging furiously. "Is this Ms Varley's dog?"

I nod affirmativel . They don't even seem to remember the time they'd caught me embarrassed by the AGO, so far from home. It does not matter to them. Each day is fresh and new in their lives. There is something about the protests that erases lines of distinction and separate histories. It almost, momentarily, erases time itself, and the pain that accompanies time.

Mrs Navaratnam is very happy to meet them all, and the last of my awkwardness dissipates as she engages in small talk.

Letting my eyes wander, I see a sea of dark brown faces and red T-shirts. Earlier, when we came up the Spadina ramp, some cops on bicycles had formed a chain and tried to stop us. But there were so many of us, behind me, ahead of me, that we surged ahead and broke through. The police looked so comical in their bike shorts, yellow jackets, and bicycle helmets that I almost forgot about Niranjan for a moment. For the first time, the cops were the extras in our movie instead of the other way round. The whole spectacle was a movie set, a production whose budget had spiralled out of control.

I think of my father, and a small, yearning part of me wants him back. Would he have liked it here, on the Gardiner? Probably not. With his death, an age has passed, some old school version of what it is to be Tamil. Something that is strict and colonized, to use Lynn's terms, but rails against its colonization. Ineffectual, unhappy.

I still feel guilt over his death. Perhaps more than anything, it is our fights that have killed him. Gradually, inch by inch, drop by drop, second by second, we have bled the life out of one another. The slow hand on his watch, interminably moving round that dial.

Now past and present, east and west, converge. I had thought of the Tigers as our boys, our fighters over there. Far removed from our lives, with fatal politics and fatal policies, they are vindictive and uncompromising young men. Men with collection boxes to be avoided. Now that will, that surge has burrowed into the ground, has bored like a cosmic force right through the centre of the earth and gushed out here. I am a Tamil, and no matter where I go, that cannot be excised. My hands are Tamil, my legs are Tamil, my tongue is Tamil. My very brain is Tamil, no matter what my father said.

Raising my hands, I look at them. The skin has gotten rough, exposed, its blackness seems normal. The hands are burnt from the sun and do not tremble anymore. I hold them up in front of me, the hands that briefly drove the Yutani on that fateful day. Yesterday. The hands that pressed the red button at my father's funeral. A month ago. I inspect them for even the slightest tremor. As calm as anything, my palms stare back. And then, amidst all the chanting, even more people pile up the ramparts and push onto the Gardiner, and we – my students, Thambi and his mother, Chuck – are pushed forward in the surge. How will we ever get off? The tide swells and bursts with feeling. Cars are stuck. When they can, the cars move forward. They have to drive gingerly to avoid the Tamil mothers and strollers who have boldly taken their positions on the asphalt.

The cops try to reach a politician who can do something on this godforsaken Mother's Day. The cars honk and people shout and curse, but the crowd's chanting eclipses them all. We are a red surge pushing forward, growing so that the protesters cut out the noise of the traffic. Who would have thought that there could be so many Tamils turning out to claim the highway, the very same highway belt that, further east, has claimed Niranjan's life? Who thought that there could be so many of us in this corporate and cold city run by its clinical traditions? That we could bring it to a stop and force it to take notice for just a moment?

Just a moment.

I am a drop of red in that huge swirl. I am sure that the police chopper circling far above cannot see me individually, with my doubts and infractions, my ambiguities of feeling and devotion. I am a red blood cell like all the other red blood cells filling onto this stretch of highway, this main artery along the Toronto waterfront, this red mass of ganglia that manifests the Tamil heart. Pumping the vein of highway with a surge of blood. To them, up there, it must seem as if a vein has just popped. The arcing spray has become alive with pressure, conviction, and vitality. And in Sri Lanka, the blood is also let, in gallons. Into waters, into lagoons, into oceans. It flows out of the bodies into the ground, pools and runs downhill in rivulets, streams, coagulating into thick rivers until it evaporates and rises into the air. Like a red mist, the blood vaporizes to ascend into the sky, forms into clouds, comes down as rain upon the people.

DANIEL

It is later in the day now, and the sun is on its westward arc. The clouds throw great shadows upon us and the expressway, as the dog bolts and runs around protesters. The jeering and chanting, the honking of vehicles, the cops vainly shouting, trying to maintain order all disorient me. It's much easier for Chuck to make his way in between people's legs than for me to fight against the prevailing direction of the crowd. My resolve begins to break. I have to get out of here. I am not a protestor. I don't belong. Like someone who has subsumed Niranjan's atavistic tendencies, I try to avoid cops.

All those people at the protest. What was I doing there? I see my father's face in every other man – his balding dome, the fringe of white hair, the sharp and flaring nose. He is in every look, every gesture, and he calls out to tell me I am not an authentic Tamil, that I don't belong. My confidence seeps awa .

We head westward where I can buy food and get water for Chuck. I am exhausted. It is early evening by the time I find food. We have been out here all day. Walking through one of the alleyways west of Spadina, we come upon an abandoned house and peer in.

The place is filth . Squatters have used it before us, but thankfully no one is here now. The Subway sandwich wrappers and the cardboard coffee trays and the plastic bags and an old soiled sweater in the corner next to beer empties tell the tale. There is no electricity of course, but the window's glass is broken on the ground floo , and the night chill comes in along with the light and glare from the streetlamps and the tenements surrounding the back yard.

Oh, Chuck, what have I done? Was it all just to prove a point to Lynn and Badlamenti? To my father? What caused me to be so bent out of shape and broken? I am broken and do not wish to be human. Tell me what it is to be free from this pain and sorrow, to not feel this doubt and confusion.

The dog raises his head, and despite the darkness I can see his fur pulse blue. His eyes gleam phosphorescent red like the day I saw him rise upon hind legs.

The voice comes to me like a fish flipping its fins inside my brain.

Lie down on the floor and take o f your T-shirt.

I have no choice but to obey. Slowly, I kneel down on the hard, splintered floor and take off my red T-shirt. It is sweaty, long damp from all the excitement earlier in the day.

The dog walks around, his voice, his thoughts incomprehensible like a buzzing inside my head. He laps my hairy shoulders with a raspy tongue. The hairs on my shoulders and arms begin to burn, dissolve and diminish. Patch by patch, swath by swath, the follicles pull back into my body, a time lapse sequence in reverse.

The shoulders are clean and bereft of hair.

Close your eyes and grow new fur, comes the voice.

I obey, my eyes shut, imagining new strands of hair, the spirals of protein sprouting from new follicles. Push them with effort and will out the pores of my skin. Profusely drenched in sweat. My hair has been replaced by thick, shaggy grey tufts of fur. Like being draped by a rug.

Tuck your legs in. Bend your hips. Further! Good. Good. The power must go to your thighs. Move your eyes further apart. Push them away from your nose. The nose must become shorter – pull it into your face. Good. Now lick it with your tongue. Smell the things around you! The teeth need to be longer and sharper. Balance yourself on your palms and bring your shoulders into your body. Feel your strength and stand up!

I open my eyes and get used to the surroundings. Everything seems larger and above me now – the peeling paint of the window pane, the shattered window, fixtures on the wall that do not work. The walls tower and the floor recedes in an impossible perspective. Everything comes in a smoky opulent black and white. Like an old film on silver nitrate stock, the images are in shades of charcoal and pearl. As if everything is filmed with a wide-angled lens, the room curves away on either side, distorting distance, my relation to things.

Slowly, the smells come to me, powerful: I can pick and sort each one. The mouldering olives and onions from the Subway wrapper. The fumy rank on my clothes where I can smell my sweat, the dust from my shoes, the oils from my fingers in the shoelaces, spots of dried urine on my underwear. The dust and the mildew in the abandoned house, the plaster in flakes upon the roof. A dried and oily burnt smell from the old stove in the next room, long corroded into rust. A thousand different types of dirt all over the place.

Come, take a look at yourself.

I pad over on my four paws behind him, press my snout up to a jagged piece of glass still left in the corner of the window. My body is covered in grey-black hair. I have a wet black snout and piercing dark eyes. I bare my fangs and marvel at their beauty. I shake my left paw, and the reflection shakes his right one. I wag my tail enthusiastically, and it wags its tail in mimicry.

Come on! We're suddenly crashing through the window and into the street. The jagged glass tears at my body, cuts through my fur, but it is pleasurable, the wounds closing up almost immediately, flesh s nutrients and healing agents kicking in high gear. I had no idea how powerful I really was – my haunches like bent bows, springing me forward, my whole body a twist of pure muscle, no fat. My frame seems to fly rather than fall. I'm on my feet before I even land, bounding like Chuck through the night.

We race through the side streets with the large poplar trees and the low lights, banging around garbage cans, avoiding the smell of people. My sight is distorted, grainy, greytone, no good. Other things kick in. A sense of smell overpowering, that I never knew I had. I can sort out metal, garbage in various states of decay, foliage both wet and dry, a thousand different foods and poisons all over. My tunnel of hearing has flattened lower to the ground and broadened out. Like a sonar echo, the wind rushes past me bringing with it human voices but also myriad other things: the rustle of caterpillars, the sharp cry of a fruit fl , wasps hovering then gone, a shuffle of porcupine as he uncurls and roots around. The moon sings to me with golden-throated pitch, a subtle and sublime hum, throwing its beams into everything. Other living things pulsate with life, different coloured streaks moving at different speeds, a feeling to be noticed or avoided.

I wish to stop and smell everything, to explore, but we move ever faster, pushing my haunches to their very limit and beyond. I did not know such speed was possible, such pain, such beauty, such abundance. The ATP energy burns within my muscles, racing through sinew, a catalyst for thought to action. I burn with so much pleasure. We curve and swoop and edge around corners, taking streets until we are above Bloor, running east to meet the moon, into the Don Valley. We run down the escarpment into the Don without fear, sweep around a homeless person sleeping in a tent. We bound down the hill, scudding around the tent flaps, and then we're galloping through lanes of traffic. I dodge them easily, able to turn direction with fine and unerring sense. We're running north now along the disused train tracks, and the thin Don River runs south against us. The moon just hangs, large, coppery, yellow, a ripe fruit bursting. The pleasant smell of the sumac, berries, and grass. Damp earth and lime chalk underneath the exhaust fumes from the viaduct above us, the deafening rumble of the exposed subway train.

Chuck glows with such beauty. I can sense the feeling, the energy enter his bloodstream, shoot through his capillaries and veins. Nerves like a fine spray all over his body. His bones aglow with hollow, supreme, musical whiteness that has not seen the sun. It is pure, crystalline, perfect. He is a glowing blue cloud. He pads down to the river and runs against its current. I stand on the bank and watch him, uncertain,

What is it? The water's the quickest way to get to where we need to go – when you move underneath water, you can connect yourself to anywhere in the whole world. The connection between us is so clear, as if his mellifluous voice is coming through crystal wires. A flick of his stubby tail to indicate I should jump in.

My joints twist at the elbows, and I balance myself on my forelegs, leap in with precision and agility. The water rushes against me, fast and cold. What sharp joy! What affection! The feeling of love and privilege that floods such a moment. I nuzzle his flank, and he licks my side, bites my ear. The blue life shoots all through him like liquid fireworks

We are at the bottom of the water. We might as well be at the bottom of the ocean. Fronds of seaweed flow past, the water no longer the sickly brown trickle that I saw during all those trips, first east, then west, as I journeyed to work and back. The water churns and roils and rises, threatens to strangle its banks. Rises with a green spume that stands out against the greytone of everything else. It sweeps me up so that I'm crashing, paws struggling, tail propelling furiously. It makes no difference. I'm swept up and forward so that I crash into Chuck, and then we're both underneath the water, rushing forward again. We move even faster this time, bolts of lightning radiating through space. Sound waves quivering in the ocean. Electricity crossing the gap.

Move through the water, through the Don Valley, through the adjoining system of ravines, the taste of foliage, leftover rime hardening its leaves, lime, anemones the most fleeting of taste, lifeforms like a grain of salt, floating through the Rouge Valley. Eventually, a calm overtakes me and I can feel him keeping pace, but I can't see a thing. We slow down. We're moving with such ease, but then we're standing still. Where are we, and why is it so dark?

Lie down, he tells me. Gather your mind. Collect your thoughts. I become aware of my body again, the stiffness in my legs, the heavy mind. The abrasive skin where my hair once grew. Ache in my belly. Sadness. A stinging sorrow lacerates me, leaves me in anguish. I had forgotten that I am a man. I must live and age, have lived and aged, must die and pass away.

With time's arrow, things decompose. The best years are behind me. Slowly, the fur, the muscles retreat and shrink. They fall away from my body. Fat settles itself on my lean frame, hangs onto my stomach. The last of the hair falls off like pine needles, leaving a smell of resin all around me. There is such a strange pain in my head that I must curl into myself, my head against my chest.

Where are we? We are underneath the ground, and though I sense that my normal vision has returned, I can see nothing. It is as dark as poppy seed. And warm. And moist. The fertile febrile earth covers us wholly. I can sense the alkaline acidity of the soil, the tender spread of taproots from the maple and pine trees above us. Worms burrow around my muscles, digesting the nutrients and sugars at a tender pace. Ladybirds crawl into hollows between the damp soil, eating aphids that flit over and brush against bacteria. I can hear the thud of sparrows above us as they land, the soft burbling of a one-note brook, the daisy chain of weeds circling the flowers that stretch and grow. An endless field of grass, blade after blade, touched with dew and reaching for the moon. I feel the tall trees of the ravine, their spindly branches jostling and sighing, giant nerves of a huge and extensive brain.

Rest now, says the dog. Let the taproots and filaments rebuild your body. Replenish, regrow, relive. In the mud, the poppy seed dirt, I feel a million fibres brush and join my pores, take root in my body, shoot life into the capillaries. A soft blue pulse moves through my tissues and recovers, rebuilds my flesh. It feels clean. The sensation is soothing, and my mind reaches out further. I sense the pebbles, the gravel and sand of the racetrack circling the football field. I sense the low squat building, orange brick, sooty with the exhaust of radiator fumes. Sodium lights. Pleasant streets with small houses. Throw my mind the other way and I sense an industrial playground, the decaying apartment buildings, rust and pigeons, the sound of TV. I know exactly where I am.

There's something about this place that's ancient. The ghosts of Seneca and Mohawk Indians pass me, running through the forest, teeming in the field

Just as there are some families who do not take care of their children, just as there are some schools that do not take care of their students, there are some countries that do not take care of their citizens. To be Tamil is to suffer. We are squeezed from all sides.

Our race, if it can even be called that, is about to be decimated. I try to think upon the tens of thousands massacred in the last few months, and my mind cannot comprehend the notion. What is it to be a far flung spore in a distant land, to be blown to the end of time?

The roots and filaments detach one by one. Slowly I am released, and my body starts to float upward, moving through the earth.

At the end of the world, everything will be stretched to its limit, the universe will collapse instead of expand, time will flow backwards. Fish will swim downstream, rivers will run backwards, and water will seep out of the ground, condense and flo , curl up into clouds. Ink will lift off the page, and words will be as if they were never written.

Bodies will lift themselves out of the ditches, their blood will collect and flow back into their wounds. We will heal instead of hurt each other. Cows will move their mouths in reverse, the food in their various stomachs recomposing. The world will grow new instead of old.

We will start out unhappy and become joyous, instead of the other way around. We will start out tainted and become pure. Broken vessels will repair themselves, as if by a magical hand. We will be born old and die young, stripping off our memories and experiences as if they never were. Melanin will lift from the skin, and calcium and marrow will cleave from the bone. Semen will separate from ova, and we will swim backwards, furiously, swivelling our tails through time.

Everything will flow back to its source. We will be neither male nor female, black nor brown, this nor that. We will be pure spirit rising to Heaven on waves of light.

I come up out of the dirt, scooping away handfuls of mud from the hill that looks out onto Leonard Cohen Collegiate. There are a couple of lights still burning in the school, and it is the first thing that I see. I know now that I will return to my job and pick up my duties as a teacher, tie the discarded strings together, or at least attempt to.

The dog is gone. I am covered in dirt, whole and alive. I can't smell Chuck's fur or hear his mellifluous voice in my head. I feel as clear as the wind that blows around me, but I am alone. The pain and sadness come back. The only thing that radiates blue is a lone iridescent flower that rings with a pale vibrancy among the moundfuls of dirt I have dug up. It shimmers for a while, and then it too is gone. The only things that shine now are the windows of the Tuxedo towers, with their cadaverous glow, and the bare light of Leonard Cohen Collegiate.

The small flower is dead. The lattices are locked. The blades of grass intersect to keep me out. The dog is completely gone. Oh Chuck, I am a part of you – I always was. You are more ancient than all the other dogs. I am what I am because of you. I am only a distant echo of your growl.

I exist because of you – even though I know you do not exist.

AFTERWORD

I heard much later that they finally came down off the Gardiner in the late evening. Bill Blair and George Smitherman reached out to someone leading the protests. Everybody came back down the ramp safely and catastrophe was averted. Of course, the catastrophes and massacres continued in Sri Lanka for a long time after that.

The link between the protests and Tiger Command could not be clearer than it was on that Mother's Day in 2009. Even if people didn't support the Tigers, they had shut their mouths and gone along with things. The whole population, the remaining living population, walked out onto a cliff above the battle plain, above the killing fields, and then narrowly walked back.

It was not opposition so much as an end to something. The last gasp of a desperate surge, now spent. All those people who had been galvanized, made desperate by the end of the war, nowhere left to go, had to back down off the highway and return to their regular lives. Pick up the pieces and go on living. Traffic resumed, and Toronto returned to its cold mechanical thrum. What an anticlimax – it was the bottoming out of some long exasperated feverish dream. I had only ever been on the fringes of it, yet I still feel its drum-like insistence beneath the tarmac of the pavement, the industrial girders of the highway shaking and wobbling as people stamped their feet and shouted their chants.

It was difficult to imagine the tens of thousands dead. The only way I could do it was to use Raptis's Fermi problem. Raptis again. Even when I used Raptis's conception of postage stamps on a football field, pure arithmetic – my father's sums – it was impossible. Imagine a family of four in Sri Lanka, mother and father, two children, uprooted and running for their lives. Multiply that by twenty-five. Twenty-five families and you have a hundred people. Ten groups of a hundred and you have a thousand. A village. Could you fit them onto our school football field? No, you could not. Maybe two football fields. Take those two football fields full of people with all of their dreams and desires and hopes and bonds crushed, and multiply them by ten again. Twenty football fields full of people and you still wouldn't have all the deaths over the last few months, never mind the encompassing war. Multiply it by ten again and you start losing sight of the faces, the individual definitions of their cheekbones, the way those people wore their hair. But you'd have to multiply it by ten again, or a hundred, or a thousand, as the war and its problems on just this little island stretched back throughout history. We are ground down, powdered, atomized by history. I tried to keep going, but it was too much. The mind cannot comprehend such pain and devastation.

They announced on May 18 that the war in Sri Lanka was officially over. I swayed as I looked at *The Globe and Mail* that day. It was finally over. Charles Anthony was dead, as were commanders Soosai and Pottu Amman. Everything seemed unsolid, insubstantial, broken into subatomic particles. The green and white checkered tiles of the magazine store's floor seemed to extend forever. Even after the war, the violence continued in one form or another.

The Western nations were relieved once the fuss was over. The atrocities simply continued in Sri Lanka with the rehabilitation camps, the torture, the suppression of freedoms, the intimidation and killings: politics and economics could return to normal with the wholesale corruption of the country on a scale never before imagined, presided over by the Rajapaksas. People were afraid to say anything. The North and the East were completely shattered. I'm sure Lynn did not feature this when she talked about the greatness of the Obama administration.

Thambi's father, thankfully, was one of the people who survived. He was imprisoned at Manik Farm. One of the lucky ones, he got out in a little less than two years, then found a way to rejoin his family. I went back to teaching of course – what else was I going to do? I wasn't going to enter the film industry at this point. Badlamenti did indeed send me to a school for Section 23 students, the kind of school Niranjan would have ended up at had he lived.

I applied myself and worked hard. In a few years, I'd been transferred out to a school at the other end of the city, Margaret Laurence Secondary School, which also had a significant Tamil population. It was like returning home. It felt a little bit like a neighbourhood in decay and I liked that: there were a lot of different elements. I even found a cheap apartment down there.

My mother, also limited in her choices, moved in with Malathi and her husband in their big house on the Bluffs. My sister had her first child, a girl, and my mother has been relegated to a helping hand, no longer a matriarchal force. She has softened to things, a little. I don't see much of them, but my sister has become a very fierce little mother in her own right. She still has a Napoleon complex, is quite sharp and demanding with her daughter. Sometimes I look at the five-year-old girl and feel an inner cringe, a sense of defeat at the expectations heaped upon her by generations. A sadness that reminds me of her mother at that age, the way she was both spoiled and controlled. When I see my sister play the martinet, I look at my young niece and offer a sympathetic smile, but I have no idea if it is received. At five, she already has a tight, faraway, distant look, girding herself for the pressures and expectations that will surely follow. My sister's become much more successful as our father's heir than he could have imagined.

I walk with my mom sometimes along the Bluffs, not too far from Badlamenti's house, but I never see my old tormentor. He became a superintendent, and Lynn became a vice-principal at another school, and they've gone on to bigger, more important things. I'm sure they don't think of me, but I sometimes think of them. The scars in my life and the ghostly impressions are things I can still feel when the Rajapaksas come across my news feed.

Mahinda Rajapaksa was finally ousted from government in January 2015, but the lasting damage is done, and he still has supporters. A strong army presence occupies the North and East. The climate is ugly and cronyism is rampant. People's attentions are short, and nobody remembers what happened to the Tamils except of course the Tamils who lived through those events. It was impossible to conceive of all the people who died in the final days, caught between the government and the LTTE. I imagine them all, ghostly and wailing, filling out the coaches and cabooses of some endless train rattling across the plains, my father in his decaying uniform conducting them to a destination they will never reach. Niranjan stands at the back of the column. I can do nothing to save him.

My mother asks me if I remember what happened during those days, those crazy days after the death of my father, when we all acted within the spheres of our private madnesses. I do. I do, I tell her. My mind drifts back to that day on the Gardiner Expressway, the sun beating down on me, people chanting all around, and it feels as if time has stood still. Though we walk around and speak, nothing really changes or moves, does it? I can remember exactly what happened to me on that Mother's Day, although I cannot prove anything. It is something only remembered by me, in the dim neurons and recesses of my mind. I am like a cockroach, I tell her, a cockroach peering into the light.

My mother looks at me and takes my elbow. "What are you thinking?" she asks.

I shake my head.

She nods and looks away to acknowledge that she understands. She is still a woman with grief, but she has picked up the pieces of her life and moved on, as have I.

Everything is normal now. Although once in a while, I'll sense an occasional shadow moving just beyond the corner of my eye and wonder what it is. Where is that dog?

It is fully dark, though the early summer air is fragrant with the white and pink blossoms of crabapple and cherry trees that are blooming for a second time. The dark night is punctuated by the light of distant stars. This part of the neighbourhood is in darkness, though there are some streetlights up the road. Cars whizz by, their tail lights an electric streamer to let me know the world's heart still beats. There are the sounds of a party down the street.

Wilted cherry blossoms drift from a neighbour's garden, blowing across my face. The whole world smells like a wet canine. The sky is black except for tiny pinpricks, rents in the heavens that allow light to fall down to earth.

As if escaping through these cracks, the cherry blossoms drift and fall, landing on my outstretched fingers and face. I am never far from the sad, sweet realization that one day, all this will end. The beauty and purity of this moment. My forty years honed to this immaculate shine. I try to reach my students at school. I honestly do. The teacher's credo: if we can reach just one student, it is enough. How many have I reached? Not just helped, but truly reached?

That scrap of verse by Leonard Cohen, inauthentic perhaps, in the foyer of my old school haunts me. As I remember the words, they make me think of Niranjan, Lynn, Chuck, my father.

> *As a branch shakes*
> *when a bird alights/departs*
> *So I continue trembling*
> *long after you are gone*

The departure of our old way of life.

This is the only moment we will ever have. Let us then be closer. If we are bodies, we are also thoughts, ideas, electricity. What is it that differentiates me from my father? Me from Lynn? Me from anyone else? Let us remember that we are fire and spirit, that the burning of thought and flesh makes it hard to discriminate between lover and that which is loved. If we must enter each other through words, let us do so with the totality of our bodies instead of the mawky plodding that passes for human interaction. Let us go through the pores, trip across the bridge of the nose, let us ride a protein spiral into someone else's mind. Let us burn against each other so that thought and action are no longer separable. Let us remember that men, women, nations, cultures, and their words are not so much like prisoners, jailors, and the bars between them, but like lovers with a letter on the table, the origin of love forever indistinguishable between he who sent love and she who received it. Let us remember the chemical combustion of spirit, and not be so quick to put it out.

I close my eyes and imagine myself to be on one of those cherry blossoms, giant, turning in the wind, a dirty lotus floating upward towards the forbidding heavens.

Petals blow all around us. We move against gravity's pull, time suspended, everything reversed. We will be pure spirit rising to Heaven on waves of light.

As if upon waves of light, I hear and feel the sounds of the surrounding neighbourhood coming to me: the honks of traffic and the bells of bicycles and wind chimes. Somewhere in the distance, a visitor enters a home. The sounds of the party down the block come to me clearly, as if through crystal waves, enthusiasm undampened by the blackness of night, voices raised in cheer and amusement. Telephone cables overhead hum and buzz with stray ions, shooting out in frenetic direction. Copper transmitters and their wire sheaths ripple with beautiful electricity. Everything is infused with a cacophony of sound that somehow comes together, as if part of some notable musical wave. Identity and communion where before there was dissonance, the sounds merge into an amplified concordant whole.

I know that I will only have this sweet experience for a few more moments, but it is enough.

To be Tamil and alive is enough.

Oh God, it is so good to hear your voice again.

ACKNOWLEDGMENTS

I thank both the Ontario Arts Council and the Toronto Arts Council for their assistance, in terms of grants, which allowed me to take time off work to complete this book.

Thanks to Luc and Allan and Sonia and everybody at Quattro. Thanks also to Carolyn Zapf (copy editing) and Jared Shapiro (book design) for going beyond the call of duty.

My gratitude to Kumar Sivasubramanian and Terri Favro for taking the time to read and comment on this manuscript at different times in its development, Drummond Wilson for allowing us to use his photo for the cover, Jacob Hoffman and Maxine for the author photo, Val Lem, librarian extraordinaire, for his help and support, and John Higgs and Chester Brown for their kind blurbs.

It's impossible to name all the influences, small and large, which have contributed to this project, but some of the obvious conscious resources/inspirations I must mention are Channel 4's investigative documentary *Sri Lanka's Killing Fields*; *The Cage* by Gordon Weiss; *Pain, Pride, and Politics* by Amarnath Amarasingam; David Simon's book *Homicide* and series *The Wire*; Franz Kafka's *The Metamorphosis*; and Alan Moore's work on *Saga of the Swamp Thing*. ♥